PRAISE FOR BARBA[RA]
AWARD-WINNI[NG]

FOLLY DU JOUR

"Cleverly's fine seventh 1920s historical to feature Scotland Yard's Joe Sandilands (after 2007's *Tug of War*)...[an] engaging sleuth...a puzzling whodunit." —*Publishers Weekly*

THE TOMB OF ZEUS

"Award-winning author Cleverly debuts a captivating new series.... In the tradition of Agatha Christie, the characters are complex and varied.... Riveting." —*Romantic Times*

"With a spirited, intelligent heroine, a glorious exotic setting, a clever plot, loads of archaeological detail and a touch of romance, there's nothing not to like in this crisply told first book of a new series by the author of the Joe Sandilands mysteries." —*The Denver Post*

"The crisp writing and depth of characterization should please traditional mystery fans." —*Publishers Weekly*

"*The Bee's Kiss* . . . certainly satisfies." —*Entertainment Weekly*

"Intriguing . . . another enjoyable read." —*Mystery News*

"Cleverly combines a colorful historical setting . . . with a complex plot and well-developed characters. . . . Make[s] a natural for fans of Elizabeth Peters' Amelia Peabody." —*Booklist*

"Atmospheric . . . intricately plotted, with red herrings and a denouement that depends on a Lanvin dress." —*Kirkus Reviews*

THE DAMASCENED BLADE

Winner of the 2004 CWA Historical Dagger Award—Best Historical Crime Novel

"Introduces an intelligent author and an interesting investigator. The Indian setting is expertly exploited and the climactic scenes are full of satisfying twists." —*Morning Star* (UK)

"[*The Damascened Blade*] is set to bring the author into the big league. . . . The writing and accuracy of scene are astonishing." —*Bookseller*

"This marvelous historical delivers." —*Publishers Weekly*

"This excellent historical mystery gains immediacy in light of the recent events in the region." —*Booklist*

AN OLD MAGIC

"Spellbinding." —*The New York Times*

"A pacy and evocative novel. Well-researched historical detail combines with an intriguing contemporary story line. An enjoyable read." —JANE ADAMS, author of *The Greenway* and *Heat Wave*

"A compelling tale." —SIMON SCARROW, author of *Under the Eagle* and *The Gladiator*

ALSO BY BARBARA CLEVERLY

A DARKER GOD

A Laetitia Talbot Mystery

BARBARA CLEVERLY

BANTAM BOOKS TRADE PAPERBACKS
NEW YORK

A Bantam Books Trade Paperback Original

Copyright © 2010 by Barbara Cleverly

Published in the United States by Bantam Books, an imprint of The Random House Publishing Group, a division of Random House, Inc., New York.

BANTAM BOOKS and the rooster colophon are registered trademarks of Random House, Inc. MORTALIS and colophon are trademarks of Random House, Inc.

Library of Congress Cataloging-in-Publication Data
Cleverly, Barbara.
A darker god : a Laetitia Talbot mystery / Barbara Cleverly.
p. cm.
ISBN: 978-0-385-33991-9 (trade pbk.) — ISBN: 978-0-440-33905-2 (ebook)
1. Talbot, Laetitia (Fictitious character)—Fiction. 2. Women archaeologists—Fiction. 3. Athens (Greece)—Fiction. I. Title.
PR6103.L48D37 2009
823'.92—dc22
2009004141

Printed in the United States of America

www.bantamdell.com

2 4 6 8 9 7 5 3 1

Text design by R. Bull

To my good-humoured, eagle-eyed editor, Kate Miciak

PROLOGUE

Mycaenae. 1200 B.C.

The watchman fastened his sheepskin cloak more tightly around his shoulders before he set about climbing the ladder up to the palace roof. It was autumn now and the wind off the sea was a flenching knife to his old carcase these nights. He crept on all fours, staying below the line of the pediment as he'd been instructed, to reach the wool-stuffed cushion he kept up there. He lowered his skinny buttocks onto it, grateful for the warmth it had retained from the day. Cross-legged and stiff-backed, he sat exposed in the northern corner, training his gaze on an arc of hills running between north and east.

The queen herself had told him in which direction to look and what he was to watch out for.

Back in the summer when he'd been glad enough to be posted up here, she'd even climbed the ladder after him, fancy oiled-wool skirts bundled up around her knees, linen undergarments rustling, sandaled feet slapping, unhesitating, on the treads, so eager was she that he should not misunderstand a word of her instructions. A sudden blast of the hot royal breath on his ankles as he hauled himself upwards had almost caused him to miss a rung but he'd held tight and made it up onto the roof.

"Never mind the moon and the stars, you old goat!" she'd told him. "I know what you shepherds are like! Stargazing zanies, the lot of you! It's *fire* you're to keep an eye out for. The signal. It will start far away on Mount Ida, above Troy, and from there will bounce across to the rock of Lemnos and on to Mount Athos." She counted out the names, holding up her fingers in front of his face, mouthing the words as though he were a child learning his lesson. "Mount Makistos will take up the tale, then Messapion, Kithairon, the headland over the Saronic Gulf, and finally it will flare on the head of the Black Widow over there."

She'd made him point out the peak she had in mind to be sure he'd understood. And then the curt instructions were followed by an appeal to his Achaean honour. "You, my man, are the final link in a long chain of vigilant and dutiful men. Do not fail your compatriots at the last." She had sighed, staring with distaste at his rheumy eyes and bony frame, assessing his competence. Her voice took on a brisker tone: "The fire will be of brushwood and heather. You can expect it to be bright, but it won't last long. The moment you see the summit of the Black Widow ablaze, you run and tell *me*. No one else. I don't want you screeching the news all over the palace. Do you understand? If you fall asleep... if you miss it... I'll have you impaled."

She hadn't explained—just delivered orders and threats as usual. But he'd worked it out anyway. It was the prophecy, of course. This was the year, they said. Her lord, the High King of Mycaenae, would come sailing home victorious from Troy before the year was out. How many summers had it been? Too many. Some had said it might even stretch to ten. Now, that was an exaggeration, surely? A nice round sum of years that would trip off the tongues of the storytellers. But there were boys running around the town with wooden swords, boys who'd been squawking babies when their fathers had sailed away in their black ships.

Agamemnon's queen, Clytemnestra, would have made a bloody good general, the watchman often thought. She got things done. Had to, of course; with her man away at the war, she'd had the running of the kingdom. And it had survived. After a fashion. It hadn't been easy, with the men of fighting age (with one glaring exception) off besieging Troy and only the useless old men and a few young lads left behind to keep things going.

Little news of the war got back to the city. Occasionally, a trading ship would put in to the home port or to Aulis, one of those opportunists, more pirate than trader, who'd made it into the war zone carrying supplies in and spoils out. They were always eager to report the bad news: "Won't be long now! Word has it that there's been a nasty spat between King Agamemnon and one of the generals—Achilles it was. All over possession of some girl. Naw! Not that one! Some other local charmer…Tetchy blighter, Achilles! He was threatening to pull his Myrmidons out and bugger off back home. And if that happens…well…it doesn't look good. Men'll be back soon—what's left of 'em!"

But mostly the accounts were dull: "…bogged down…no sign of defeat or victory. A little light skirmishing going on in the lands around Troy but the city walls stand strong while the ships of the Greek fleet moulder to dust on the beach. Nothing more than worm-eaten hulks, most of 'em…Some have been upturned to make housing of a sort for the men of the army…and their native concubines and fresh litters of children…Very pretty, you know, some of these Hittite women…" The remarks were delivered with a slanting and cruel smile. And the reports always ended with the same rigmarole: "Any good—all right, then, they'll settle for any *bad*—

carpenters available? How about *you*, laddie? You're needed up there at the war. Fancy working your passage? What about it?" And, last and most tantalisingly: "Well, then. The bit you've all been waiting for...Anyone recognise any of this lot?...Cost you—don't forget! You know the rules: If you touch—you keep! If you keep—you pay!"

The contents of a leather bag would be casually emptied onto the beach and the women would press around, eyes devouring the mass of clay objects, demanding to see one or another more closely, turning them over, throwing them back into the sand, most often, in disappointment. Sometimes, with a gasp of delight and relief, a wife would hold out a hand for a tablet bearing the imprint of her husband's seal stone and, fondling it, she would try to squeeze from the trader more news than he had or her small fragment of silver would buy.

The watchman grinned to himself. His old wife was too smart to part with a honey cake, let alone a hen or a tenth of a silver bangle. At every docking, she'd be down there, rummaging through the bag-loads, and every time she'd find one—a tablet sealed with a ram's horn. He'd carved the simple device himself on a piece of soapstone and handed it to his son before he sailed. Thersites never failed. Clever lad with a quick tongue on him. A tongue and a brain to direct it—the boy got that from his mother. She'd never been content for her son to waste his life watching sheep. It was a good thing he'd been taken off with the army before he could get himself into more trouble. Pushy little bastard...Oarsman, carpenter, general dogsbody, it didn't much matter what he was doing...at least the lad was away adventuring. He'd have stories to tell his own children, as long as he lived to have children, that is. And always assuming there'd be some girl desperate enough to have him. Not exactly favoured by Apollo, Thersites. With his narrow shoulders and hair like sheep's wool, he'd never been much of a catch. But it was that stroppy mouth of his that would wreck his chances! He could talk himself out of any good deal. Still—so far, so good. At least he was still alive. The tablets kept arriving. Thersites's mother spotted them all right, but she never picked them out and paid for them. She stirred them up and put them back. Enough for her to see that they were there. Still coming. Thersites would have laughed at her trick and approved. In fact, they'd probably hatched the plan together.

And here the citizens were, placing all their hopes on seal stones and a prophecy. But also on the determination and devotion of a queen who had the foresight to set up a chain of mountaintop bonfires to warn her that her husband was returning. How much warning? The watchman had little idea of the distances involved, but he'd discussed it casually in a tavern with a seaman who'd worked the Egypt-to-Troy trade route and he'd reckoned that with a following wind and no storms, ten days should do it from Troy to the Bay of Argos. But the bonfires—they could zip across the island-dotted sea and hop from peak to peak down the coast in a single night. What was the queen intending to do with her ten days' warning? How long did it take to slaughter the beasts, pick the figs, and mix the wines for a banquet? Time enough for all that when the king's ship was sighted off the point. Even if he drove his chariot at a fast lick from the coast, she'd still be ready, every last bangle in place, every instrument tuned, the bath filled, all the lamps lit.

It was no business of his to know the reason behind her urgency, but the watchman thought he could guess. The sky and the mountains weren't the only things you could see from this vantage point. The palace courtyards were full of movement on a summer's night. Lamps skittered like dragonflies from one room to another. Forgotten up here behind his concealing frieze of decorated bulls' horns and bored out of his wits, he'd followed the lights and, with his shepherd's instinct for order, his alertness to wayward behaviour in the flock, he'd worked out a pattern. A disturbing pattern.

He longed to tell someone what he'd seen, to share the burden of his suspicions, even with his old wife, but he'd said nothing. "I have the weight of an ox on my tongue!" he'd muttered, reminding himself. "And there it must stay!" If he ever spoke of it, she'd have his poor old tongue out, and his eyes. Before she impaled him.

"Agamemnon! Where are you? What's keeping you?" the old man wondered with a rush of anguish. "Hurry back! Your kingdom's rotting from the core!"

He allowed himself the swift satisfaction of picturing his lord arriving in triumph at the palace, striding ahead of the army, trailed by a retinue of spear slaves and carts laden with booty. A head taller than his men, long-haired and massive-shouldered, Agamemnon would be instantly recognisable. He'd have taken the time to put on his boar's-tooth helmet and his best armour, polished for the occasion. And the lion's-skin cloak he always wore on state occasions? Thrown casually over his left shoulder perhaps, to reaffirm his kingship...To remind them: The Lion of Argos is entering his city through the Gate of the Lions. All is as it should be. In his fantasy, the old shepherd saw himself on his knees before Agamemnon, who recognised him and spoke his name and thanked him and his son for their loyal service. Every inch of him a kingly Atreid, he would play his part, do his duty. The people would be acknowledged, the gods honoured, and lastly, he would look for the attentions of his dutiful wife. That's how it would happen.

The watchman fumbled with the faïence beads he kept, out of habit, on a long string at his belt. For years he'd told the numbers of the flocks with them, click-clicking as he counted them in to safety at the end of the day. A grunt marked a stray ironic thought: All his days had been spent with the herds and flocks out on the hilltops, protecting them from wolves. And now, at the end of his life, where did he find himself? Atop the royal citadel. Still keeping watch.

But the wolf was already inside the fold doing his deadly work.

He crushed the treacherous thought before it could take hold and freeze his mind with terror. He began to count the stars. It helped him to stay awake as the beads slid over and over between his busy fingers.

The wind was rising, finding a gap in his cloak. The end of the sailing season, surely? The seaways would be closed for traffic any day now. The Greek army would have to stay in Troy, if that's where they were, or shelter until spring on one of the islands scattered like stepping-stones between there and here. It wasn't safe to be caught in mid-ocean with the sea god in a bad mood. No, they'd be holed up in some snug billet if they had any sense. Before the week was out, the queen would call him down from the roof until the next spring, acknowledging she must live through another winter without her husband. He yawned and began to hum the songs of his youth as he stared into the darkness.

It was his string of beads falling from his hands with a clatter onto the stone roof tile that woke him. Guiltily, he looked about him. How long had he slept? The sun was showing over the horizon already. No...it couldn't be...He collected his senses, trying for calm. The palace below was silent. The moon was still high. The red glow he was seeing was in the northeast.

Alert now and mewing with panic, he scrambled to the edge for a better view. A bonfire was flaring on the peak of the Black Widow, right there in front of his eyes, not five miles away, and there, further to the north and fading fast, was the dying echo of an earlier signal fire.

A surge of triumph and pleasure and affection oiled his limbs, easing his movement towards the ladder. "He's on his way!" he told himself, remembering to preserve a strict silence. "All will be well! Our lord, our shepherd, is coming home! Agamemnon, High King of Hellas, sails for home!"

CHAPTER I

May 16, 1928. London.

George the Second, High King of the Hellenes, was decidedly not on his way back home to Greece. He would have been turned away at the border had he attempted to enter the country, his passport confiscated. He was striding about his room in Brown's Hotel in the heart of Mayfair, dressing for the evening's performance at Covent Garden. He hummed a snatch of the opera he'd seen the night before: *Siegfried*. To-night he would enjoy *Tannhäuser* and, after a day to recruit his strength, *Götterdämerung*.

He posed himself before the cheval glass checking his tailcoat and white tie with a critical eye. His valet stood by anxiously with a clothes brush in hand. After a well-judged interval, an imperious finger pointed to a thread, a speck, a flake, invisible to any but the kingly eye. The valet silently flicked with the brush, tilted his head and surveyed the royal shoulder afresh, administered a second judicious flick, and stood back. Brooking was on loan from the Marquis of Melton to the King of the Hellenes for the duration of his stay in London, and Brooking was longing for the Wagner season to be over.

The evening clothes were perfect and perfectly fitted the

elegant figure. Fussy bugger, was Brooking's opinion of his temporary master—but a rewarding man to dress. He knew how to wear a suit, all right. In the prime of his life—thirty-eight years old according to his passport (Brooking had checked)—his spine was as straight as a flagpole, his shoulders square, his bearing reflecting his formative years in the Prussian Guard. Unable to challenge the valet further, George lingered in front of the mirror, as he always did, apparently finding surprising and rather distasteful the image of himself in anything other than uniform. An active soldier, he had risen to the rank of Major General in the war against Turkey and had been devastated when he had been stripped of his military rank, along with his Greek nationality and his possessions, four years before. Forced out of office and into exile by a Revolutionary Committee. A committee led by a man who had become his personal enemy, his cynical tormentor.

But it could have been worse. At least he'd fared better than his Russian kindred; George II Oldenburg still had his handsome head on his shoulders. And the courts of Europe, many of them stocked with German relations of one sort or another, welcomed him. With Queen Victoria as his great-grandmamma, what doors would not open to him? He was a notable and sought-after figure on the social scene. "And, of course, George of Greece will be of the party…" were the words every hostess longed to utter.

"Your Majesty will be unaccompanied this evening?" Brooking thought he'd better check arrangements.

This evening, George would be sharing a box at the Royal Opera House with a crowd of like-minded Wagner lovers and he did not for one moment give any sign that he pined for the presence of his dark and beautiful queen at his elbow. His wife, Elisabeth, had elected to live out the years of exile in her own country of Romania, where from time to time, and increasingly rarely, George joined her. They had no children and were no longer *intime*. He remembered with a shudder one of her more reckless pronouncements. With a face like Medea she'd said: "I've committed every vice in my life except murder, and I don't want to die without doing that either." And she'd smiled at him. George had no intention of providing the means of fulfilling his queen's last desire.

"I go alone," he told Brooking with satisfaction.

A brisk tap at the door prompted a curt "See who that is."

The valet returned, unable to conceal a slight tension. "A gentleman wishes to see you, sir."

"At this unreasonable hour? Everyone's dressing! Why have they let him up?"

"I have explained that you are engaged for the evening, but he is most insistent. A young gentleman of Teutonic bearing, sir. Name of Kellerman. A Major Kellerman."

A card was handed over.

George studied it, his face expressionless. "Show the major in and leave us. Do not return on any pretext until you see him depart."

Brooking performed his duties calmly, then scurried down the stairs to take refuge in the Snug Bar of the pub opposite. From there, he could keep an eye on the door and be ready to hurry back as soon as the young gentleman left. He was taking the last swig of his pint and beginning to wonder whether he'd missed the visitor when he spotted him striding back down Albemarle Street towards Piccadilly.

When he returned, he found the king deep in thought. His long face was invariably lugubrious, but his unscheduled meeting had given him something of the appearance of a colicky horse, Brooking thought. Unusually, he was seated. He seemed not to notice that Brooking was back in the room and hovering anxiously. Finally, with a discreet cough, the valet decided to move things on. "Your taxi, sir? Would you like me to go down and have the doorman whistle one up for you? You have half an hour before the curtain goes up."

"No. I find I have to cancel my evening. No time to change. Get my theatre cloak, will you?" Suddenly resolute, he got to his feet. "I'm going out. To St. James's. I shall walk. You may expect me back by ten o'clock."

As Brooking held the door open, George paused and muttered:

> " *'Mine honour is my life; both grow in one;*
> *Take honour from me, and my life is done.'*

"Wise words, don't you think, Brooking? A sentiment worth having?"

"Indeed, sir." Brooking had grown accustomed to responding with a fitting remark to the Challenge of the Quotation. "Would that be your German hero, Siegfried, speaking, sir? On contemplating a little dragon-slaying?"

"No." George shook his head. "That would be your English King Richard the Second, on contemplating his imminent death...But your mention of dragon-slaying is not inapposite."

The king's lips twitched in something very like a smile, and with a flash of unprecedented humour, he held out his arms for attention. "Yes, Brooking! Pass me my breastplate and helmet, would you? George has another dragon to slay!"

CHAPTER 2

May 30, 1928. Scotland Yard, London.

Chief Inspector Percy Montacute waited to hear the discreet *click* as he gently closed the Assistant Commissioner's polished mahogany door behind him. He squared his shoulders and, with a suave smile and a greeting for all he encountered along the carpeted corridors of the third floor of Scotland Yard, Montacute made his way back to his own more modest office.

Once safely inside, he let out a roar, threw his file onto the desk, and aimed a fly half's mighty kick at the wastepaper basket, sending it careering across the room, spilling torn papers and envelopes as it went. Next he aimed a vicious right jab at the hat stand and knocked it to the floor. The stream of inventive oaths accompanying this activity would have raised admiring eyebrows amongst the men of his squad. Percy's explosions were not frequent but they were famed throughout the Force, and from the first rumblings announcing one, men gathered to listen. A safe procedure, since the Governor had never been known to vent his wrath on his own men. The targets of his fanciful and anatomically taxing suggestions—villains, politicians, and superior officers—always deserved it.

Red with rage, he fought to open the window and stuck

his head out to take a few calming breaths of air. A hot May, a southerly breeze over the Embankment, and a low tide on the stinking Thames combined to frustrate him and had him slamming shut the window again. He stalked to his desk and rang a bell. The door opened at once and the young detective constable on duty looked in. He'd clearly been waiting close by, drawn by the sudden noise.

"Ah! Constable! Bring me a mug of tea, will you?" The voice was controlled and friendly. D.C. Perkins was reassured that he was in no way the object of Percy's murderous impulse.

"Right you are, sir. Got a pot brewing right now. Be with you in a tick." The young copper paused and lifted his eyes discreetly from the paper-strewn carpet. His voice took on a musing tone as he enquired: "Er...would you like me to send for one of the cleaning ladies? Looks as if they missed you this morning, sir? There's one of 'em just down the corridor rubbing up the nameplates. I can divert her up here for a spell..."

"Thank you, Constable. No need. *I* made the mess. And I'm still relishing it. I may yet add to it. I'll clear it up myself when I can bear it no longer. Now, what about that tea?"

Even the tea, served up in his special pint mug, did its bit to fan the flames of Percy's anger. He pictured the Assistant Commissioner sipping coffee from a Wedgwood china cup and his lip curled. He cursed his superior officer once again for an overbred, overpromoted, overconnected nincompoop. The man was unaware enough to be reporting back to the Chief Commissioner right now between sips of his fragrant Blue Mountain that the interview had gone according to plan. In fact, Chief Inspector Montacute, he might be saying—and Percy imagined their conversation with no difficulty—didn't appear to be quite the oik some people made out. (This use of the vernacular would be accompanied by an apologetic laugh.)...A nobody, of course, who'd reached the high-water mark of his career—and damned lucky to have got so far...

a man of *his* dubious background...(Percy knew that "dubious" was probably the most polite description of his antecedents they could come up with. He was used to much worse.)..."It could never have happened before the war!" they'd have told each other, shaking their heads. Nevertheless, a surprisingly able detective. Chestful of medals, if he ever cared to parade them. Educated, too. Not many chaps about these days who could make a joke in ancient Greek...If it *was* a joke? If it *was* ancient Greek? One couldn't always be certain with Montacute. Could just as easily have been playing the smart-arse...

They might have concluded with the thought that, at any rate, the oik had agreed, with some reservations it had to be said, to fall in with their suggestions. Yes, his secondment to Greece was in the bag. They hadn't left him much time to consider it—quite deliberately—and the officer was most probably packing his tropical kit already. Yes, on the whole, it had gone well. Two birds killed with one stone. And the royal families of two countries would be graciously thankful...

An ominous unfinished comment which, in its oily and suggestive way, succeeded not in tantalising Percy Montacute but in raising his hackles.

"Sod the royal family!" he thought traitorously. "And sod their Greek cousins!" He snorted with derision. Greek! They were no more Greek than he was! German, weren't they? Or Danish? Throneless, anyway. Their King George was swanning around the capitals of Europe making mischief. In London right now, if Percy wasn't mistaken. Enjoying the Wagner extravaganza at the Opera House. In exile these four years. Kicked out for the second time. Surely they'd at last taken the hint? The modern Greece clearly considered itself a Republic as well as a Democracy. Percy couldn't imagine the circumstances in which a deposed royal family would have any cause to be "graciously thankful" to *him*.

He concentrated and tried to pull together his sketchy political knowledge. The king and his archenemy, the Cretan hero, Prime Minister-in-waiting Venizelos, were like figures in a Swiss weather clock. You never saw them both at the same time. One popped out as the other popped in. Sun and rain. Perhaps as well they didn't have a face-to-face encounter? Now, hadn't Venizelos also been here in London...? There'd been something in the newspapers...A wedding photograph? Yes! Yes, that was it! Several years ago now...The elderly statesman and revolutionary had been getting married. In a Highgate registry office. Percy had almost shed a sentimental tear with the rest of the nation at the report. Twenty-seven years after the death of his adored first wife, the old feller had been getting hitched again to the resounding congratulations and back-slapping of admiring Londoners who loved nothing so much as a nice love story.

And what a plum he'd picked! Venizelos's bride was a younger and very rich and lively Greek-English lady. Percy had been intrigued to note that the happy couple had set off for California after their marriage. Tireless travellers, the pair of them. Percy approved. She was a politically ambitious lady, the second Mrs. Venizelos, by all accounts. And with her on his arm, the past and perhaps future prime minister of Greece was preparing to return to his homeland. To take up the reins of power after the summer's elections? Percy was uneasy. Did these events have any bearing on his own coming assignment? He didn't welcome a political element to crime-fighting. Diplomatic skulduggery was someone else's province.

And what had all that been about—the business the Assistant Commissioner had sneaked in towards the end of the interview? Percy frowned as he recollected the increase in speed of the man's speech, the dismissive delivery, the refocusing of the attention to a point over his shoulder, the accompanying bland smile—all signs, to Percy's experienced eye, that they had arrived at the crux of the matter at last.

The remarks slid in innocently enough, eased by the usual references to acquaintances in common: "You were in the same regiment as my old friend so-and-so, I think? Good! Good! You should look him up—he's presently in Athens at the Embassy…Oh, and by the way…there's a chap out there we'd like you to meet…bit of a live wire—ha! ha!—just your type…Does the name 'Merriman' ring any bells? A distant tinkle? Thought it might. He's quite the scholar but a man of action, too…rather too active for comfort, some do think… You'll have a lot in common. We'll give you an introduction. Understand you trod the boards, Montacute, during your stint at Oxford? Familiar with the playwright Aeschylus, are you? To be specific—his *Agamemnon*? Excellent! Excellent! Funny how these things work out, isn't it? Look—there's just a possibility our chap Merriman may be in need of a bit of sur-veillance, er…guidance, firm hand under the elbow, don't you know? Or even…um…direct action. We'll arrange it."

Direct action? The words were open to a sinister interpretation.

"Ah…Is this the moment, sir, where I say—along with King Agamemnon—*'I pray that no ill fortune befall me from the eyes of jealous gods afar'*?" Percy had enquired. "Line nine hundred and forty of the play," he improvised, "just before His Majesty gets his comeuppance…" His explanation was accompanied by a kindly smile and a soldier's swift stabbing gesture.

Percy was bemused. His shadowy superiors clearly had no intention of committing themselves further for the time being. Perhaps they were intending to send him sealed instructions by special messenger to be delivered as he stepped onto the boat train? Percy was bemused. What the hell did Agamemnon have to do with anything? And—a bit of guidance? What did

that involve? The steady hand under the elbow they were proposing could assist some old codger across the road; it could
just as easily shove him under a bus. Percy's suspicions had
been aroused. He'd been approached in much the same spirit
some years before when they'd tried to recruit him for the Special Branch. He'd turned them down. Those bruisers, half-
military, half-political enforcers who carried their brains in
their boots, weren't his style. His own bully-boy days were over;
he'd hung up his thumbscrews with relief. Percy was more
comfortable with the less morally equivocal routine of the
C.I.D., where the only villains were the home-bred villains.

But, really—he'd had enough of this stinking city. The
black hills of his mother's land were bothering him again,
muttering in his ear. Their voice always swelled and grew imperious after a run-in with his superiors. "Chuck it in, boyo!"
they were saying. "Come on back up here, buy some land, and
breed some badger-faced mountain sheep!"

For the umpteenth time he composed in his head a stately
letter of resignation. The words never made it onto a sheet of
writing paper. Police work was what Percy Montacute did best.
In fact, it was all he did, all he knew how to do apart from soldiering, and nothing would drag him back in that direction.
Too old by now anyway. Thirty-five. Too old to be changing
horses in midstream.

He drained his tea, rang the bell for Perkins, and picked up
a pencil from the floor. Scrambling about, he found a large envelope, smoothed it out, and began to make notes. His best
planning had always been done on the back of a used envelope
or discarded ammo wrappings. And now he'd jot down the essentials of the ridiculous proposition he'd just been presented
with while it was fresh in his mind. He had no intention of
committing himself to a scheme he'd discover to have been
subtly modified by the time the official papers made their way
to his in-tray for his signature.

Departure in a fortnight's time. Brief but adequate to familiarise himself with the task they were setting him. And a hellish task, by the sound of it! Destination: Athens.

"Ah, Perkins. Just remove the tea things, would you?" He looked thoughtfully at the younger man, watching as he stepped in a disapproving manner over the recumbent hat stand. "Forgive my asking, Constable…er…Harry, isn't it?… You're too young to have fought in the war?"

"Missed it by a year, sir. I'm twenty-five."

"So you've no personal experience of enemy action? Never killed a man?"

"Oh, I couldn't say that, sir…" the constable disagreed mildly. "Where I come from, on the Old Kent Road, there's enemy action in full swing every Saturday night. Knives, broken beer mugs, rolling pins…Not guns so much since the crackdown. I've been taking care of myself since I could toddle. With four older brothers in the house and the Jubilee Court thugs out on the street, I had to learn to handle myself in a barney. And I *have* killed a man. Just the one."

The constable timed his pause and, on catching the lift of Percy's black eyebrows, he added: "It's on the record, sir. In the line of duty. A peterman cracking his last safe. No blood spilled. His mates had all legged it and left him on his tod to carry the can. I chased him to his death, you could say. Daft old bugger should never have run! I gave due warning in the correct way. Loud and clear. Dropped dead of a seizure. Apoplexy, my old ma calls it. Croaked as I put the cuffs on him. Never quite been easy about that…"

Percy's eyes narrowed in interest. "Remind me, Harry—you're not married, are you?"

The constable showed no surprise at being asked the personal question. That was Montacute for you—took an interest in his men, encouraged them to speak out and actually listened when they spoke. Remembered to ask after the wife and kids and the granny, getting their names right and all. His men would follow him anywhere, and "follow" was the operative word—however fast your feet, you'd always find the chief inspector a few strides ahead.

"Married? Me? Naw! Never taken the plunge, sir. Though I've had my offers. What about you, sir?"

"Lord, no!" A shout of laughter where most officers would have called him to attention for overfamiliarity. "Not even an offer! Still footloose and fancy-free. Right, then, Constable... That's good. And that'll be all for the moment."

As the door closed, Percy made another note and his thoughts slipped back to Athens.

What did he know of Athens? Plenty about the ancient city in its glory days, but about the modern capital—nothing. End of the world. A sleepy, one-donkey town where not much of note had happened since Alexander of Macedon's rough, tough highland regiments had laid claim to Greece. He'd admired Edward Lear's watercolours and that was as close as he'd come to an interest. A gleaming, austerely beautiful temple poised on a high outcrop of rock and a froth of red-roofed, white-walled houses below was as much as he could recall.

Percy loosened his collar. It was warm enough here in London; God knew what the temperature was in Greece. Greece! He'd had enough of Greece for a lifetime. The dust and the flies of Salonika were still there somewhere, lodged at the back of his throat and in his belly, never to be entirely scrubbed or swallowed away. Percy had tried to object that he didn't speak the language. But the Assistant Commissioner sitting smugly in front of him with his records open was not deceived. He'd pointed out Percy's degree in the Classics. Arsehole didn't even realise that modern Greek was not the same animal at all. If Percy had gone on protesting he'd no doubt have told him to just shout loudly at the natives like everyone else. But hadn't the Chief Inspector shown a wartime facility for languages?

the Assistant Commissioner had enquired mildly. Bulgarian? Serbo-Croat? And—what was the language they spoke up there in Salonika, where he'd been based for two years...could Montacute recall? Demotic Greek? Ah, yes, that would be it—demotic Greek.

"Mainly Spanish and Turkish," Percy had objected.

"How very cosmopolitan!" The bland smile again. "Well, there you are, then—you'll be bound to be speaking the lingo fluently in a month or two, Montacute. And plenty of time to get to grips with it. Your secondment is to be for a minimum of a year. Or however long it might take..."

Warning bells had sounded in Percy's head on hearing that smoothly spoken phrase, slipped in with a smile and a shrug of the shoulders. And what was all that nonsense about his war record? Mutinously, Percy had clammed up when the Assistant Commissioner had tried to draw him out, disguising his truculence as the becoming modesty of a tongue-tied Englishman.

"Quite the adventurous young captain in Salonika, it would appear?" his questioner had mused, running a finger down the page. "Something of a trench-raider? 'Devising and effecting raids on enemy positions and leading dashes into occupied territory for the purpose of snatching prisoners for questioning,'" he quoted.

Percy had muttered that on some days he would have raided Hell to relieve the boredom. But at least his forays provided him with someone intelligent to talk to. The enemy of choice at the time were the Bulgars...His dark eyes had trained on the Assistant Commissioner a steady double-barrelled challenge. "Sportsmen like ourselves, good sense of humour and excellent conversationalists," Percy had added.

The Assistant Commissioner had cleared his throat, hesitated, and changed the subject. "And all this on top of a distinguished performance in Flanders during the first year of the war...Hmm...You're just the chap to assume duties in a young and turbulent state like Greece, I'm thinking."

Half of Percy's anger was directed at himself. He'd failed again. He'd waited too long. The words he ought to have voiced half an hour earlier came to him now: "Sir, you must be aware that you are sending me out of the country at a pivotal moment in my career. A certain position is about to become vacant in the next month or two. We both know that I deserve this promotion. This next step ought, by right of ability, to be mine. By posting me to Athens you are deliberately denying me the opportunity."

What had prevented him from speaking out? Cowardice? Percy required himself to consider this. He had medals and commendations enough, on the military and civilian stage, testifying to his courage. Old opponents on the rugby pitch still grimaced when they passed him, playfully giving his imposing frame a wide berth. If it ever came to a physical duel with his superior—anything from fisticuffs to pistols—Percy would prevail. But when the contest was a one-sided bout of aristocratic shadow-boxing with its underlying shibboleths, prejudices, and acceptances, he felt himself outclassed, anxious, the angry and impotent loser in a struggle he despised. Perversely, he'd have thought less of himself if he *had* been able to fight on their chosen terrain.

And so, unable to voice his true objections, he had cravenly quibbled about the small print—the language, the local police, the political implications, even his lodgings. And he didn't give a tinker's cuss about any of that. Percy sighed. It was done and dusted. Kicking the guts out of a wastepaper basket would get him nowhere. There was very probably a rosy side to all this if he could consider it calmly.

After a minute or two, the only thought he could come up with was that he was lucky to be still unmarried. He wouldn't have wanted to find the words to tell a wife she was to pack their trunks, that he'd been posted to the Balkans. If that was where he'd find Athens. He'd have to think of something to tell Vesta, of course. It didn't have to be utterly convincing—she was hardly likely to wait for him anyway. Might as well tell her the truth.

The truth? Percy was quite certain he hadn't been told the truth himself.

Athens—secondment to ... That much was true.

"Old so-and-so's already there ... You're bound to run into what's-his-name ... Systems, you'll find, are in place ... The new Prime Minister's expected ..." It sounded as though someone were planning a sort of awful house party. No, that wasn't quite the flavour ... And then Percy had it at last! It had sounded to his ears like the click of ivory chess pieces being set up on a board. He was being taken out of the box and dusted down, ready to play his part. Doubtless as a pawn in the front rank. Vulnerable. Expendable. But on whose side? Black? White?

Well, the game, any game, would find Percy, if confused, at least battle-ready. Pawns had been known to make it through to the far side.

He made an external phone call to a newspaper editor who owed him a favour and arranged a lunchtime drink at the Cock Tavern in Fleet Street. Might as well establish the lie of the land. He toyed with the notion of ringing down to Records to ask what files they had on interesting residents of Athens, but decided against it. He wouldn't go through the switch-board; he'd go down after the top brass had gone off to the golf course or home for tea to their cosy nooks in Surrey. Then he'd personally charm whoever was on duty—with a bit of luck it would be Phoebe Carstairs—into leaving the material out on her desk while she went to powder her nose. Next, he seized a second envelope and began to make a list of hot-weather clothing to take to Lillywhites. And boots. He wondered if there was time to get his bootmaker to make up a couple of stout pairs. It seemed they had activity of a physical nature in mind, and if they required him to go chasing brigands over rocky mountainsides, he wanted something more substantial than police-approved Oxfords on his feet.

He took down an atlas from his shelf. How in hell did you get to Athens these days? Maritime nation, Greece. Cut off from the rest of Europe (with its blessed railway network) by a tangle of mountains, it looked depressingly unapproachable by anything other than a boat. With dire memories of sweltering days on troop ships in the Mediterranean, Percy began to track his way overland, his finger hopefully following the railway lines. He made it as far as Rome, then crossed over to Brindisi. From there, the last leg—he drummed his fingers in irritation—would appear to be by ferry, either into Patras and on by train or through the Corinth Canal into Piraeus, the port of Athens.

The picture of himself arriving in port, seasick and sunburnt, triggered a certain self-deprecating humour in his situation. He took down his well-used copy of Alexander Pope's translation of the *Iliad*, tugged off his tie, and settled back at his desk, putting up his feet rebelliously on the leather surface. He rummaged in his drawer for a cigarette, found an old pack of Senior Service, and lit one. It was crumpled and dry and bits of tobacco prickled his tongue, but he enjoyed the first coarse blast of smoke rasping its unaccustomed way down his nose. He retrieved his wastebasket and, against all the rules, flicked his spent match and tapped the ash from his cigarette into it. Now he was ready to squander a half hour of the Department's precious time in silent mutiny.

Wherever his book fell open, he found inspiration and consolation. The most magnificent English ever written, Percy reckoned, and it always made his heart sing. And Homer's ancient story, heroic yet pulsing with humanity, still awed him.

In that magnificent welter of blood, vengeance, and valour he could lose himself and his petty problems. It was no wonder to him that his hero, Alexander of Macedon, had taken a copy of the *Iliad* with him when he set out to conquer the world. Along with a dagger, he'd kept the scrolls by his bedside when on manoeuvres. And what a copy! In the margins—they said—were handwritten notes added by Alexander's tutor, the great philosopher Aristotle himself. The scrolls had most probably gone up in flames on one of the occasions the library at Alexandria had caught fire, Percy reasoned, but his rational conclusion was always swept away by a rush of rebellious speculation. He still dreamed that one day the papyrus, crackling with age, would come to light, preserved in some dark space. Alexander's own tomb perhaps? The book had never left his side in life—surely the conqueror's grief-stricken generals would have buried his most prized possession with him? Historians seemed certain that Alexander's last resting place lay hidden away in Egypt's desert sands. It was to be hoped so. Everyone was, these days, aware of the almost magical power of the sands to preserve delicate artefacts. Well, why shouldn't the book come to light again? All manner of wondrous things were turning up on people's spades these days.

Percy, like everyone else, had been thrilled by the recent discoveries of gold, jewellery, and precious pieces of workmanship from antique times. But it was the written word he prized. Whether carved in stone, stamped on clay, painted on plaster, or—best of all—written on papyrus or vellum, words transmitted ancient thoughts and deeds. "In the beginning was the Word," many religions agreed mystically in their different languages. Percy chose to take that literally. Words were more precious to him than philosophical ratiocination. The world could get by (and had for millennia) without looking on the face of Tutankhamen, but where would it have been without the astonishing words of Homer, the sonorous phrases of the Old Testament, the stupendous story of the Babylonian hero Gilgamesh, a thousand years older even than Homer?

He balanced the spine of the leather-bound *Iliad* in his hand and wasn't surprised to see it fall open at the second chapter—the list of Greek ships setting sail for the war at Troy. There was a lifetime's historical and geographical research to be done from those pages and he'd promised himself that if he ever retired, or had the luck to win a fortune on the football pools, that was the kind of detective work he'd spend his days on.

Percy noted again that, among the invading Greek fleet, quarrelsome old Agamemnon was top dog, managing to raise the largest number of ships for the punitive expedition.

> *"Great Agamemnon rules the numerous band,*
> *A hundred vessels in long order stand."*

The Great King's friend, wise Nestor of Pylos, came next, contributing ninety. The island of Crete had brought in a contingent of eighty. Lagging about halfway down the list came Athens with an undistinguished fifty.

With a mischievous apology to the poet, Percy improvised:

> *"Fierce Percy led the London squadrons on,*
> *Percy the Less, Montacute's valiant son.*
> *Sick-bag in hand, he plows the wat'ry way,*
> *Queazy of stomach and with feet of clay."*

Good humour restored, he grinned. "Greece, land of flawed heroes! Shove over, Achilles—here comes Percy!"

CHAPTER 3

Late June 1928. Athens, Greece.

The golden death mask of Agamemnon gleamed, alluring yet menacing in the filtered morning sunlight.

Two men strolled towards it from opposite sides of the display cabinet in the Athens Museum and leaned forward at the same moment to examine it more closely. The dark head and the fair one bent, forming a triangle with the golden face. And what a face! This was the dark man's third visit and would not be his last. Spectacular, barbaric, beautiful, and mysterious was Percy Montacute's verdict on the old warrior. But was he indeed—Agamemnon?

Percy turned and murmured as much in a knowing way to the other admirer.

The fair-haired Englishman burst out laughing. "Almost certainly not, I fear. Probably his great-grandpapa. But I *can* identify *you* correctly! Captain Montacute, isn't it? Percy! Salonika! We played the Ugly Sisters, you and I, in the Christmas panto for the troops in '17. Well, well! Montacute's son. How is your father? Haven't seen the old bugger for years!"

Percy appeared genuinely surprised and pleased. "Good Lord! Colonel Merriman! Sir! My father was well when last I saw him. But how are *you*?"

"Be delighted to tell you, my boy, but not here." Merriman glanced around him. "Ladies beginning to direct Gorgon stares in our direction. This place gets worse than the London Library. Not the spot for two raucous fellows like us with ten years of life to catch up on! You *are* still a raucous fellow, I hope? I had heard you were enforcing the Law? That could dampen the spirits somewhat. Come on! There's a café just along the street... why don't we...?"

When they'd settled with their coffee at a table in the shade of a parasol, Merriman leaned to Montacute and asked: "Now, before we start chewing the fat, tell me straight: Were you following me?"

Caught off balance, Percy hesitated for a second. Had he been so obvious? They'd warned him that Merriman was nobody's fool. He was pleased with his reply. It had just the right degree of offended incredulity. "Certainly not! But, professionally, sir, your question troubles me. Do you suspect you're being followed? If so, as a copper, I may be just your man—unless it's a more serious matter and a psychoanalyst might be what's called for?"

Merriman grinned. "Still got all my marbles, I'm glad to say. And sincerely glad to hear *you're* not on my trail! Slight case of the jitters these last few days, though, I have to confess. Survival instinct. You know... you look up and out of the corner of your eye you see a face, a figure you're sure you saw a minute or two ago hovering some yards away... With me, the phantom usually takes the form of a taxi driver!"

Percy laughed. "Lucky man! It takes the rest of us half an hour with a megaphone to attract one in this city! No, if I'd been following you for any clandestine motive, you wouldn't have noticed me. I'm rather good at that. But I prefer to announce myself to my friends. I've been meaning to drop my card in at... Kolonaki Square, isn't it? I've been somewhat engaged since I stepped off the boat..."

"Ah, yes! I've been following your exploits on the front page of the *Athens News*! Exterminating bandits in a spectacular way. More heads for your mantelpiece, I understand? You've lost none of your Celtic dash, Captain!"

"I'm Detective Chief Inspector now, sir. With the C.I.D., Scotland Yard. Seconded to Athens. My recent history, in a nutshell. And you, Colonel?"

"Now Professor—Sir Andrew, if you can believe it! Digger, classicist, and writer. Writer..." The professor looked thoughtfully at the smiling younger man and walked straight into a trap Montacute had been planning to set before him at their next meeting. "I'm working on something that might interest you. An enthusiasm we have in common... Still travelling with your *Iliad* under your pillow?... Agamemnon! I'm hacking out a translation of Aeschylus's play with a view to staging it. No shortage of willing actors in this city. It's stuffed with classicists of all nationalities. A lively young chap like you needs to extend his social life... take an interest in something other than his work. Shall we have another of these? Delicious stuff, Greek coffee... a thimbleful's never enough."

Merriman ordered more coffee and settled in for a deeper conversation. "You must come and meet my wife, Maud. She'll propel you into Athenian society! Maud knows everyone! Look, are you free to come to dinner on Saturday? Maud's cousin is arriving from England to spend the summer with us, so you won't be the only new bug there. And we'll see if we can't rustle up some pretty girls to sit opposite. There are some particularly fetching American nurses in town. Am I tempting you?"

"Delighted!" said Percy. And he was. It had been so easy. But he was remembering also, and with pleasure, the all-too-rare boozy evenings in the Mess when Colonel Merriman had breezed through, raising the spirits of men like him. In the doldrums militarily, enfeebled by dysentery and malaria, sweltering in heat or shivering in cold, the young officers felt the better for the colonel's optimism, the connections he made for them with the world outside the fortifications, and, not least, his risqué stories. They'd laughed themselves sick at a play he'd sketched out on the back of an ordnance list and produced within sight of the enemy who, they could be reasonably certain, were watching. Soccer and theatre always caught their attention and no hostile shots were ever fired for the duration of the performance. Percy remembered, the morning after the rowdy musical performance, unhooking a sheet of paper from the barbed wire of the compound fence. In Bulgarian *and* English it had complimented the British on their performance. Much enjoyed. And would they please supply them with the words for the song "Boris the Bulgar"?

Percy was glad that Merriman was back in his life again. He just hoped it wouldn't fall to him to push the charming firebrand under a bus.

Andrew Merriman bade a cheery good-bye to his refound friend, exchanging addresses and promises of further contact. With narrowed eyes, he watched the tall figure of the inspector shouldering his way along the avenue through the crowds. Merriman resented surveillance, even from someone as congenial as young Montacute. A bit of a thug, the professor remembered, and a bonnie fighter. A man you'd want at your shoulder, not at your back. Well, the best place for an undeclared foe was within range of your sword arm. Andrew would keep him close.

He made his way back to his grand double-fronted house overlooking Kolonaki Square. "Finished my research, my dear," he said to his wife, putting his head round the door of the morning room, where Maud was taking a late breakfast on a tray. She'd clearly had another of her bad nights. "I'll just pop up to the library and put a few last touches to the translation while it's fresh. The second act I thought was a little stilted, didn't you? Could do with a bit of polish before we go public with it. Oh ... by the way ... I met an old friend while I was communing with Agamemnon. I'm quite certain the meeting was predestined! I asked him to dinner on Saturday. Scholar. You'll like him. I haven't mentioned it to him yet—and perhaps I'll leave this to you—but I've marked him down for a part in the play. Wonderful voice! See if you aren't enchanted when you meet him."

Neatly sidestepping any of Maud's attempts to engage his attention further, he bustled off.

The professor had been telling nothing less than the truth when he complained to Montacute of a suspicion of scrutiny. Any malignant interest directed at him, whether from inside the house or external to it, raised the fair hairs on the back of his sunburnt English neck. And his hairs were telling him that he was at this moment being overlooked.

His reaction to the unseen stimulus was a purely physical one, the mind somehow being left out of the circuit: the chill between the shoulder blades, the tension in fingers that crept, undirected by him, towards his waist, where he'd grown used to feeling the reassuring weight of a gun belt. He was experiencing the same feeling that, more than once in the war years, had drilled into him like a phantom bullet and sent him diving for cover. It had earned him a reputation for luck with the men—the most valued attribute in battle—along with a ready following and a rude nickname. His years of soldiering had honed this natural protective mechanism to a fine edge but it had always been there from his childhood, a gift, not to be called on, but calling him.

He was eager to get started. His desk stood ready: research texts; dog-eared books in German, French, and Italian; maps and photographs in orderly piles; a ream of fresh paper laid out, awaiting his pen. The feeling of foreboding struck him again as he closed the door, and he held tightly to the handle until the shudder passed. The order had been delivered to his household along with his regular daily instructions: "no interruptions until two o'clock." The servants would respect it but his wife never paid attention to requests or commands.

He'd told her a cheerful lie when he'd announced he was busy with the *Agamemnon*. He'd brushed aside her offer of help. Maud was reasonably happy for him to slip off to work on the play; you could say she was heart and soul behind the project. She saw it involving her with the cream of the expatriate society of Athens and planned to while away her summer co-directing the amateur dramatics. She would be deferred to, admired, consulted, busy: a personage on the Athenian scene. His wife wasn't so happy to see Andrew whiling away his time on his other task: his true magnum opus.

He calculated he'd be allowed a half an hour to settle, then she'd sidle in with a discreet cough, a placatory smile, and a bunch of flowers for his desk. She'd make a fuss over the placement of the wretched vase, taking care to cast her slanting glances over his shoulder to catch a glimpse of what he was writing. As a variation, she might flutter in with a cascade of apologies, hunting for her spectacles. And, sure enough, she'd find them in whatever improbable place she'd planted them the previous evening. But not today.

With a grimace, he turned the key in the lock. He'd be made to pay for that defiant gesture later.

He rebelled less frequently these days against the constant marital surveillance. But he'd played a trick on her last week. Maud knew he'd been in consultation with his man of law here in Athens. Such things always agitated her. On a sheet of his best writing paper, he'd written the address of his lawyer and followed it with a fanciful change to his will:

*Benedict——We spoke of this earlier. I'd like you now to
recast my will as agreed, viz: All resources of which I die
possessed to be divided between the Home for Lost Dogs,
Battersea, London, and the British Museum.*

Maud hated dogs and had had a row with the Director of
the B.M. He'd left the paper for her to find.

He'd regretted it. Schoolboy humour. Was this to be his
last defence against the increasingly suspicious woman he'd
married? Was this the pathetic depth to which she'd reduced
him? Maud hadn't been deceived or amused. She'd silently
turned up the basilisk stare a notch and doubled her vigilance.

At least the prospect of the forthcoming visit from her English cousin had raised her spirits. Maud was beginning to
grow weary of Greece and talked more and more frequently of
her longed-for return to London. The new arrival would provide someone fresh for her to show off to. Someone to hold
handcuffed by her skeins of wretched knitting wool, a captive
audience for her endless tittle-tattle. Andrew checked his
watch. Oh, Lord! Had he left orders for someone to call him in
good time to get out the Dodge and motor down to the port
to meet the boat? He relaxed as he remembered leaving a note
for the housekeeper the previous evening. For a moment he
wondered about this London cousin he'd never met. Some
mystery there. He'd been introduced to all Maud's other sane
and living relations: appalling chaps, every single one—fellows
who had no interests other than golf and making money to
spend on building villas next to golf courses in Surrey. If this
unknown cousin (at least never spoken of by Maud until very
recently) was considered less palatable even than those, then
Andrew was in for a miserable summer. But Maud had hinted
at some scandal... a court case narrowly avoided... change of
scene an absolute requirement until the clouds blew away...

Andrew grinned. A scallywag might at least enliven the scene. Ah, well—in the half-hour drive back from Piraeus they'd have time to get acquainted. For better or worse.

A fly buzzed languorously and irritatingly in the quiet room. Merriman swatted it and walked over to the tall window to dispose of it. Always such a battle to get to the fresh air on the Continent! Impatiently, he dragged back the fine net curtains and opened the two glass panes, then threw back the shutters and stepped out onto the balcony. The temperature was still bearable but in an hour's time it would be oppressive. For a moment, he longed for the cool silence of the London Library Reading Room. June. He wondered what the temperature was like over there and decided that the English were probably only just thinking about discarding their winter vests.

Better get started before his brain began to simmer.

Delaying one last moment before turning to his task, he leaned over the wrought-iron rail to enjoy the lunchtime bustle in the square below. Customers were beginning to drift in to the café tables, calling out orders for their thick black Greek coffee, lighting up their Turkish cigarettes, and opening their newspapers. They were men, all of them, clutching and fidgeting with their strings of worry beads. For a moment, Andrew thought of joining them, escaping into an inconsequential but involving discussion of the latest scandal or a lively argument about the coming elections. He was well known and always welcome down there. It had become his refuge.

He was unable to duck back inside fast enough to avoid being seen and greeted by a man he knew—a visiting and very distinguished Italian professor on his way up the hill to the British School of Archaeology, where he was giving a series of lectures to students and staff. Andrew should have been up there waiting eagerly in the front row of the audience, not lounging about on his balcony. Ouch! This breath of air was going to cost him dear. There'd be fences to mend. The two men acknowledged each other, exclaiming in Greek and Italian—*"Kathigitis! Professore!"*—with a show of joyful astonishment, and the Italian went on towards Lykkabettos swinging his walking cane.

Andrew's eye was caught by another middle-aged man who, like him, was observing the flamboyant Italian greeting the ladies with exquisite politeness as he passed. The stranger was loitering in the shade of a plane tree, and as Andrew watched, he finished his cigarette, stamped the stub into the grille under his feet, and looked about him. Becoming conscious that he was under scrutiny, he raised his eyes and saw the professor. The men held each other's gaze for a moment, then the one below tipped his boater and walked off. Andrew, who had tensed with foreboding at the encounter, breathed out, calming himself.

For a moment he'd thought he knew the man. He cursed himself for all kinds of idiot when he realised that, of course, he almost certainly did. The gaily beribboned straw boater worn at a rakish angle proclaimed the fellow below to be one of the increasing flock of taxi drivers who haunted the square. They seemed to have adopted the raffish headgear as their uniform this year. Professor and Lady Merriman had no doubt used the man's services frequently. Perhaps he'd hurried forward on spotting Andrew in the anticipation of a summoning whistle from the balcony. Entrepreneurs, the Greeks, Andrew thought, approving. Greeks didn't sit about scowling and truculent like Londoners. They came after their customers with a polite phrase or two. But Andrew disapproved of the excessive use of these motor vehicles by his rich and lazy neighbours. The spluttering cabs polluted the air with fumes and noise. He himself took pride in walking everywhere in this accessible city, when not encumbered by Maud. A lithe and energetic man, he spent the digging season working in the trenches and his physique was still, in early middle age, more like that of a Greek hoplite than a deskbound academic. Perhaps he wouldn't be picked for the front line of the Three Hundred at Thermopylae any longer, but he could certainly skirmish to good effect on the back row if called on, he thought.

But now, his desk was calling him. He could delay no longer.

With the ritual gestures of a priest tending an altar, he approached the resplendent gramophone he'd had shipped out at great expense and lifted the lid. He changed the needle, then selected an electric recording from his collection and slipped it from its cover. He waited to hear the first bewitching notes of Alexander Borodin's piece of lush romanticism, *In the Steppes of Central Asia*. Written to celebrate the accession of Tsar Alexander III of Russia. Alexanders! How they haunted him! In came the flutes and the horns, and Merriman was instantly transported, travelling the endless desert sands. He listened as the caravan conjured up by the composer drew near, entranced him with its exotic lyricism, passed by, and then disappeared into the heat haze. With a sigh of satisfaction, he put the recording on again and went to his desk.

He sat down and took a new packet of pencils from his drawer. He sharpened one. He rolled back his sleeves and wiped his already damp palms on his handkerchief.

On the first page he wrote with a defiant tilt of the head:

DEDICATION:

Illustrious acts high raptures do infuse,
And every conqueror creates a Muse.

The author dedicates this *Life and Death of Alexander of Macedon* to the Conqueror who is its subject and also to the Muse who is its inspiration.

In the centre of the following line he added, with a grin: *"Alexander. Laetitia."*

She wouldn't like that. In fact, she'd hate it. It would alarm her. The colour would rise in her cheeks, her eyes would spark like flint. She'd flourish the word "hubris" about. And she'd be right. Professionally at least, the girl had always shown taste and a sense of proportion. There would be no persuading her to accept a dedication that bracketed her with a man she considered the world's greatest megalomaniac. "Alexander! But he killed more men than the Kaiser! More than Napoleon! A power-crazed, egocentric, drunken butcher whose only redeeming features were a love of literature and horses" had been her diagnosis of the young god's condition.

Alexander. He'd been the occasion of Merriman's first quarrel with Laetitia. The least deferential of any of the students Andrew mentored, she'd seized with delighted vindication on the information that Alexander considered himself descended from the mysterious sloe-eyed young man-god from the East: Dionysus. "Well, that explains a lot! Remind me, Professor, of his attributes...God of Wine, Drama, and Revelry, was it? Your hero certainly emulated the god! Nightly debauches for weeks, culminating in his death. According to his secretary, the Lord of the World was actually in mid-gulp when he was struck down with whatever was to kill him days later. Ruptured liver is what I'm betting! And the uncontrolled outbreaks of orgiastic frenzy? It's not recorded that he actually tore men and animals to shreds with his teeth like the followers of Dionysus, but he did stab his friend Black Cleitus in a drunken fit of rage. And I prefer not to think about the thousands of innocents he had crucified and tortured." She had constantly advised: "Look elsewhere for a subject, Andrew. Alexander is irredeemable!"

And her opinion was unalterable. Ah, well, plenty of time

to change the dedication later. After he'd drawn out the pleasurable teasing.

He touched a letter pushed deep into his trouser pocket. Her latest news. She was doing some worthwhile work in Crete and managing to have a happy time with that ecclesiastical sheepdog of hers. William Gunning. Renegade priest. Extraordinary pair! A highly unsuitable relationship and Andrew wondered if he'd done the right thing in encouraging it. It was he who'd brought about their separation initially, for selfish reasons he'd disguised as concern for Laetitia and then, regretting his action, he'd engineered their reunion in Crete. He'd pushed them onstage together like cardboard characters in a child's toy theatre. Playing God—he knew he enjoyed the role more than was good for him. But perhaps one action had cancelled out the other? And perhaps it was all up to Fate anyway. And it did seem to have turned out well in the end. Andrew liked to know his friends were happy. He particularly liked to know Letty was happy.

And, this morning, behind his locked door, he was going to have some fun with his writing.

The first two thirds of the book were ready in manuscript form and sitting with his publisher in London. He'd dealt with the life and career of his subject, Alexander of Macedon, and he'd done it well. It had taken years in time snatched from an active life but it had been meticulously researched. Started in the trenches of Macedonia during the Great War—1915, he remembered—some of his early pages of notes were difficult to read under the brown blotches of mud and blood. He could remember the exact moment when he'd had the idea. He'd taken a copy of Plutarch's *Lives* to war with him in his backpack and, finding himself stationed amongst the silver-fir-clad slopes of the very mountains where Alexander was born and raised, he'd begun to reread the conqueror's story. Stormed and retaken from the Ottoman by the Greek army only a few years previously, this northern province beyond the shrugging shoulder of Mount Olympus was now accounted a part of Greece, though not many people nowadays were entirely convinced that this was a political certainty. According to Prime Minister Venizelos—there could be no doubt! It was now firmly in the territory of the New Greece. And, in Alexander's day, the boy king himself showed no geographical confusion whatsoever! Alexander had had the confidence to write to his enemy Darius, King of the Persian Empire, a letter of intent—intent to invade Asia—and the reason Alexander gave was, just like the man himself, blunt: *"Your ancestors came to Macedonia and the rest of Greece and did us much harm . . ."*

Good point, Alexander! A telling sentence. It was clear from this that he regarded Macedonia as the prime province within Greece and not separate from it. And also that he took the sufferings meted out by the Persian invaders on two occasions to the string of Greek city-states as a personal insult. Alexander saw himself not, as many critics had claimed, as "a barbarian" but as a Hellene. A Greek speaker, a Greek thinker, and an avenger of Greece.

Crouching amongst the crags and the glens of those northern fastnesses where the only creatures about him apart from the military whose presence scarred the land were sheep and eagles, Andrew had had a vision of the young highland soldier more than two thousand years in the past. Raised in a tough school, a warrior among warriors, loved by his loyal kinsmen, the prince had been driven by ambition—and probably by rivalry with his father, Philip—to conquer the world. They said his favourite line from Homer was *"Ever to be best and stand far above all others."* They said his mother Olympias was descended from the hero Achilles, who had so plagued and defied King Agamemnon, his war lord. And Alexander had grown up intending to rival Achilles in glory. Like his ancestor, the boy king had chosen to trade the chance of a long

and dull life for a brief but glorious one which would ensure his eternal fame. His choice certainly made for a gripping
biography.

Andrew's research was incomparable, his style modern,
flowing, and involving. And now at last he'd come to it: the
nub of the book, the point, the culmination of the last ten
years of effort. Ten years he'd spent off and on exploring the
desert sands, not in the hope of making a sensational discovery in the style of archaeologists like Schliemann or Howard
Carter, but always with fingers crossed and—bizarrely—half
hoping for a nil return. He'd been bent on eliminating possi-
bilities, dutifully pursuing trails into the dust, laying the foun-
dations for his coup. Such was the tenacity generated by an
idée fixe. But he was conscious of the weaknesses, the traps
that opened up at the feet of men who sought to make the
facts fit their theory. Dangerous self-deceit, he knew. Self-
deceit could be his undoing.

He'd had considerable success. It was hard to stick a spade
into the sands of Egypt without success of some sort and he'd
made the most of his, using his skill and his scientific background to shape the young discipline of archaeology. He
couldn't rival Howard Carter's astonishing discovery in the
Valley of the Kings, but Andrew knew he had on his side
three attributes Carter could never boast: an aristocratic background, an impeccable education, and a "good war." His
scholarship and his independence were trusted by the Academic Establishment—as far as those prima donnas trusted
anyone. Andrew Merriman was the man governments chose to
consult when problems arose and they needed to quote advice
from an impeccable source who had the world's approval.

They would read his final chapters and swallow the hook.

Andrew sighed with anticipation. His time was coming!
He could pull it off!

And he wouldn't have recourse to ancient curses, dogs

howling in the night, unexpected deaths, and suchlike vulgar attention-grabbing devices! The King Tut Music Hall obsession had entertained the world but he would manage his show much more skilfully. With the understanding of a director for his audience, he would present to the world a mummy of a splendour that would push the insignificant young Pharaoh of Egypt to the back pages. A golden mummy. The embalmed remains of the Son of Zeus. Or so Alexander of Macedonia had thought himself. And oracles, soothsayers, priests, and kings had hurried to support his pretensions. The world had prostrated itself at the feet of its young conqueror. And would again!

The Death of a God. (Who murdered Alexander?) And his Entombment. (Where Do His Remains Lie?) Hard not to scatter the capital letters about. Andrew thought he knew the answers to both questions. And his readers, from the most eminent classical scholars to the man on the London omnibus, would—carried along by the impeccable prose and irrefutable facts of the body of the book—accept in its entirety the astonishing conclusion.

And now for the *bonne bouche*! The finger-tingling climax of his writing. For inspiration, Andrew propped the drawing of Alexander's magnificent golden funeral carriage up in front of his inkstand and stared at it. A hypnotic image.

Borodin's caravan swayed out of sight in time with Andrew's vision. A flute gave one last plaintive flourish. The bells on the golden sepulchre fell silent. The professor smiled with satisfaction. A moving temple, fit for a god. Time for it to make its glittering appearance in his pages!

Ignoring the surreptitious movement of the door handle, Andrew Merriman began to write.

CHAPTER 4

Soulios Gunay strolled to the café fanning himself with his straw boater. Ridiculous headgear! He still felt comfortable with nothing but his red fez. He felt more comfortable with his true given name: Suleyman . . . but, when in Athens . . . He joined three men at their table. They looked up eagerly.

"*Kalimera, sympatrioti*," said one. Was the Thracian greeting sincere or a sly and indiscreet reference to his northern origin? Soulios returned a stiffly polite reply. He looked at their drinks, signalled the waiter, and ordered more ouzo all round with mint tea for himself.

"I shouldn't indulge you," he commented with distaste when the four drinks arrived. "You should be keeping a clear head. That's what I pay you for."

"Oh, come on, now, we got it right this time, didn't we? That was him, wasn't it? You saw! You knew him, or you wouldn't be celebrating by standing us another ouzo," one of them reasoned.

"Give me the photograph."

The oldest man, his cousin, took a battered sepia photograph from his briefcase and put it in the middle of the table.

They all considered the image, matching it with the features of the man they had witnessed briefly.

"Hard to tell. I'd know the *horse* if I saw it again," the cousin commented. "But the arrogant poser in the saddle? Still has that swagger about him...if it *is* him we saw just now. All that bowing and scraping! It's possible. He's aged, if so... It's been how long? Ten years?"

"Eleven," said Soulios firmly. "The year of the Salonika fire—1917. That's when I first encountered him. But it's five years since he rode up to my door with his pockets stuffed with gold. It's him. That's all I need to know."

The three men relaxed and exchanged congratulatory smiles. "Then you'll be wanting us to...?" The youngest of the trio mimed unsheathing a knife.

Soulios stopped him with a peremptory gesture. "No. The next bit is delicate. I don't mean to offend you but I have things to do, things to check...It will take time. My permit runs out next week and I must return...home." The word always caught in his throat. He dislodged it and spat it out again: "Home...to Turkey." He listened politely to the expressions of sympathy his show of emotion had triggered and concluded: "I'll return when I can and prepare you for a busy summer. Meantime—you may stand down."

His cousin shrugged. "Five years, Soulios. Strike while you still have the venom in you. Leave it any longer, you'll start to forget. You'll make yet another fortune, marry another wife... grow fat and easy sitting under your olive trees. Could be your last chance."

Soulios smiled. "Oh, no. The poison distils. Or rather—it improves with keeping, like a good brandy."

They looked at each other with the agitated disappointment of muzzled hounds shown the hare. "Well, when you need us you know where..."

He did. He owned their businesses and their homes.

"Thank you. There is one thing . . . Cousin, your boy—he is how old now?"

"Twelve, Soulios. Well grown. He's a big, strong boy."

"Time he was earning a wage?"

His cousin shrugged. "It's not easy. The city's awash with cheap labour, you know that. Lads that'll work for a day to earn a crust of bread."

Soulios glanced back up the street. "I think a job should be found for him. And I have one in mind. Send Demetrios to see me this evening."

He smiled and rose to his feet, drawing the meeting to a close. "That will be all for the moment. You've seen him. You will know him again. You can go now."

The bleak features invited no argument or comment. Respectfully, the three men finished their drinks, slipped away the banknotes he offered them, bowed briefly, and left together.

Soulios watched them walk away, eyes narrowed in speculation. He decided he had chosen well. The men were bound to him by the double tie of family allegiance and financial interest. The two older cousins had acquired a ruthless competence during their spell in the Greek army during the Balkan wars. They had not yet sunk into the mire of postwar lethargy; their spirit was not yet quenched by domesticity. They could handle weapons. They could kill. The youngest had a naturally vicious streak and a cockiness that pushed him to outdo the two others, whom he jokingly called his "uncles." They would need careful management, but their talents, Soulios calculated, would be quite adequate for carrying out the first stage of his plans. The simplest.

His ultimate goal, a coup so ambitious and so satisfying he could scarcely bring himself to believe it attainable, his cousins had no conception of. And they must catch no whisper of it.

They would have no sympathy for his plan. In fact it would horrify them. They would refuse to be involved with it at any price. Soulios could understand that. No—for this a professional operator would be brought in from a foreign power. It would be expensive but Soulios was prepared to put his last drachma behind it. It would be tricky but, at last and surprisingly, there'd been a breakthrough. He'd learned to wait. And waiting had thrown up support from an unexpected quarter.

He'd discovered there were people in the city more fanatical and madder than he considered himself. Reckless, impetuous, wild-eyed people he wouldn't trust as far as the end of the garden, but they had in place exactly what he needed: a network that threaded Europe. At the centre of the web was Athens, and from here it looped its way from glittering capital to glittering capital in a tangle of telegraph and telephone wires. He'd made discreet use of these people and what he suspected was their leaking sieve of an organisation. They were eager to help. And they'd found exactly what he was looking for in London.

London. The irony pleased him.

When he was sure he was not overlooked, Soulios sat down again, ordered some more tea, and took from his wallet another photograph. He placed it over the first. Dark brown with weathering and much use, the subject was barely distinguishable. Three dark heads close together, six bright eyes, a white streak which might have been a pearl necklace around a slim throat. Three innocents dead.

But it would take four lives to pay the bill.

His loving eyes made out the fading features with painful clarity. His wife, his six-year-old son, and his two-year-old daughter. Their image was still there, etched forever on his mind, as, clasped in each other's arms with not even a burial sack to cover their dead faces, livid and lost, they sank slowly beneath the grey waters of the Bosphorus.

CHAPTER 5

October 1928. Athens.

n an ancient scoop of land, a sheltered hollow on the southern slope of the Acropolis where the rock was still warm from the day, a man's scream ripped through the gathering darkness.

The scream followed the unmistakable sound of a blade thrusting into flesh.

For a few seconds all other sounds were pushed to the edges of perception; the rumble of traffic, the pealing of a cracked church bell, the squabbling of a pair of birds were discounted by everyone within earshot as listeners strained to make sense of what they'd heard.

It came again, the same butcher's blow, accompanied this time by a grunt of effort. A second piercing shriek of surprise and outrage turned abruptly into a guttural rasping: the gargle of a dying man whose lungs refuse to function, whose air passages are filling with blood. And yet the unseen victim went on fighting to snatch one more breath.

The Little Summer of Saint Demetrios had settled over Greece, smiling a blessing. It looked as though they were to have a gentle October. But the harsh heat of the past months lingered on in the citizens' minds, a recent and scorching memory. The memory was too easily triggered by a glance upwards to the contorted shapes of trees outlining the hills and the occasional whiff of charcoal carried down on the breeze. September rain had quenched the sporadic fires and already underbrush was shooting fresh and green amongst the blackened stumps, a premature taste of spring.

As the sun set, the evening sky began to flush with the grey-purple light that the slopes of Mount Hymettus bounce back with some optical witchery to stain the heavens for a few moments over the city. Athens, the violet-crowned, was settling gratefully for the night under a single silken sheet.

It should have been a moment of deep peace but, somewhere just out of sight, a man was screaming in his death throes.

A grey shape, hooded and masked, detached itself from a crowd of similar grey shapes standing frozen in horrified tableau within yards of the butchery, and with a wide gesture called for silence. "Quiet!" The voice was deep and authoritative. The crowd stopped its murmuring at once. And then the same voice came again: "There's been murder done here!" The comment was sepulchral in meaning and delivered with an awed intensity, yet it was so superfluous, following the blatantly obvious nature of the assault, that it risked provoking an explosion of nervous laughter from two women who were sitting at ease on the hillside, listening, a short distance away.

This was no time for levity. The dying man's pain was evident to all who heard it; his dogged refusal to surrender to whatever horror was staring him in the face aroused a sympathetic agony. A third slicing blow and a low gurgling sob had them twitching in response.

Was it over now? They longed for it to be over.

The two women stirred uneasily, listening on, wanting to block their ears yet not daring to miss a sound. Their tension, stretched beyond its limits by fear and pity, frayed and fell apart at a further vocal onslaught, unravelling into strands of impatience and anger. Enough! Enough! Was the victim now attempting to call for help? Surely not! The man knew he must die. Why couldn't he just bow to Fate, give up the ghost and slide away, putting the listeners out of their misery?

Laetitia Talbot, seated in the centre of the first row of marble steps, turned to whisper as much to her companion but closed her mouth, censoring the ungracious comment.

"Lord! Geoffrey's really hamming it up, isn't he?" Maud Merriman had no such compunction. "Where on earth does he think he is—the Torture Chamber at Madame Tussaud's?" Maud's commanding English voice risked disturbing the action even when produced, as now, in a whisper. She sighed and hunted for the spectacles that dangled on a gold chain on her bosom. She popped them onto the tip of her nose and turned the face of her watch to the dying light from the west but shrugged, unable to read it. "If I rightly remember the play, I reckon we've got three hundred lines more to come...Now—*you've* got the script, Letty. Aren't you supposed to be prompting? Just have a look and check I'm right, would you?"

Laetitia knew that she needn't bother. Maud knew every line of the tragedy by Aeschylus, whether in this new English version of *Agamemnon* they were hearing or in the ancient Greek.

"Good thing they invited *us* to their rehearsal, my dear! They can depend on hearing our informed opinion—delivered with unsparing honesty." The relish in Maud's tone promised a stinging application of the renowned Merriman honesty.

"We must tell them to speed things up a bit before the actual performance...Somewhere between lines nine seventy-five and thirteen-forty, I'd say. Wouldn't you agree, Letty? Mark it up in your copy. No! There! There!" An imperious finger flipped over two sheets of the script in Letty's lap and pointed with unerring accuracy to line 975. "One hesitates, of course, to edit dear old Aeschylus and I'm quite certain the suspense is just what the author intended at this point—keeping us on the very edge of these uncomfortable seats—but all the same . . . An hour and a half should be the *absolute* limit for a modern audience. Great Heavens! This could all take another twenty minutes!" Maud hurried on, not requiring a comment. "Fifteen if they dash through it—longer if Geoffrey indulges himself in another death rattle. Don't, I beg you, Laetitia, call for an encore! He's showed off quite enough for one night."

Maud pulled her woolly cardigan more tightly around her shoulders, shivered, and muttered to herself: "For goodness' sake! Still moaning on? What's the matter with you, Geoffrey? *Die*, man! Supper's in half an hour."

Offstage, the victim obliged. Geoffrey Melton, M.A. (Oxon.), attaché at the British Embassy, in his guise of Agamemnon, King of Mycaenae, fell silent at last, lying stabbed to death in his bathtub. Letty could envisage the mad scramble backstage to help Geoffrey out of his resplendent purple Agamemnon outfit and into the dark robes of his wife's lover, Aegisthus, his next role, ready to storm onstage again and throw his weight about. But the audience demanded a sight of the corpse, then as now. Lined up to represent him in the bath was the tailor's dummy Letty had worked on with such glee that afternoon.

Acquired from a gents' outfitters in Syntagma Square, the mannequin, once divested of its smart Parisian suiting, had proved a disappointment. Slender, smooth, and white-skinned, it was no stand-in for a leathery Mycaenean warrior just off wartime manoeuvres. Jokily, the stage manager had approached Laetitia with the suggestion that since she had a pleasing combination of artistic sensitivity, historical knowledge, and a capable hand, and seemed to have nothing better to do that afternoon, she might be just the right person to transform this waxen ephebe into the dead Agamemnon.

He'd judged rightly. Letty was eager to please and delighted to be asked to make a contribution, however insignificant, to the amateur effort. She'd used all her imagination and energy. A thick black wig bought from the same obliging tailor had been stuck in place, a coat of the suntan brown appropriate for an ancient fighting man applied to the stiff limbs, and gouts of stage blood dribbled down the arms. After much argument, it had been agreed that the body should appear without a mask so that Letty could retain the glass eyes of an unnatural green, leaving them in place and open wide to glare back in the torchlight at the audience.

Moments ago in the ancient Theatre of Dionysus, open to the late afternoon sky, Agamemnon, fresh from his conquest, had come sailing in, after an absence—they said—of ten years.

Caked still with the blood, sweat, and soot of battle, the king was returning to the bosom of his family, to the House of Atreus, to his palace in Mycaenae, rich in gold. And his loving wife, Clytemnestra, warned in advance of his arrival, had produced the traditional comforts for the home-coming victor: a bath and a feast. In front of the palace, reaching for his hand, she offered a most royal welcome:

" 'Come now, my darling. Step down from your chariot but—wait a moment! The feet that stamped the city of Troy to dust shall not be allowed to tread on the common earth again.' "

And, clapping her hands to summon the servants: " 'Where are the staff? Ladies—do as you were instructed. Bring out the red carpet! Line the king's path with tapestries!' "

Agamemnon attempted a rejection of the notion. " 'What on earth do you take me for, wife? Some vain foreigner, peacocking about? It's the gods who deserve stuffs dyed with Tyrian purple, not mortal kings,' " he'd protested. He made a token show of unwillingness to commit the act of hubris but, in the face of Clytemnestra's blithe encouragement and flattery, he conceded. " 'Oh, well, go on, then . . . but at least let me take my boots off first!' " he grumbled.

The women spread embroidered cloths, flowing in a bloodred stream beneath his feet towards the palace. The air was scented with Syrian myrrh, roasts were on the spit, wine was being poured. The stage was set.

But all was not well in the House of Atreus. Loving the queen might be, but no Greek audience would be deceived by her soft words. They knew the story. They'd heard it countless times since they were infants. The queen's affection was all for her husband's cousin, Aegisthus, who had ignored the call to war and stayed behind in the palace working his mischief. The pair of lovers had determined that this bath of Agamemnon's would be his last, and Clytemnestra, bursting with long-suppressed hatred and resentment of her husband, had insisted on delivering the death blow herself. What better moment? The servants dismissed, his armour set aside, the battle-ready watchfulness of ten years washing away, the king lolled offstage in the scented water, exposed. His dutiful wife, clucking sympathy, had gently rubbed oil into the silver tracery of scars etching his naked body.

And now, his bath over, she approached, offering up a robe she had woven, like a good Greek wife, with her own hands. As Agamemnon stepped, one foot out of his bath, towards her, Clytemnestra threw the diaphanous yet strong fabric over his head, wrapped it netlike behind his body, trapping his arms by his sides, and plunged her two-edged bronze sword into his unprotected flesh. And plunged again. And a third time.

It was over.

Letty stretched her spine and eased her bottom from the

unrelenting marble. The ghastly old story had lost none of its power to bewitch after three thousand years. Antique it might be, but this tale of hatred, betrayal, and revenge had been played out down the ages. The truth of it was undeniable and every succeeding war had thrown up its own similar horrors. Letty wondered if Agamemnon's dying screams could have been much different from those of Sergeant Wilcox, who'd lived in her village near Cambridge. The local carpenter, Fred Wilcox, had come swinging home, unscathed, from the war ten years ago in the confident expectation of resuming his domestic situation. He'd been found, hours later, not in his hip bath still brimming with scummy water, coal-tar soap suds, and drowned fleas in front of the fire in the back kitchen, but in his garden workshop, hacked to pieces with his own adze. Mrs. Sergeant Wilcox, expressionless and silent, had held up bloodstained hands for the manacles. Letty smiled sadly at the memory of her father's reaction. Lord of the Manor, Magistrate, and senior officer of the village, Sir Richard Talbot had stormed about ineffectually in much the same way as the leader of the chorus here onstage was now storming. Sir Richard chided himself likewise: surely he ought to have foreseen the tragedy . . . everyone in the village knew about Mrs. Wilcox's fancy man, after all . . . But where did one's loyalties lie? One ought not to forget that Wilcox was a notorious wifebeater . . .

The two women fidgeted slightly on their marble seats and drew in breaths of thyme-scented air, cool off the hill. And immediately they stiffened with tension again. More faintly now, but carried towards them by the efficiency of the ancient acoustics, which, miraculously, were still capable of transmitting the merest murmur to the audience, Agamemnon—still clinging to life, apparently—gathered his pitiful strength to deliver one last exclamation.

From the thicket of olive trees to the left of the stage the

Little Owl of Athens heard him. She called out a mocking comment, and was joined by her mate on the right, hooting his derision.

"The work is done!" proclaimed the grey-clad leader of the chorus with a detumescent gasp.

CHAPTER 6

D id you hear that, Maud? That wasn't in the script, surely!"
said Laetitia, running a finger down the page of the book
she held open on her lap. "Drat! I can't make it out. What
did Agamemnon say? He sounded a bit surprised..."

Maud Merriman took her time replying. The older woman
seemed puzzled; her interest in the play suddenly sharpened.
Her response, when it came, was slow and considered: "As you
rightly observe, Letty, that was not in the script. I didn't quite
catch it either, I'm afraid. Greek? English? Not sure. A rasping
squawk, I'd say."

"Those wretched birds! Did someone cast them as an extra
chorus, I wonder? Were they birds, indeed? Eerily, they seemed
to be repeating whatever it was Agamemnon was saying! Don't
you think? *To-whit-to-whoo*?" said Letty. "Or—*coo-coo-vay*?"

"Well, whichever language he was using, I hardly think a
bird call makes a dignified exit line! But that's Geoffrey for
you! A law unto himself, that young man! He may be a highly
competent actor but he's not someone you'd pick for your
cricket team—I've heard the view expressed." Maud sniffed her
disapproval.

"I expect the poor chap stubbed his toe as he was dashing

round the bath, changing costume. 'Ooh! Ooh!' You know…
something like that…Anyway, all will be revealed in a second…Here we go…the coup de théâtre. This is the bit I've
been waiting for. I'm longing to see my corpse appear!"

Maud smiled a slow indulgent smile and murmured, "Of
course, my dear. We are all anticipation."

The chorus of old men whirled about the stage in a dance
of despair, fluttering their robes, full of foreboding, shouting
contradictory orders and advice to each other. Then, in a cho-
reographed movement, they lit torches and dashed here and
there like demented fireflies, holding off the moment of revelation and screwing tight the tension. Finally, beside himself
with anxiety, the leader rushed to the central doors of the
palace, the closed doors behind which the murder had just
been perpetrated. He flung them open. The audience of two
gasped in astonishment, carried away by the theatricality of
the moment.

"Oh, bravo!" breathed Maud.

"That's the stuff!" said Letty.

The torches had settled into a line on either side of the
doors, a last guard of honour forming up for the king. A silver
bath, an old-fashioned Victorian hip bath painted to resemble
a decorated metal cauldron, swept forward on silent runners
into the circular orchestra space.

Maud leaned close and whispered so as not to spoil the effect: "The *ekkyklema*! It's worked! But so it ought—they've
been tinkering with it for a week! I never can quite bring myself to trust in these mechanical devices and—truth be told—
they've no idea how the ancients worked it, though they'll
never admit it! But some clever cove—come to think of it, it
might have been that William Gunning of yours—borrowed a
hospital trolley and stripped it down to its wheels. He got a
chappie up from the street of coppersmiths and had him weld
the bath onto it and hey presto! What a tableau!"

Letty wished she could have been left, just for once, to absorb the scene without asides from Maud. It was certainly dramatic. Following on the shattering effect of the sounds of murder still ringing in their ears, it was enthralling. The bath, gleaming fitfully in the torchlight, contained a body. Slumped sideways, one bare brown arm trailing over the side, Agamemnon lay, shrouded in white fabric. The net wrapped around his head and torso was stained hideously with blood. Letty was proud of her contribution to the scene of slaughter, but this very minor rush of feeling was swept aside by other emotions. Her lips parted and her eyes flared, in astonishment and admiration for the stagecraft but also in pity for the character. Just as the playwright intended, she was contrasting the picture still in her mind's eye, of the kingly figure of Agamemnon arriving, a warrior in the prime of his manhood, towering over his men and eagerly awaited by his subjects, with the presentation of this huddled creature before her. Within minutes the golden monarch of Mycaenae had been reduced to a side of dead flesh, netted and speared, a temple offering, bleeding into a bathtub.

"Ox blood," explained Maud. "They brought it here in a flask."

Clytemnestra entered, reddened sword in her right hand. She strode towards the distraught old men of the chorus ready to defy them, eager to challenge their judgement of her. The role of the queen was being played by a tall girl instead of the traditional male actor and was all the more terrifying for that, Letty thought. Men were never convincing squeaking away in an attempt at a woman's voice. And this actress had a powerful contralto that Lady Macbeth would have been proud of, along with a stage presence that fitted the part. Though clad in heavily embroidered silk robes and wearing a tragic mask like the others, her every gesture spoke directly to the audience. She conveyed pride in her royal status but with a suggestion of her femininity. The audience didn't doubt that under her rich robes she had breasts and a body that had given birth. But she was about to reveal also a heart of steel.

"*'At last my hour came...'*" Letty heard her gloat.
"*'Here I stood firm. Here I struck the blow.*
There was no way he could escape or flee his fate.'"

Letty hated and feared her.

The queen flourished her sword and tugged at the knots restraining the limbs. She began to peel back the folds of cloth.

"*'... So down he fell, and the lifeblood spurted out of him—*
In showers. And this deadly rain has dyed me black...'"

Clytemnestra turned to the audience and, with a clatter of cascading golden bracelets, thrust up her arms. The wide sleeves of her robe fell back to her armpits, revealing shapely limbs stained black indeed in the twilight by gobbets of blood.

"*'... and I? I revel in it!'*" Her voice rose to an unholy shout, the white mask she wore directing the force of her triumph straight to the audience.

Letty's hatred deepened.

Unrepentant, implacable. Surely some god or other would take offence and strike her down? Letty felt as one with the leader of the chorus of citizens when he bravely summoned up the spirit to chastise his queen. A worthy opponent. His baritone rang out, fearful yet determined, channelling, at the risk of his own life, the outrage of the classical audience:

"*'Woman! Loathed abomination! Whatever possessed you to do this deed? You deserve to be banished from the city, forever cursed!'*"

Emotion had stripped away a layer of the actor's smooth, upper-class English and Letty thought she detected something more raw, more musical, beneath. A Welshman perhaps? His heartfelt outpouring was scalding, and the perfect foil for the cold precision of the queen's reply:

> " 'My heart is steel, you know that. You may praise me,
> Or blame me as you choose. It's all the same to me.
> Here is Agamemnon, my husband, murdered
> By my right hand—a perfect piece of Justice.' "

In pursuit of her flourish of "Justice," Clytemnestra was distracted for the moment from her unwrapping of the corpse: a bit of business designed to prolong the suspense. The ancient writer himself, father of stagecraft, would have admired the device, Letty thought. The queen launched into a tirade against her husband, enumerating his many appalling sins against her. With each accusation she tugged at the cloth and, inch by inch, the guilty man was revealed.

Well—fairness in all things. That was the Greek way. Balance. Hear both sides. Letty could not help but agree with the queen that she had much to complain about. Foremost of the charges was that Agamemnon had offered up as a human sacrifice their young daughter Iphigenia to placate the gods and ensure a following wind to take the Greek fleet to Troy. And all with the intention of chasing after his brother's wife, the lovely Helen, who had eloped with a Trojan prince. In pursuit of a whore, Agamemnon had sacrificed a virgin. The audience sympathised with the queen. Clytemnestra objected to his long absence from the family hearth. Ten years. That amounted, surely, to desertion? And, most recent of his offences, and most bitterly resented—he had brought back, as his concubine from Troy, his spear prize, his share of the booty: the princess Cassandra. Agamemnon had fallen in love with the Trojan girl and had returned to Argos treating her with all honour, as his wife and the mother of his two small twin sons, rather than as his slave.

And, here also, Clytemnestra has a devastating revelation to make to the citizens:

> " 'Here lies the man who dishonoured his wife.
> And there' "—the queen gestured offstage—" 'lies his slave,
> His fortune-telling concubine.
> Cassandra—this superfluous bride,
> This foul new interloper in our marriage bed,
> His lover—lies dead! And her whelps with her.' "

She brandished her sword again.

Cassandra and her children: three innocents dead by the queen's hand.

The chorus cringed and moaned at the cruelty. But the queen's greatest sin in their eyes was the murder of Agamemnon. A king was inviolate, and a husband all-powerful. He might have concubines and bastard children by the hundred, he might have killed his own daughter: no matter. The moral law was clear. A woman guilty of the double sin of killing such a man was anathema to the good citizens of Mycaenae. Or Athens.

The chorus went on with its breast-beating while their leader remonstrated with her on their behalf, threatening dire consequences.

> " 'For this flood of slaughter
> The full price shall be paid.
> For sacrifice of children.
> Flesh for flesh, blood for blood,' " he warned.

To no avail. The queen had an answer for everything. Obdurate and ruthless and a mistress of timing, she stood by her husband's corpse, clutching the last fold of the cloth as though she would hold on to him forever, her trophy, the victim of her sword. Finally, judging her moment of revelation had come, she leaned in close to the body, a lowering Nemesis, and delivered over his head a mockery of a eulogy:

> " 'A wonderful swordsman, you thought yourself!
> Well, don't think of showing off your skills in Hell,
> Now you've got what you deserved—
> By the sword you lived, and by the sword you died!' "

With a practised flick of the wrist she snatched the remaining length of cloth from the corpse and, turning as she did so to the audience, she sought to involve them in her triumph as she revealed their dead master to the citizen chorus.

Letty gasped, not in response to the queen's gloating but in mortification that her so carefully applied wig had been wrenched loose from the dummy's head by the gesture and, with an obscenely comical air, was now resting at a drunken angle over the upper part of the face. She could hardly bring herself to look.

"Ah! We descend into bathos ... But don't take it to heart, my dear," advised Maud. "This is, after all, exactly why we have a dress rehearsal. Something always goes wrong. This is it. You'll have plenty of time to reinstate the wig before the actual performance."

The old men of the chorus ought to have wailed in shock and pity and held their hands before their eyes as though unable to bear the sight. So the stage directions instructed. But they stayed silent and still. Torches wavered and drooped. Then, with the sudden flashing movement of a shoal of fish, the members of the chorus made a concerted advance on the bathtub.

What on earth was going on? Letty, for once, would have been glad of an explanatory footnote from Maud. One or two of the actors snatched off their masks, the better to see what lay before them. Gasps exploded, comments were muttered. Letty thought she heard an injudicious and very Anglo-Saxon exclamation. Weirdly, still behaving as a chorus and moving with purpose together, they began to close ranks, packing themselves in a double circle protectively around the corpse.

Clytemnestra, sensing herself being physically edged away from centre stage, hesitated. "What *are* you doing? What *is* all this?" Letty heard her hissing and then, receiving no response, her voice rang out, imperious and angry: "I say, you chaps! Have you all gone barmy? Get out of my way, you clowns! I've not finished yet. This is where I spit on the corpse!"

No one moved an inch to accommodate her. The queen raised her sword and advanced on the grey figures. Confused but still apparently acting in role, she picked out the tallest. The leader of the chorus. She jabbed him in the ribs. "Hey! You! Bossy Boots with the loud voice! I'm talking to *you*!"

The man moved reluctantly to one side with a shocked protest: "No, madam, no! Believe me—this is not a sight for…" And, in firmer tone: "Madam, I'm afraid I must ask you to leave the stage…"

Clytemnestra ignored him and pushed herself swiftly forward into easy spitting distance of the corpse before they could close the gap. She peered down at the bloodstained wreck. Her regal left hand went out and grasped Agamemnon by the shoulder. She shook him.

"Geoffrey? Is that *you*, Geoffrey? What on earth do you think *you're* doing there?" And, surprisingly: "This isn't the time for playing stupid games!… Oy! Geoffrey!"

The warrior's muscled brown arm flopped, lifeless, over the edge of the bathtub, knuckles grazing the rough slabs of the orchestra floor as the naked body, unbalanced by her shaking, folded at the hips and lurched forward.

"Oh, my God!" wailed Clytemnestra, and she slid in a silken whisper to her knees.

CHAPTER 7

The young lighting manager, hidden behind the scenes in the buildings to the rear of the orchestra, came suddenly to life. Confused and wondering how he'd managed to lose his place in the text—had he nodded off? turned over two pages at once?—he decided the sensible thing to do was to respond to the drama of the moment. He turned on the additional stage lighting and bathed the scene of confusion in an unkind glare.

A second later, Letty found herself distracted from the events unfolding before her by the arrival at her side of a large and very welcome masculine presence. William Gunning settled on the stone bench and leaned across her, managing a fleeting but affectionate squeeze of the hand as he did so and whispering: "Lady Merriman...Laetitia...I've brought the car. Thought you'd appreciate a lift back. Ah—I see the *ekkyklema* worked...Now—where've we got to? Running a bit late, aren't they? Good Lord! What's going on?"

Maud replied, "You may well ask, William! They've gone mad. They've all forgotten their lines and they're inventing their own rubbish. I believe on the London stage it's called improvisation...Isadora Duncan has much to answer for! The queen has launched an unprovoked attack on the leader of the chorus and has now sunk to her knees yelping over the king's corpse. Where's the stage manager? Where's Hugh? And where's my husband? I can't believe he authorised this. Someone must fetch Andrew to deal with them." She looked pointedly at Gunning.

Letty had to agree. Professor Sir Andrew Merriman, director, scriptwriter, and moving force behind this amateur entertainment, should at this moment be striding around the stage, boxing a few ears.

"William, my dear—would you mind? Go and roust him out! I'd go myself if only..." Maud's voice trailed away and they filled in the unspoken: "...if only it weren't for my weak heart...my palpitations...my arthritis...my nerves..."

Gunning had got to his feet and was standing tensely absorbing the scene. Letty was sure he hadn't heard a word Maud said, but he was already starting towards the stage. Letty put down her script and scuttled after him, aware that Maud was staying firmly in her seat, tut-tutting with exasperation and clutching her bosom. Obviously, this was a palpitations day.

Gunning stalked to the centre front of the stage and held up his arms like a conductor. "Quiet! All of you!" he commanded. "Stand still. Stay exactly where you are." The response to the crisp officer's voice was automatic and immediate. "No one is to move until we've got hold of Professor Merriman. Now...anyone know where he is?"

"Sir...he'll be backstage having a nip of brandy before the last scene," offered a tremulous voice. The young man who'd been playing the part of Cassandra came back onstage again. He pushed up his white mask and looked over his shoulder towards the higgledy-piggledy arrangement of tents and wooden huts that served for a *skena* behind the orchestra. "He keeps it in the dressing room. Er...would you like me to go and do a recce?"

"That would be kind of you. It's Simon, isn't it? Thank you," said Gunning, dismissing him with a nod. "Steady, the rest of you." And then, tentatively: "I think you're all aware that we may be looking at something of a problem..." He turned to the queen, who was still on her knees gasping and moaning in front of the bathtub, and held out a hand. "We haven't yet been introduced, Your Majesty. William Gunning...loosely attached to the British School of Archaeology."

The queen stifled her gasps long enough to mutter: "Thetis Templeton. How do you do?"

"Would you mind moving aside, Miss Templeton?"

At last she took his hand and, suddenly clumsy in her long robes, struggled to her feet.

With the queen's presence removed, Letty had a clear view of the bathtub. She stepped closer, expecting at any moment to be ordered away by some bossy male voice, most probably William's.

She'd guessed what the tub contained.

The slumping movement of the body seen from the audience benches had not been that of the stiff-jointed mannequin she'd worked on a few hours earlier. She'd become intimate with every limb of that doll and knew that she was not looking at it now. These legs and arms were not the smooth white waxen ones she'd daubed. They were tanned and muscled. This torso had flopped with what she imagined would be the heavy downward and forward motion of a real man who'd suffered a real death.

Fearful but drawn on towards the horror, she braced herself for the sight of Geoffrey in his agony. The recently exposed face was bloodstained and almost obscured by the black wig, which had slipped its moorings and been dragged down over the nose by Clytemnestra's jerky unwrapping.

Someone was going to have to remove it.

Laetitia felt a residual responsibility for the contents of the tub, whatever or whoever they were, and she readied herself for the task.

Within two yards of the body, she stopped. She gasped and stared and her limbs began to shake. With a low moan of disbelief and protest, she flung herself the last few feet, sinking to her knees in front of the corpse, in unconscious repetition of Clytemnestra's performance. Murmuring softly, she reached out to remove the wig, but her arm was firmly grasped by a strong hand before she could touch it.

The leader of the chorus spoke gently in her ear: "I'm awfully sorry, Miss...er...Talbot, isn't it? You really mustn't disturb anything, you know. I'm afraid there's been a terrible disaster...In fact, I rather think we ought to clear the stage." He released her into the protective custody of Gunning's arms before leaning over to search with expert touch for a pulse behind the right ear of Agamemnon. After a few moments he stood up again, shaking his head in an unmistakable gesture. "Gunning, would you...?"

William took Letty by the waist and led her as far away as she would allow him, then he turned to face the leader. "I'm sorry...you have the advantage—and the additional concealment of a mask. You are...?"

The actor fished about under his grey cape and produced a card. He held it out to Gunning, and there was a distinct but instantly suppressed flash of irony in his voice as he announced: "Deus ex machina. At your service. I think you're going to need some divine help. I'll be glad to be of assistance."

He swept off his mask, revealing features which, though certainly not godlike, were impressive. A clever face with a decisive nose, was Letty's first impression. Intense eyes below straight black brows were the most striking feature in a face moulded in strong, smooth planes. Not in the first flush of youth, he had frown lines between his brows, but this severity was offset by a slight ironic lift of the mouth. It was a face the equal of the voice she had admired. The slyly confident face of an opponent who is just about to pronounce "Checkmate!" A face ruthless enough to make her want to look aside.

Gunning looked from the card in his hand back to the man, who was quietly watching for his reaction, and he read out, loudly enough for Letty to hear and clearly struggling to master his disbelief: "Chief Inspector Percival Montacute, Scotland Yard, Whitehall, London. Well, I'm blowed!"

"Percy," said the leader affably. "Or Chief Inspector...depending on how our relationship develops."

"You're a long way from home, aren't you? But what the devil...? How on earth do you come...? I don't understand..."

Gunning was cut short by Montacute. "Later. We'll go into all that later. There are excellent reasons for my being here, lurking in the shrubbery so to speak, but first things first, eh? Corpse on our hands...Sure you've realised that much. Where's that Greek boy assistant got to? The one who does the lighting effects?" Montacute shouted his name and when the lad appeared he instructed him in fluent Greek to run to the police station, alert the officer in charge, and request backup at once in the form of a murder squad.

"And now, I think Miss Talbot was showing us the way... preparing to take the next step...We all know what has to be done," he said. "Gunning, would you join me at the tub? You know the cast, I believe? You will be able to identify the poor fellow who's concealed below that frightful wig."

The two men went to stand one on either side of the bathtub, and carefully Montacute began to peel the fall of black hair upwards over the forehead. With a last tug, he separated it from the thick mass of greying fair hair underneath.

A chorus of exclamations burst from the spectators, and Gunning, shaken and trembling, made the sign of the cross over the body, murmuring instinctively the ritual phrases of farewell to the departed.

Identification had been at the forefront of everyone's mind—an imperative—and yet, strangely, with the familiar features exposed for all to see, no one breathed his name. The discovery had the effect of silencing every member of the group, isolating each in his own shock and disbelief. Grief and mourning would come much later, with acceptance; for now, all they could do was stare and look aside, praying that their senses were misdirecting them, and stare again and be forced to confront the truth.

Stage left, Clytemnestra made low keening noises into a trailing sleeve of her robe. Stage right, Letty stood frozen in an unnatural rigidity, eyes huge in her pale face and focussed on the bloodied body, making no sound.

The inspector looked from one to the other with interest. And looked again.

"That's quite *enough*! You've had your fun! Now will you please all stop larking about and put an end to this." The clarion voice rang out, sounding a note of farce. "It's an absolute disgrace! I resent wasting another moment on your buffoonery! Whatever will you come up with next? Pigs' bladders and water pistols? This is a drama, not a satyr play..." Maud Merriman had, at last, decided to make her appearance. She advanced, with a torrent of complaints, limping along with the aid of her stick (a support on those days when arthritis struck), and the cast moved aside to let her through. In minutes, all roles had been reversed and the audience was onstage, acting out a tragedy, while the actors could do no more than look on, aghast, dreading the outcome.

Maud joined Gunning at the bathtub and peered in.

"I thought as much! This prep-school humour is undignified and has to stop!" She struck the side of the bath with her stick and the ringing note triggered a quiver of distaste that ran through the crowd. "Get up! Ugh! The man's quite naked under all that paint! Will someone please pass him a robe?" She bent her head and spoke directly to the body of Agamemnon in an eerie echo of the queen's waspish address to her dead husband.

"Andrew! You begin to be an embarrassment! Joke's over. You're to get out of there at *once!*"

CHAPTER 8

t was Montacute who moved to respond to the first of Maud's commands. The inspector took off his own grey cape and draped it, shroudlike, over the limbs.

The formality of the draping and the finality of the age-old gesture seemed to convey its stark message and Maud fell silent. Her face showed the fearful resignation of someone who has seen a flash of lightning and is now waiting for the thunderclap that must follow it.

"Lady Merriman..." he began.

"Montacute," she interrupted, "you knew my husband. In Salonika. You came to dinner with us...What are you telling us?"

"I did indeed know him, madam. And I can, of course, identify him myself. I counted him my friend. But it would be more fitting, perhaps, if you were to confirm that the man you have just seen is your husband—Professor Sir Andrew Merriman?"

"Of course I can. I recognise my own husband!" And then, softly: "He's not play-acting...he's dead, isn't he?"

"I'm afraid he is."

"This is ludicrous! Andrew has no business being in the

bathtub! Why isn't it that obscene dummy of Laetitia's in there? Or Geoffrey? Geoffrey Melton was the one supposed to die...Geoffrey!" Maud called out, rapping her stick sharply on the stone flags. "Where are you?"

"I'm here, madam. Did I miss my cue?"

Already nervous, the cast jumped perceptibly as the voice that had only minutes before shaken them with its prolonged death screams responded to her challenge. Geoffrey Melton, still adjusting the black velvet robe of the villain Aegisthus around his shoulders, made his way out of the shadows and onto centre stage. The other players instinctively shuddered away from him as he moved between them. He stalked on careful feet to the bath and there was a rustling sigh from the gathering as Aegisthus with terrible inevitability produced his entrance line:

" *'What a brilliant day this is for retribution! My eyes feast on this man, this victim, snared by the vengeful Furies' net!'* "

He paused and peeled off his linen mask, though Letty thought he might just as well not have bothered; the face beneath was no more revealing than the emotionless, chalk-white painted fabric.

"Hey! What's going on here?"

"It's *you* who must answer *that*, man!" Maud snapped. "How do you account for this? What do you have to say for yourself? You were on the spot. Andrew's dead. You must have seen or heard him expire. Could you not have called for assistance? Did you just stand by and let him die? Were you too involved with your own dramatic death rattle to notice his dying gasp?"

Her staccato demands betrayed to all onstage an irrationality out of character with the calculating and correct lady they knew, and their drooping heads and averted eyes expressed a quiet understanding. The challenge on Melton showed a certain mad gallantry which impressed but alarmed

Letty. Geoffrey Melton was not one to tolerate such an attack, even from a distraught woman. He was a splendid actor, but he kept himself apart from the rest of the cast by means of a cold and supercilious attitude. And here he stood, improbably tall in his built-up leather theatre sandals, towering over Maud, even dressed as the very figure of villainy.

Letty moved forward to stand protectively by Maud's side, though she could not rationally explain her impulse. She was not alone in feeling the threat, apparently, as Montacute held up a warning hand and stepped himself between the widow and the object of her scorn. Once again, the London police-man found himself, in rôle, squaring up to a figure of royal authority.

There was obvious relief when Melton chose to make a soft response. He leaned over the body, his gold chains clank-ing, and moved the cloak aside to take a close look at the re-mains, taking his time. Then he straightened, made the sign of the cross, and murmured in his light baritone:

" 'Who dies in youth and vigour dies the best,
Struck through with wounds, all honest on the breast.'

"A fine man, Lady Merriman. I am truly astonished and devastated to see Andrew like this. A huge loss."

"We thank you for your sentiments, Mr. Melton," said Montacute, responding for all. "But now, may I ask you to step aside, join the rest of the cast, and hold yourself ready for questioning?" He turned back to Maud and took her comfort-ingly by the arm. "Now, madam, you may have heard me send for my colleague in the Athens police force. The moment he arrives, we will instigate an enquiry into the circumstances of your husband's death."

"The Athens police force?" Maud's eyebrows shot up. "I

wasn't aware they had one. And why would you be needing them? You should summon a competent doctor." She shrugged off his arm. "May I recommend, Montacute, since you appear to have put yourself in charge of some sort of an enquiry, my friend Dr. Peebles, who has his offices on the Queen Sophia Avenue? He is Andrew's doctor also, and if you send for him he will be pleased to come along and ascertain the circumstances for you."

A swift skirmish with Scotland Yard seemed to be just what Maud needed to put her back in control of herself once more. Rallying, she went to take a further look at her husband and no one had the nerve to stop her. Tugging the cloak to one side, she stared down, expressionless, at the blood-slathered corpse.

"Heart attack," she pronounced. "You'll find he died of a heart attack. Now—William? Where are you? You were about to run me up to the villa in the motor, I think?"

Montacute exchanged an imperceptible nod with Gunning.

"Military men," thought Letty. "How easily they recognise each other."

Clearly on the point of collapse, Lady Merriman put a hand on Gunning's arm to steady herself. She paused to look over her shoulder and direct one last instruction at Laetitia. She even managed a stiff smile. "Do feel free to stay on and be of any assistance you can to the inspector, Letty, my dear. I appoint you my stand-in. I'm sure you will be able to provide answers to any questions he may have about the professor. And some answers which might even be outside my own experience and knowledge." She turned on a sweet smile and directed it at the inspector, adding: "Laetitia is an archaeologist, you know. One of her many skills. And she likes to make herself available. You'll find her very willing, Inspector."

They all stood, heads bent in quiet respect, as the widow turned and tapped her way offstage, hearing her say conversationally to Gunning: "Ox blood. They brought it here in a flask, you know. I was just telling Letty..."

The silence rolled back as they left and were lost to sight in the thick stand of trees and bushes that cut the theatre off from the Avenue of Dionysus.

The cast looked at one another, wary and uncertain. The London policeman seemed to catch their mood and began to speak to them in a reassuring tone.

"For those of you who don't know me yet, let me introduce myself: Detective Chief Inspector Montacute of Scotland Yard. Criminal Investigations Department. I'm here in Athens on secondment. I and two British colleagues are working with the Athenian police force at the invitation of the Greek government to establish a certain Britishness of practice in the local force and train their detective branch in the latest forensic methods. Not for the first time—there's a tradition of cooperation between the two forces going back half a century."

He paused, aware of a shuffling of feet and increasingly agonised glances drawn ever towards the bathtub. He was losing their attention. With the stage sense of an actor, he walked off to a point on the floor away from the body. They turned automatically towards him, backs now to the distraction, eyes fixed on his face. Having captured his audience, he kept them. He abandoned his lecturing style and addressed them with a change of tone and speed of delivery. "But Aeschylus? Do policemen spout Aeschylus?" he wanted to know. "Well, here's one who does! But let me assure you, because I'm certain some of you will already have begun to wonder, that my appearance here is entirely fortuitous—"

"Oh, yes?" drawled a wearily sceptical tenor voice from the chorus. "Is that what you're saying? In that getup, some might well suspect there was a bit of cloak-and-dagger work going on. An extraordinary coincidence? A certain inexplicable anticipation of a tragic event, perhaps? Anything you'd like to confess, Montacute?"

The speaker, still masked, was taking no trouble to hide a scorn, a dislike even, that Letty found ill-timed and ill-judged. Whoever this character was, she would have liked very much to rap his knuckles.

"Masked and caped I may have been, but hardly under cover!" returned the inspector, unruffled. "You're all free to inspect *my* ugly mug. May I suggest you return the compliment, *Louis,* and show yourself to the assembled company?"

The young man unmasked himself and sketched a sarcastic bow.

"Thank you. Now, as some of you will already be aware, your original chorus leader came down with a bout of malaria. Andrew was relieved to find that someone with experience of the play happened to be seconded to Athens for the weeks in question," Montacute continued. "He gave me a copy of the script, knowing I was familiar with it, and asked if I could possibly mug it all up and perform. You've heard his wife mention that we knew each other. We were in the same regiment during the war, the Northumberland Fusiliers. He was a superior officer but we were drawn together by shared interests."

Sensing he was saying more than they needed to hear and repeating facts most of them already knew, he let his voice trail away to be absorbed into the dutiful silence, and he looked over with concern at the cloaked body. "I'm sorry indeed that this should have happened..."

"*On your watch,* were you about to add?" jibed his heckler. "Slipped up there, I think, Montacute? Or were you looking the other way deliberately?"

He was silenced by the crowd, who turned on him with angry hisses and threats of a walloping.

Montacute's eyes narrowed as he judged the gathering anxiety and turbulence. Letty was relieved to see him make a schoolmaster's decision to regain authority by a simple means: the distraction of a routine task in hand. "Anyway, may I ask you all to remove your masks—if you haven't already—line up, and give your names to Miss Talbot in the time-honoured way?" the inspector finished decisively.

"Who? *Me?*" Letty was taken aback.

"Yes. *You*, Miss Talbot. We all heard Lady Merriman's tribute to your efficiency and dedication! She volunteered you! We count ourselves fortunate to have you among us at this stressful time. Take this notebook. And here's a pencil. As the one of those here assembled with the least strong connexions with the cast and the play, perhaps you will allow yourself to be recruited as my aide until support arrives? I'm sure we're all hoping that nothing untoward has happened, but we must wait for our hopes and fears to be resolved by a medic. In the meantime, I'm taking the precautions you might expect a police officer to take at the scene of a crime."

"Ah! You're saying it's murder?" The challenging voice again.

"I say! That's a bit hysterical, isn't it?" someone else protested. "This is Athens. You're not stirring about in the cesspits of Whitechapel now, you know. I'm betting her ladyship's got it right! Well—is she ever wrong?" He looked for support from his fellows.

"Oh, put a sock in it, you chaps! You never know. Could all turn nasty and then we'll be glad we did it by the book. And we'll all thank you to show a little respect! Henry Beecham, by the way, sir. Chorus, fourth from the left... I'm sure I speak for everyone here when I say we've all lost a dear friend, colleague, patron... our inspiration... You, too, Louis... And we owe it to him to do whatever we can to resolve this tragedy." Beecham's voice faded and then resumed awkwardly: "Well, you know what I mean..." And, more briskly: "Now, where do you want us, Percy? Or should I call you Chief Inspector for the duration of the enquiry?"

With varying degrees of cooperation, the chorus, the leading actors, and the remaining backstage crew of two lined up to give their names to Letty. She opened up the black leather Moleskine journal she'd been offered and found a clean page. Finding a folding campaign chair, she settled down with her back to the arc lamp and required the actors to line up in alphabetical order and stand in front of her with the light shining on their faces. She'd learned a thing or two about police work in the last couple of years, she reckoned. She'd been the subject of some sneaky interrogations herself.

There was a farcical moment when, like a herd of prep-school boys, they pushed and jostled one another.

"*J* comes after *G*, you twerp!"

"Hey, miss—can you do me first? I'm going on somewhere—late already, don't you know."

"I simply *must* be at the Embassy by eight or there'll be the devil to pay!"

Letty, her hair an unnaturally gleaming halo of gold in the light, surveyed her flock. She remembered her nanny's brisk way with crowds of children at parties: *Start as you mean to carry on, dear—and take no little prisoners.* Letty stabbed her pencil at the anxious crowd and announced: "No excuses. No privileges. No exceptions. Alphabetical order by surname. *Anthony,* did you hear me?"

Anthony Wardle shuffled disconsolately to the rear.

Work began. She was sorry to see that the dismissive Louis had the surname of "Adams" and therefore presented himself legitimately at the front of the queue. She looked for some misdemeanour as an excuse to send him to the back but, aware of her watchful eye on him, he behaved perfectly.

"Ah! The Recording Angel!" he said with an ingratiating smirk, smoothing down his own floppy blond hair. Blue eyes bleached and splintered to diamonds by the harsh light glittered disconcertingly. "Adams. Louis Fortescue Adams. At your service. I may be contacted at the British School. You know the address."

He made to leave.

"A moment, Mr. Adams," she said sharply. Tall and handsome, he had spoken to her with a languid condescension. This was exactly the kind of Englishman who raised Letty's hackles, reminding her all too keenly of the treacherous Cambridge don who'd engineered her dismissal from the university. Determined not to let him off so easily: "The inspector will need to know exactly where you were positioned at the moment of Agamemnon's death," she invented, deliberately to detain and irritate him. "Perhaps you could give me the stage reference...you know...stage left, six feet from central point...I'm assuming a twenty-foot radius."

"What do you mean—Agamemnon's death? It's a work of literature, my dear," he explained slowly and clearly, playing to the crowd. "Like Robin Hood. Or King Arthur. You've heard of them? The king didn't *really* die. At least not here, not now, not on this occasion. We would calculate the old rogue in actuality to have slipped this mortal coil towards the end of the Bronze Age—1200 B.C. or thereabouts."

"The queue is waiting, Mr. Adams."

"Stage right. Perimeter. End of the chorus line rubbing shoulders with Dicky Crawshawe," Louis Adams contributed briskly, then, apparently unable to pass up the chance of tormenting her a little further: "At least I think it was Dicky. Hard to tell. Could just as easily have been Count Dracula in that cloak." He leaned towards her confidentially. "Have a care, miss, when you get to the *D*'s."

"Thank you. Next!"

Letty noticed that Adams did not leave in spite of his affected haste. He quietly drew aside and sat down on the front row of marble seats, watching the proceedings, his blond Anglo-Saxon head flaring like a beacon in the arc lights.

She had been kept afloat by her rush of anger with Adams and with his departure was, for a moment, almost swept away by other emotions. She found herself fixed here taking notes like a school matron at the bedtime roll call—*Hands? Teeth? Bowels? Tick. Tick. Better luck tomorrow, dear*—when what she wanted to do was express her shock, to share her grief with William Gunning. He too would be feeling devastated. He'd grown to admire Andrew Merriman—owed his present situation to him. Letty owed the professor that and much more. She looked wearily down the line of actors and wondered how many of these people, most of them students, were themselves trying to push their feelings to a lower level, to disguise their affection behind a stiff upper lip and clipped English formulae of regret. Warm, witty, and juggling his immense learning with a blend of skill and insouciance, Andrew became dear to everyone he met. He had launched many careers; he had sabotaged none. It seemed only his wife despised him. But then, Letty acknowledged, his wife had good cause.

"Beecham. Henry Beecham, miss ... er ... stage left. Fourth from the end in the lineup. British School of Archaeology. Student digs. That's all? Thank you. Got to dash."

Letty wondered whether she ought to insist on their staying. Montacute hadn't passed such an order. In the end, she asked the two who needed to leave early to report to the inspector before they went off-site. She looked in the policeman's direction, wishing he'd walk back over and take the reins from her hands. She caught sight of his barrel-chested figure in its khaki shirt and linen trousers apparently beating the bounds of the theatre, moving in and out of the shadows. Head bent, he was tracking over the ground in ever-widening circles. He disappeared for a few moments into the clutter of wooden buildings that stood for the *skene* and continued his survey of the scene of crime. The sight of his solitary effort made Letty ashamed for her lack of dedication. She had to suppose that a man of his rank was used to directing a whole squad of trained hounds back in London, spearheading the advance of forensic science, a world authority. And here he was alone for a vital half hour until reinforcements arrived, in a foreign country, in the dark, with a grotesque corpse on his hands, twenty skittish witnesses to control, and no one in support but a feeble, heartbroken English girl.

With a sudden insight, she realised why Montacute had set her to catalogue the dramatis personae. Queuing up to supply information was something they understood. They had been doing it all their English lives and could be expected to fall in with the procedure with no demur. Even Adams had not seriously challenged the authority bestowed so surprisingly on her. They would stand quietly to one side, out of the inspector's hair, while he roamed about unencumbered, trying to establish what he could in the important minutes after the—could she bring herself to say the word?—murder. The inspector's professional behaviour certainly indicated that they were looking at just that. Someone had murdered Andrew.

Shuddering as the suspicion belatedly struck her, Letty looked along the queue of actors, standing passively waiting for her attention. Someone had killed Andrew and could be at that very moment waiting patiently in line, ready to tell her his name.

CHAPTER 9

She beckoned the next actor forward.

One by one they chose, on leaving her, to go and sit down with Louis Adams, huddled together, waiting on events. Although not generally liked—Letty noticed—Adams seemed to attract a following. People listened when he spoke and had no objection to keeping him company on the stone benches.

The stage manager, Hugh Lattimore, presented himself, perplexed and defensive. He risked becoming garrulous, Letty thought, as he launched into a self-justifying account of his evening: He wouldn't be held responsible ... Couldn't possibly be everywhere ... He'd no idea what villainy had been going on backstage—his eyes had been trained on the performance from the wings and the front side of the audience benches, judging the effect of the torches and timing the advance of the twilight. Oh, there was so much more to stage management than people realised! Surely she'd noticed him? He'd been no more than twenty yards away, to her right? Letty admitted the truth of this and steered him back to the vital moments.

"Ah! When my cue came—that is, Melton's screeching—I did my duty backstage. I made my way to the bathtub, whisked off the length of muslin covering the king…someone had already poured the blood over him…and pushed it forward just as we'd practised. I didn't notice anything untoward, but then neither did Clytemnestra at first and she had much closer and longer contact with the body than *I* could have done. Speak to *her*!"

Letty, irritated and unsympathetic, heard him out. "Thank you, Mr. Lattimore, that's all…If you will just tell me where you're staying in Athens?"

She was poised to write him down as yet another British School student but he gave an address in the exclusive new northern suburb of Kifissia. He acknowledged her surprise with a deprecating smirk. "A rather splendid situation, I'm sure you'll agree! Cool, green, and elegant. And hoi polloi nowhere in evidence. Do you know it?"

"I visited once, last spring. General Konstantinou was throwing a tennis party at his villa."

He began to thaw at once. "You know the General! Small world, indeed, the city of Athens! I'm staying with his family. Tutor to the children—his grandchildren mainly. But also to the household. We practise at mealtimes. The General is very concerned that every member of the family should be able to converse in English. But all that leaves my evenings free for cultural activities of this nature."

Was it the fear and suspicion swirling all about that was making Letty see all her interviewees in such a bad light? She couldn't wait to get rid of this self-serving and snobbish little twerp. She felt a twinge of pity for the General's grandchildren. But then, looking over his shoulder at the next in line, she saw that things were going to get worse.

"Next, please. Ah, yes, Mr. Melton."

She hoped her voice had not betrayed the dread she had been feeling at the thought of facing the figure of Aegisthus in his spreading black and gold regalia. To her surprise, he made her brief interview unremarkable. He waited for her questions, answered them smoothly, and immediately fell silent. Though not appearing evasive, all he revealed about himself was that he could be contacted at the British Embassy. His eyes, she noticed, never engaged with hers, remaining trained over her shoulder into the bushes beyond. She dismissed him and watched him glide away with the same relief she might have felt on seeing a king cobra decide she was not worthy of his royal attention.

"And you are . . . ?"

"Patterson, Miss Talbot. Zoë Patterson. I know who you are, Laetitia—I may call you Laetitia?—and I've seen you from a distance but no one's had the time to introduce us yet. I work with Sarah. She's at the back of the queue under *W* for Williams. She's a student at the American School of Classics and I'm next door at the British. We do the wardrobe together—you know, repairs and that sort of thing—and we help the double-ups out of their costumes and into their new ones."

"Tell me about Geoffrey Melton, Zoë." She looked about her to check that he hadn't stayed in earshot. "He walked off the orchestra as Agamemnon, to have his bath backstage—we saw all that from out front—but he was supposed to get ready to come onstage again almost at once as Aegisthus, wasn't he?"

"That's right. When he's finished with his sound effects—you know, the screaming-in-his-death-throes part—he changes the purple silk for the black velvet and the gold necklaces. From king to villain. Sarah and I heard him yelling and rolled our eyes—we always thought he enjoyed that bit a little more than was natural—and stood by in what you might call the robing room with the Aegisthus outfit. He took longer than usual to arrive and Sarah and I were just standing about making silly jokes about him having been picked off—with a bit of luck—in the shrubbery by bandits. Hoping he'd never turn up." The girl gave an exaggerated shudder. "There's something about the way he stands there with his arms stretched out, just waiting for us to attend to him . . . I mean, he could easily put his own jewellery round his neck but he insists on us doing it for him . . . He tells us to tighten the laces on those boots of his—can you imagine? He has us on our knees like serving maids!"

"Hang on a minute! 'Picked off'? Zoë, what did you mean by 'picked off'?" Letty had been all attention at the words.

The girl shivered and looked anxiously about her, then leaned in closer and confided: "Been attacked by thugs. I don't exaggerate! There could be anyone hanging about in those bushes. Quick exit from the theatre, straight onto the avenue. I've seen strangers wandering in just to see what was going on, and out again, unchallenged—it's completely unfenced and unguarded. There are two watchmen on duty at night and the three wooden huts have locks but in the afternoon, when we're all performing, everything is left open."

"The three huts are used for what purposes, Zoë?"

"The big one in the centre, at the hub of everything, is Andrew Merriman's room. He sits in there whenever we're here in case we need him, but he doesn't throw his weight about . . . not always poking his nose in, you know. The second is the one on the right, which we call 'Wardrobe.' Rather grand name for a cupboard where we hang the cloaks. No need for makeup or changing space—people just come along in something light and summery and pop a cloak or a robe over the top. Then they put on the mask they've brought with them . . . they hate using each other's masks and they've written their names on the inside to discourage borrowing. We keep a few spares in case of forgetfulness. The third is for the mechanical stuff. Ropes, pulleys, axle grease, you know the sort of thing."

"It's guarded at night, you say. Is the site under threat of some sort, would you say?"

"Oh, yes. Leave any sort of building unattended and you'll

find six families have moved in. It can be pretty lawless about here, you know. Plenty of desperate people on the streets—all those refugees from Asia Minor...a million and a half have been sent over with nowhere to go. And then there are men displaced by the war—fighting men, dangerous men, some still armed, not all willing to just curl up and die quietly... Dodge City, Sarah calls it! At least it *was* before the British advisors got here. I must say they've worked wonders! They've hounded out most of the gangs and tamed the traffic. It used to be a free-for-all in the streets, cars everywhere, ramming one another, running over pedestrians. Now it's a ballet! Smooth and orderly and a handsome young Greek officer in white gloves at every junction. People come in on Sundays from the country just to stand at the crossroads and admire them!"

Zoë looked over her shoulder, tracking the inspector. "*He's* advising the criminal brigade. World authority, is what they say. Attached to the International Criminal Police Organisation and all that. They're setting up a CID squad, I believe. You know—like the one they have at Scotland Yard. If this should turn out to be a crime...well...it could be the very first of its kind the new department has had to deal with."

"Reputations to be made—or broken?" Letty guessed.

"Or repaired," Zoë commented thoughtfully.

"Repaired?"

"Yes. The inspector was unfortunate enough to arrive in Athens in the middle of the most awful crisis! You weren't here in the summer, were you? No? In Crete? Ah, then you very probably won't have heard...Most distressing! Towards the end of June, a bunch of foreigners—English, American, and French—were kidnapped during a Cook's tour to Delphi. Hard to imagine. In this day and age! A repeat of something dreadful that happened fifty years ago, they say. They were marched off at knifepoint, poor souls! The brigands responsible held them to ransom. The international outcry was something formidable, of course! Montacute got straight off the boat and joined the chase through the mountains. He's very...um...*fit* for a policeman. Don't you think?"

Zoë's eyes were drawn again to the magnetic figure of the inspector, at that moment striding between two blocks of polygonal masonry. "Well, they caught the kidnappers, hiding in the back of beyond. Albanians, was it? From over the border, apparently. I'm not sure—but somebody from over some border. Borders are a bit confusing out here, you know. Anyway—hand-to-hand fighting broke out. *He* shot two of the bandits dead, by all accounts. Two got away but the others surrendered. Well, you would, wouldn't you...with the inspector waving his Browning at you?" Her eyes skittered sideways again, keeping the policeman in view.

"But what happened to the tourists?" Letty was anxious to hear the outcome.

"Ah...too late, I'm afraid. They were all found in a shepherd's hut, dead, with their throats cut. In no way his fault, but they say the inspector took it badly."

"I see," Letty murmured. "A man with something to prove?"

"Hey! Will you get a move on up front! This is no time to be swapping gossip!" someone called rudely from the rump of the queue, putting an end to a conversation Letty would have liked to pursue.

"Next! Ah. Clytemnestra. Miss Templeton, I think?" said Letty, scribbling down the name.

She was uneasy at the prospect of coming face-to-face with the queen in her distressed state. At close quarters and without her mask, the woman was even more impressive than Letty had guessed. She moved forward and stood before her, undisturbed by the bright light, her black hair hanging in gleaming coils onto her shoulders and dark eyes ablaze. Her nose was as straight as a statue's, her forehead broad, her mouth generous.

And Letty could not turn those features into the cold killer's face of Clytemnestra. She had last seen that profile in a carving on a Gothic cathedral in France. Not on the etiolated outline of an austere saint but on the rounded shape of one of the more roguish female characters of the Bible. One of the beauties whose inclusion in Holy Scripture was licence enough for the medieval mason to display his earthy appreciation of womankind. Salomé? No, there was a nobility as well as strength about this face. And then Letty remembered. The likeness was of Judith, the virtuous widow who had, at risk of her life, crept into the camp of the Assyrian general besieging her town, seduced him, and beheaded him with her sword to save her people. Letty almost looked for the linen bag, dripping blood, in which she'd carried his head back in triumph.

The woman gave no sign that she was aware of Letty or that she intended ever to vouchsafe any information. Her focus was on infinity, and Letty's presence in front of her was at best an irritating distraction.

"Miss Templeton?" Letty asked again.

"Thetis Templeton." A mechanical response, followed by silence.

"Wonderful performance, Thetis! May I say how much I was enjoying…" Letty heard herself, with confusion, nervously filling the conversational void with unthinking chatter. She stopped, taken aback by the ferocity of the glare turned on her.

"Do you hear what you're saying? Must we next expect to listen to you heaping praise on Andrew for his convincing portrayal of a corpse?"

"I'm sorry, Miss Templeton. So sorry. I intended no offence. I was merely gauche and thoughtless. I am hardly trained for this...The inspector asks too much, I believe. Would you like me to call him over to take your details himself? I'm sure that would be the more professional approach."

Thetis Templeton shrugged. "We're all stretched to the limits this evening," she whispered, unbending a little. "I'm sorry I snarled...not your fault." She extended a hand and touched Letty's briefly. "Keep going. You're doing well and the inspector needs all the help he can get. Don't distract the man on my account—he's doing what he must do and with some skill, it seems, in the circumstances. Carry on with this pantomime. Let's get it over with, shall we?"

"Would you mind telling me where you're staying in Athens?"

"In Kolonaki Square, number twenty-five."

"But that's the Merriman house!" Letty's astonishment was evident.

"And I am their guest," said Thetis Templeton. "Where else would I be likely to be staying? Maud is my cousin."

CHAPTER 10

etty was watching for the right moment to present her completed notes when the eagerly awaited contingent from police headquarters arrived. Two or three heavy motor vehicles rumbled to a halt on the Avenue of Dionysus: a presence more substantial than the couple of gendarmes on bicycles she had been expecting. She threw a speculative glance at the inspector, this foreigner who had influence enough to call out the big guns. Doors banged and heavy boots crashed through the wooded area separating the road from the theatre.

"Harry! You thought to bring my murder bag! Good man! Quite lost without it!" Letty thought she heard the inspector say. And then: "Sarge, a light over here, if you would?"

Montacute picked up his Gladstone bag, tracked his way to the centre-front of the orchestra, and sank to his knees, peering at the floor. The sergeant followed, torch in hand. Satisfied that he had the right spot, Montacute opened his bag, plunged in up to the elbows, and selected from the contents a small paper envelope, a pair of tweezers, and a magnifying glass. He slipped on a pair of gloves and set to work. No one could make out exactly the nature of the tiny objects he was picking up with such care and slipping into the packet. The audience peered down, intrigued by this bravura display of detective behaviour. Apparently oblivious of their interest, he took a ball of cotton wool, dampened it with liquid from a small bottle, scrubbed it around on the interesting patches, and popped the resulting mess away in a screw-capped jar.

"And for an encore, they tell me, he polishes the brasses," drawled a voice from the audience.

Letty was inclined to share Louis Adams's scepticism. From her brief association with the inspector she could quite believe Montacute was putting on a performance calculated to distract and reassure his audience. If so, it was a manoeuvre much appreciated by the god of the place.

Dionysus himself was presiding over the day's dramas. Set up by Andrew in position of honour, not in the central altar place in the orchestra but off to the right, perched on a six-foot-high stone column, the tutelary deity sneered down. Letty had no idea how Andrew had come by the marble bust and she couldn't even be quite certain that the subject was, as he had claimed, the God of Theatre. The traditional ivy leaves crowned the god's luxuriant curls and his expression of slightly crazed merriment was authentic, but his was not the bloated face of the elderly lecher which Letty associated with Dionysus. This god was in his prime. In control. Manipulative and up to no good. An agitator if ever she saw one.

Hearing Louis Adams's quip, Montacute raised his head and grinned. Amused? Surprised? Menacing? All of those. Letty was relieved not to be the target of that brief baring of teeth. Was she the only one who'd noticed the resemblance? Stick a wreath of ivy leaves on the inspector's handsome head and he could have sat as model for the dark god.

He got up from his knees, took off his gloves, and squinted into the light, grunting: "See more in daylight tomorrow morning, I hope. Ah! Now, who've we got . . . ?" he said to no one in particular.

Two older men in civilian clothes—dark suits and hats—were arriving together at a more dignified pace than the constables had, and they held back at a careful distance, taking in the scene. One carried a soft bag, the twin of Montacute's, the other a doctor's attaché case.

"Gentlemen! Come around this way, would you? Glad you're here. Superintendent Theotakis," Montacute announced to the crowd. "My colleague in the Greek C.I.D. Over to you, Markos!"

The superintendent took in the situation, raised his hat, and bowed briefly to the gathering.

"And Dr. Petropoulos!" Montacute greeted. "Pathologist extraordinaire. Delighted! Sir, if you wouldn't mind stepping over here? Our problem is centre stage. I think a swift preliminary examination of the deceased would answer some essential questions. I believe you know him?"

Petropoulos, oblivious of the crowd, went straight to the corpse and delivered a series of staccato exclamations in Greek, so fast Letty could only just follow.

"Good Lord! Of course I know him! It's Andrew! They didn't tell me it was Merriman...Poor chap! What a barbaric scene! How on earth did he end up like this? In a bathtub?" The doctor flung an accusing glare at the inspector. "And with *you* here, Montacute, in the thick of it, I'm told? How could you let this happen under your nose, man?"

"Steady on, Doctor!" Montacute replied in the same language with what seemed to Letty's ear a perfect accent. "It looks worse than it is. Dramatic performance, don't you know...He died offstage. The widow declares her late husband to have succumbed to a heart attack. If she's right, then we may all disperse and go home with no further ado. We wait on your decision, Doctor."

Petropoulos began to mutter, stating the usual caveats concerning a postmortem. Poor conditions...inconvenience...lack of equipment...no guarantees. Montacute conveyed the gist of this in English and he was heard with nods of acceptance, all willing the pathologist to press on and pronounce the hoped-for words: "natural death." Everyone noted that he approached the corpse and set about his task before he had even finished speaking his preliminaries. The two inspectors stood at his shoulders, quick exchanges of question-and-answer batting between them in two languages as Montacute put them in the picture.

Letty was aware of a practised efficiency and camaraderie—even friendship—and aware also that all three men were perfectly conscious that their every syllable was being relayed to the audience with clarity. No swearing, no exclamations, the very minimum of information was exchanged. After several minutes of grumbling and sighing, redirecting of arc lights and flourishing of shining and mysterious pieces of surgical equipment, the doctor was ready to pronounce his initial findings.

"The gentleman's heart did indeed—and in this his widow was expressing nothing less than the literal truth—stop beating," he began. "But not as the result of an infarction or any natural cause. No, no! He's suffered a penetrating cardiac injury. It's the single thrust with a blade of some sort through the chest that did for him. Here, you see? Wound looks like a closed-up doll's mouth. Haemorrhaging occurred, but there's a complication. Yes, this is odd...The rest of this...um..." They consulted briefly over the choice of word and Montacute came up with: "Muck?" The doctor waved a dismissive hand at the red stains on arms and legs. "...*Substance* is not associated with the death wound. And there's rather a lot of it...Any ideas?"

"Ox blood," said Montacute. "Or so it's asserted. We'll need to have a sample tested."

"So—poor old Agamemnon meets his fate again," said the doctor, shaking his head sadly. "And just three hours ago."

"What was that? Are you telling us he's been dead three hours?"

"Does that surprise you? Well…as far as I can tell—yes. Again I say it…I'll know more later. For now, shall we say death occurred between two and four hours ago? And, to be on the safe side, I'll say—nearer four than two. That is to say at about your teatime. Five o'clockish. Well, if you can get a squad of your stout fellows to help out, Markos…" The doctor looked down dubiously at the body. "We have to get him to the morgue…lucky we came in the hospital van. Look, why don't we just carry him off in the bathtub? Agreed? It'll keep any evidence intact and in one place and it seems to have done a good job of containment so far." He began to pack his equipment away.

Superintendent Theotakis, dramatically moustached and authoritative, took over with a few clear gestures of command, assigning four of his men to bathtub transport duties. The Greek inspector turned in surprise as the witnesses on the audience benches, without a word spoken, performed their last act as a chorus. As the policemen, two on each side, lifted the tub, the actors rose to their feet in silent homage and remained standing while the professor was carried offstage. Theotakis fell in with their observance, taking off his hat and bowing his head as the cortège staggered in front of him. He then set other constables to seal off the area and stand guard in shifts until first light. He himself, he announced, would take the opportunity of going over the crime scene for his own satisfaction and would confer with Montacute when he'd dealt with the assembled witnesses. If the chief inspector was agreeable, they might all just as well be sent off home after a routine search for concealed weapons by his officers, of course, and not left at large to trample over the theatre, compromising potential evidence.

This was greeted by a sigh of relief from the actors but they stayed in their places, docile and watchful. Some were murmuring, some were weeping, and no one protested when Montacute gave the expected advice to hold themselves available for interview and not to contemplate leaving the city until further notice. They finally began to shuffle off when released, after running the gauntlet of two Greek policemen who patted them down with brisk efficiency. The three ladies, Montacute had improvised as an afterthought, could well present themselves to Miss Talbot, who would perform the same service.

Thetis, Zoë, and Sarah came to stand in line in front of Letty, each raising her arms with a conspiratorial smile and a forgiving shrug. They'd endured greater indignities at school. Thetis even murmured: "Poor you! Here—let me save you the trouble." She held out her sword, presenting the jewelled hilt. Letty checked that it was the stage piece being offered, a confection of wood and glass, and she handed it back. None of the three girls was concealing anything sinister under her light summer clothes. No blade bulged in bra or knickers or garter. Letty discovered not so much as a nail file when they turned out their pockets.

Laetitia was agreeably surprised that Montacute had taken the time to make certain no one was about to attempt to walk home alone. All, he insisted, must be part of a group of no fewer than four. This seemed to fall in with the group's own desires since, without an instruction given, they lined themselves up and sorted themselves into teams.

"Anyone for Kolonaki? Join us, then. We're going as far as the British School..."

"Syntagma, anyone? I'm off to the Grande Bretagne for a stiff drink. What about it, Johnny?"

Laetitia was pleased to hear Zoë and Sarah calling over to her: "Hey! Laetitia! Come with us. We've found two strapping fullbacks to escort us up the hill. Are you going our way?"

"I'm afraid I must detain Miss Talbot a little longer," said Montacute. "But don't worry, I'll be certain she gets home safely."

Letty's shoulders slumped at the thought of her prolonged detention, but she sat back down in her place in the central wedge of seats. The inspector joined her and they both watched the movements of the Greek officer covering the ground Montacute had recently covered. Letty handed him his open notebook and watched as he ran his eye down the pages she'd filled.

She explained succinctly as he read. "Twenty names, including me and Maud Merriman. I allowed two men to leave early. They both had appointments at the Embassy and I've noted down where they may be contacted. I sent them to you and I thought I saw you having them checked?"

He nodded. "Beecham and Melton. Clean, both of them."

Montacute flashed a keen glance at her. "I see. Oh, this is very well done, Miss Talbot! Names, addresses, but more than that—positions onstage at what we had all assumed to be the crucial time. Well anticipated! And additional information confided to you by some of those involved... I shall have to spend some time absorbing all this."

"Come off it! A waste of time!" Letty was too tired and too distressed to mince her words. And she was not in a mood to be humoured by the inspector. "I mean—in view of what we now know: that Andrew was already lying dead while you lot were prancing about onstage. Three hours? That takes us way back beyond the death scene with that awful screaming and gargling and to a moment before the start of the play. Let me think... Five o'clock. Everyone was frightfully tense. You'd expect that. Very self-absorbed... they only noticed each other to quarrel about masks and gowns: 'That's mine, you swine! Hand it over!...No! Maurice has got yours...' You know... that sort of thing..." Letty fixed the inspector with a direct look. "Yes. You were right there, in the middle of that back-stage circus, weren't you?"

"I didn't notice *you* lurking behind the scenes, miss. Why were you there?" he asked, batting back her own question.

"Perhaps you were preoccupied with other business, Inspector." Letty didn't quite like his tone of unemphatic suspicion. "I was only there for a minute or two. Everyone had gone out into the open—too stifling in the huts and tents. Most of the actors had found their own bit of space—standing about in corners behind rocks or trees, mugging up lines they hadn't yet learned properly. I think you must have been one of those?" She gave him a moment to explain himself but as he stolidly resisted her silent offer Letty continued: "I'd slipped backstage, over-officiously you could say, to check my mannequin was in place. It was. I'd draped a discreet length of muslin over the whole lot—it was too distractingly grotesque to just leave exposed."

"Did you check...?"

"Oh, yes, I peeked underneath. It *was* my dummy. I looked for Andrew to wish him a broken leg and all that stagey rot. All was left ready for him."

"So you left the dummy in what I might call a 'dry' condition?"

"As I said. I'd applied the brown makeup—lashings of Leichner—earlier in the afternoon. The liquid from the flask was to be poured on nearer the time of presentation by Andrew or Hugh."

"Why wait until that late moment to make the final libation?"

"They wanted it to look fresh—shiny and red and convincing. I believe they added something...glycerine, was it? To keep it fluid. Plenty of people in the audience would have known the difference...sadly, from recent personal experience. Half the chaps are likely to be ex-military types, half the girls Red Cross nurses...Not an easy lot to fool in the matter of spilt blood. They would have been insulted to be presented with a daubed-up mannequin figure."

He nodded understanding and encouragement. "This was to be the climax of the play. The show-stopping moment."

They exchanged glances, then Letty hurried on: "You must have noticed the careful timing. The sun sets at six-fifty but it's nearer half past when it sinks below the Attic Hills. Andrew was using the natural light of an open-air theatre much as the original playwrights might have done. Though the classical Greeks preferred the morning hours, I believe. The daylight faded as the onstage tension increased—the shadows gathered literally as well as theatrically. With all the grey and white, the gloom, and foreboding, it was Andrew's intention to create a yearning for colour in the audience and then to assault their senses with a burst of it, switching the arc lights on at the moment of revelation. Bloodred, silver, bronze. Gleaming and glinting. It was meant to take everyone by surprise. He wanted to hear gasps and whimpers. And—on a more practical note— we weren't forgetting the flies! The weather's still warm—you don't expose a pint of ox blood to the elements.

"Well, I was just getting in the way so I left everyone to it backstage. I'd arrived far too early, as usual. It must have been just before five...ah..." Letty paused and frowned. Montacute waited, giving her time to order her thoughts. "I went to find a place front of house where I'd arranged to meet Maud. I was sitting reading the scripts when she wandered over about half an hour later, a decent ten minutes before curtain-up."

"Ah, yes, Lady Merriman. She and Gunning are the only two apart from Melton to have hopped off without a search." The inspector ground his teeth in irritation.

"Don't blame yourself, Inspector—you could hardly have searched the distraught widow in the middle of the orchestra. You'd have been torn to bits by the cast! Maud's not everybody's cup of tea but she has her following. So, you'll have to take my word for it and I give it now—Maud had no bloodstained dagger secreted in her corset. I think I would have noticed. And her bag"—Letty smiled at the thought—"her reticule, was a tiny thing of calfskin . . . just about big enough for a hanky and a pair of spectacles. Gunning didn't arrive until the body had been pushed onstage. 'The body'—I hate to refer to Andrew like that! I never saw him again . . . in life. If only I . . ." she added quietly, her voice beginning to break up.

"Hindsight's a wonderful thing, Miss Talbot," said the inspector comfortingly. Then: "Oh, what the heck! Why do we say that? Irony? Kindly platitude? Whatever it is, it's dashed irritating. You should take no account of hindsight unless it can teach you something." He tapped her pages of notes. "And here's an example: This information, so meticulously gathered, may now strike you as being beside the point in the light of what we're now told about the time of death, but the very fact that you decided to record it tells me that you're a thoughtful and sensible woman. I'm glad you were there."

"Keeping the herd from swirling about and stepping in something they shouldn't? Something you might want to swab and bottle up?" she teased gently.

"Yes. And I'm not insensitive to choreography. I was pleased to see you timed your own performance to the second. Again—well done! And this wasn't the time-wasting exercise you seem to think it was. Police investigations are divided into three parts, Miss Talbot: Observation. Interrogation. Information. They normally occur in that order but I'm adaptable—not a stickler for routine. I've done just enough observation to be able to make sense of any information you may have gathered. I have to confide that, embarrassingly, it's the last of the three aspects that clinches most cases. The general public solve more murders than the élite detective division … though we take the credit. People tell you things. Can't seem to help it. You've heard the initial responses from this lot, raw and delivered under shock with no time for editing out inconvenient elements. I should like to hear your impressions … your insights into the behaviour of members of the cast. They are your class and age—*you* would understand them. You would be alert to any false notes. Were any of them acting more strangely than they normally do? Did anyone break down and confess under the gaze of your grey eyes, shining with innocence?"

"Will I be class sneak, you mean?"

"If you like. Though I think Andrew Merriman, in the circumstances, might have found a more dignified term to define the activity. We're not seeking to establish which bounder stole the sticky buns from Smith Minor's locker."

Letty regretted her own unconsidered response.

"You haven't yet confided the nature of your relationship with the Merrimans," Montacute said. "Professional? Family? I don't wish to assume too much—or too little. I'm sorry I have to ask indiscreet questions—prying is part of the job."

"Part of my job too, Inspector," Letty replied. "We're both in the business of solving mysteries. Though my dead are long dead and, in studying them, I don't risk annoying the living."

"Not what I hear, miss," he said with a grin.

Letty glowered and wondered from where exactly the inspector got his information. "My relationship with Andrew was professional, certainly, but more than that. He's an old family friend … of my father's. Archaeologists tend to be men of action and resource. To put down a pick and take up a Lee-Enfield is an easy gesture for them. Scholars and soldiers both, he and my father were drawn together by mutual interests and passions.

"Andrew was wounded, and for him the war should have

been over but he insisted on doing his bit. His particular talents were recognised and he was sent out to the Middle East. Indeed, I believe he spent some of the war years here in Greece. But you probably know more of that than I do."

"His talents?"

"Knowledge of ancient languages...hieroglyphs...He was of use in the cypher department out here. Encoding and decoding—that sort of thing. And I believe he was given some light survey work to do while he was recovering from his wound. Andrew was never a man to sit twiddling his thumbs doing nothing, especially when the world was burning around him. You know what the military are like..."

He nodded and smiled.

"They gave him a horse and sent him off into the country around...oh...up north in Macedonia."

"Salonika?"

"That's right. *Thessalonike,* Andrew always called it, pedantically. Named for the sister of Alexander the Great. With his background, Andrew was appointed Surveyor of Ancient Monuments, Northern Division...or some such. And he had a wonderful time! He may even have had plans to dig there one day but he never discussed them with me. 'Macedonia, Rich in Gold,' I've heard him chortle. 'Letty, I wonder, how would you look in a headdress of Thracian gold?' He knew I despised Schliemann for making a dolly of his wife."

Her voice wobbled in distress at the memory of Merriman's enthusiasm for a fancy never fulfilled and she fell silent. Andrew's following words were only ever to be replayed for herself alone.

"And presumably he made contacts that would prove useful in later life?"

"Presumably."

"And after the war?"

"He picked up the threads of his academic career and made fast progress."

"Ah, yes. Many chairs left empty at the high tables of Academe. A talented man *would* move swiftly towards the centre."

Letty was not entirely comfortable with Montacute's questions. She felt there were implications in each one that she was intended to refute or confirm. She was being invited to give away more than she felt she had any right to do. Her best defence was attack; she would turn his queries back onto him.

"Dead men's boots? No doubt you've tried a few for size yourself, Inspector, judging by your eminence in the Force?" she commented, closing down that line of enquiry. "But you were asking about dubious behaviour among the cast," she said, steering him back onto safer ground. "It's hard for me to judge. I only know one or two of these people slightly. Students come and go... The staff at the Embassy washes in and out with every boat... I was here in Athens staying with the Merrimans for six weeks early in the spring. I was being prepared for an expedition to Crete—my first chance to direct a dig, and Andrew was determined I should do him credit. He put me through an intensive course in Minoan and Mycaenean archaeology and culture. I left in March and returned only last week, so my knowledge of the Athenian social scene is a bit patchy and out-of-date."

"You hadn't met Lady Merriman's cousin?"

"No. I've only just settled back in... I hadn't realised she even had a girl cousin. But a lot can happen in eight months' absence. *You've* happened, Inspector—a new star in the Athenian heavens, I understand?"

He shrugged dismissively. A discussion of his stardom was not tempting enough to distract him, apparently. "You know the Merriman family well?"

"No. And it's hardly a family. They have no children. I

don't count Maud my friend. Maud is...I have always found her uncongenial...cold. She's a good deal older than I am. My mother's age, in fact. She's always made a parade of maternal interest in me." Letty shuddered. "You'll find this with Maud— she categorizes people. Pops them into a pigeonhole at first acquaintance. It's very annoying. She'll most likely have *you* marked down as Policeman Plod, the Bumbling Bobby. For her, I'll always be a sort of delinquent daughter, one who trails after her carrying the shopping and can't quite be trusted to behave herself."

"Shows a lamentable lack of judgement?"

Letty looked at him suspiciously and pressed on: "She's older than her husband. Forty-five, perhaps? Andrew is... was...about five years younger. They married before the war, when he was quite young. Maud is well-off and well-connected and was reckoned to be something of a beauty in those days. It was a good marriage for him, I think. At first. Maud has grown more and more ill over the time I've known them, which must be nearly ten years. And her temper has declined with her health."

Montacute nodded.

Letty realised that he had what she had come to recognise as the best quality of a police officer: He was an intelligent listener. He would go on hearing her confidences for as long as she was willing to make them. A danger. Policemen were not to be trusted with confidences like priests and doctors. They heard what you had to say and then used it in evidence, almost always against you. She fell silent and tried ostentatiously to consult her wristwatch.

He caught her raised arm and tucked it companionably under his. "It's ten past eight. Past your bedtime, are you thinking? Well, listen! Before I take you home I'm going to tell you a story. You're from Cambridge, aren't you? Then you probably know this one. Or a version of this one. Stop me when you realise you've heard it.

"Once upon a time, in a university city through which a green river ran," he began with a confidential dip in his voice that she found intriguing despite her hostility, "a group of learned gentlemen—dons, they called them—formed a secret society. Innocent enough pastime, you'll think, when I tell you that their entertainment consisted of gathering on those warm Sunday mornings before the war at a secluded spot along the riverbank to re-create scenes of their boyhood. In pursuit of the modern fad for Naturism they met at the river to bathe in the buff—naked!"

Of course she knew the old story. Letty smiled encouragement and he went on: "One Sunday an innocent young lady of the city, accompanied by three of her equally unworldly friends, set off to explore the riverbank. They made their way through the overhanging willows along a far reach of the river. Imagine their astonishment when they came upon a dozen dons *en déshabillé,* leaving the river and making for the clothes they had left hanging on a branch!

"The reaction was instant! Shrieks and confusion amongst the ladies, of course. And the gentlemen? All the dons, with one exception, automatically put their concealing hands over their private parts. The exception chose to put *his* hands over his face."

Letty was intrigued by his version of the well-known tale and waited for the dénouement.

"When the danger had passed, the dons turned on their fellow and asked why he'd behaved differently. 'I'm not entirely certain how *you* chaps are known about the town,' he answered virtuously, 'but *I'm* identifiable by my face.'"

"Ah—that might well have been my father," murmured Letty, unsure where the inspector was going with this. She feared she could guess. And if she was right, she saw clearly why she'd been singled out by him from the herd.

Suddenly serious, he turned his dark eyes on her and said softly: "I was struck just now by an unexpected reaction within the group. An oddity. Omissions, differences, and changes, Miss Talbot, are always interesting to me. Now, let me tell you what struck me—though perhaps I shouldn't: Of the assembled crowd, only two people recognised the dead man for who he was from a glimpse of the naked torso. Even William Gunning, who was standing very close by and knew the deceased intimately...am I right in supposing this?"

"You're right. Gunning knew Andrew well," Letty whispered, now certain she knew what was coming next.

"Even Gunning had to wait until I removed the concealing wig from the features before he recognized him. You, Laetitia Talbot, were one of the two present who was able to identify the professor from...um...the neck down," he finished delicately.

He looked at her, not with accusation but with sympathy.

She nodded dumbly. "*Two*, you say?"

"The other was Queen Clytemnestra."

CHAPTER II

For a moment Letty was silenced, then: "Great heavens! So she was! I believe you're right! Thetis Templeton. Yes, she did break down before it was clear..." she breathed, remembering. "Oh, gosh! No wonder the poor girl looked shell-shocked!"

She squirmed in embarrassment and tried to withdraw her arm, disturbed by the contact, but the policeman held fast. "Look here—if you're trying to take my pulse rate, Inspector, I have to tell you—you're missing the spot by a mile. If this is some newfangled way of checking my level of agitation, I'll tell you straight—it's high! I'm agitated all right! I'm devastated and furious."

"You mistake me, Miss Talbot. Just offering a little comfort in your uncomfortable circumstances." He did not release her.

"It's all right," she said. "I'm not going to try to effect an escape. You can relax."

She waited in vain for him to pursue his fanciful accusations. He'd made his play; now he was leaving an expanse of silence into which he expected her to leap. With what? A confession? An accusation? Letty was mystified. She remained stonily staring ahead.

Dissatisfied with her response, he changed tack. "I'm sorry. It must be a double shock for you. To find your lover not only is dead but has been unfaithful? Though perhaps a girl expects no less from a man who has, by his very relationship with her, demonstrated his capacity for infidelity?"

The gently enquiring smile that softened the austere features, the purr in the musical voice, made the scything rudeness even more intolerable. Letty drew in a sharp breath. "Very well, Mr. Policeman. Against my better judgement, I'll allow you to sting me into a response to your impertinent question. Did you hear me? I said, 'I'll allow.' Be quite clear that I know what you're up to! Andrew was my lover off and on for some years until a year ago last spring. When…when…"

"When your affections were transferred elsewhere?" he supplied.

"When I went abroad to dig in the pursuit of my career, Inspector." She was pleased with the calm hauteur of her squashing response. She'd learned squashing from Maud, and though she found very few targets for the skill, here was an intrusive and perfectly objectionable policeman testing her goodwill to the very limit. "If this interview is intended to reveal the character of the victim to you—and in a bad light—as I must suppose it is, you should understand, Montacute, that Andrew was not a wicked seducer of young girls. No, no! He had affairs but in all the cases of which I am aware, he was approached, invited into it even, by the girl or woman in question. And he chose carefully. The vulnerable, the naïve, the overprotected, were never in danger. He was a very attractive man. Hard for other men, I think, to appreciate this quality but every woman he met was aware of it…the kindness, the interest, the sparkle, the roguishness."

Feeling her lips begin to tremble, she bit them together hard before she could go on.

"And when things moved on . . . ?" the inspector prompted.

"As they do . . . he distanced himself with lightheartedness and friendship. I know of none of his amours that has ever turned sour. His conquests stay on as friends. Perfectly understandable in this day and age when there are available the means of avoiding the potentially disastrous consequences of extramarital affairs," she said, flaunting her worldly knowledge deliberately to shock him. "Andrew was a lively and energetic man with a great sense of fun. And he had an unfulfilling marriage."

"Seems to me I've heard that line before, miss. At many a murder scene."

She turned the iciest of eyes on him. "He was my friend, my lover, my mentor. I owe him more than I can say. If anyone threatens his reputation—whatever the scoundrel's position— he will answer to me. And, equally, if someone is guilty of doing my friend to death, I'll strain every sinew to find out his—or her—identity. I had understood that you too, Inspector, were his friend?"

"An investigating officer is allowed no friendships," he replied curtly. "But what loyalty the man commands, even in death! Must I expect a posse of avenging lady friends getting in my way? Tell me, Miss Talbot, how well do you know Clytemnestra? Um . . . Miss Templeton? You met in London?"

Letty looked at him suspiciously. "I don't know her. We had never met each other before this tragedy. I speak only for myself when I say that, if I uncover someone's guilt, then he'd better take cover."

"Ah! Is this the moment where I confiscate your Luger?"

Enjoying her astonishment, he grinned and added: "Your reputation goes before you. A quick temper and a quicker trigger finger is what I've heard. Do you wonder I take your right hand into custody when I'm about to say something provoking? *You* have searched the ladies, but who searches the searcher?"

She froze, expecting at any moment to have to struggle for her privacy, but he chuckled and went on in a businesslike way: "Now, one or two small mysteries I'm hoping you'll be able to help me clear up before we pack it in for the night... Will you come backstage with me for a moment? Don't worry—I keep a strong electric torch in my murder bag and we're chaperoned by half a dozen policemen."

He led her over the orchestra and beyond into the deep shadows of the *skena*. Lining himself up with the double doors of the palace of Mycaenae, still lying fully open, ready for the last act, he lit his way to a solid oak table standing in one of the tents and pointed his torch beam at it. In the blue glare, the appearance of the mess on the tabletop threatened to turn Letty's stomach. She was reminded, sickeningly, of the livid thorn-punctured flesh of Christ in an altar painting she'd failed to admire.

"Were we expecting this?" Montacute asked. "I'm sure there's an entirely convincing explanation for it and I think I can probably work it out from my brief acquaintance with the performance, but I'd like you to confirm my mad idea. The knife? The disgusting mound of flesh? What sort of butchery's been going on here?"

"It's exactly what it looks like," Letty answered. "It's flesh. A side of pork, to be precise. Bristles and all. The texture most resembling human, according to Geoffrey, who by all accounts is very knowledgeable on the subject."

The inspector waited for further elucidation, a hint of amused disbelief in his eye. Letty found she was irritated by his conscious use of silences and raised eyebrows to encourage his subjects to speak. Ah, well, if he wanted information, he ought to be given what he wanted... after all, the man was doing his job and working towards the same end as herself. She could not explain her resentment of his attitude other than as a tetchy reaction to his not-well-concealed suspicion of her own motives and her involvement with the dead man.

"Geoffrey got it from the butcher's at the far end of Ermou Street. He's ordered another one for the first night, Zoë tells me. Now, what is to be done about the superfluous carcase, I wonder?" she rattled on. "I must say, from where I was sitting it was completely convincing to hear him do it. When he came off as Agamemnon, he made straight for this point—carefully placed for the best sound effect—and stabbed away at the pork, howling and screaming in time with the blows. Like a madman. Still, I suppose you'd have to work yourself up to a pitch of dementia, wouldn't you, or you'd just fall about laughing. And there's the knife he used. Are you going to take it away?"

"Yes. We'll study it. Not that we're looking at the murder weapon here."

Montacute picked up the knife carefully in a gloved hand. "A serious, functional blade. You could certainly kill someone with this. Look at the profile. This is a sort of *gladius*... a short stabbing sword the Roman army used. Two-edged and two inches wide. Perfect for reenacting the murder of Agamemnon, but Merriman's wound looked to me to be much slimmer. Though, I have to say, delivered in the legionary's manner—one short stab in the area of the breastbone by someone with a knowledge of anatomy, pull out and on to the next target. Neat. Quick. No nonsense."

"The weapon was more like a dagger? An inch wide, would you say?" Letty tried to recall the hideous image.

"About that. Though some stab wounds are wider than the blade if the killer's waggled it about on withdrawing it. On the other hand, some wounds seem to shrink a bit after they've been inflicted, as the flesh— Well, no matter. Not the stuff for a lady's ears. Let's just say—I've seen similar wounds caused by the blade of a bayonet. I'll get someone to carry this away." The inspector threw back his head and called out: "Harry! Over here!"

The keen-looking young British officer she'd noticed earlier looked up, left his fellows, and, with a nod for Letty, stood waiting for instructions. "Sergeant Perkins, Scotland Yard. My aide," announced Montacute grandly. "And, Harry—this is my new assistant, freshly recruited this evening: Miss Talbot. You're to be nice to her. I want you to arrange to have the stuff you see on the table conveyed to the laboratory for testing. Fingerprints, blood, whatever you can get. And then resume the search of the *skena,* will you?"

"Can they distinguish animal blood from human?" Letty wanted to know.

It was Harry who replied. "Oh, yes, miss. A doddle. They can even tell you the type of human blood as well. Four different kinds they can identify to date." He began to busy himself noting down the contents of the tabletop.

"One, Two, Three, and Four, they call them, imaginatively," Montacute added. "And tell me—after Geoffrey had tormented the pork to his satisfaction, what did he do then?"

"What he was supposed to do was get himself into the costume of Aegisthus with the help of Zoë and Sarah backstage and then come on again. It's all there in my notes. Zoë reports he was late arriving this evening. But Maud and I heard him make a startled exclamation of some sort—we thought he'd stubbed his toe on the bathtub."

"Or taken a critical look at the contents?" suggested the inspector.

"Good Lord! It…it…hadn't occurred to me." Letty stammered in her confusion. "The dummy! I mean…enough on my mind…but the dummy's missing as well. Someone took it out of the tub where I left it…"

She started forward towards the space where the tub had

stood before the performance. The area was marked out by a hastily assembled square of tape held down at its corners by stones, and she took care not to alarm the inspector by approaching too close.

"Someone put Andrew in there, then covered his upper body with muslin. There was a lot left over—on that roll over there." Letty pointed to a shelf on the wall of the hut a few feet away. "Plenty left ready for tomorrow's performance. And, of course, everyone walked around him thinking it was my mannequin . . . thinking what a spectacular job I'd done . . ."

"The killer took the time to pour the blood from the flask all over him, so no one would have got too close," Montacute suggested. "The sticky mess was quite repulsive." He pointed to the taped area. "So I'm assuming the scuffmarks in the dribbles of blood spilled around the tub were made by the feet of whoever killed him."

By a huge effort of will, Letty looked straight ahead and not down at her own feet, a betraying movement which she was sure the inspector was waiting for. She replied lightly: "Then you've left it a bit late for a baring of soles, Inspector. You should have had the chorus line up at once for a foot inspection. They've dispersed. There won't be a trace left after a few strides through the dusty streets of Athens."

She decided she didn't quite like his narrow smile and the slight mocking tilt of the head as he acknowledged her reprimand.

"But, to return to our dummy, Miss Talbot—no one's been reported walking down Dionysus Avenue with a life-sized doll over his shoulder oozing gore. So it must be concealed hereabouts." He looked around, seeing nothing but a labyrinthine straggle of shadowed masonry. "We'll just have to wait for first light before we can do any more searching. There must be a hundred hidey-holes around here. What are we looking at?"

"Five tents, three semipermanent wooden huts, piles of masonry and rubble, an open trench or two. It's not so much a theatre as an open-cast mine! An abandoned dig."

"Recently abandoned?"

"I don't believe so. There was excavation done some seventy years ago but the work was never finished. Dr. Dorpfeld, the German excavator, took an interest but it's been neglected for a long time. Andrew thought that by staging the play here, he'd rouse some enthusiasm, attract some cash, and be in a position to fund a new and more skilled attempt to reveal the original structure. He used his own money to put the area in some sort of temporary order..." Letty waved a hand at the orchestra floor. "The pavings were reinstated, smoothed, and repaired. Not perfect, but at least no one fell over and broke an ankle at rehearsal. The front few ranks of seating are just about useable. A number of the carved chairs for dignitaries are, as you see, still ready for business on the first row."

"Ah, yes, dignitaries...You were aware that a very eminent person—persons, perhaps—was due to be in the audience for the first performance?"

"I'm sure the authorities are more familiar with the guest list than I am, Inspector," she replied evasively. "And I'm sure any dignitaries would be offered one of the rugged marble seats reserved in ancient times for the priests. One of those fronting the orchestra, with the best view in the house. But anyone coming to the performance can find somewhere to settle down in the amphitheatre. It's all part of the fun. Bring a picnic basket and some cushions. People don't mind roughing it—it adds to the fun."

"Mmm...not sure my officers will see the fun even if I send them out with a hamper from Harrods."

"I have to tell you I'm not keen, Inspector, on the notion of a small army of gendarmes fossicking about in the theatre.

We're looking at a many-layered construction dating from pre-Lycourgan times through Classical to Roman. Untrained and undirected diggers could do untold damage to an evolving and complex site."

She heard her crisp rebuke die away because he deliberately left her words hanging while he considered them. Then his teeth gleamed briefly in the torchlight as he grinned at her. "Lord! For a moment I could have sworn Lady Merriman had joined us," he teased. "Well, know that I share your concern, miss—as a classicist and as one who has grown deeply fond of this city. My father may have passed on to me a Norman Viking ancestry, but I don't believe I've inherited their deplorable ways with cultural artefacts. The Director of the British School is a valued friend and I shall, naturally, seek his advice and take it."

She acknowledged his set-down with a cool smile.

"Sir! In here!" The eager but muffled voice of Harry Perkins came from the interior of one of the wooden huts, the largest one close by the centre stage entrance.

"Merriman's office?" Montacute confirmed with Letty.

They entered to find Perkins had lit an oil lamp, revealing a bleak space having all the atmosphere of a general's campaign HQ on the move. The furniture, such as it was—table and chair—was of the folding variety. On the table a neat pile of books and one or two sketches, a carafe of water, and two glasses, both used.

Montacute pointed to the glasses. "He had company. Harry—would you...?"

"Sir! We'll decant the contents into separate containers, bag and box the lot, and lift the prints," said the officer, clearly with the intention of impressing Letty.

"Seems to have been a working area and not a convivial space," Montacute remarked.

"No room to hold parties in here," said Letty. "No space for the traditional back-slapping after the performance."

"But a party had been planned," Montacute reminded her. "To take place after the first night's performance. You were invited, I take it, Miss Talbot?"

"Oh, yes. I was looking forward to meeting...um...well, I expect you know who was to be guest of honour? We aren't supposed to speak of it. They were planning to have champagne and canapés out on the orchestra by candlelight, right under the nose of the God of the Theatre. The statue of Dionysus. Andrew was planning on lifting a glass to him. And making a witty speech, no doubt."

"But he did have a surprise guest in here," said Harry Perkins, and he went to stand beside a curtain which he swished back with the air of a music hall conjuror to reveal a wardrobe in which a few men's clothes were suspended. Perkins tugged these aside; suntanned, red-stained limbs and green eyes gleamed in the inspector's torchlight.

"He didn't go far!" said Perkins.

Montacute handed his light to Letty and went first to examine the light linen jacket and trousers hanging in the wardrobe.

"That's what Andrew was wearing when he arrived," Letty confirmed.

"And here's his unmentionables, in a pile on the floor," Perkins pointed out.

Montacute picked up a bloodstained shirt and looked at it closely. "Bag these, will you, Harry? Do you see this? Stab wound clear through the front of the shirt. So—someone came in here, killed Merriman, and instead of just legging it, went to the trouble of peeling his clothes off and putting him in the bathtub? Well, that was just standing conveniently to hand by the door—but why take the risk of being spotted manhandling a body?"

"It's personal, vindictive...wouldn't you say? His killer hated him enough to put him on display. Poor Andrew was the coup de théâtre in his own play. Lit by a blaze of limelight, centre stage. A bloodied carcase." Letty shuddered.

"As Agamemnon? The character of the man—could that be significant, do you think?" suggested Montacute.

"Aw! It could be entirely practical, sir, miss," offered Harry, and she noticed that Montacute encouraged him to go on with a swift nod.

"Well, if the Prof was knocked off well before the opening, the killer could guarantee that no one was going to mess about with the body until some time into the performance."

"An hour at least," said Letty.

"So, that gives the villain between one and two hours to get away or establish an alibi or just blend with the crowd, going about his usual business," said Perkins thoughtfully. "That means it was done by someone who knew his routine. What time he'd arrive...where he spent the time before and during the play."

"Well, that reduces it to a couple of dozen or thereabouts," muttered Letty, and then, more helpfully: "Andrew had given rather particular instructions that he wasn't to be alerted for anything other than a dire emergency," she remembered. " 'Over to you, Hugh,' he'd said. 'I'm not your puppetmaster. This is the final rehearsal. Just think for yourselves and turn in a damned good performance,' he said to everyone."

"And someone did," said Montacute. "Someone he knew came in and closed the door, then stabbed him with a weapon he'd brought along for the purpose. And, to gain time—I think it must, as you say, Harry, have been a practical impulse—undressed him, bound his head, and put him in the tub outside, hiding the original occupant here in the wardrobe. It would have been hot in here, mid-afternoon. Merriman was working in his shirtsleeves, so—not too taxing a job to get him out of his loose summer gear and into the bath. At that point the attacker could have slathered the corpse with stage blood without making a mess of himself. And then he went about his business for anything up to two hours unchallenged before Clytemnestra shook the corpse by the shoulder."

"So what are we saying, then, sir?"

"That this crime was either carefully worked out to the last minute by a cool and—one almost inserts the word 'professional'—character..."

"Or was an impulsive attack which just happened to be accompanied by a huge amount of luck," Letty corrected.

The inspector flashed her an approving smile. "As you say!"

"By a man or a woman," added Perkins disconsolately. His shoulders slumped in mock despair, then he grinned. "In other words—"

"Harry! Don't say what you're going to say," reprimanded Montacute. "Lady present!"

"Well, now, if there's nothing more the lady can do, Inspector—I'd really like to return to my lodgings." And Letty added silently, "To bury my face in my pillow and be alone with my grief."

"Remind me where you're staying... Oh, Lord! Not with the Merrimans, I hope?"

"Not on this occasion. I'm just passing through Athens on my way home to Cambridge. I was to report to Andrew on the success of the dig he fixed up for me in Crete in the summer. My travelling companion and chauffeur—the Reverend Gunning—has been given a room at the British School and I'm in digs with an English landlady and her husband not far away—just off Stadiou Street, near the British Embassy. Mrs. Rose and her husband were, until three years ago, in the employ of the Embassy. A housekeeping couple. To the joy of many, when they retired they decided not to return to England but to buy a house and set up as a private hotel. Their business is flourishing."

"I know the lady you speak of. Just round the corner from Klafthmonos Square. The neat house with the green shutters? Handy for the police station."

"And the Embassy."

"I think I'd better try to stop a cab for you on the avenue."

"Don't trouble yourself, Montacute." Gunning's voice broke in before Letty could reply. The vicar appeared out of the shadows, smiling, concerned. "I left the Dodge up on Kolonaki at Lady Merriman's disposal but—as the lady says— it's not far and we're used to walking it. I'll take Laetitia home now."

Instead of the relief she'd expected to see at the offer of saving the inspector a precious hour of his time, she saw indecision. Montacute chewed his lip and hesitated, a beady eye on Gunning. Finally: "Look here," he said, "you'll think me an awkward old cuss but I'm not comfortable with the thought of the two of you wandering off through all that scrub and then making your way north through the alleyways of the Plaka after dark— No! Listen to me ... I know more about the underbelly of this city than either of you. I'm going to send you off with an escort. Sergeant Perkins. Harry!"

The sergeant appeared and stood by ready for further instructions. "Harry, you know where the Embassy is—would you accompany Miss Talbot and Mr. Gunning as far as Klafthmonos Square and then come back here?"

"Right-oh, sir. Forty minutes the round trip?"

"Sounds about right. You may take my torch," the inspector said, handing it over. "Armed?"

Letty thought this question was asked not to check up on the sergeant but to reassure herself and Gunning.

Harry Perkins tapped his right hip and grinned. "Service Browning, as usual, sir." He put on his cap and squared his shoulders. Letty thought he looked frighteningly effective. "Madam. Sir. If you'll kindly follow me..." And he set off down the overgrown pathway at a brisk march.

rat!" said Gunning, leaning close to Letty's ear. "I thought that just for once we were going to be able to snatch a few minutes by ourselves. So much to say and now it'll have to be a series of 'And how are you enjoying Athens?...Wonderful weather for the time of year...' and suchlike stuff. Grr!"

"I thought we'd go as straight as we can through Plaka—which is about as straight as a dog's back leg..." commented Perkins when they had cleared the confines of the ancient theatre. "Come out on Voulis, then take Stadiou up to the Embassy. More brightly lit, not quite so dusty."

Letty saw in his eye the same knowing gleam she'd seen in many a London cabby's.

"And how are you both enjoying Athens, may I ask?" the sergeant went on blandly. "We do seem to be having rather wonderful weather for October, don't you think?"

Stifling a laugh, Letty trotted forward into the widening pavement to take Perkins's arm, carefully choosing his left. "You're awfully young to have made it to sergeant," she said. "Congratulations!"

"Oh, thank you, miss. Yes, four months ago I was just a constable. But then this Athens job came up—riding herd on the Chief Inspector and generally tidying up after him. That was the way *he* described the job, you understand." Perkins hurried to dismiss any suggestion of criticism of his boss. "And the promotion went with it. I'd have snatched at the chance anyway...always wanted to travel the world, and I missed out on the war."

"Have you got a good billet in the city or have they put you into barracks?"

"I'm a guest in the family of one of the Greek coppers, madam. Inspector Montacute insisted. Best way of learning the language, he reckons. And he's right. I love the Greeks... well, those I've met outside my professional sphere, if you take my meaning. The lady of the house is cut from the same cloth as my old ma—honest, house-proud, tough as last Sunday's joint, but she's a much better cook." He smiled at Letty, and seemed about to be wondering whether he could make a confidence.

Guessing his secret, Letty asked casually: "And are there daughters in the household, Sergeant?"

He laughed. "I'll say! Three beauties!"

"Then I think I should offer some really practical advice: It saves a lot of trouble if you pick the eldest! Were you aware that the poet Byron of scandalous repute spent some time in Athens with a family much as you describe? He went too far with his versifying and had to flee the country when he was assumed to have made an indiscreet declaration regarding the youngest daughter—Theresa, I think her name was—"

" 'Maid of Athens, ere we part

" 'Give, oh give me back my heart!' " the sergeant intoned. "His lordship was a fool not to take up the offer, if you want my opinion, madam. Might have saved himself a lot of inconvenience in later life...with a good Greek wife to keep him on the straight and narrow. She wouldn't have put up with his nonsense."

Gunning smiled and sighed and settled to bringing up the rear guard as they made their way through the narrow lamp-lit streets of the Plaka. Perkins glanced back anxiously.

"Don't be concerned for Mr. Gunning," Letty advised. "He knows the way and he has a fine right hook."

Perkins grinned. "Did I hear someone call him a vicar? Funny, that...I'd have taken him for a military man, the way he walks."

"He's seen his share of action. He was an Army chaplain serving on the front line. Gunning's a tough man...much decorated. He frightens *me* sometimes."

Café tables still crowded the pavements and were filling up with predinner drinkers ordering their ouzo or their wine. Strong tobacco vied with scents of spicy cooking and from most of the oil-lamp-warm interiors came the sounds of native instruments tuning up for the nightly sing-song. In this street the plaintive, plucked notes of the Turkish *outi* remembered its Asian homeland with sorrow, anchored, in the background, by tambourine and shepherd's flute. Crowds of thin children, large-eyed, hands extended, dogged their steps and Gunning began to empty his pockets of the coins he always carried for the purpose.

Perkins, becoming aware of the excitement behind him, turned with a reproving smile for Gunning. "We'll make faster progress, I think you'll find, Reverend, if you keep your hands in your pockets. Give to one and you find there's another hundred in front of you. I don't know how they pass the signal down the line. Poor little whippersnappers! Immigrants, most of 'em. Still homeless after five years. Fair makes your heart bleed! I always advise those of a giving nature to put their money where it'll do most good—into the hands of the American Ladies. Perhaps you know them, madam?"

"The nursing charity, you mean? Yes, I've met one or two of their organisation. Splendid women! I was thinking of offering my services while I'm in the city, though I'm not sure exactly what I could offer."

The sergeant looked at her, assessing her appearance. The well-cut skirt and jacket, the handmade ankle boots, the silk blouse and pearl necklace, told their tale. "Only two things worth the offer, madam," he said. "Money and energy. You can't feed thousands of starving nippers with a pat on the head. I've not got much of the former but I've got plenty of the latter and I spend my day off working at the orphanage. Perhaps you'd like me to give you the address...?"

"Thank you, I'd like that," Letty said quietly.

The journey passed quickly in Perkins's company, and Letty was not surprised that Montacute had chosen this man to be at his side during his spell in Athens. But she did rather wonder if the sergeant would be still by his side for the return journey. He looked to her like a man who has unblocked his ears and listened to the Sirens' voices. Everything about the city seemed to please him. The food, the wine, the architecture—all came in for a few glowing words from Perkins.

"Ever been to Paris, madam?" he asked. "Never been there myself, but the Guv'nor says this is every bit as smart as Paris in places. Truth is, I think he was as surprised as I was when we fetched up here. Hadn't been expecting sights like that, for instance..." He paused and gestured towards a house occupying every inch of a corner site. Its perfect proportions, restrained decorative details, and elegant balconies made Letty sigh with admiration. "And that's nothing special," Perkins went on in his proprietorial tone. "Ten-a-penny these grand houses... streets and streets of 'em."

"And have you seen the Schliemann mansion?" Letty was interested to hear his opinion.

"Mansion?" He grunted. "Palace, more like! A trifle overblown for my taste, madam. And all that indecent statuary posing about on the roof in full view of anyone who passes by!

If I were Greek I'd suspect the old feller was 'aving a larf. Surprised they put up with it." He sniffed.

But the British Embassy, when they turned off Stadiou into Klafthmonos Square, received an approving comment.

In spite of their eagerness to be home, they all stood for a moment at the gates, peering into the courtyard like three urchins, enjoying the spectacle of the Legation building en fête. Under a full moon bathing the scene extravagantly in glamour, the dark pine trees of the garden were silhouetted against brightly lit windows; ranks of lanterns marched up the wide steps leading to the grand entrance. Both doors were standing wide open onto the great hallway and footmen were greeting late arrivals, ushering them forward into the pool of light cast by a chandelier. The scene had all the allure of a Bakst setting for some magical ballet—*Cinderella* or *The Nutcracker*, perhaps.

"They never asked us to the ball," grumbled Perkins, staring in fascination.

They stood listening to the bursts of chatter and gusts of laughter as doors opened and closed; they enjoyed the sound of a string band which was suddenly joined by a bandonéon, guiding the players seamlessly from the *Merry Widow* waltz into a throbbing Argentinian tango.

"No," said Letty. "We weren't invited, but two of the cast told me they were expected here for a party. They weren't deceiving me, evidently."

"Probably on their third tango by now," Gunning commented.

"I wonder what's going on," said Letty.

"Some shindig or other," said Gunning. "They don't need much of an excuse to shake out their epaulettes, starch their ties, and slip into their glad rags. I think it's to do with an anniversary of something international...the Entente not-so-Cordiale most probably. Diplomats!" He spat out the word.

"Oozing around, flattering and fascinating each other...oiling the wheels of their own state's juggernaut! Do they ever notice the vehicle they're servicing so assiduously is heading straight for a war zone?"

"William! I don't think..."

"Sorry, Letty! It's my theory that if you got rid of all the embassies in the world you'd have a better chance of peace. They're probably all in there negotiating alliances, planning invasions, redrawing borders, arranging transfers of populations. Doesn't it occur to you that all those starving scrappits we passed on the way here were uprooted from their homelands by bureaucrats and their political masters?"

"William!"

Again he ignored her. Hadn't even heard her, she thought. "How would you like your nationality assigned by a new line drawn on a map? One day you go to sleep knowing you're Greek, speaking Greek, your family has tilled the land around you for generations, your friends and neighbours are all around you, but you wake up and find that overnight, you've become a Turkish citizen and must return to that homeland, leaving everything behind. And it's all been decided according to your religion. If you worship in a mosque—that does it. Off you go. And, no—you can't suddenly change religion...not allowed...not playing by the rules...

"If someone's omitted to sharpen his pencil before the planning meeting, which will, of course, be convened thousands of miles away in a congenial place—like Lausanne—your village is no longer Greek and Christian, it's Turkish and Muslim. And vice versa. You take to the roads in your donkey cart. And you pass other displaced souls coming in the opposite direction. Life or death at sea doled out by the pencilling-in of an arrow. Peacemaking? Warmongering? Do they make any distinction? Do they care so long as they get their patent-leather dancing shoe on the next rung of the ladder?"

Letty was speechless with embarrassment at his outburst, and it was the sergeant who picked up the pieces.

"Oh, I don't know, sir," he said, puzzled by Gunning's bitterness. "I think it's just a bunch of nobs in there getting as drunk as skunks, having a good time. Dressing up. Showing off. Harmless enough sort of entertainment. And at least while they're in there annoying each other with their gossip and scandal they're not out here bothering us in the real world. That's what the inspector thinks at any rate. Good luck to 'em, I say."

CHAPTER 13

The butler tracked down his quarry, spotting his highly polished size twelves tapping in time to a tango behind a lemon tree on the terrace.

Sipping his third glass of champagne and flirting merrily with the wife of the French ambassador, Thomas Wentworth, His Britannic Majesty's First Secretary at the Embassy in Athens, was not pleased to be found. The mischief died in his eyes, the smile slipped from his lips, as he became aware of the discreetly coughing presence at his elbow.

"Excuse me, Your Excellency," murmured the butler, with an apologetic bow to the Countess. "I have a message for Mr. Wentworth."

Wentworth concealed his rush of alarm behind a tetchy sigh. Notes would be delivered during an Embassy soirée only in the utmost urgency and then by a footman. If Grant had taken it upon himself to appear with his silver tray, then the piece of folded paper being offered to him must contain something of moment. Wentworth bit back an urge to make a jocular and nervous remark... "What ho, Grant! Serbs and Bulgars decided to have a go at each other at last, have they? Balkans on the brink again?" He tightened his lips. Might just as well chuck a grenade into the middle of the floor. Any indiscreet remark, even delivered in jest and under the influence, would be picked up by these raucous vultures and passed around the Foreign Offices of Europe to be picked over, swallowed, or spat out by the hundreds of spies and hangers-on who infested them.

"Pull yourself together, Wentworth!" he silently told himself. Three glasses, was it? He counted them up, then remembered the large glass of Talisker he'd shared with the Ambassador before the junket had started. He had mentally taken himself off watch for the evening and here was Grant with his granite features putting him on the spot, warning him to raise his guard.

Inspiration struck. "The Wellington Cup at Newmarket... got a horse running, my dear..." he muttered to the Countess. "I only hope the result warrants the interruption to my evening, Grant?" He accepted the note with a convincing show of disapproval.

The butler caught his cue. "You asked to be informed, I believe, sir. It came through on the wire moments ago. I trust the news will in no way detract from your evening. Sir." Grant permitted himself a reassuring smile.

Wentworth gave the note a brief perusal and put it away in his pocket. "No, indeed! Felicitations in order, it would seem! I say, would you excuse me for a moment, your ladyship? This requires an instant response. London can never seem to work out the time difference... they think the whole world runs on Greenwich time... Ah! There's young Clarendon arriving. The well-set-up chap with his arm in a sling—javelin thrower, don't you know. Have you met him? Come and be introduced. Vastly entertaining young fellow. I'll leave you in his capable hands— um, hand," he finished vaguely, and beckoned the young man over to him. Introductions made, with a neat bow he headed for the door. The butler eased his passage through the crowds of guests, flushed and chattering in many languages.

"Bloody hell, Grant!" spluttered the First Secretary when they were out of the reception room and he was sure they were unobserved. "Was that necessary? And—*Newmarket*? That *is* where they run in October, isn't it? Do I have that right? Better check the results of one of those damned races." They hurried through deserted corridors, leaving the sounds of jollity and the string band behind them. "The lady's mad keen on horse racing... It occurred to me that might be just about the only reason she'd be ready to swallow for my pushing off in a hurry. But she'll check up on me, that's for certain! She's much more on the ball than that husband of hers. The *on dit* is that she's the one who's really in charge in Vassilis Sophia Avenue. Attractive woman, too. Curse you, Grant, for interrupting!"

"I'll get straight on to it, sir. And if verisimilitude is a priority, why don't I order up a few copies of the *Racing Times* for you to be discovered studying?... I put the gentleman to wait in your office. People swarming all over the building... it seemed the safest thing. He could hardly appear at the soirée— he's not dressed yet. Still in his acting gear." Grant forged ahead, throwing muttered phrases over his shoulder. "Cool as a cucumber on the surface... writhing with tension underneath. Not sure whether he's come to report success or failure. Hard to tell with him—not the usual style of Invisible Fixer. A touch histrionic, sure you'd agree?"

"A touch *touched*, if you're *really* asking me," grunted Wentworth. "Nutty as a fruitcake. Gives me the creeps! Can't imagine who thought it was a good idea to ship him out to us. Do you suppose every embassy is allocated one like him? Or have we been specially selected? Who've we annoyed? Let's hope he's clocked in to confess to *failure*, then we'll have every excuse to post him back home on the next boat or shunt him up the line to...Salonika! Or, better yet, Mid-Balkans...What's that dreadful place where I came down with the dysentery in '25? Pishtush? No—Slopsi Blob. That's it! We'll send him up to Slopsi Blob...Over Mount Zlatibor...By *mule*," he finished with evil emphasis. "That'll make our friend a little more respectful." Wentworth checked himself, suddenly aware that he was chattering nervously.

"But he does possess the essential qualities," Grant conceded.

"Well, I suppose you'd be likely to recognise them, Grant. Past master at skulduggery that you are."

Grant replied with the slanting grimace that, with him, signalled displeasure: "He is so quietly effective, so alarmingly professional, isn't he? It's rather like owning a not fully tamed predatory creature—a hawk, or a very superior ferret—"

Wentworth shivered. "Polecat, I'd say—polecat," he muttered. "Sleek, vicious, and uncontrollable."

Reaching the door of his office, he hesitated. He cleared his throat and fumbled with his white tie, wasting time. Reluctant to walk into his own territory and face the temporary occupant of his bolt-hole, he turned to Grant. "You're going to sit in on this?" he asked, trying for a neutral tone. He was reassured to see the majordomo's swift nod and his automatic gesture as he checked the pistol he kept below the well-padded shoulder of his uniform jacket.

"Wouldn't miss one of *his* performances for the world," said Grant with a smile. "As good as a three-act drama at the Old Vic."

Wentworth made a bold entrance, taking in the robed figure lounging in one of the leather armchairs. One leg was casually crossed over the other; a tragic theatre mask dangled insouciantly from one finger of his left hand. The other hand was holding a glass of whisky to the light. A staged appearance. Did he fancy himself sitting in the lamplight for a portrait by John Singer Sargent, perhaps? Yes, Sargent would have been able to capture the arrogant tilt of the head, the gleam of the narrowed eyes which seemed never quite to focus on the person who was talking to him. It occurred to Wentworth that, if asked, he couldn't have sworn to the colour of those eyes. Blue? Grey? Brown? He'd never managed to look into them for long enough to know. All he could be certain of was: cold. The French had a word for chaps like this. In fact they had several: *poseur, crâneur, il se croit un peu*... The First Secretary often wondered what creature lurked behind the flawless façade.

He waited pointedly and for rather a long time until his visitor rose to his feet before saying cheerfully: "Oh, do sit down, old man. I say, may I get you a drink? Oh, I see... you've helped yourself. Islay to your taste, is it? And you've had the sense to select the twenty-year? Good. Good. Now, Grant will be sitting in on this, of course."

Grant took up a stance by the door with an air of calm menace, an attitude unconsciously revealing his years of service with a British regiment.

"Always nice to know The Branch is with us," continued the visitor with a sarcastic nod in his direction. "So—we're both masquerading this evening, Grant? If I may be permitted an observation, as one third-rate thespian to another? You really ought to work on your *deference* if you're going to go about the place butling. Not sure casting have quite got it right..." He tilted his head, affecting to observe critically. "Some might judge the craggy Highland countenance out of place in the douce getup of an Embassy butler... Like coming upon Ben Nevis in the middle of Hertfordshire... And do get

Costume to attend to your jacket—that bulge is too big to be taken for a corkscrew."

Grant acknowledged the advice with a tilt of the head and looked thoughtfully down at the right leg of his trousers where the comforting handle of his preferred weapon nestled in the top of his sock. His dagger. Three seconds was all it would take. He allowed himself a second's fantasy and smiled.

"We weren't expecting you to report back quite so soon, were we, old chap? Surely we weren't looking for news before the opening night?" Wentworth brayed loudly, sensitive to the dangerous animosity between these two. "I say, I trust this is urgent enough to justify breaking into my evening? The French Ambassadress was just about to show me her scars…" he finished on a lighter note. Into the surprised silence he enlarged: "Acquired fighting off a gang of local *apaches* with her brolly, she tells me…"

"Utter balls! It's a birthmark. We've all seen it—the whole *corps diplomatique* has been accorded a viewing. All those of us under the age of fifty, that is" was the laconic remark. "The lady is predatory. Be warned, Wentworth—this is her way of sorting out the sheep from the goats—a distinction not always immediately obvious amongst diplomatic staff. All kinds and conditions of men… those who show an interest in surveying the Promised Land more closely go down on her list as exploitable; the others: blackmailable. It's crude but effective. You've had a lucky escape. Something else to thank me for."

"Ah, yes. Your news?" Wentworth snapped back, goaded into a show of haughty efficiency. "What have you to report?"

"A death. An assassination."

The visitor allowed the words to make an impression, enjoying the look of astonishment and concern on his listeners, and added: "I come hotfoot from the theatre of Dionysus—or the 'crime scene,' as we must now call it, since it's presently in the hands of the Athens C.I.D. A Graeco-British contingent of the boys in blue are, as we speak, turning over every loose stone looking for clues. That well-oiled double act: Theotakis and Montacute, playing with their fingerprint kits. Doing a lot of agreeing. Can't tell you what a happy time they're having, sleuthing about!"

"Already? But why? Isn't this a little premature? How could this have happened? And—the police? Who on earth was so stupid as to send for *them*? Do they normally turn up for accidental death . . . the death from natural causes we look for? Surely not?" Wentworth was aghast.

"Aren't you taking all this a little lightly, my lad?" Grant's first contribution to the conversation was delivered with a mildness that went little way to disguising the steel beneath it.

There was an uneasy pause before the reply came. Information was obviously being sifted, censored perhaps. Prepared for presentation to the real authority in the room. Then: "Rather unfortunate . . . sure you'd be the first to agree, Grant . . . these things can happen despite the most careful planning—"

"Get to it!"

"Montacute was right there on the spot as anticipated. But so also was an inconveniently nosey member of the public. William Gunning. You know—Andrew Merriman's protégé. Some sort of archaeologist or architect . . . dancing attendance on Lady Merriman and the Talbot girl. He's no fool and ex-military, I'd say, judging by his bearing. Likely to know a bayonet wound when he sees one. He took one look at the body and sounded the alarm. Can't say I blame him—it was evident to all that someone had been done to death—and by a professional hand."

"Bayonet?" Grant could contain his anger no longer. "What a fiasco! This was never intended! Whatever have you *done*, laddie? You're telling me you've despatched someone, without authority, in a flamboyantly murderous way in full view of a man of the cloth? An English vicar?"

"And no doubt our young friend had the editor of the London *Times* standing by, pen at the ready," said Wentworth, a warning hand going out to pat the bristling Scotsman on the tightening muscle of his upper right arm. Grant's slow-boiling temper terrified Freddy even more than Geoffrey Melton's snakelike menace. Really, he deserved better, Freddy thought. Why had he been sent these two when he'd put in for a couple of perfectly nice Magdalene men? Hey ho! Perhaps if he arranged to lock them up together in a room, neither would emerge?

The First Secretary's next question was more in the nature of an accusation, and he just managed not to cast a triumphant glance sideways at Grant. "What you're telling us is that you've made a confounded mess of all this! God knows what the Greek military are going to have to say about it! You've queered their pitch—do you know that? I don't like to think what that appalling old man-eater Konstantinou will have to say to me. And it will be *me* they call in after breakfast to stand to attention on the carpet and suffer a mauling. Not you. Not Grant. They are supremely unaware of the presence of either of you two buggers on Greek soil. *I'm* the face of the British Government. The face that gets slapped. Oh, couldn't you have—? We were assured you were adept at flushing out and disposing of...at arranging accidents."

"Certainly I could have....It was all in hand. You approved my plans for a swift theatrical exit. It would have worked out well," the visitor said thoughtfully. "At the given time. Nothing easier. Tonight, in the backstage mêlée, I could have done away with half the chorus line and got away with it." The words slowed, a note of puzzlement creeping in. "It's just that someone jumped the gun. *I* didn't kill him."

"Are we glad to hear that?" Wentworth's icy tone indicated that he had had quite enough of the games. "Are you requiring us to congratulate you on a *non*-assassination? Perhaps if you were finally to disclose the identity of the unfortunate victim we could decide whether to pat you on the back or kick you up the arse . . . ?"

A rare smile of devastating charm lit Geoffrey Melton's austere features briefly as he further confided: "Most odd! I wasn't the killer and the victim wasn't the victim—at least not the one any of *us* has in mind."

CHAPTER 14

The moment her doctor left, Maud Merriman changed into the long black evening dress and single row of pearls she judged suitable for her new status in life. She returned to the drawing room and seated herself in a brocade armchair, alone and brooding in the lamplight. Waiting.

She looked at the clock on the mantelpiece when she heard her cousin stamping up the stairs to the second floor, and began to speak the moment Thetis came into the room. "Of course one could never say as much with that bloodhound of a policeman sniffing about, but Andrew would have been very much a target for violence, you know." It was the voice of a woman eager to express the thoughts that had clearly been occupying her for the past hour. "He risked his life every time he walked unaccompanied down an alley or into the country-side. Salonika, you know . . . He would never have risked going back north to that hated place. But perhaps Salonika, at the last, came to him?"

Thetis stared at her, uncomprehending. "What on earth are you talking about? A target for violence? Andrew? What's that supposed to mean?" Her voice was slurred by fatigue. And then, enlivened by a touch of suspicion: "Didn't I hear you say you thought he'd died of a heart attack..."

"Oh, come now! I couldn't help noticing the wound in his chest. It seemed to me more dignified not to point it out. Draw a veil over the unpleasantness—that would always be my way. Let the policeman do his ghastly job...the poking and prodding business. Everyone saw it; no one mentioned it. I expect you were aware of it, too? You did spend quite some time peering into the bathtub, Thetis...And *you* of all people might be expected to recognise a bayonet wound when you clapped eyes on one."

Her cousin stared straight ahead and ignored her.

Maud pressed on, sweetening her tone: "Yes, poor thing, you must have realised at once. How perfectly dreadful for you! William Gunning certainly was aware—he took it upon himself in his kindly sacerdotal way to explain the situation to me as he drove me home. I smiled and nodded and took his words in the spirit in which they were offered. But I'm not quite the silly old woman Gunning—and others—take me for."

"Maud, you've had the most awful shock. Will you let me call Dr. Peebles and ask him to prescribe a sedative?"

"He's already seen me. About an hour ago. You're very late." The older woman's voice took on its familiar martyred tone. "I've had time to make a few telephone calls, send off a few messages...The caterer had to be stood down, of course—that was a priority. I've started another list which you may care to help me work through when you're feeling a little sharper." She paused, running an eye over her uncommunicative cousin. "But, Thetis, my dear, you don't look wonderful yourself...In fact, you look done in. You're barely listening to me. I hope you didn't allow yourself to become too *embroiled* with the detective branch? And I trust that they behaved themselves? I can understand that, as you *were* the only one of the cast actually armed with a sword at the *moment critique,* they were bound to show a particular interest, but if they have been overzealous, believe me, I shall take it up personally with the Minister. And you're still in your stage clothes? They might at least have allowed you the opportunity to change."

"Maud, I must say, you rush to judgement—as usual. That Inspector What's-his-name—"

"Montacute. You did meet him here at dinner soon after you arrived. He was at the other end of the table."

"Ah, yes. I didn't take much notice, I'm afraid. I heard he was a policeman and switched off."

"Montacute. It's an ancient name—Norman, you know. Are we to assume—the Shropshire Montacutes? Or the Northumberland branch?"

"God Almighty, Maud!" Her outburst made Maud flinch. "Does it matter at a time like this?" Thetis could no longer hide her exasperation. "Norman Montacute, whoever he is, seemed to know his trade and, indeed, he appears quite the gentleman. I'd already decided I liked him as an actor and I even liked him when he finally unmasked himself and revealed the policeman tonight. They are, as you know, no favourites of mine! Several of us were quite impressed with the way he conducted himself. But, in the end, having taken the roll call, the police couldn't get rid of us fast enough. They said something about contaminating the crime scene as little as possible," murmured Thetis. "We all had to make our way home as best we could and wearing whatever we were standing up in."

"You came through the streets in that bloodstained robe? And your stage jewellery? An open invitation to robbers!" Maud was aghast. "And with your sword stuck in your belt, like Boadicea? You might at least have left *that* behind! I'm only surprised they didn't seize it in evidence." Her shoulders quivered delicately. "No—don't sit down yet...all that red paint on you...you'll ruin the new covers. And I see you couldn't be bothered to wait in the hall for the boy to dust down your boots…" And, sighing: "Why don't you pour your-self a gin and tonic and take it up to your bath with you before supper?"

"I'd rather have a cup of tea, Maud. And I think I'll give supper a miss if you don't mind. I'll confess I've had a drink—or two—already. I found myself caught up with a crowd who were heading off for the Grande Bretagne for a quick one to stiffen the sinews."

Maud tutted her disapproval. "Drinking in mixed company, dressed as you are? And the management tolerated it?"

"There was a fancy dress party passing through the cocktail bar…we blended in," said Thetis wearily. "My companions were chaps from the British School up the hill. They may have been a bit tiddly but at least they delivered me to my own front doorstep safe in wind and limb. Don't fuss, Maud. I've got a headache. Haven't got one of your aspirins handy, have you?"

She sank down with a mutinous face onto the sofa, raising a cloud of dust.

Maud got up and tugged at a bell pull.

Making an effort to gather her thoughts, Thetis frowned and asked: "But what were you implying about Andrew when I came in? That he was a target? Whose target? Everyone loved Andrew."

"Very nearly everyone, I agree. You may find it difficult to imagine, but there *are* people who wouldn't hesitate to put a dagger in his heart. He wasn't only and wasn't always the charming boulevardier. He had his dark secrets."

"'Dark secrets,' Maud? Please stop being so mysterious—I'm too tired for all this. If you have serious suspicions you should confide them to the inspector."

"Well, I would if I knew what to suspect! A secret is a se-cret, silly girl! Though perhaps it would be wise to share my concerns, such as they are." She collected her thoughts and declared: "It is my opinion that Andrew was the subject of *surveillance* of some sort for the past few weeks. Expert surveillance, I would say, since he confessed himself unaware of it when I mentioned the matter. He claimed he hadn't remarked the same face of notably Levantine appearance hastily averted in the café on the square whenever we passed by, the presence lurking in the bushes behind the house, the to-ing and fro-ing of a man in a dark felt hat on the pavement in front." She nodded towards the window which stood half open and added lugubriously: "He may be down there now, as we speak."

Thetis rolled her eyes in exasperation. "*Expert,* you say? Can't have been *that* expert if *you* noticed, Maud! And Andrew would feel bound to deny it so as not to scare you. And—*Levantine*? This *is* the Levant, for goodness' sake! Or very nearly... People *do* have olive complexions and large noses. And had you noticed that half the men in Athens are wearing dark felt hats? It's October! Now, if you'd spotted a red-haired Scotsman in blue bonnet and furry sporran I might have been intrigued. And look here—if a clandestine killer was waiting his chance to do away with Andrew, then he's been successful, hasn't he?" she explained. "I'd say he'd be well advised to make himself scarce and not return like a dog to its vomit. He's not likely to have done the dirty deed, then come up here to camp out on your doorstep, thumbing his nose at you, is he? Unless *you're* on his shopping list too, Maud..."

Thetis gasped and put a hand over her mouth. "Oh, I'm sorry! I didn't mean to scare you! That was a really unfeeling remark. But the whole idea is quite ridiculous. And I can reassure you—there was no one skulking about when I got home."

Further irritated by the exaggeratedly fearful glance Maud cast towards the window and the nervous clutching of the string of pearls at her throat, Thetis got to her feet and stalked across the room. She threw wide open the tall double panes and leaned out over the low wrought-iron balcony. "...Ninety-nine, one hundred!" she called. "Time's up! You can come out now! We know where you're hiding! Show yourself, you villain!"

Maud winced in embarrassment, took out her handkerchief, and sniffed into it.

The familiar street sounds below—chatter, laughter, the chug of taxis skirting around the square, the Athenian evening promenade—continued uninterrupted, apparently well able to resist the nursery-room challenge to play hide-and-seek with Thetis.

"Well, all the same, I've made my mind up to mention it in the morning when the inspector comes to call," Maud conceded. "I shall tell him that it most probably all goes back to Andrew's escapades in Salonika just after the war. He was up there in northern Greece working in a diplomatic rôle off and on from the end of the war until just recently. Spying, most probably! He made some questionable decisions and upset quite a few people, he told me once. Had to return home to London in something of a hurry...pursued by the Furies, you'd say...Yes, I'll say something. And don't concern yourself, Thetis—you are not involved. Ancient history. After all—I'm not talking about his grubby *little* secrets like...his love affairs. I wouldn't dream of boring the police with all that. You know, I've never been certain whether Andrew knew that I was conscious of his infidelities. I am quite certain he wouldn't have cared."

"Love affairs? Infidelities? Whatever next? And you say you *knew*?" Thetis said faintly. "Surely you're mistaken?"

"Oh, no...Ah—Maria!" she called as the maid entered. "I want you to go down and tell Dorothea to cancel supper. Instead—would you bring up a tray of tea, please? And don't forget to top up the sugar basin. Miss Thetis is suffering from shock. Something hot and sweet is what she needs."

The maid bobbed and went out.

"Mistaken? Never! Now, how can I convince you? I'll give you a name, shall I? A name...oh, how to choose one from so many...?"

"Maud! Really! Your husband is hardly cold and you lightly seek to destroy his reputation? You must rest and reconsider. It's all been too much for you, but it will look very different in the morning. And I promise not to remember a word of what you've just said. Andrew was a fine man—I really can't sit here and listen to you maligning him even though you're, naturally, distressed."

"*De mortuis nihil nisi bonum*? I've always thought that a rather silly maxim. Nothing but good of the dead...Let me think...He was, I admit, a fine soldier in his day and an inspired and lucky archaeologist. But apart from that it's hard to think of anything virtuous about Andrew. Fortunately for him, *I* shall not be delivering his eulogy." Maud gave a narrow smile. "Though I could always say, with Clytemnestra: 'You lived by the sword and you died by the sword.' Yes, that wouldn't be bad. But I will not have you sit there affecting to disbelieve me! Let me see...there must be one of his lovers close to hand, someone who could confirm his villainy...Yes, of course! Letty Talbot!"

"Who? That archaeologist girl? I met her tonight...after the event...A perfectly proper young lady, I thought. We got off to a bad start but I liked her. She was kind to me in the circumstances. I was quite rude to her but she answered me softly. I would have said she might well become a friend..." Thetis's voice trailed away, then rallied. "Laetitia Talbot and Andrew?" She gave a shout of derisive laughter. "Maud, I say again—you're barmy!"

"There, you see! You are quite astonished. *You* were unaware, Thetis, because I confided in no one, but I've suffered silently for years, knowing what was going on between those two. My fool of a husband thought himself madly in love. Heaven knows what he might have sacrificed for that little minx! His reputation? That certainly. His career? His marriage? All too likely. And when I think of the kindness and consideration I've lavished on that motherless girl ... !" Maud clutched at her bosom to calm a heart pounding with indignation and, gasping, was unable for a moment to continue.

She rallied and began to speak again with venom: "But proof of his folly will soon be out!" She looked speculatively at Thetis, a cold-eyed warrior selecting her most lethal weapon. "It will be revealed to the world when the terms of his will are made known. He had the insolence to tell me only last week that he had made the wretched girl the recipient of a fat slice of his personal wealth. *That* will set tongues wagging! Always allowing that he was telling the truth, of course." She sniffed. "His candour was frequently a deceit."

Apparently satisfied by the incredulous expression swiftly followed by one of dismay that her revelation caused, Maud gathered herself for her next assault. "Astonishing when you recognise, as do I, that the wretched girl proved to be every bit as frivolous and manipulative as himself. She took what she wanted and spat out the rest. No—Letty Talbot didn't hesitate to distance herself once she'd got what she really wanted from him, and that was not his money."

"Oh, Lord! I shouldn't encourage your tittle-tattle but I can see you're going to tell me whether I want to hear or not! What exactly did Laetitia Talbot want from Andrew? Apart from the chance to get up your nose, Maud?"

"An impeccable entrée into the world of archaeology, which, for some unfathomable reason, would appear to be her heart's desire." Maud paused for a moment, her head on one side, genuinely mystified. "Strange girl! Good family. Wealthy in her own right, they say, as well as pretty. A little too *knowing* for most men's taste, however. And, they say, she has political opinions so strong as to verge on the Bolshevik . . . though I, of course, make a point of refusing to have them voiced under *my* roof. It's said she embarked on a course at Cambridge, though they had the good sense to send her down. Still, she could have any man in the kingdom at the snap of her fingers. And what does she choose to do but dig about in holes in the desert in the company of sweaty native workmen and a disgraced clergyman."

Thetis raised a weary eyebrow but let the remark pass unchallenged.

Maud chuntered on. "I remember Andrew's words: 'That young girl's flying with her own wings now. She doesn't need me anymore.' But it wasn't two minutes before he'd found consolation in other quarters, of course." She picked up her knitting and pretended to count the rows. "Shall I name more names, Thetis, to amaze and entertain you?"

Thetis gathered up the hem of her dusty robe and struggled to her feet. Ashen-faced, she went to tower over her cousin, who remained seated, chin raised in defiance. Her voice was controlled but cold: "Maud, I've been meaning to tell you—I've held my tongue for too long but you force me to say it—you get more like our mad old grandmother every day! Remember her motto? 'Anything to cause a little pain,' she used to say. And she practised what she preached. I've heard enough of your filthy innuendoes. I won't stand by and hear another disrespectful word about Andrew. Be quiet! I'm leaving!"

Maud's sly voice followed her, snapping at her heels as she strode to the door. "But he learned his lesson! None of his other lightskirts has taken him seriously . . ."

"Lightskirts? Where *do* you get your vocabulary? The *Gentlewoman's Journal*? Maud! I've heard enough! *Shut up!*"

"They knew what they were to him...An afternoon's romp at the Café Royal. Stolen moments behind potted palms at the Savoy. Nothing more. *Playthings. Passing fancies!*"

At the last waspish words, Thetis growled, turned, and tugged the sword from her belt. The gold bangles clanked and clattered down her right arm as she raised it high and let out a fearsome shriek of uncontrolled fury.

CHAPTER 15

I n a corner of the office shared by Superintendent Markos Theotakis and Percy Montacute a telephone rang. The two men working in shirtsleeves at the cluttered central desk looked up and glowered at it, annoyed to be disturbed. They were engaged in a heated but amiable discussion in a mixture of English and Greek, poring over a sketch of the theatre of Dionysus, a sketch covered in dots of various colours and sporting heavy directional arrows. In the centre of the *skena* and opposite the stage entrance, a red cross marked the position of the evening's corpse. Montacute's notes and Theotakis's notes were piled up and the Moleskine journal lay between them, open at the pages Laetitia had filled in.

Theotakis looked at his watch. "A bit late to be rung up? I asked the switchboard to note name and business of callers but avoid putting them through to us..."

"Couldn't be the doctor already, could it?" Montacute said, struck by a hopeful thought.

"Philippos—take that, will you?"

They bent their heads again over the plan but both were listening in to the exchange.

Philippos spoke with exaggerated clarity into the mouthpiece. "This is the office of the Criminal Investigations Department, Athens," he announced. "Good evening. Sergeant Georgios speaking. If you wish to speak to Superintendent Theotakis or Inspector Montacute, you may deliver your message to me. The gentlemen are both occupied at the moment but I will pass it as soon as is possible."

The moment he stopped speaking, a rattle of Greek, in a woman's excited voice, was clearly heard across the room.

After a few repeated requests to slow down, consider, speak more quietly, the young policeman was ready with his information: "It's Dorothea Stephanopoulos," he hissed. "She's the housekeeper at the Merriman house in Kolonaki." Wide-eyed, he added: "She seems to have something important to tell us.

"When was this, Kyria? I see...Yelling and screaming... Doors banging...A domestic dispute, would you say? The *usual* domestic dispute? Where?...The bootboy made the discovery? Great Heavens! Just tell me what you saw there..."

The voice gave a machine gun burst of words that had the sergeant recoiling from the earpiece. Several times Philippos tried to interrupt but was ignored. Finally he shouted into the instrument: "I understand. I've got that! Thank you, Kyria. Tell me—has anyone thought to summon medical aid? Dr. Peebles, her own doctor. Good. Good. Now, you'd best return to your duties. I'll send someone over to you at once."

He replaced the handset and looked thoughtfully at the two officers, almost reluctant to speak. "The housekeeper was reporting an attack on her mistress. There's been an attempt on Lady Merriman's life. In her own drawing room!"

Theotakis groaned and tugged at his moustache in irritation. "Over to you, Percy! They're *your* countrymen—go and stop them from doing whatever it is they're doing to each other, will you? Bang heads together, slap wrists, wag a finger...settle it and get straight back here!"

CHAPTER 16

A decorous shake of the hand was all Gunning could permit himself as he said good night to Letty in the front porch of Mrs. Rose's boardinghouse for the respectable travelling gentry.

After saying good-bye to their police escort, they'd spent a precious hour pretending to have dinner in a small restaurant on the square. Neither had much of an appetite for anything other than hushed conversation. Letty stirred up her salad and nibbled at pieces of cheese; Gunning made better inroads on his dish of spinach pie. The student meals at the British School were meagre and predictable and Gunning had got into the routine of eating out every evening in Laetitia's company.

"You're sure you'll be all right, Letty?" he asked gently, before knocking on Mrs. Rose's door. "We could have taken a room at the Grande Bretagne. They're very discreet. I'd be ready to risk it . . . I don't like the idea of leaving you alone tonight. You must be feeling raw . . . I know what the man meant to you."

"Then you know I need time by myself to grieve. My feelings and memories aren't the sort I can, in all decency, share with the man I'm currently in love with."

Gunning winced. "If we weren't standing here with the estimable Mrs. Rose on the other side of the door, preparing to take your coat and hat, I'd pick you up and shake you till your teeth rattled for being so infuriating. I never know whether you're being ironic or just plain rude! Why do you go on tormenting me in this silly way? Can't think why I bother with you."

He turned to leave.

Letty couldn't think why he bothered, either. She couldn't understand and couldn't control the impulse constantly to annoy and test him. It was a year and a half since they'd met in Cambridge, a year since he'd told her he loved her, but the man was still a mystery in too many ways. She knew that one day he would walk off without a backward glance and she'd be too proud to call after him. Perhaps this was the occasion?

Catching a stifled sob, Gunning turned back, threw caution aside, and hugged her close to him, murmuring regrets and soft endearments.

"I say—I'm sorry to break in on this tender scene."

Gunning looked up, startled, as someone tapped him on the shoulder. "Great Heavens! What the . . . ?"

"A bad moment. Life's full of such this evening, don't you find? I'm really here to have a word with Miss Talbot . . . That *is* Letty Talbot in your clutches, isn't it? Ah, yes, there you are, Miss Talbot. Hello again! Unforgivable of me to barge in like this at this time of night but I wonder if I might have a word with you . . . in private."

Letty and Gunning stood in silence looking at the trim figure before them in its smart linen suit. A wide smile from under the dipping brim of her hat acknowledged that she understood she had not been recognised. "It's me, Thetis Templeton." She gave a formal bow of the head. "Clytemnestra. How do you do? We met earlier this evening at the theatre."

"Oh, of course. Thetis. Yes," said Letty. "How nice—but

how surprising to see you again." She glanced down at the travelling bag the girl had put down at her feet. "Oh—I say—are you off somewhere? Is that a good idea? The inspector told us all we should hold ourselves . . ."

"I'm not leaving," interrupted Thetis, and she added, mysteriously, "In fact, I may be arriving!"

With sudden insight into the girl's situation, Letty turned to Gunning. "William. You were just off, I think? Thetis and I have things to discuss. *Female* things. You would be bored to hear them. Will you come and collect me in the morning?"

Clearly puzzled but murmuring polite phrases of understanding, Gunning detached himself and set off to walk back to his room up the hill at the British School.

"You've run away?" Letty suggested.

Thetis nodded.

"I'm only surprised you've stuck it out for so long. Sorry—she's your cousin, I know, but . . ."

"That's why I'm here. You know Maud. And knew Andrew. You're probably the only person between here and London who would understand what I have to say. Something really rather awful's happened. Do you think we might have a talk? And do you think your Mrs. Rose would have a spare room for a benighted guest?"

Letty sighed. "Oh, dear! I know she hasn't. The house is full. But look—leave it to me. Come in with me and meet her."

She rang the bell, and the door was opened by a stately and very English-looking lady. Mrs. Rose looked down her nose and made a show of consulting the watch she kept pinned to the bosom of her black silk dress.

"Two minutes after ten o'clock, Miss Talbot," she sniffed. Then, breaking into a broad smile: "That's a full half hour earlier than you managed last night! Weren't you having a good time?"

"I've had a perfectly dreadful day, Mrs. Rose," Letty said,

ushering Thetis into the hallway. "I shall have to tell you all about it at breakfast. Meanwhile—an emergency! This is my friend Miss Templeton. She's the cousin of Lady Merriman, whom I believe you've met, and she's staying with her in Kolonaki Square but, on account of circumstances not in the least in her control—and which you will be horrified and fascinated to hear—she's had to leave in a hurry and seek refuge elsewhere. That is—here."

Mrs. Rose opened her mouth to speak but Letty rushed on: "I know you have no free rooms but there are two beds in mine—do say Miss Templeton may bunk up with me—at least for the night?"

"Well, of course, Miss Talbot. Your friend is very welcome. You will show her the facilities and—"

"Yes, yes, I'll do all that, don't worry."

"Cocoa? Would the young lady like to join you in your bedtime cocoa?"

Thetis nodded dumbly, then murmured her thanks.

"Let me take your bag," said Letty. "The room's just up here on the second floor."

Letty settled in the one armchair and watched as Thetis kicked off her shoes, tugged off her hat, and slumped down on the bed Letty invited her to use. For an anxious moment Letty thought the young woman had collapsed in exhaustion or fainted. Her blouse was badly buttoned up and one earring was missing. Her face was pallid under streaks of makeup and her dark hair clung damply about her face. And still the wretched girl looked beautiful.

"You all right, Thetis?" Letty asked. "You look as though you've just been thrown out of a Roman orgy."

After a gurgle of laughter and a few deep breaths, Thetis raised her head and grinned at Letty. "It's quite like being back in the dorm here! And cocoa on its way! You're rather spoilt, I think."

"Mrs. Rose is someone you can quickly get fond of. She and her husband kept house at the Embassy for years and now, in her retirement, she offers an oasis of Englishness and respectability in Athens. It's known to be a safe place for single travellers and vulnerable young girls—like us. She loves to hear news from home, and scandal from her guests is most welcome—I should prepare a few stories for breakfast tomorrow morning, if I were you! They needn't all be true so long as they're entertaining. But—don't worry—you can tell her anything you like. She is herself the soul of discretion."

They chatted on, making general conversation until the tray containing cocoa pot, two mugs, and plate of digestive biscuits made its appearance. Thetis, unexpectedly, drained the mug Letty poured for her with relish and reached for a biscuit. "Jolly good cocoa! I haven't eaten or drunk anything but alcohol since lunchtime," she confided. "Two rum punches at the Grande Bretagne on the way home and that's it . . . Home! Huh! Where *is* home now? I have no home!"

Letty was startled when her guest burst abruptly into racking sobs, hands over her eyes and fighting noisily for breath. She watched as Thetis moved to sit up on the edge of her bed, found a handkerchief, blew her nose, and bent her head, trying to regain some control.

"Here, have my cocoa" was all Letty could think of to say, disturbed as she was by the emotion on display. "No—really . . . you're very welcome."

"Sorry! Self-indulgent nonsense!" said Thetis critically. "How insensitive of me. You must be feeling pretty cut up, too? In the circumstances." She gave Letty a meaningful stare from under her wet lashes, then apparently decided on bluntness. "A helpful little bird tells me you were very close . . . to the professor?"

"You know about Andrew and . . . me?" Letty said tentatively. "About our . . . affair? Ghastly word! But 'friendship' doesn't stretch quite far enough, perhaps. Whatever it was, it's long over, you know."

"Yes!" The reply was instant and delivered with relief. "You obviously caught on faster than I did! Perhaps you heard a warning screech from the same little bird...Huh! Liver-pecking vulture, should I say? I'd no idea until my dear cousin took it upon herself to enlighten me. With considerable plea-sure. You can imagine. So. We each know about the other's ex-ploits. And we're no doubt intended doubly to suffer thereby. A refinement of cruelty, typical of my cousin. She's probably calculated that we'll kill each other on sight in a fit of jealousy. Lord! How Maud would chortle at the thought of the two of us sharing a room. What wouldn't she give to be that fly on the ceiling!"

Letty went to sit on her own bed, opposite the tear-smudged face. She felt she had some understanding of the girl's tumbling emotions. But her own enlightenment had, at least, come in the guise of an entertaining story told with com-passion by an uncensorious man. She'd had time to deal with the shock and bitterness. She'd even arrived at the prospect of reevaluating Andrew and his place in her life. Thetis was still raw and spinning rudderless. She had no Gunning close by with quiet offers of unconditional love.

Letty took Thetis's cold hands in hers and spoke quietly. "I see no reason why we shouldn't grieve together. This is not the moment—and we aren't the people, I think—for destructive ri-valry and jealousy. We both loved him. It might compensate—if anyone up there is taking account—for the meagre amount of concern his widow is able to squeeze out in his memory. Weep for him all night if you want to—I'll understand."

She was encouraged to feel a reciprocal squeeze of the hand; then Thetis looked up with a sudden smile. "What? Cat-erwauling all night? What a dreadful notion! The saintly Mrs. Rose would have to evict us both." Back in control of her emotions once more, she changed her tone to one of hesitant intimacy: "I say, Laetitia, that was a pretty steamy scene I interrupted just now. I'm most awfully sorry. Sorry too that I guess we shall all have to cross the heavenly William Gunning off our lists of eligible men about Athens... Does everyone know? It hadn't reached *my* ears!"

"No. It's not generally known. And I'm not sure 'heavenly' is quite the word for William."

"Ah. Well, I have to tell you—that little secret is out! At least Maud knows—which means the whole of Athens knows—that your Gunning is...um...professionally speaking, somewhat lapsed. As a priest, I mean. I'm sure he's in good standing in all other respects! 'Lost his faith on the battlefield' is what Maud's saying. Like a pocket handkerchief! And she's proposing herself as his spiritual guide to help him retrieve it! You'd better warn the poor chap she intends to make a project of him! Maud likes to surround herself with a retinue of younger men, you know."

"Thetis—I'd prefer you to keep this thing to yourself."

"Of course. Whatever 'this thing' may be..." Her bright eyes invited a confidence.

Letty smiled. "It's very simple. I love him. He says he loves me. My father's threatened him with dire consequences involving horsewhips and steps of London clubs if he rejects me, but he's turned me down."

"*You've* asked *him* to marry you? Have I got that right? Well! There's a novelty! And he's turned you down, you say?"

"Three times."

"Great heavens! A catch like *you,* Letty? The man's mad!"

"You may be right. I sometimes think he is—a little bit mad. The war, you know. He suffered mentally as well as physically. Not neurasthenia but something more subtle... He's still fighting some monstrous fallen angel of his own invention. It's not a battle I'm invited to join or even witness." She gave a rueful smile. "Sadly. Because I love him very much and I'd stride through Hell and confront Satan on his behalf if he asked me to."

"Have you thought . . . ? Have you wondered . . . ? I mean—he may well be struggling with dark angels in Hades and all that, but is there a possibility that his reticence might have a much more earthy cause? I'm trying to say—do you suppose he's found out about *Andrew*? Could that be the reason? 'Damaged goods' and all that rot? You know how even the nicest men can entertain such medieval notions . . ."

"He does know. Andrew told him himself at a crucial moment in our relationship. A piece of meddling for which I haven't forgiven him and now never will be able to. Nor will I be able to thank him for his subsequent change of heart. But that's not the reason. William isn't an example of your narrow-minded, prejudiced English gentleman. In his way, he's a man of the world . . ." She paused for a moment. "Though don't ask me what world . . . it's not a place into which he's invited me yet. And he was fond of Andrew. He actually stayed with him and Maud for some months in London last year. It was Andrew who slotted him into a position where he could use his talents—in Crete. We've been working there together for seven months. We were to spend a week or two here in Athens reporting back to Andrew on the success of the dig he set up for us."

Letty stopped talking. She had resisted all Montacute's attempts to draw her out into a declaration of her circumstances and here she was, blurting out her deepest concerns to this stranger. But the stranger's eyes were sympathetic and knowing and they were not judging her.

Thetis seemed to accept that Letty had said as much as she was prepared to say, and decided not to pursue the conversation. She got to her feet, and began to fish about in her bag, unpacking a small toilet bag and a white cotton nightgown.

"You haven't brought much with you. Here—let me hang up that dress . . . Will you have to return tomorrow to Kolonaki for the rest? Face Maud again? I'll come with you if you like," offered Letty. "And did you tell anyone where you were coming?"

"No, I didn't. I had no idea myself where I was going when I left. I made an exit! I just swept out in a marked manner. Very marked. Wish I hadn't lost my temper, but you know what she's like!"

"Drives you mad! What did you say to her?"

"It wasn't so much what I said as what I *did*! Pushed to the very limit, you understand—I paused in the doorway, turned, and hurled my Parthian shot! All too literally! I threw my sword at her!"

"Your sword?" said Letty faintly, recalling the determined and righteous face of Judith the Beheader.

"I was still wearing my stage gear with the sword stuck in my belt. 'Like Boadicea,' my cousin remarked." Thetis grinned.

"Another sword-wielding lady! History's full of them."

"Well, the image was a good one, I thought! Now, there's a woman who would have stood no nonsense! 'Right, Maud!' I said to myself. 'You've conjured her up, now you can have a taste of the Warrior Queen's wrath!' The snarl and the screech, the jangling bangles, the whole business—I really turned it on! Played it for terror! And then I shied my weapon at her head! Drew blood! Regret that. Stupid thing to do . . ."

"Remind me, Thetis," said Letty carefully. "It was made of wood, wasn't it? You couldn't possibly have harmed anyone with that?"

"Of course not! Wood? Yes, I think so. It was very light. Well, you would know—you frisked me, I think the word is among the criminal fraternity. You handled it yourself. But a jolly convincing piece of stage stuff, whatever it was! Jewelled hilt, silver-painted blade, but you couldn't have cut into a blancmange with it, don't you agree? I was surprised to see it had drawn blood. On her right cheek." Thetis demonstrated. "Nothing serious—I think it might have been a sharp bit on the hilt, one of the glass gems, perhaps, that cut her. She didn't even squeal. Still—a disgraceful scene. Andrew would have been horrified. He hated scenes."

"What did Maud say?"

"Nothing. She just stared at me. She touched her cheek where the blood was trickling...looked at her fingers...and then..." Thetis shuddered at the memory. "...and then she smiled. Horrid smile, Letty! Like a cat licking cream from its whiskers. You'd swear she was pleased she'd riled me to such a pitch. It's more than likely that she'd achieved her aim—getting rid of me without appearing to be vindictive or inhospitable herself."

"Of course. And now, in the eyes of the world, *you* are the thankless, treacherous cousin. The woman who deserted her in her hour of need."

"Exactly!" Thetis agreed, and then, with unaccustomed hesitation: "And it's worse than you realise! It's worse than even Maud realised. The eyes of the world, I'm afraid, are going to slam shut in horror when it all comes out...I've got something dreadful to confess...Oh, Letty! How strong are your shoulders? This could turn out to be a very long night..." She lapsed into silence, lost in her thoughts.

"But, anyway, you managed to get out of her clutches?" Mystified, Letty tried to put her back on track again.

"Oh, yes...I went straight downstairs to the front door. I left it on the latch and went into the square to hunt for a taxi. Always make sure your line of retreat is clear—not a bad maxim to live your life by if you get into trouble as often as I do! I was in luck—there was one loitering nearby while the driver stopped for a smoke. I told him to get his cab and come along to the house to pick me up at the door in ten minutes. I raced back up and stuffed some things into a bag. I ran a flannel over my face and got into a respectable suit."

"Maud didn't try to stop you?"

"No—not a squeak from Maud! Didn't *really* expect it. She wouldn't have wanted to detain me! The drawing room door stayed shut. She'd achieved her aim, I think, in casting me loose...All the same..." Thetis mumbled with unaccustomed hesitation. "She may not have wanted me around but perhaps it was my duty to stay? I do wonder if it was a bit heartless of me to sneak off like that, leaving her by herself for the night."

"I shouldn't worry too much about Maud. She always lands buttered side up," said Letty comfortably.

"But she was in such a nervous state..."

"Nervous state? Maud? She's about as nervous as a doorstop! Look—mentally and emotionally the old girl's made of steel. She's very tenacious of life. I've learned to take all her creaks, groans, and palpitations with a pinch of salt. No, Thetis, don't worry! Whoever else suffers around her, Maud always comes out on top."

"No, it's not that...This was different, I think. I tried to make light of it, but I did wonder...She had some mad idea that the house is being watched. She thinks some misdemeanour of Andrew's from his past has come back to haunt him. I thought she was genuinely frightened—spooked by some character lurking under her window this evening. She kept saying a name in that tone she uses for her portentous prophecies of doom...'Salonika!' That was it." Thetis repeated the word with a perfect rendering of Maud's booming contralto.

"Andrew was up there in Macedonia in the war years," murmured Letty. "But how extraordinary! You'd better tell the inspector tomorrow, just in case, but it does sound to me like one of her attention-gathering stories. In which—I remind you—she always features as the heroine! If there really were anyone so unwise as to lurk under Maud's balcony, my advice to *him* would be—put your tin hat on, mate!"

"Well, there certainly was no one around but me and the poor little boot boy who was hovering about, scared out of his wits by the screeching. Oh...and the taxi driver I whistled up when I left," said Thetis, remembering. "I didn't know myself where I was heading until the driver asked me for an address. You had just been in my mind, Letty, and I remembered you'd told me where you were staying when we mumbled at each other at the theatre this evening. Awful imposition! I'm sorry. Nowhere else to go. No home here or in England now. And no bolt-holes in an emergency—this very definitely isn't Brighton! Always hard up, I'm afraid—I can't afford the Grande Bretagne prices! I know a few other smaller hotels, all rather sporting when it comes to welcoming clandestine couples but they're not the kind to take in unaccompanied women, especially after dark."

"Well, I'm glad you thought of me," said Letty. "We'll dream up something to tell Mrs. Rose in the morning after breakfast. You'll enjoy breakfast...a touch of home. And—don't worry, Thetis, you'll be quite safe here."

Thetis smiled and sighed and helped herself to a second mug of cocoa.

CHAPTER 17

The man in the shadows pulled his hat further down onto his forehead and tipped the brim to hide as much as he could of the impressive hooked nose below it. He paused under a lamp to light a cigarette, his eyes squinting into the flame but taking in the arrival of the police car. It screeched and swayed to a halt in front of the house and a man got out. He identified the lithe figure of the Englishman at once. Yes, there was no mistaking those devilish dark features.

The Greek sergeant driving the car manoeuvred for a moment to direct the headlights onto the front of the house, then got out and stationed himself, back to the building, hands on hips, facing the street. Well trained. The officer moved forward to talk to the housekeeper and the young boot boy who were keeping watch over a hunched shape lying on the paved area that divided the house from the street.

The housekeeper's piercing babble reached him in bursts: "Demetrios found her...He was just about to lock up... Right here under the drawing room window...She's not dead. I rang for her doctor before I called you but you've got here first...We've covered her up but we've not dared to move her.

I think her back's broken . . . She's said nothing . . . just groans with pain."

Montacute knelt by the side of the still form and checked for signs of life. He raised his head and called urgently to the sergeant. "Philippos! Go inside and ring for an ambulance. Better be one of ours, I think."

He turned back to the recumbent figure. "Lady Merriman, it's Inspector Montacute. Can you hear me?"

Only her head was visible; the rest of her body was shrouded in a woollen blanket. On the ground beside her, someone had hopefully placed a glass of water, a bottle of brandy, and a towel. The slightest nod of the head and a gurgling sound encouraged him to continue. "Medical aid is on the way. Try to keep calm. I'm going to switch on my torch so that you can see my face and I can see *your* face more clearly."

Percy did this, sheltering the injured woman's eyes from the first sudden light with one hand. He made an attempt to smile reassuringly, holding the beam high, aware of the effect his strong features often had on those of a nervous disposition. Underlit, he knew he looked like Beelzebub himself and he had no wish to frighten the poor lady to death. But all was well—Lady Merriman's eyes, he noted, were still bright and were focussing on him with recognition and understanding. The mouth, on the other hand, was set rigidly, a trickle of blood from one corner betraying internal injuries, the lips glued together.

"While you are still conscious, tell me—was this an accident?"

The eyes told him—*No.*

"Did someone push you from the window . . . deliberately?"

A nod of the head confirmed.

"Did you see the person who pushed you out?"

Another nod. Weaker this time. Montacute, sensing that

he was losing her, hurried to ask: "A name? Can you give me a name?"

The eyes closed. The narrow lips twitched, then struggled to part. With swift fingers, Montacute took out his handkerchief and dipped it in the glass of water. Gently, he sponged the trembling mouth, sensing this was what the woman herself wanted. She was clearly fighting to stay alive, straining every sinew to communicate some awful truth to him, and he would fight with her against the encroaching paralysis to receive it. He leaned closer, murmuring encouragement.

A cold touch pricked his cheek like the tip of an icicle as something slid up from under the enveloping wrap. He recoiled in horror as he understood that the dying woman was using the last threads of her strength to push towards him an object she was clutching in her hand. Her eyes pleaded with him to notice it. He nodded and gently pulled a fold of the wrap aside to reveal the jewelled hilt and then the blade of a short sword that he recognised.

The blood-caked lips came unstuck at last and Lady Merriman whispered in his ear.

The watcher strolled by on his way to the taxi rank at the corner of the square, catching the exact moment when her head lolled back. Unconscious? Certainly. Dead? Most likely. It looked as though the Englishman was going to have his hands full for the next day or two. Time to give Soulios the news he'd been waiting for. Husband and wife dead within hours of each other. With unbelievable luck.

There only remained the daughter.

CHAPTER 18

reddy Wentworth chose to bite the bullet and do his duty before breakfast. A swift telephone call established that the General was already at his desk and expecting that someone would call. Freddy sighed, straightened his tie, and set off for Konstantinou's headquarters.

The Chief of Security held court in a smart modern office on Queen Sophia Avenue. Handy for the consulates, the banks, the Royal Palace, and the government offices, and not the least military looking. Lulled by the atmosphere of a busy office about them, the clack of typewriters, the ringing of telephones, and the coming and going of serious-faced young men, the General's interviewees could almost put themselves at ease. Almost. No one could ever count himself at ease standing before the General, Freddy thought. And the General was notorious for preferring to conduct his interviews standing.

The elderly, aristocratic figure, in impeccable uniform, rose from his chair to greet Freddy when he entered and sat down again, gesturing to him to take a seat on the other side of the desk. Bad sign? Freddy made out the sketch of a charming smile under the luxuriant grey moustache, even a flash of teeth. Freddy looked aside. He really didn't want to see the

General's teeth. He always tried to avoid meeting his gaze also, though he was ashamed of his lapse into what must appear unpatriotic shiftiness. The piercing grey eyes were the only clear feature in a face which always looked to Freddy like a relief map of highland terrain. Crags, valleys, scars, and sinkholes provided cover for the surprisingly youthful and un-rheumy eyes which glared out, chilly and somewhat hypnotic. It was not surprising to Freddy—the frequency with which people changed their views in the General's presence, came to an accommodation, and crept out backwards wondering what on earth they'd promised. The man was now retired from active army duty. Officially. But the stories of his wartime exploits continued to do the rounds of the embassies and the clubs. Freddy hoped they were exaggerated but feared they were no more than faithful illustrations of the pitiless nature of this formidable old warrior.

"Oh, it's you, Wentworth. I wondered who they'd send," said the General. He had no small talk. "I was rather expecting that new Scotsman of yours . . . Grant, is it? Haven't yet had the pleasure. Perhaps someone will bring him round to show me. Now, before you start accounting at length for the murder of one British citizen by another on Greek soil, I will say—leave it to the police. We have no interest in domestic squabbles. Our C.I.D. have this in hand. Clear?"

Freddy opened his mouth to confirm, but the General didn't wait to hear his agreement.

"Two points, Wentworth: First—I express my dismay that this should have happened in such a public place and in this particular public place. For obvious reasons. And I hold your Embassy responsible." This time he waited for Wentworth's acknowledgement of guilt. Apparently satisfied with the nod and grunt he received, he pressed on: "Secondly: I have reaffirmed my original advice on the planned appearance of the Prime Minister at the opening night of these English revels.

And I remind you that this advice is clear and consistent: Mr. Venizelos should not attend. He does so without our blessing and with all our forebodings. This, however, in no way affects our professional attentions. The Prime Minister will be as effectively protected by my men as he has been on the occasion of all other assassination attempts."

"One could wish the protection squads of other countries were as diligent," said Wentworth, regretting at once his remark, which sounded unduly obsequious to his ears.

The General took the compliment as no more than a statement of fact. "You're thinking of that near tragedy in the Gare de Lyon in Paris? Supreme carelessness! Two bullets he took. And survived! The man's made of steel!"

"Indeed. Admirable constitution for a man of his years. I understand he's just been released from hospital. A touch of the dengue fever is what they're saying..."

"Came out far too early! And why? Had to get a train to... Belgrade...Salonika...Constantinople...God knows where! Never stops! And that wife of his is just as bad."

"Work hard, play hard, what!"

"It's the *playing* that gives me indigestion. Unnecessary risk-taking in my book. Now—I've personally reconnoitred the site of his next little outing and declared it a security nightmare. Theatre?" The General showed his teeth again. "Shooting gallery, more like! Space for ten thousand assassins, all able to draw a clear bead on the P.M. And he, I understand, is to be conveniently picked out by spotlight? The guests would have to be searched for secreted arms before entry. These guests! All dolled up in evening gear. As many women as men. Again, I say: nightmare!"

He listened with half an ear as Wentworth murmured his agreement. And then, with barely concealed wrath: "A frivolous entertainment! But I have word from on high—and I mean as *high* as you can go—that the frivolity on offer is to be staged as planned. With a week's grace to get the funeral out of the way. We are speaking of next Saturday. Got that, Wentworth?"

Freddy nodded. "Right you are, sir. That's three points then. All noted."

The General glared. "Then I look to you to expedite the matter. There are some who value the Greek-English cultural links…and who fancy a night out at the theatre…regardless of the cost to me and my men in…" He broke off and chewed his moustache in frustration.

"You were saying, sir?"

Konstantinou looked again at Wentworth, eyebrows raised in slight surprise to find him still sitting opposite. Freddy got to his feet and, mumbling he knew not what, shot out of the office, doing his best to remember what he'd agreed to.

CHAPTER 19

A hammering at the front door interrupted the breakfast party in Mrs. Rose's dining room.

To Letty's surprise, Thetis had rejected the idea of having a tray brought up to their bedroom and had joined the other guests downstairs. She had listened to the introductions to the five hearty English people gathered there and offered in return the quiet, polite phrases expected of a newcomer to the communal table. Conscious of the discreet scrutiny she was under, she'd exclaimed with pleasure at the sight of a large brown pot full of Lipton's tea circulating around the table and had admired the effect of the sunlight streaming through a jar of marmalade.

"We always bring supplies from home for Mrs. Rose," confided Mrs. Colonel Armitage, flattered by the remark. "Cook makes wonderful marmalade—good and bitter. So difficult to find abroad. Do try some, my dear."

Letty fussed about finding for Thetis on the sideboard the scrambled eggs, toast, and glass of goat's milk she'd asked for. The choice surprised Letty and made her feel queasy, but she was pleased in a nannyish sort of way that her guest had an appetite. Thetis seemed to have weathered last night's emotional storm and emerged determined to move on. Letty approved.

"You'll enjoy the milk," Colonel Armitage had assured Thetis cheerfully. "Put roses in your cheeks!"

"Well, of course," his wife added kindly. "And you may drink it with confidence. It's good milk. Good enough for the Embassy! 'We drink milk from the same goat'—you'll hear that said—it's a charming way of saying, here in Athens, that we are neighbours. They milk the animal right here on the doorsteps every morning before daylight so it's bound to be fresh. You've just arrived, have you?"

Thetis listened to Mrs. Armitage's hints and wrinkles on Athenian life with patience and even managed convincingly to slip an ingenuous question or two into the conversation. Letty looked at her freshly cold-creamed face, hair still damp from her bath, the luxuriant curls combed straight, parted in the centre, and tucked neatly behind her ears. The green linen dress she'd brought in her bag was flattering and not too badly creased, and she smelled unobtrusively of Letty's eau de cologne. The embodiment of proper English womanhood. Very far from the tearful, abandoned girl who'd talked through her despair for most of the night, and even further from the vengeful Queen Clytemnestra. A many-faceted personality, Letty decided, and wondered how many more sides would be revealed.

Mrs. Rose came in and caught Letty's eye. "There's a gentleman at the door asking to speak to you, Miss Talbot. Will you come?" Oddly, she didn't announce his name, though Letty noticed she was holding a calling card in her hand.

"A gentleman?" Letty wondered. Not Gunning, then, whom she had been expecting. Mrs. Rose would have put him straight in the guests' parlour and stayed to chat with him and not left him standing about on the doorstep.

"The parlour's empty—you may use that if it looks as if you're in for a long interview. Call if you need me—I shall be in the office," Mrs. Rose finished mysteriously.

"Crikey! You look awful! Have you been up all night, Chief Inspector?" Letty said unguardedly.

"Well, I can't return the compliment," he replied easily. "*You* look as bright as a buttercup, Miss Talbot. Yellow suits you." He put his hands on either side of his head and squeezed. "I looked in the mirror this morning and saw a pumpkin head. Sorry to frighten you! This is what two hours' sleep on top of two murders can do for you. Tell me—is there somewhere we could..."

"Come in," said Letty. "We can use the guests' parlour. Unless you want to drag me off to the clink?"

"The parlour would be wonderful." He sniffed the air as he closed the door behind him. "I say—is that coffee I smell...?"

"It certainly is, Inspector Montacute," Mrs. Rose called flirtatiously down the corridor, advancing on them with a tray in her hands. "Fortnum's best. I'll put this on the sideboard in the parlour. You can wait on yourselves, I think?"

Best coffee. Best china, too. Mrs. Rose apparently judged the inspector worthy of her Wedgwood. Letty wondered whether she might be the only woman in Athens who had not been charmed by the man. Perhaps she should make an effort. "Let me guess—milk, one sugar lump?" she said sweetly, pouring out. "I thought so. But—Inspector! This is too much! *Two* murders, did I hear you say? *Another* one? Poor you! I'm very sorry and all that for the second victim, whoever he may be, but I hope you won't find yourself too distracted by his case from Andrew's death? I'm not at all sure how you manage these things."

"Not distracted at all." He took a sip of his coffee, unusually silent, and looked around the book-lined room, wondering where to settle. In the small parlour, with its chichi collections of reminders of home—Doulton vases, Staffordshire figurines in a row on the mantelshelf, embroidered fire screen, spindle-legged chairs—the inspector appeared dangerously large and intrusive. At a gesture from Letty, he moved to sit at the central table the guests used for work or games and she joined him.

"Is there something I can do for you?" she prompted him.

"Probably not, but I thought I'd better check...on the off chance...You see how desperate we are...You had some conversation last night at the theatre with Thetis Templeton. I noticed the two of you exchanging more than addresses, it seemed to me?"

"Not much more. We made a few rude and thoughtless remarks—you understand the tension that gripped us both—though neither of us realised at that moment that it was a grief we had in common that was turning us waspish. Then we apologised and began to get along more easily," she said, trying to remember accurately.

"Did she confide anything about her circumstances here in Athens? In her cousin's household?"

"Nothing more than the address in Kolonaki."

"She didn't give you an inkling of where she might possibly— Oh, dammit! I'll come to the point. The girl's run off! She's a missing person. We've got people looking for her all over Athens. Hotels...railway station...the seaport. We haven't a clue where she might have hidden herself and wondered if you...well, no...you can see we're clutching at straws."

"Well, I'm glad you've come clean! You only had to ask. I do know where she is. Don't worry—she's safe and well. Has frightful old Maud got the wobbles and repented? 'Come back, Thetis, all is forgiven.' Huh! She must have been alarmed to have rousted out the police force to do her retrieval for her! But it won't get her far. Thetis is never going back, you know."

Montacute croaked something unintelligible.

"Very well, I'll fetch her and she can tell you that herself. She arrived late last night, running away from Maud."

"She's here—in this house?"

"Yes. She shared my room."

"You're telling me you spent the night in close proximity to Clytemnestra?"

There was more than surprise in the inspector's voice. Concern? Alarm, even.

"Well, yes. If you'd call the three-foot gap between single beds close proximity. And I'd call her Thetis Templeton. She was perfectly comfortable. You can check for yourself—she's only a few yards away, tucking into her scrambled eggs. She won't want to see you! And I insist on sitting in on the interview. For propriety's sake, naturally—this is Greece, after all, where an unmarried girl may not speak to a man unless she's accompanied by six male cousins and her granny. But also to make certain you don't bully her. I think I know your sneaky ways...armlocks and suchlike."

Letty hurried off to beckon at the dining room door, indicating that Thetis should accompany her to the parlour, and the girls entered together.

"Ah. Your Majesty." Montacute shot to his feet, opening with what sounded to Letty like a flourish of embarrassed bonhomie, and she rather wished he wouldn't. But then she remembered she'd seen the two as actors striking sparks off each other. They must, inevitably, have arrived at some kind of an onstage relationship, if not an understanding. An understanding Letty was not privy to.

"Oh, hello there! It's old Bossy Boots, isn't it? I poked you in the ribs...I say, I'm most frightfully sorry about that."

Thetis sailed in and approached the inspector, genuinely pleased to see him, Letty would have sworn. She stared up into his face and her smile vanished. "Oh, dear! Poor old thing! You look as though you died last Tuesday. Are you investigating your own death, Percy?...Tell me, Letty, when was it we last saw the inspector alive?" She seemed eager to enjoy a joke with her old sparring partner.

He was unable to find an immediate response to her overtures. Thetis tried again: "Have you caught him yet?"

"Caught whom?"

"Well—the killer...Andrew's killer. Geoffrey Melton. Surely you've worked it out? Everyone else has. They were all putting money on it last night over the pink gins. And we've all decided that if you can't get him for murder you should nab him for some other misdemeanour. You've only to look at the man to know he's guilty of something."

Montacute was not entertained by Thetis's slant on crime-fighting and he replied stiffly: "It is believed Mr. Melton has taken refuge in the Embassy where he works, and we are hoping to be granted an interview shortly. I'm not here to talk about the killing of Professor Merriman, miss. I'm afraid I am the bearer of further bad news." The tone was formal, even chilly.

"'Miss'! For goodness' sake—I'm Thetis, she's Letty, and we both intend to call you Percy. Or Percival if you're inclined to prance about on your high horse," said Thetis. "Oh, do settle down and tell me what exactly you want to talk about. Though I think I can guess! And if I'm right I shall need a cup of fortifying coffee." She went to the tray and poured out a cup for herself. "How about you, Letty? No? More for you, Percy?"

He shook his head, uncomfortable with the girl's familiarity. She sat down opposite him at the table and they stared at each other.

For rather a long time, Letty thought.

"Maud's sent you, hasn't she?" said Thetis, deciding to break the silence.

"In a manner of speaking"—Montacute hesitated—"you could say that. Can you run over for me the events of last evening, please? I'm aware that you spent some time in the bar at the Grande Bretagne and I know what you drank and in whose company. You arrived at your cousin's house at just after nine o'clock. Take it from there."

But Thetis wasn't prepared simply to take it from there. She slammed a fist angrily on the table, making the coffee cups rattle. "I thought as much! Didn't I tell you, Letty? She's a vindictive old cow! She's not trying to get me back—she's sent the hounds after me to slap a writ for Grievous Bodily Harm on me. Do they have such a thing out here? That's what they called it in London when I clouted a chap round the ear for getting too fresh. She's reported that I was drunk and incapable, hasn't she! Not true! And this was only a nick on the right cheek, for goodness' sake, not a broken jaw! About as harmful as a shaving cut on a man's face . . . I notice you've got two such on your own craggy features this morning, Inspector. It gives you a certain buccaneering allure." She leaned forward and smiled up admiringly into the inspector's face. He looked aside and fiddled with his coffee cup. "But—imagine—if your barber did that, would you bother to chase all over town to arrest him? Surely you took a close look at the alleged wound before you decided to hunt me down?"

"I have no recollection of the scratch you mention, Miss Templeton. It went undetected, I'm afraid, but taken alongside the other horrific injuries to her body, I may be forgiven, I think, for overlooking it."

His dry voice silenced the two women. Thetis made a small noise in her throat and at last could find no words.

"I think you're going to have to enlarge on that remark, Inspector," said Letty. "Injuries? What injuries?"

"The ones she received at about ten o'clock last night as a result of falling through the open window of her second-floor drawing room over the balcony and onto the paved area below. Not a huge drop and some might have survived with no more than a twisted ankle, but Lady Merriman was not strong and she fell awkwardly. Her skull was cracked and her spine, we believe, broken. From initial investigation, I deduce that she was thrown out headfirst. But we'll know for certain shortly. A pathologist is even now working on it."

"Pathologist?..." Letty managed to breathe. "You're saying she's dead? And—'*thrown* out'? Murdered, you mean? That's quite an assumption! How sure can you be of that? Shall I tell you what *I'd* guess, Inspector? Maud jumped out of the window herself. Didn't that occur to you? So recently and tragically widowed—it's likely that the balance of her mind was disturbed, isn't it? With Andrew gone, she had little else to live for, you know. They didn't get on, everyone knows that, but—you know—when the oak tree is felled, the ivy that's lived on it withers and dies, too."

Montacute listened patiently, understanding that she was still absorbing and trying to make sense of the shattering news. "As you say. That would, of course, have been our first thought but we were summoned to her side moments before she died. We do not need to rely on guesswork for an account of the events."

He turned sad eyes on Thetis. "I'm saying that death was not instantaneous. The lady struggled gallantly to the last. She lived long enough to communicate with me. She was conscious and able to summon the strength to tell me she had been pushed through the window. She told me the name of the one who had pushed her. She was holding in her hand a clue to her assailant's identity."

His voice took on an even colder formality: "Miss Thetis Templeton, I have to tell you that I am placing you under arrest for the murder of your cousin Lady Maud Merriman. And further, there may eventually, at the completion of my enquiries, be some question of your involvement in the killing of Sir Andrew Merriman, your lover. For discretion's sake, I will accompany you from here to the police station and there lay out all the charges necessary and explain the legalities of the situation in which you find yourself. You will be held there under arrest until the situation is clarified. You may wish to summon a lawyer."

Letty sat in shocked silence, waiting for the explosion.

CHAPTER 20

There was sure to be an explosion but Letty couldn't guess which of these two incandescent characters would flare first. There they sat on opposite sides of the table, mirror images, locking dark glares, their hands held in front of them like opponents in a card game. In their onstage battles, Letty had thought them well matched: the arrogant, unassailable queen and the chorus leader, her subject, swept by moral outrage to a state of bravado which lay beyond fear. And if it came to a showdown here in this room in real life, could Letty be sure where her loyalties lay?

Of one duty of care she was in no doubt. She got up and deftly removed the half-drunk cups of coffee from their elbows. If handy weapons were to be pressed into use by this volatile pair, she knew she didn't want Mrs. Rose's tasteful décor to be the victim of a sudden assault. They paid no attention to her stealthy movements. They simply sat on, deep in thought, showing the intense but sharply circumscribed concentration of arm wrestlers.

It was Thetis who broke the stalemate.

She leaned forward and reached across the table, covering the inspector's clenched hands lightly with her own. "What a perfectly foul job you have to do, Percy! You look so tired and miserable...Don't worry—I'll come quietly. We've all caused you quite enough trouble...And poor old Maud! Not my favourite person in the world, but she didn't deserve such an end." Her dark eyes gleamed with tears, holding his, hiding nothing. Her voice was silken and sorrowful. The inspector leaned closer to hear her murmurs. "I didn't kill her, Percy. And I'm sure I can explain everything if you'll listen to me. Do you think Letty could come along with us? That is, if she's willing to, of course? It may be the last thing she would want to do. But she is a witness of a sort—she did hear my confession last night when I loomed up out of the dark, shattering her peace. No—not a confession to murder—but there are other things I'm guilty of, I'm afraid. Things which may have a bearing on the case."

The inspector detached his gaze and found his voice. "Certainly. It would be most convenient. We'd be grateful. The central police station is just across the square...very handy." He turned to Letty. "What about it, Miss Talbot?"

To her surprise he made no attempt to hustle them off, sitting on quietly, still hand-clasped and bemused.

"Of course. I'd be glad to be of help. Look—give me a moment to speak to Mrs. Rose. I shall need to leave a message for William Gunning, and I'll tell her to expect us both back for supper, Thetis," she finished with a show of confidence she couldn't feel.

"Has Miss Templeton brought an overnight bag with her, I wonder?" the inspector asked Letty, directing the question over Thetis's head. "She has? Good. Would you pack it for her and bring it down?"

Letty was suddenly angered by the way the policeman had distanced from himself, had rendered impersonal, in the space of seconds, a woman who had just shown him a surprising understanding. Thetis was now merely a prisoner and only to be addressed for the business of extracting information, apparently. Her personal welfare was to be the concern of others.

"Why don't we ask her permission, Percy," Letty said sweetly and turned to her. "Thetis, my dear, would you mind awfully if I were to go up to our room and see to your things? He doesn't say so but I think our friend here suspects you capable of scrambling through the attic skylight and showing a clean pair of heels over the rooftops if you go up yourself."

Thetis gave her a shaky smile and murmured her agreement. As Letty reached the door, she added: "Oh, Letty... while you're at it..." She bit her lip in confusion, then went on: "I must ask Percy to forgive me if I mention female unmentionables but I can hardly ask him to leave the room. He will just have to close his ears." Her voice took on its more usual light tone as she spoke: "Could you check that I packed spare knickers? I have a sketchy recollection of stuffing in there last night a handful of green shantung ones with lace edging. Ones I bought in Paris. In the circs, they may not be quite suitable for what the inspector has in mind for me for the next few days...I don't think his plans involve spiriting me away to that little hotel by the beach at Glyfada...though you never know your luck!"

Montacute tugged his hands hastily out of her grasp, and if that severe face had been capable of showing such emotion, it would have blushed with embarrassment, Letty thought.

"Got it!" she replied. "Know exactly what you mean. Luckily some of my campaign gear's come with me. Trench-digging undies...elastic tops and bottoms...mosquito- and snake-proof...just the thing for a police station. Won't be a tick!"

Once in her room, she tugged Thetis's bag from under her bed and placed it, opened, on the luggage stand. She bustled about collecting toiletries and added from her own collection a cake of Yardley's lavender soap, a fresh flannel, and a bottle of cologne. She folded the travelling suit and put it on the bed ready to be placed on top, then fished out from under a pillow Thetis's wispy white nightgown. Thoughtfully, she put this into the laundry basket and substituted a pair of her own striped flannelette pyjamas. The nights would be cold in a Greek jail, she supposed. But—knickers? What had all that been about? So unnecessary to mention it—except of course as a means of annoying and embarrassing the inspector. Well, that had certainly worked! And serve him right, too!

Letty rummaged about in the depths of the bag and came up with two surprises. The first made her frown. A blue leather *coffret* with gold lettering discreetly on the underside. The name and address of an expensive clinic in Switzerland. Letty had a very similar box from their London branch. With a stab of irritation she wondered how many girls were wandering the world with just such a souvenir of Andrew. She put it back in the bag exactly where she'd found it. And she began to wonder about Thetis.

The second discovery made her gasp. Three pairs of green silk knickers just as described. But it wasn't the quality and the Paris label that impressed her. It was the object they were wrapped tightly around—a black and purposeful small revolver. Letty inspected it with careful hands, recalling all her brother's training on handling weapons. A Webley Mark IV. British Forces issue. Its snub four-inch barrel made it perfect for close-range work. Some army men had not been so impressed, even calling it the "Wobbly," scornful of the way it tended to spray its deadly bullets around when aimed at a more distant target. Colonel Lawrence had confessed that he had accidentally, whilst dashing about the Arabian desert, shot his own camel with his "Wobbly." But in a confined space, with your enemy at close quarters, it was unbeatable, they said. Trench raiders swore by it. It even had a device at the side by which you could attach a short bayonet in case you preferred a silent approach.

Struck by a sickening thought, Letty swallowed, breathed deeply, and upended the bag onto the bed. She inspected the contents, finding nothing sinister, and then ran her fingers gingerly across the bottom and along the seams as she'd seen customs officers do. To her relief she dredged up no blood-stained blade, but she did find a Harrogate Toffee tin full of ammunition.

Letty used the stirrup-type barrel catch to break open the gun. Not loaded. But it had been used. And recently cleaned, she thought, wiping streaks of gun oil off her fingers. Where on earth had Thetis come by such a gun? Had she brought it with her from England? Or had she acquired it in Athens? Either way—not difficult. Europe was awash still with ex-war-issue pistols if you knew where to look. Letty smiled. Andrew had offered *her* a palm-sized Beretta for self-defence when they'd been digging in Egypt. He was never quite at ease abroad—his soldier's instincts, she'd assumed, urged him to ensure that the women in his life were adequately protected from whatever nightmares he pictured for them. Her father and brother had demonstrated the same concern; military men were all too aware of the terrors that lurked not far below the veneer of civilisation. Letty had to allow, but refused to contemplate, the horrors they must have witnessed.

For a moment she wondered if Andrew had ever offered a handgun to his wife when she accompanied him to foreign parts and, remembering Maud's vaunted inability to master anything more mechanical than a tin-opener, thought probably not. She'd have pretended to faint at the sight of a pistol.

Letty held the Webley for a moment, thinking. Even unloaded, the gun in her hand could kill. It was as good as a death warrant. Letty understood the older girl's concern that she check her underwear. It hadn't been mentioned merely to annoy and reprimand the policeman. A murder suspect taken along to the clink with such serious armament hidden away in her luggage was risking her life. Letty had no doubt the meticulous inspector would order the usual searches and the gun would be found. And Thetis had seen this. It could make all the difference between a charge of killing on the spur of the moment while the balance of the mind was disturbed and a charge of premeditated murder. Letty could imagine the mocking disbelief in the voice of the prosecuting counsel as he sought to establish intent: "It would appear, Miss Templeton, that you came to a civilised and friendly capital armed and prepared for some eventuality, would it not? The question we all ask ourselves is: What eventuality exactly did you have in mind?"

The gun in Letty's hand marked the difference between a life sentence in jail and a death on the scaffold. Did they use the noose or the guillotine out here? Or perhaps the firing squad? Letty had no idea.

She didn't conduct a debate with herself. There was no question of what she should do. She simply wiped the revolver and the toffee tin clean of previous prints with a towel and was about to slide them into her own underwear drawer when she hesitated.

She was comfortable with guns, had grown up in a country house surrounded by them and respecting them. Although she'd never killed a man, she had learned two years before in Burgundy that she was capable of it. Violence and unexpected death were creeping up on her like jungle beasts and suddenly the little black gun seemed very desirable. Thetis would have no use for it in jail. And Gunning need never know she had it. She didn't have to think very deeply about Andrew's reaction to the seduction she was feeling. With his imagined encouragement ringing in her ears—"Do it, Letty!"—she broke open the gun again and reached for the toffee tin.

Her arrangements complete, she took out three pairs of sensible cotton bloomers and put them in Thetis's holdall.

On reflection—what *did* you pack for a friend on her way to jail?—she added a bag of fruit drops, a notebook, and a pen. She took her precious copy of *The Three Musketeers* from her shelf and wrote on the flyleaf: "Gunning and I are with you!" Well, Alexandre Dumas would keep anyone's spirits up, she reckoned.

Letty fastened up the bag, grabbed her own battered leather satchel that went everywhere with her, and hurried downstairs to the parlour. "There! All done," she announced into the charged silence. "The inspector may rummage in total confidence. Everyone's blushes spared!"

"You're a godsend, Letty," Thetis said quietly.

CHAPTER 21

"Well, for a start, her name's not Templeton and, to go on, she's not 'Miss,'" Montacute confided as they left the police station.

Letty had done what she could to mediate with the forces of law and order on Thetis's behalf. She had enough knowledge of Athenian society to come up with the name of a lawyer of whom she'd heard good things spoken and insisted that he be fetched at once. A slight nod of encouragement from the inspector reassured her in her choice and the prisoner was led away by the duty officer and a local woman hurriedly brought in to act as wardress. Letty did wonder if the prisoner had helped her cause, though, when she'd turned dramatically at the last moment and smiled back at the inspector. "Don't worry about me, Percy," she'd announced in throbbing tones. "I know how to be brave!" Then, with a wink for Letty, she'd disappeared, all gracious smiles for her escorting jailers, into the depths of the building.

Montacute had admitted gruffly that he was not yet ready to conduct an official interrogation; he needed more hard evidence and this he intended to comb from the scene of the crime in Kolonaki Square. He'd invited Letty to accompany him there; in a house where she was very much at home, she might well have insights helpful to his study of the case. And with, doubtless, a clutch of domestic servants to interview, a respected female presence at his elbow would be essential. Letty sighed at the prospect of more hours of her time being commandeered by the inspector. Did he envisage her trotting at his side, smiling reassuringly at his female targets until the moment the case was resolved?

Probably. But first—he'd reminded her—he had an appointment at the Embassy and she was very welcome to attend with him. He'd looked at his wristwatch. "We're a little early. Take a turn with me around the square, will you?"

She had had the feeling that refusing was not an option.

"Crikey! She's not Miss Templeton? You don't say! Well, I think you'd better tell me—in whose company *did* I spend last night?" Letty asked, confused. "Is she—at least—*Thetis*?"

"Yes. That bit's accurate. Named for the sea nymph… silver-footed, shape-shifting Thetis…" He paused and grinned. "Huh! Very appropriate! Fast mover if ever I saw one! And you're never quite certain who exactly you've got. The original Thetis was a nymph favoured by Zeus. The mother of Achilles. She's Thetis all right. But not Miss Templeton. Her real name is no deep secret, I understand, but I bring all this to your attention as a warning. I observe you to be a kindhearted and accommodating sort of person, miss. Someone likely to stand by her friends—or anybody—experiencing difficulties with the forces of law and order. But I'm obliged to tell you that you ought not to rush to take people on trust, as I see you do."

"I don't have the benefit of your underhand methods, Inspector, to inform me. Where on earth do you get your facts?"

"I check with London on every British subject who looks like staying for any length of time. That way I can head off a

lot of trouble. You'd be surprised how many problems are cre-
ated by us foreigners. I like to know who I've got on my patch
and what they're up to."

"And what was Thetis 'up to'—apart from putting in a
splendid performance as the wicked queen?"

"You'll be surprised! And don't wonder that her acting
was impressive—it's what she does. It's her occupation, I mean.
It's what she does for a living. She's on the stage. An actress."

Letty had the impression that he was stumbling somewhat, watching for her reaction.

"And doesn't *that* explain a lot!" she said. "She didn't confide any such thing over the cocoa last night. I wonder why?"

"It's the sort of information that's not always found di-
gestible by people of your standing in society, Miss Talbot. I
imagine that cold shoulders, blank stares, and chilly set-
downs are the order of the day for ladies of her profession."

Letty couldn't deny the prejudice of her class. *She's on the
stage* . . . The phrase was nearly as condemning as *She's entered a
house of ill-repute*. It was generally assumed that the exit from
one was the entrance to the other. Unless an actress was elderly, ugly but stately, and had the protection of married
status—*Mrs. Brewster Langdale-Price makes an unforgettable impression in the role of Cleopatra, Queen of Egypt*—she was regarded
as "no better than she ought to be and a disgrace to her family . . . if she has a family . . ."

"I think it's very intriguing. I go often to the theatre . . . I
wonder if I may have seen her performing in something?" she
asked, confident that the omniscient inspector would have an
answer.

He did not disappoint. "She toured the country with a
repertory company after the war. Comedy or tragedy—she
could turn her hand to anything. A chirpy Eliza Doolittle one
week, a soggy Ophelia the next . . . you know the sort of thing.
Then her talent was spotted and she graduated to the London

stage. *Love Your Enemy* at the Savoy...*A Lady of Easy Virtue* at
the Duke of York's—wonderful reviews for that one! '*A revelation!*' the critics said of Miss Templeton's performance as
Chloë, Lady Brunswick-Plaice. '*Her charm of appearance and
beautifully flexible voice are matched by a swift intelligence and force-
ful personality,*' the theatre critic of *The Times* enthused. I don't
think we could argue with *that*, could we, miss?"

"No, indeed," Letty agreed, amused. "But, Inspector—you
are full of surprises! I had no idea you were a masher! You lack
only the moustache to twirl. I trust you took the opportunity
of getting her autograph while you had her under restraint?
Look—I don't see why this ability and success of hers should
make her interesting to the police—or the government—whichever is sticking its nasty suspicious nose into her affairs."

"Just background," he muttered.

Letty stood and faced him on the pavement. "Which you
wouldn't have bothered to trail before me unless you were
about to stun me with the foreground. Do get on with whatever character assassination you have in mind and leave me
free to make my own judgement."

"Bit of a firebrand, that young lady," he said tantalisingly,
and began to walk off on a second tour around the square.
When Letty caught up with him, he was flowing on: "...fol-
lower of Mrs. Pankhurst, seat on the board of the Suffragist
movement, Bolshevist agitator...you understand I quote
from the file we hold on her, and I speak in confidence and
without implied criticism...I'm aware that such behaviour
has its admirers among what they call the upper-class intelli-
gentsia...She marched down Piccadilly with the coal miners,
carrying a banner, in the '26 strike that brought the country to
a standstill. You may well have seen her photograph on the
front page of the *Herald*, Miss Talbot."

Letty glanced at the face of the inspector, carefully composed in neutrality, and decided to annoy him. "No, I wasn't

aware of that. But how disappointing! They didn't take *my* photograph!" she said. "Not on that occasion."

"*Someone* did," he replied quietly. "Don't imagine that you went unnoticed."

His reply chilled her.

"I'm wondering, miss, if I were to pick through the photographic evidence on file, whether I might find you and Miss Templeton in the same shot? Two known female agitators... It would be surprising if you'd never met before you both turned up on the same stage set in Athens. Chummy lot, the Sisters, I understand? And you do seem to be hitting it off rather well...perhaps too well for women so recently acquainted?"

"What a sinister world you inhabit, Inspector! I think we've had this conversation before. You obviously have a short memory. The last time you asked me if I knew Thetis, I said no. I say again: I had never set eyes on Thetis Templeton's face until the moment she took off her mask onstage last night. And—photographic record? What are you telling me? That all my father's warnings about the fanatical nature of the present régime at home—the surveillance he hints at, the sabotage of reputations he suspects, the gagging of opposition he has experienced—are well founded?" Letty challenged wildly, expecting no answer.

Suddenly oppressed by the deadweight of the postwar male hierarchy she had been struggling against for years, she turned on him—the immediately accessible, flesh-and-blood representative of the all-powerful but shadowy forces of the Establishment. "It would be interesting to hear this confirmed—and by an employee—a minion, a tool of the oppressive authorities that run our country. I do not lose sight of your chain of command, Inspector. *You*, Montacute, are a pawn in the State's game and you are ultimately answerable, at the highest level of your department, to your king-piece—the most damaging, most retrogressive Home Secretary we've had for decades. Do you feel no shame, being a cog in the machine of that prejudiced, vindictive homebred Napoleon? That narrow-minded little peacock?"

Letty ran out of breath and she waited, expecting to hear the clink of handcuffs. With that speech she had earned a place next to Thetis in the cells. Halfway between the police station and the Embassy, he would be wondering to which authority he should deliver her up on a charge of treason. She cut short her tirade, distracted by the contortion of his facial muscles. Grinding his teeth in fury? Bristling at her insults? In the end she decided he was trying to fight back a smile.

"A fine mixture of metaphors there, miss," he commented mildly. "Good effort. But my 'ultimate authority' as you call him, my boss—the Home Secretary, Sir William Joynson-Hicks, I think we're speaking of—has had much worse opprobrium heaped on him. It always slides off," he said comfortably. "Water off a duck's back! I'll disregard your abuse of my superior but I will pick up your original question and answer it directly: yes. You *ought* to pay attention to your father's warnings. You should listen to his advice. Sir Richard's suspicions are not ill-founded."

Letty was silenced. This was not the language of a devoted Servant of the Law. Montacute disturbed and puzzled her. She'd heard of agents provocateurs who sidled up at demonstrations and, with a show of friendship, drew one out into making statements against the government, and she wondered whether she was faced with one such now. The police force with its right-wing, anti-Jewish, anticommunist leadership was riddled with Fascisti, it was rumoured. Men who put on black shirts and shorts and paraded at weekend rallies, confident that their antics were shielded from criticism by gangs of their paid bully-boy supporters. She would be wise to hold her tongue. For a C.I.D. man, even one at the forefront of his profession, Montacute seemed to have access to knowledge that she would have reckoned outside his sphere.

Letty resolved to struggle with the telephone system to put a call through to her father. With his connexions, Sir Richard would be able to make discreet enquiries about the smiling sleuth who'd now tucked her arm companionably under his as they made a second tour of the square.

"What did you tell me about Maud Merriman?" he mused. " 'Takes people at face value, puts them into pigeonholes and there they stay…' Something on those lines? You've been learning from her! Don't assume you know me on two minutes' acquaintance, miss. But your rush to judgement illustrates neatly the point I was about to make regarding Thetis Templeton and her activities."

"Ah, yes. I did wonder what had tempted her to come to Athens. It sounds as though things got a little too hot for her back home in London?"

"I'll say! But, in the end, it wasn't her political activities that got her into trouble last spring. Oh, no. The stage-door Johnny she claims to have had an altercation with in the alley behind the Drury Lane Theatre didn't just suffer a reproving tap on the cheek with a fan. She decked him—right there in front of a gang of his roistering cronies. Even worse for her, the bloke happens to be related to the Home Secretary. Yes, the gentleman of whom we were just speaking: your hero and mine, Death-Warrant-a-Day Joynson-Hicks himself. Or 'Jix' as he is playfully called by one and all."

Letty shuddered. "Jix indeed! Is that supposed to endear him? I once knew a Rottweiler called Cuddles."

"Well, you can imagine the fuss that ensued. An arrest was made for Grievous Bodily Harm—the man's jaw bone *was* broken, so there were grounds. There was the suspicion that she'd used some concealed instrument to deliver such an injury—"

"What? I can't see Thetis sporting knuckle-dusters! Can you?"

He grimaced at the image. "Whatever the circumstances, there was no shortage of well-connected witnesses to support the injured complainant. Miss Templeton was contemplating a guilty verdict. Probably delivered with sententious regret by a beak at the Old Bailey who just happened to be a member of Jix's Club, don't you know…" His supple voice slid mockingly into an aristocratic accent. "But no one thought it was a good idea to hear that girl stand up in the witness box to give evidence in a court of law—she's got a tongue like a hedge clipper and knows how to manipulate an audience! And newspaper editors of the sensation-seeking kind—and who pack the public galleries of the courts—would hang on her every word! And report them!"

"So—face-saving negotiations were conducted behind the scenes?" Letty guessed.

"Exactly. A deal of some sort must have been done. It does happen. Threats and favours doled out in the right measure—the usual. No apology was forthcoming from the lady—they were mad to expect it—but she agreed at least to go abroad for a while, in the traditional way, to cool off."

"Couldn't she just have gone to Brighton? Everyone has an old aunt mouldering away in Brighton. An aunt who'll make you welcome and ask no questions."

"No aunts, gaga or otherwise, I'm afraid. Not much in the way of family. Parents both dead. She has two uncles and five male cousins who've all disowned her. And a fearfully decrepit old granny tucked away years ago (for very good reason, Miss Templeton assures me) in an institution of some kind on a cliff top near Eastbourne. Our Miss T's been something of a black sheep for some time now. Her family didn't much care for her activities and she's had no contact with them for a few years. It was Lady Merriman who did the decent thing—probably talked into it by her husband, who's well known for his kind attentions to young ladies—and invited her to stay in Athens with them for a few weeks until it all rolled away."

"I wouldn't put it down to good nature. Maud always liked to have someone around to torment," said Letty. "And no paid companion would have stuck it for longer than a day or two. But it does seem odd to me that a spirited girl like Thetis would have submitted to such coercion."

"Five years' hard labour in Holloway prison or a summer with Maud in Athens? A difficult choice." He grinned. "But with her cousin, I think Maud had taken on more than she could handle. A woman of experience and self-sufficiency. Not one to stand any nonsense from Lady Merriman, I think. Very modern." He paused to give her what she could have interpreted as an approving smile. Definitely warm. "Not unlike yourself, I'd say, miss. I expect a lot of agreeing was going on last night . . . ?"

She didn't pick up his invitation to bare Thetis's soul without her knowledge or consent, though Letty had heard a confidence which would have stopped the man dead in his tracks with astonishment. He could stay in ignorance as far as she was concerned. She was no longer surprised by masculine assumptions that women were always ready to blurt out any information or opinion they might have, the moment it flitted through their mind, but she scorned them. The inspector, she was pleased to note, hadn't the faintest idea of the depths of his victim's degradation. He hadn't heard the desperate confession and he hadn't plumbed the depths of her overnight bag, either. Letty really wouldn't want to hear his judgement, which might well have recourse to the Bible for its expressions of disapproval. "Moral turpitude" might feature, and "heinousness" and "sink of iniquity." No, Letty would leave him in comfortable ignorance with his illusion of slightly risqué modern womanhood.

"Sleeves-up-and-set-about-it types, the pair of you! Miss Templeton hadn't been in Athens two minutes before she was spending her days working with the American ladies who run the refugee charity."

"Very laudable!"

"And as good a way as any of getting out from under Maud's feet," he suggested.

"You are too cynical, Inspector," said Letty. "How *do* you think a lively woman should choose to spend her time in this exciting city? Sipping tea with the Archbishop or stirring a steaming cauldron of stew in a soup kitchen?"

"I know she did neither," he replied quietly.

Then he knew more than Letty had supposed. She thought she'd test the extent of his information, editing out of her account anything which was not complimentary to Thetis. "No. A surprising and admirable girl. I'm sure you're aware also that it was the war that opened up previously blocked avenues for her. As it did for many girls of spirit. She tells me she trained as a nurse and worked her way through the last years of the war up to her armpits in pus and gore. *I* couldn't have done it even if I'd been old enough, but I remember as a young thing—nine or ten years old—longing to kit up in headdress and apron and take off for the battlefields. I had a much-loved brother fighting there. It was my dream to snatch him and his friends from the jaws of death and nurse them back to life…you can imagine…Thetis is five or six years older than I—she scraped in halfway through the war. And she actually did it. I envy her courage."

"And it's her medical knowledge she puts to good use over here. But it took a strange turn: Somewhere along the line, Miss Thetis turned her attention to midwifery. Yes—

midwifery. Not much call for that in the front-line dressing stations, I'd have thought. Bit of a puzzle there...And my records are silent at this point. She helps out, not in the street canteens like most of the foreign women in the capital, but in the refugee mothers and babies facility. Always a demand for that. And she's been working with Mrs. Venizelos, who's putting a good deal of money into establishing a maternity unit at the hospital. But perhaps the interest has its origins in those war years?" he said with apparently sudden speculation.

Letty sensed she was about to be astonished by his next revelation.

"She married hastily—suspiciously hastily—at a young age during the war. It was one of those rushed weddings performed a couple of days before the groom goes marching off in uniform. Her husband, a Lieutenant Chandos, was hardly much older than she was and disaster ensued. He died on the Somme and the baby she was expecting died soon after birth. Could account for her rather special interests, wouldn't you say? Mrs. Chandos has had a tough time for the past few years. A hand-to-mouth existence. She's got by on a meagre widow's pension supplemented by her earnings from appearances in plays on the London stage."

"Good Lord! I had no idea! Poor, brave Thetis!"

"The lady has, indeed, shown much courage and enterprise."

"I wonder why she's never remarried? She's intelligent and very beautiful."

"And there you have it! Too challenging for most." He shrugged. "Good men aren't exactly thick on the ground after the last lot. And there aren't many Agamemnons left in our postwar world, Miss Talbot. You'd be looking for a bloke with some considerable resilience to take on such a wife. And a stout lock on his bathroom door."

He gave a shout of laughter, struck by an entertaining notion. "And never forget the prophecy! According to the story, the original Thetis was fated to bear a son who would grow up to be more illustrious than his father. That certainly put off a few contenders. Zeus himself prudently bowed out of the contest for her favours."

"And the son turned out to be Achilles, hero of the Trojan War and the Great Alexander's inspiration. But you're right, Percy...or the prophecy was...I can't remember the name of the father. Is it recorded?"

"Homer mentions it—Peleus, I believe."

"And our Thetis kept her maiden name?"

"That's right. It's her stage name. Her husband's family wouldn't have been pleased to see their name plastered over theatre billboards in London."

"Then that's the one I shall use, as it's the one she's chosen to be known by."

"Quite so. I tell you these things to alert you to the possibility of exploitation and deception. It would not be wise to invest too much sympathy in her cause. A little distancing is called for, I think."

Letty tapped him lightly on the arm. "You'd do well to take your own advice, Percy. And watch out for that knuckle-duster," she said, and was pleased to see that she had, at last, managed to silence him.

Much of last night's magic had faded from the scene at the Embassy. The gravel was being raked, the trees watered, pots lifted back into line, and candle-grease stains scrubbed from the marble steps.

At least, in the middle of all the bustle, they were expected. With a warning to tread carefully on the black-and-white chequered floor, freshly swabbed, Montacute was greeted by name. The inspector acknowledged the smart young aide who'd hurried forward and presented him to Letty, making it clear that the lady would be accompanying him. Charles Devenish was for a moment disconcerted and seemed prepared to question her presence. Letty was intrigued to see the steel beneath the bland exterior as Montacute, with a smile and a few short sentences, got his way.

"Ah…in that case…you should know, Montacute, that the First Secretary has himself asked to see you for a moment before your…er…interview with Mr. Melton." The aide looked uncertainly at Letty.

"Always a pleasure to see Freddy!" Letty smiled reassuringly.

They followed Devenish along a corridor to the office of the First Secretary, turning into a silent and heavily carpeted area of the building. He tapped on a door, paused for ten seconds, opened it, and announced DCI Montacute, accompanied by a lady: Miss Laetitia Talbot.

"Laetitia! My dear! What a charming surprise!" came the exclamation as they entered. "I say, bring up another chair, would you, Charles?"

Frederick Wentworth sprang forward from behind his desk to kiss Letty on both cheeks and shake Montacute's hand. He looked at his watch. "Now—where've we got to? Tea? Coffee? May I offer you some refreshment?"

They both declined and sat down on the chairs provided. He dismissed Devenish with a nod.

The First Secretary was somber, Letty noticed, beneath his smooth good humour. He was gracious in his condolences on the death of Andrew, who was well known to him, and his sorrow and outrage were heartfelt. Consular facilities were to be made available to Montacute, cooperation assured. The killer must be brought to justice, and as soon as possible. The professor was an admired figure here in Athens as well as London. Questions were being asked. The phone hadn't stopped ringing since the news broke! Retribution was demanded. Public confidence simply had to be restored…Couldn't have it thought that there was a killer out and about on the streets of the city, a knife-wielding assassin at work in the shadow of the Acropolis itself…The First Secretary was quite sure Montacute understood the implications?

Montacute murmured appropriate responses for both himself and Letty into the pauses.

"I can't tell you how disturbed I was," Wentworth continued, "to receive the news of Lady Merriman's death just an hour ago when I got to my desk, and thank you for sending in the details, Montacute. You must have worked through the night, man? Still, people don't arrange to do away with themselves to suit the police duty rosters, do they? And you—such a close friend of the family, Laetitia! How sad you must be! His Excellency was stricken by the double tragedy and asks me to convey his condolences."

Letty mumbled her thanks.

"It's early in the investigation, I know, but are you able to confirm, Montacute, that it was—as everyone supposes—a case of suicide?"

"No, sir. It was murder. We have a suspect under lock and key."

"Murder, by God! And you have the man in custody already? Excellent! I'm relieved to hear it." He shot a triumphant grin at Letty. "Nothing like the Yard when they get going, eh? And in Montacute here, I'm assured we have the finest."

The inspector glowered and waited for Wentworth to get on. "But—a *double* killing, you're telling me? Is that what we are to assume? How extraordinary and distressing! Can you be certain you have the evidence to nail the ruffian responsible?"

"In the case of the second death, there can be no doubt," Montacute replied warily. "The victim survived the assault long enough to declare herself to have been pushed from the window and, with her dying breath, she confided to me the name of her assailant."

"Good Lord! What a drama!"

"As you say, sir."

"And whom do you have in manacles for this foul deed?"

"Her cousin, Miss Thetis Templeton."

Freddy Wentworth was for a moment speechless. His mouth opened and no words came. His eyes bulged and he harrumphed. Finally he managed to say, eyes skittering away from Letty: "Montacute, may I speak to you privately for a moment? I hope you won't be too offended, Laetitia, if I have the inspector to myself for a bit? Things to declare, not entirely suitable for a young lady's ears ..."

"Of course, sir," Montacute agreed.

Letty was disappointed to hear the inspector's ready capitulation on her behalf, the manly understanding as he rose to his feet to show her to the door. "Miss Talbot, would you mind? Do excuse us."

Once on the far side of the closed door, Letty looked up and down the corridor and, seeing it was clear, firmly put her ear to the woodwork. Nothing. Perhaps the slightest murmur of two men conferring, she thought ... one short explosion from Montacute ... but she wasn't able to make out a single word of the conversation that followed. She was discovered examining a portrait of Queen Victoria six feet away when they emerged.

She went back inside with the inspector while Wentworth, with a hurried farewell, went off to summon Geoffrey Melton.

As soon as they'd settled again, Montacute leaned to her and whispered: "I don't suppose you caught much of that? Thick door, Miss Laetitia? Just wanted to warn me that there were more things going on in the world than I knew of. Jokily suggested I restrict myself to chasing a few more bandits over the hills ... Still two villainous kidnappers at large, he reminds me—why not finish the job? More useful than getting involved with what he called 'politically sensitive areas.' Did you realise that was where we were—in a politically sensitive area? And I don't mean the Embassy! Funny thing, when I told him it was Miss Templeton I'd arrested he didn't like it. Not one bit. Did you notice? Advised me to release her as soon as possible. Told me to imagine the damaging headlines if the news were to get out. Bad for the national image, he claims. The wretched girl cuts some ice with the Greek establishment, it would seem. Present and future international relations endangered at the highest level. You can imagine the sort of thing. He definitely put the diplomatic boot in!"

Letty was uneasy that the inspector was so readily revealing a confidence. There was something alarming about the degree to which he was so casually involving her in the proceedings. It had echoes of the last chapter of a two-penny thriller where the villain smugly reveals everything in the sure knowledge that he's about to shoot the detective dead with the gun hidden in his pocket the moment his vaunting confession is over. If she was being allowed the knowledge, then either the knowledge didn't count for much—or *she* didn't.

Her unease deepened at the sight of Geoffrey Melton sweeping into the room.

He greeted them and came to seat himself, perching on the front edge of the desk, long legs in neatly pressed linen trousers extended towards them. A pose which suggested reassuring informality whilst affirming his precedence. They were being accorded an interview. He offered them a cigarette from the First Secretary's silver box and when they shook their heads in refusal he selected an oval Turkish one for himself and lit it, inhaling the fragrant smoke and assessing them through narrowed eyes.

He put them at their ease, conveying his shock and sorrow at the news of the second death. "Frederick tells me you've made an arrest already? Excellent news! Then I can stop working on my alibi? I was calculating just how many foreign dignitaries I would have to parade to satisfy you, Montacute. I imagine about twelve will remember seeing me here at the do last night. The Serbian ambassador's wife will retain a painfully clear imprint of my presence. On her feet. I'm not the most skilful of dancers." He gave a deprecating laugh. "I'm quite aware that I'm the popular choice for *Andrew*'s killing! Makes a fellow wary!"

"Yes. It's the death of Sir Andrew I'm here to discuss," Montacute said, cutting him short. "We're here this morning seeking further information on last night's events, Mr. Melton. Would you mind retracing your steps, as it were, from the moment you walked offstage for your bath?"

"Of course. Look—is your charming assistant taking notes again? We can supply paper... No? Right-oh, then... Off we go! There's never a great hurry to change—there are two hundred lines between my death screams and reentrance as the villain."

" *That was the King, groaning. I fear*
The worst has happened. Sound the alarm!
Break in at once and catch them red-handed!' "

Montacute quoted his own chorus lines. "Take it from there. You didn't yourself happen to catch anyone red-handed backstage?"

"I'm afraid not. I performed the sound effects, and as I strolled off towards wardrobe I paused to look at the dummy. You know—as you do when you subconsciously notice that something's not right. Someone was at that moment supposed to be anointing it with blood and removing the cover, ready to push it forward onstage. It wasn't being done. I investigated. I tweaked back the outer edge of the muslin wrapper and saw what lay below. Human limbs where there should have been celluloid. Poked at an arm and encountered human flesh. Recoiled in horror, emitting an unmanly and unscripted exclamation."

He directed an enquiring smile at Letty and waited a second or so, expecting a response.

Determined not to assist him in any way, she smiled back politely and remained silent.

"I dropped the muslin back in place," he went on, "not being quite sure what the protocol might be in such circumstances—to stop the play or not to stop the play? Had I prematurely taken the wraps off some practical joke? Some of these young things *will* go to extraordinary lengths to startle and annoy in the name of humour." He sighed and shook his head, every inch the jaded housemaster. "Did I risk making a fool of myself by interfering? You know—'Trust that spoilsport Melton to ruin everything!...Perhaps one of us should have told him...' I'm not the sort who develops an intimacy with his fellows on short acquaintance—you may have noticed that? Well, you can imagine what was going through my mind...In the end, I decided—none of my business...let them have their fun. I went mechanically through my rehearsed movements until I came onstage to find Lady Merriman stirring about in the cauldron with her stick! Thought for an awful moment I'd fetched up in scene one of the Scottish Play and we were all to be accursed! But no—the old witch was merely pronouncing the last rites over what was now revealed to be an actual body—and, moreover, the body of her husband."

Letty glowered at Melton, hating him for his lack of feeling, but he glanced away, refusing to acknowledge her disapproval.

As a reaction to the stony silence of his audience, he allowed his face to melt into an expression of what he intended to be a blend of incredulity and sorrow. "What a loss! A wonderful man!"

Letty didn't believe a word he said.

"And the rest you witnessed for yourselves. All I have to tell you, I'm afraid. Do let me know how you get on with all this. You're bound to stumble upon the wretch responsible sooner or later. I expect you'll find it was some vagrant straying onto the set…Knives two-a-penny to be had on any street in Athens, of course. Must make your life pretty difficult, Montacute? But the sooner we reach a solution the better, of course. I'm sure the First Secretary has made that clear."

Letty couldn't imagine why Melton was lying and didn't care if they knew it. Or why Montacute hadn't challenged him.

CHAPTER 22

They'd decided to walk the short distance to the Merriman house. The inspector had asked her to accompany him politely, not forcefully, allowing her the illusion at least of a refusal. Letty thought she made a good show of disguising her eagerness to visit the scene of the crime, convinced that she would see something, experience some insight that would prove Thetis's innocence. She realised that an accusation made with the dying breath of a lady who was well known to be a firm Christian and pillar of society must be held incontrovertible, but she was prepared to try at least to question it. And she had a feeling that, strangely—since his was the ear that had heard the dying denunciation—in this she would have the inspector's unspoken support. And now, here was the Embassy throwing its weight behind a swift release. It was beginning to look as though Thetis would be out of custody before the end of the day.

They stood for a few moments on the opposite side of the square, looking up at the Merriman house. Montacute confirmed that Maud had fallen from the open second-floor window on the right. Letty identified the room next door with the matching window and balcony as Andrew's library and workroom. She was able to give the purpose of each of the rooms in the house, which were very likely unchanged since her eight-week stay in the early months of the year. On the top floor, under a grey-gleaming mansard roof: maids' rooms and storage. On the third floor: master bedroom, Maud's room and small sitting room, guest rooms, and bathrooms. The second floor was the grandest, with spacious, well-decorated reception rooms: the drawing room and library, and a wide landing leading from the stairs. On the ground floor, the usual domestic offices: kitchen in the rear, Dorothea's apartment, butler's pantry, though they kept no butler.

The housekeeper greeted Letty with warmth and Montacute with deference, waiting until the boy Demetrios had whisked a perfunctory feather duster over their shoes—a service delivered with mechanical politeness, and not so essential in October when the summer's dust had largely abated. Mrs. Stephanopoulos ushered them inside, glad, she told them, chattering away in Greek, to have someone in the house to make a few decisions. So much to be done and no one there at the helm with Miss Thetis run away... And the telephone ringing and ringing... The lawyer! Dr. Peebles! The funeral director! Mr. Gunning! They'd all called and she'd hardly known what to say.

She waved at a silver bowl on the hall table, a bowl filled with calling cards. The old-fashioned but charming custom was extensively used in the city by sociable residents with time on their hands and was the most effective way of spreading news and gossip. "Here I am in town and I'd love to talk" was the simple message of the cards delivered at the start of the day, a message to be picked up with pleasurable anticipation or, in some cases, with dismay or boredom. The number in the bowl this morning indicated a lively response to the death of Andrew, but people had surely not woken to the news of the second death? Letty turned over one or two, noting brief messages of condolence addressed to Maud on the back, and promises of visits.

Dorothea presented one she had kept separate from the others. "This was delivered by messenger." Her voice lowered in awe. "With the respects of the Prime Minister's lady herself!"

Letty took the card, looking first at the elegantly engraved *Mrs. Eleftherios Venizelos,* and, on the back, in her own hand: *Maud, my dear, What appalling news! Let me know when I may come and see you to convey our respects and condolences. Helena.*

Letty calmed Dorothea in a few reassuring phrases and promised to telephone Helena Venizelos to thank her for her card and break the news of Maud's death. She confirmed that she would stay and do whatever she could in the distressing circumstances, until such time as Miss Templeton returned and took up the reins. Yes—Miss Thetis had been found—had, in fact, been spending the night with Letty. For the moment she was helping the police with enquiries but Letty had no doubt that she would be free to take charge of her cousin's household this afternoon.

Montacute had listened with some relief, she thought, when Letty launched into Greek in response. Not wonderful yet, not accurate, and having something of a Cretan accent, but Letty made up for her shortcomings with a show of confidence and many hand gestures.

Montacute picked up one word from Dorothea's outpouring. "A lawyer, you say?"

"Yes. He's telephoned twice this morning. Wanted to speak to the mistress about Sir Andrew's will. I had to tell him the bad news about Lady Merriman. Then he insisted on speaking to someone about *both* their wills. Well, *I* couldn't say... I wrote his number and name down here, sir, if you'd like to—" Montacute had seized the paper and was dashing upstairs to find the telephone.

"It's in the library!" Letty shouted after him and, pausing to reassure Dorothea and ask her to bring up some tea, ran upstairs in his wake.

He was replacing the earpiece, looking pleased. "They'll be sending round a man in a few minutes," he told her. "Efficient firm of international lawyers. Offices in London, Paris, and Athens. The wills of both the deceased were still in their in-tray, you might say—combed over in the last few weeks—so didn't need to be hunted for and dusted down. Always interesting to take a close look at the wills of those who've made an unscheduled departure from this world. Inheritance! It brings out the rawest of human emotions. Greed, ambition, vengeance. In any walk of society. People kill to inherit a dukedom or a pocket watch."

Letty was for a moment disconcerted to see the inspector ensconced in Andrew's chair behind Andrew's desk. Still in her memory were the fair hair and merry blue eyes, the swift, gracious gestures of its rightful occupant. She could hear the laughing protest—"And who precisely *is* this police hound sitting in my chair? Letty—chuck him out!" She didn't care to see Andrew's image eclipsed by this stranger. She turned abruptly away, ambushed by a rush of grief, excused herself, and went to the drawing room next door.

Footsteps on the landing. Montacute? Why was he following her? Surely he could give her a moment to herself? Insensitive? Or just making sure she tampered with no evidence? Letty decided—both.

She had to do it. A ghoulish impulse, she recognised, but she could not resist retracing Maud's steps last night. She found Maud's place on her sofa, where, Letty noticed, her knitting still lay abandoned, halfway through a row. Odd. A fanatically accurate knitter, Maud would never leave a row unfinished. On many occasions Letty had been made to wait, stamping and fuming by the door, until Maud had completed her row, stabbed the ball of wool with her needles, and tucked it safely away in her knitting bag. Something of urgency had interrupted her.

Letty sat briefly, picked up the knitting and put it down again, then got up and walked across the floor. She checked the Persian rug that covered the centre of the polished parquet floor. It was unruffled and didn't extend as far as the window—indeed, was a good three feet short of it. There seemed no possibility that Maud had tripped. Letty kneeled and examined the polished wooden floor against the light. No skid marks. No sign of a struggle. She got up and went on towards the window.

According to Thetis's sprightly account of her evening with Maud, the window had been open, as now. Letty walked onto the narrow balcony and leaned over to see what she could see in the square. Perhaps something had attracted Maud's attention? Perhaps she'd been desperate to see what was going on down there or at her own front door? She must have heard Thetis scrambling up and down stairs, whistling up taxis, leaving the front door open. Yes, that was it! An open front door was invariably the cause of a panicking reaction from Maud. That would have worried and irritated her. And she'd leaned too far over. She'd complained of dizzy spells in the past. Letty would vouch for that. And her doctor—what was his name? Peebles? Dr. Peebles must be summoned and required to confirm it.

None of this, of course, accounted for her surprising accusation, her naming of Thetis to the inspector. Could the man have misheard? Misinterpreted a last message?

To test the degree of tilt necessary to provoke a fall, Letty began to lean over the low iron balcony, holding on to it with both hands. The top edge caught her in mid-thigh. Alarmingly easy for a tall, full-bosomed woman like Maud to topple over. One push between the shoulder blades would do it.

Letty caught sight of William Gunning below, waiting for a gap in the traffic to cross the square, and her heart thumped with joy. He looked up, saw her, grinned, and waved. She raised one hand from the rail to wave back.

She saw the grin on his face fade, replaced by an expression of horror. Across the width of the square, William howled a warning and held up two arms in a futile gesture to avert disaster. Her scream rang out as a pair of strong hands seized her from behind and thrust her upwards and outwards.

CHAPTER 23

icking with her heels and shouting in outrage, Letty found herself being swung around and hauled backwards to safety. A moment later she was set down in the middle of the carpet. White with terror, she whirled around and set about beating her aggressor on his burly chest, yelling abuse.

"My! You didn't learn *that* at the Ladies' Academy," said an unrepentant Montacute. "Oh, shush! Do stop fussing! Ouch! Now tell me—when you've got your breath back—did you catch sight of me? Did you hear me come in? Did you hear me creep across the carpet? Are you listening? Imagine—could you have turned in time to get a glimpse of me?"

The urgency of his questions and the ludicrous assumption that she wouldn't at all object to having the life scared out of her in the cause of detection caught her attention. She released her pent-up resentment in one last vicious kick at his ankle and answered: "No. No. And—no. I was expecting you to come in, but with the noise outside and the distraction of catching sight of William across the square, I knew nothing until you grabbed me. Oh, my God! If that had been a serious attack I would have hurtled over headfirst, without ever catching sight of the one who pushed me!"

"And if you'd just had a quarrel with your cousin, had gone to the window to spy on her comings and goings . . . a taxi drawing up . . . front door banging open . . . lots to draw your attention . . ."

"Enough to make you put down your knitting in the middle of a row." Letty pointed to the bundle on the sofa.

"You'd assume it was *she*—the only other person in the house apart from the staff—who'd crept up and pushed you. If you survived the fall long enough to tell the tale . . ."

Letty looked into the inspector's face. Grim and doubtful. But the darker emotions were increasingly being pierced by shafts of a brightness she could only interpret as hope. The certainty Letty felt—that whatever Thetis was guilty of, this particular crime could not be laid at her door—was instinctive and strong. And the best way of communicating this to the policeman was to maintain a quiet calm. A cerebral rather than an emotional pressure was what she would apply.

"And if you'd just picked up the sword she'd already attacked you with?" she suggested. "I think it's possible that Maud really, genuinely, perceived herself to be under attack from her cousin and assumed—and who can blame her?—that she'd been pushed over by Thetis, don't you?"

"Will you accept a grovelling apology for alarming you? I treated you with the familiarity and unconcern I would have shown to a colleague and not a delicate female. And I wonder, Miss Talbot—Laetitia—would you be prepared to quote this experience in evidence at her trial? If it should come to that," Montacute asked, almost humbly.

Quite sure she had located the inspector's Achilles' heel, Letty managed a weak smile. "I'll do my best to play down your Hunnish behaviour, Inspector—Percy. And I'll stress the experimental value of my hideous experience. For the sake of truth—and Thetis, of course."

A pounding on the stairs was followed by the eruption into the room of William Gunning.

What had she expected? An icily polite: "I say, old chap, would you mind explaining yourself?"

In three strides he was across the room and clutching Montacute by the throat.

Montacute was the younger and stronger man but, caught by surprise in a rare moment of apology and gratitude, he could not immediately summon up the strength to fight back against the blazing fury shaking and crushing the life out of him. The inspector managed at last to bring his hands up and tried to prise the fingers from his neck. Sinewy, calloused fingers which had spent the last six months gripping a pick and a shovel were not so easily dislodged; it was Letty's voice shouting in Gunning's ear that finally made him release his grip.

Montacute, purple in the face, staggered back gasping and choking as Letty flung both arms around Gunning, pinioning him in a tight embrace, murmuring to him quietly.

"Tea?" said Dorothea from the doorway. "Ah, yes! There you are, Mr. Gunning! I thought I caught sight of you arriving to join the party...I brought a third cup. I'll just put the tray here on the low table, shall I, Miss Laetitia, and leave you to get on with it?"

"Damned thoughtless behaviour! Inexcusable! Not at all what the public expects from a Scotland Yard detective officer," croaked Montacute. "Please—both of you—accept my apologies."

To save the inspector's voice, Letty had undertaken to summarise for Gunning the events of the previous evening, culminating in the arrest of Thetis in the morning.

"Yes, yes," said Gunning, impatiently. "All that you say,

Montacute. Still—your unconventional demonstration does
reveal two important things. Here, trickle some tea down the
old gullet. It may help. Ah! I see we have some Hymettus
honey on the tray...Splendid! I'll melt a spoonful in your cup,
shall I? There you are, try that. You'll be singing soprano again
in no time. Now," he went on as they settled around the table,
"I had the story of poor Maud—chapter and verse—from Dorothea this morning when I rang to enquire after her. I set off at
once to Letty's digs to tell her the distressing news, only to find
from Mrs. Rose that the girls had both been escorted to the
local jug by Montacute. No joy there!"

"But they did at least tell you where we'd gone?"

"Yes. I belted along back here in time to witness a balcony
scene worthy of the pen of Raphael Sabatini or the cameras of
Hollywood. Were you fancying yourself as Captain Blood,
Montacute? Quite deplorable—but it does establish two
things. Firstly, that Maud could well have been unaware of the
identity of her attacker and assumed it to have been Thetis,
who is, as we speak, unjustly banged up on the inspector's authority. Am I getting this right?"

"More or less, Padre, more or less," said Montacute heavily. "But—*two* things, you said? Are you going to tell me what
I've missed?"

Letty smiled. The Reverend Gunning had this effect on
people, even ones of decided character and made-up minds.
They always ended by conceding that he might just have
something there and sliding into a conversation with him.

"Secondly: Anyone below, watching the building—as I was
just now—would have had a clear view of the attacker. You had
to come out of the shadows onto the balcony and show yourself, Montacute, in order to be in grabbing or pushing range. I
saw you clearly. I think you saw me...Broad daylight, I agree,
but I note there's a light right outside."

The inspector was scribbling hurried notes and muttering.

"Yes, of course. One of those newfangled lamps. The head of it is at second-floor level. It would have illuminated the scene after dark."

Letty was certain that he would return to the house at the exact time of the tragedy, meticulously noting angles and lighting. Questioning passersby. She began to feel more hopeful about Thetis's case. With the victim's identification set aside and now the possibility of an unknown attacker being revealed, it would surely not be long before the prisoner was released—at least on bail. She said as much.

Montacute looked at her strangely. "She's safe where she is," he said, mystifying both of them. "And we'd do well to wait and see what the rest of the day brings."

The next minute brought the lawyer. Dorothea announced that a young gentleman had arrived and was below in the hall. She handed a card to Letty.

"Oh, they've sent Benedict. Show him up to the library," said Letty. "That's where Andrew always saw his business associates. We'll all go along and meet him there."

"All?" the inspector protested. "I'll see him by myself."

"Are you sure? I think you'd make him clam up, Percy," replied Letty lightly. "He knows me. We've shared an Italian ice cream at Bertorelli's in Academy Street. In my presence, he may be prepared to make confidences he would otherwise censor. Why don't we ask him?"

They moved to the library and arranged the chairs in an informal group about the desk. Letty, who had met Benedict Benson socially in the spring, made the introductions. The young man was in his late twenties and impeccably turned out from sleek dark hair to shining shoes. He favoured each with a guarded but friendly look and a handshake. The Reading of the Will was a solemn occasion—a ceremony fraught with danger for the legal profession—but, Letty guessed, he could only be feeling reassured by his reception. Here were no disturbing tears on show, no squabbling relations to put a lawyer off his stride. Simply a nice girl he was acquainted with, a British policeman, and a clergyman. All quiet and cooperative.

Montacute asserted himself by speaking first and bluntly. "Benson, your firm is eager to discuss the testamentary arrangements of Sir Andrew and Lady Merriman, who both—I take it you are aware...? Good! Husband and wife died yesterday within hours of each other. The circumstances are suspicious. It is highly likely that we are looking at one case of murder at least, probably two, and the evidence of the wills may prove vital to the outcome of the enquiry."

Benson stretched uncomfortably and made to speak but the inspector rolled on. "If you would prefer to discuss your business with me alone in the first instance, I would consider that right and proper."

"Not at all, sir!" said Benson, smiling around the group. "Do feel free to stay if you think you ought, by all means, but indeed, I would particularly like to include Miss Talbot and Mr. Gunning, as they feature in one of the wills. Miss Templeton also—if she's about—might like to come in and hear what I have to say."

Letty hurried to explain that Thetis was otherwise occupied at that moment and unavoidably detained elsewhere in the city but would find time to talk to him later.

Benson produced his briefcase, took out two folders, and laid them out on the desk. "Our firm has dealt with the Merriman estate for years from our London office...old and valued clients...It is only recently, within the last three weeks, that there has been activity in the will department. First Sir Andrew rewrote his requirements. And signed the new will, of course. Lady Merriman followed suit a week later. It was a close-run thing getting it prepared to the point of signature within her time limit, but we managed."

"Time limit?" Montacute questioned. "She was pressing you to conclude, are you saying?"

"That was our impression."

"Did you form an opinion as to the reason for her haste? Could ill health have been a factor?" the inspector offered. "It very often *is*."

Letty sighed and Benedict, avoiding her rolling eye, said tactfully: "Yes, of course. Always a possibility. But it is not my place to speculate. You must seek advice elsewhere."

"Or could it have been a reaction to the rewriting of her husband's will?"

"Again you ask me—and I refuse—to speculate, Inspector. However, some might think the timing is suggestive," the lawyer finally admitted. "But you will draw your own conclusions when I've disclosed the contents. You'll find everything becomes very clear. I don't mean to be evasive—but I think you'll find a pattern emerges. And, before you ask, I have no idea whether there was collusion between husband and wife. They did not confide such matters and I did not enquire. It is not our business to understand our clients' domestic circumstances, merely to expedite their legal requirements. So, we have here on the desk two legal, binding, and all the rest of it, last wills and testaments."

"And you can read them out to us?" asked Letty.

"No reason why not. Everyone here assembled has an interest of some sort. Others not present also have an interest, of course. But all will be explained when the contents are read out following the funerals. And perhaps someone will acquaint me with the details of that when they are known?"

He looked to Letty for an answer and she nodded.

"Sir Andrew died first, so I will deal with him first." Benson began to read out the will.

The inspector interrupted him. "I'd be most grateful,

Benson, if you'd just give us the highlights. I will, naturally, take away a copy for further and deeper study later."

"Very well. The recipients of his cash, I suppose you mean?" A tight smile accompanied the blunt remark. "Who gets what? Te tum, te tum...The staff, old retainers, both here and at home in London, are most generously rewarded. The ones here in Athens may be of some interest? Every servant, indoor and outdoor, is to receive twenty pounds down to and including the boot boy, and Mrs. Dorothea Stephanopoulos receives two hundred pounds...I say, shall I skip the smaller bequests?"

"No," said the inspector. "I think we need to know all the details of Sir Andrew's largesse. I've known poor unfortunates poisoned with arsenic over the possession of a teapot. Expectations must be judged according to circumstances. Twenty pounds to a boot boy is a fortune."

"Lucky old Demetrios!" said Letty. "He arrived at a good time. He wasn't here in the spring."

"I understand," the lawyer continued. "Well, here we have the Battersea Dogs' Home, one hundred pounds...the British Museum in London, five hundred pounds...the British School at Athens, one thousand pounds—" He broke off and gave them a mischievous smile. "They'll be relieved to hear that! Two elderly aunts in England—dependants of the professor—are to have a thousand pounds each to assist them through their twilight years. I'm skipping to the nub of all this, you understand..." He flipped to the next page. "Here we are...All properties of which he dies possessed (with one exception, see below)—that is: the London house, a cottage on the Suffolk coast, and this house in Athens—are to be made over wholly to his wife, Maud, who, incidentally, was to receive the residue of his cash when all other payments had been made."

The last page gave rise to a dramatic pause before he went

on. "To Miss Thetis Templeton (or Mrs. Chandos, as she is properly known... You were aware?...) he bequeaths the sum of twenty thousand pounds left in a trust which we are to administer, to pay out a yearly sum for the rest of her life. A handsome gift!"

Benson looked beadily around the company, taking in the dropped jaws and wide eyes. "This was one of the main changes to the will, of course."

After a suitable pause he went on: "And Miss Talbot—you do not go away empty-handed. Most intriguing! I myself took the notes for the changes, here in this room. Professor Merriman quite insisted on that. He wanted to leave you something you would truly value. 'Something that will knock her eye out!' were his actual words." Benson remembered himself and sobered his tone. He pointed to a dark corner of the room. "Do you remember the chest that he used to keep over there? The chest covered by a rug of Eastern pattern?"

Letty nodded cautiously.

"You are to have the contents of that chest. Oh, and, indeed, the chest itself. The professor was most particular about that. It is at present lodged with his bank and being kept in the strong room." Benedict smiled a gratified smile. "I'm pleased to say the professor would, occasionally, accept my advice. When he gave me an outline of the contents, I expressed my horror that he had kept them to hand here in the house for so long, hidden under a rug. I can make arrangements for the bank to deliver them here for your inspection at a time suitable for you. After that I would recommend they be sent straight back again.

"And, as we're here amongst his books... what place more fitting to announce that he has left his entire collection, in London and Athens, to William Gunning?" An elegant hand gesture around the room underlined the largesse of the bequest.

"There is a further clause inserted regarding the Reverend." Benedict ran a finger down the foolscap sheet, finding his place.

William's initial expression of astonishment was hardening into one of suspicion.

"In the event of the professor's premature death, the Reverend Gunning is to oversee the publication of his last book, negotiate with the publishers, and in turn receive not only his library but any monies accruing from his publications, including the most recent work. Of which he had great hopes."

"His *Alexander*? Good Lord! Why—yes! I'd be delighted to do that. In fact, I'd be honoured. I worked with him on the text last winter," Gunning murmured, and fell into a stunned silence.

"Is that it?" asked Montacute. "Didn't I hear you refer to 'another property'?"

"Ah, yes. Mmm ... Bit of a puzzle, this. A gift horse whose teeth I would certainly recommend giving a good inspection before accepting into my stable ... But I suppose he knew what he was about ... Look, Miss Talbot, please do not hesitate to consult us should you have the least concern ... Our property department here in Athens is second to none in its vigilance and expertise, and we have a working arrangement with colleagues up there in Salonika—"

"Steady on, Benedict!" said Letty. "You're a chapter ahead of us! What has any of this to do with me?"

"He's willed the whole ants' nest to you. The deeds of the property in question are in there with the rest of the things. In the chest. You'll need some courage and patience to sort out that lot, I'm afraid, Laetitia." He looked at her with pity. "And possibly the use of one of those armoured tanks. Rather you than me, what!" he finished with an apologetic bark of laughter.

CHAPTER 24

Letty had some difficulty in keeping her eyes on the lawyer as he moved on to the will of Lady Merriman. They would return every other moment, drawn to dwell speculatively on the empty space where had stood a small chest, hardly bigger than a footstool, with its undistinguished covering of rather moth-eaten rug. Purple, red, and amber, the faded colours had always been there, a comforting glow in the background as long as she had known the house. She missed it. There it had sat undisturbed in a cool dark corner, out of the sunshine and unremarked on by the professor, but she had noticed he never allowed any object, not even an ashtray, to be placed on it. Engrossed in a book, she had once attempted thoughtlessly to sit on it. His scream of protest had made her jump instantly to her feet. Either of his two adored house cats attempting to settle there would be swatted away at once, though he would tolerate them on his desk, curled up on his books, or in his lap.

"And now to Lady Merriman," Benedict announced. "These pages are much more straightforward. Stark in their simplicity, you might say. I could deliver the contents to you in thirty seconds. I wonder if you are aware of the composition of her remaining family?"

A look from Montacute encouraged him to expand.

"It helps to have them in focus. Influenza cut a swath through them after the war and much reduced the ranks, I'm afraid. So—Mrs. Merriman was left with the elderly maternal grandmother she shares with her cousin Thetis. Grandmama had four children: Adela, the eldest and mother of Maud; two sons, Albert and John; and finally Daphne, the mother of Thetis. Albert it is—the older of the brothers by three years—who appears to have been accepted as head and mouthpiece of the family. At least Lady Merriman deferred to him as such. I can't speak for Miss Templeton."

There was a pause while they each silently speculated as to Thetis's level of deference to her uncle Albert.

"Of these siblings," Benedict drove on, "the two men have gone on not only to marry but to produce male heirs. Albert has given Maurice and Richard to the world (a daughter died in infancy), and his brother John's sons are Richard, Harold, and George. Six people, then, in the generation contemporary with Lady Merriman, would appear to be the roll call: five male cousins and Thetis."

The lawyer cleared his throat. "Lady Merriman was a wealthy woman in her own right. Her mother, Adela, married well and was left a rich widow. A goodly sum eventually made its way into Maud's account. By agreement, she kept this family money separate from her husband's. According to the terms of her original will, which was drawn up some years ago, there was a simple transfer of the bulk of this to her husband should he survive her, after the provision of certain sums of a substantial nature which were to go to each of her cousins equally. Six nominees: the cousins I've just referred to. The family money was making its way back into the family coffers, you might say."

"And now?" the inspector urged.

"The will I have before me—which, of course, is amplified

by the inclusion of the properties and money left to her by her husband—deletes all mention of Sir Andrew. Had he survived her, therefore, he would have seen no benefit from his wife's provisions. Though he could, naturally, have challenged this in law...To put it simply: The bulk of her fortune is to be divided equally between her five male cousins."

"*Male* cousins? And Thetis? What about her?" Letty asked.

"Her cousin Thetis has also been deleted and is now to receive nothing." Benson lowered his eyes and inspected his fingernails while they absorbed this.

Letty glanced at the inspector to judge his reaction. His professional mask was in place and she could read nothing in his face. Politely, he thanked the lawyer for his kind attentions and received from him the copies of the wills, making all the reassurances he required regarding discretion.

Before he left, Benedict turned to shake hands with Letty and slipped a white business card to her. "You *will* be needing some professional help with all this," he murmured. "Don't hesitate and all that..." he added vaguely, smiled, and left.

They sat down again in their places, each wrapped in his own thoughts. Finally Letty said bitterly: "Curse you, Maud! Vindictive in death—as in life! But Thetis wouldn't have been expecting anything from her, you know...She's not the kind of girl, I think, to feel dependence on anyone, so she won't be disappointed. If she is, she'll make light of it. Still...that doesn't make Maud any less of a witch, does it?"

"Isn't that a little harsh, if what you both tell me is true—that the girl was allowing herself to be seduced by Maud's husband under Maud's own roof...?" Gunning began.

"*Someone's* roof...unlikely that there was any hanky-panky going on here," said Letty.

"'Hanky-panky'?" Gunning repeated. "Doesn't quite cover the seriousness of the sin and the betrayal, I'd have thought. Disgraceful behaviour. And it would have been reassuring to

hear a less partial opinion expressed, Letty, a little more judgement exercised. Are you incapable of seeing this through
Maud's eyes simply because she was in your eyes elderly and
infirm, and strikes no romantic chord with your bohemian
set? The woman was deceived by those closest to her. She had
a perfect right to leave her money where she thought fit."

Montacute flinched and looked uneasily from one to the
other.

"Yes, Your Reverence," said Letty mildly. "Of course you're
right. It's not my place to judge Maud and I'm sorry I spoke so
flippantly. But listen—there's things you don't know yet...
complications... At least Andrew did the decent thing and left
Thetis an annuity."

"A large one. I was wondering about that... Odd, don't
you think?" said the inspector. "Designed to put his wife's
nose out of joint? Nothing like leaving your mistresses a comfortable amount of cash out of the family pot to infuriate
from beyond the grave. Still—I'd have thought two hundred
and twenty pounds would have been *adequately* infuriating,"
he said with the precision that experience brought. "And—was
the professor a vengeful man? I didn't know him well but I
wouldn't have judged him petty. A man of generous impulses
and forgiving nature, I'd have said. And why stick at Thetis? I
can't imagine she's the sole survivor of the Siren Species who
enlivened his middle years." He had carefully refrained from
mentioning Letty's relationship with the professor, not being
quite certain of the exact nature of her friendship with Gunning, she guessed, and she was grateful for his tact.

"Well, he has left *me* a mystery box! If that counts." Letty
smiled, bringing her own relationship with the professor out
into the open. "Though it begins to sound like Pandora's un-
wanted Christmas present, if Benedict is to be believed. I
shan't dare open it! But I have good reason for thinking that

Thetis was special, and I fear I'm going to have to tell you why," she finished hesitantly.

The two men waited in silence for her to go on. "You can detect all you like, Inspector—you're not going to be able to have Thetis hanged. Not for a while at least...perhaps never...You're thrashing about in a dark room and my finger's on the light switch. I don't want to betray a confidence, but...oh, dash it all!...it will out in time anyway! Very soon now. She said so herself. And this *is* a double murder enquiry! No. Forgive me. I can't. It's not mine to disclose. I'd be interfering again, William. You'd give me another ticking-off and rightly so."

It was the more worldly Montacute who got there first. "My God! Oh, no! Oh, how bloody! Excuse me! Tell me my suspicious mind has leapt to the wrong outlandish conclusion! The wretched girl's *pregnant,* isn't she? Is that what she told you, Laetitia?"

Laetitia nodded silently, alarmed by his strong reaction.

"Sir Andrew was about to have an heir—of sorts—at last," he pressed on, thinking aloud, marshalling their own turbulent thoughts. "And, according to the absurd generosity of his last-minute provisions, it would seem he'd been made aware of it and was acknowledging his responsibility."

"There we'd be guessing. I can't say if Thetis told him or not. She didn't confide that much. I do know that Maud was unaware."

"I wouldn't bet on that," said Gunning grimly. "But it certainly does suggest a strong motive or two or three for murder. Oh, how foul!"

The inspector sighed. "And the strongest emotion—jealous rage—would be motive enough for Miss Templeton to stab her lover to death. Perhaps she was using her...er...condition... as a lever to make him divorce his wife and marry her? Just when you thought it too late...here's the son you always wanted...You only have to get rid of a wife you can't stand anyway...' Not difficult to imagine. But he refused. So she took the opportunity of topping him backstage before the rehearsal started. She's a strong girl. And women—excuse me—can be remarkably vindictive when thwarted. And, in their passion, capable of outlandish feats of strength. She could have hauled him about and tiddled up the corpse. If she appeared a trifle breathless, bloodstained, wild-eyed afterwards, who would notice? She was in rôle after all, the wronged queen of Mycaenae, just practising her speeches like the rest of us, wasn't she? And the posing of the body in the bathtub...such an obviously angry gesture—he was, for her, at that moment, Agamemnon, the faithless betrayer, and she intended everyone to see him as such—in his true place. The public spectacle of his degradation was the vengeance she exacted for her betrayal—"

"Rubbish, Percy!" Letty interrupted. "You're thinking like a Mycaenaean! And you don't believe that nonsense yourself, either. Thetis is a practical, modern woman. We all know that. She would have killed *Maud* first, wouldn't she? If she had a killing urge at all—which I don't think she has. She could have pushed the old girl over the balcony or off the Acropolis at any time—or poisoned her with her own pills and potions. Maud has a cupboard full of them and chomps them up like *cachous*. Um...used to, that is. Funny, I keep expecting her to walk in and pour scorn on us for not instantly seeing the truth. But— Thetis is clever, you know. If she'd wanted to kill Maud for the inheritance she thought might be her due, or to remove the obstacle to eternal happiness, she would have done the deed so discreetly we wouldn't be here now discussing it."

Gunning looked from one keen, speculative face to the other and narrowed his eyes in disgust at their theorising. "The baggage! The termagant!" he huffed. "Obviously swept away by ungovernable rage. Poor Andrew tells her divorce and remarriage are not in his plans. So—she curses him for a treacherous, lecherous knave, remembers she's Clytemnestra, pulls out the dagger she keeps in her stocking top for just such emergencies, and plunges it into his chest. Then, with reality for a rehearsal, she goes onstage and repeats the whole performance. Pleased with your scenario, are you, Montacute?"

They stared at him for a moment.

"Not so far-fetched, Gunning," said Montacute thoughtfully. "The lady already has a mention on her record for use of a concealed weapon. The Yard have on record her confession to a blatant act of violence committed in London. Confession! Swaggering self-congratulation might be more accurate! But it's that confounded blade that's the key to the whole business. Find it and it tells us the killer's name!...She *was* searched before leaving." He looked enquiringly at Letty, struck by an unwelcome thought.

She nodded. "Oh, yes, she was. Clean as a whistle. Nothing but a hanky and a few drachmas in her pockets. And, William, I *did* check her stocking tops."

"So—nothing found," Montacute went on, relieved. "Yet. They're still looking. But the provision he made for the girl in his will strikes me as having a sort of final-arrangement whiff to it. A 'pay-off.' And then there's Maud! Why kill *her*? Clear enough to any prosecuting counsel—her inheritance. Thetis wasn't to know that the old girl had changed the terms and excluded her. And if Maud knew—guessed—or even accused her cousin of stabbing her husband, Miss Templeton might, in a rage, have thrown her over the balcony to shut her up," he offered.

Gunning groaned. "Then, in the throes of a ravenous blood-lust, she flees into the night in search of a third victim? God! You were lucky, Letty! Her murderous rage must have evaporated by the time she turned up and tapped me coolly on the shoulder on Mrs. Rose's doorstep with a kid-gloved hand.

To think I may have scooted off, leaving you in the company of a ruthless double killer!"

"Ah, no, Gunning, there you let imagination run away with you, I think," said Montacute with lazy sarcasm. "Our girl could well have intended no more than to establish an alibi. Seeking shelter with a respectable and—I have to say, Miss Laetitia—*gullible* companion?"

"You're saying she was just trying to gain for herself a friend at court?" said Letty.

"Huh! Friend *in* court might be more apt." Montacute's voice was suddenly heavy. "You may have to resign yourself to the fact that you have been used…manipulated by this woman, Miss Laetitia. *I* already have," he admitted lugubriously.

CHAPTER 25

The telephone on Andrew's desk rang and Montacute hurled himself across the room to lift the receiver with a curt "That'll be for me, I expect."

Gunning leaned to Letty and muttered: "With a bit of luck it'll be the fishmonger!"

But the inspector greeted the caller chummily and fell at once into a conversation in Greek. He was talking to Superintendent Theotakis and they listened intently, not offering to leave the room. An accurate, as far as she was able to judge, account of his morning's work ensued, followed by an arrangement to meet at headquarters for a conference after lunch, by which time some forensic evidence was expected to be to hand, as well as the preliminary findings of the postmortems. Montacute ended by saying he was just about to call a meeting of the Merriman staff for interview.

"Your cue, I think, Letty," said Gunning.

The inspector called the staff together downstairs in the room in which they gathered to take their meals. More at ease in their usual surroundings, they would be easier to read, he'd explained to Letty. They would be more relaxed and he would be able to form some idea of relationships and hierarchies within the group. Individual interviews would follow, when the staff would feel free to indulge in the tittle-tattle which always brought something of importance to the surface.

The permanent staff of four sat in silence around the table, and after an introduction by Letty each was asked to give an outline of his or her duties. Montacute listened and then asked: "No valet? The professor didn't keep a valet?"

"No, Inspector," Laetitia replied. "Like many military men, Sir Andrew preferred to look after himself. This was a simple household from day to day. Extra staff are always available and brought in at times of greater activity. There were none such on duty yesterday."

"Then I'll ask each to account for his or her movements at the time of Lady Merriman's death last evening. Mrs. Stephanopoulos, will you go first? Followed by the cook, Petros, then Maria . . . general maid, is it? And lastly, the boot boy. Demetrios?"

Montacute spoke to them in Greek and heard their evidence with understanding nods. He seemed happy for Letty to make the running, seeing that, although her version of the language was giving rise to some smiles and questions, they accepted her and were comfortable with her presence among them. Dorothea had been in the kitchen with the cook, discussing the next day's menus, and Maria had been in the dining room laying the table for breakfast at the crucial time. Petros, who did not live in, had, after his chat with Dorothea, gone home for the night. Nothing apparently had disturbed anyone's routine.

Demetrios, too overcome to speak, sat close to the housekeeper and needed encouragement to explain that he'd been going about his nightly duties. The boot boy was feeling nervous, she explained protectively, because he was the one who'd found the body. He was afraid he might be held responsible for some misdemeanour . . . not closing the windows earlier and suchlike silliness. It had been a shocking experience for the young lad, finding her like that, and they might like to be a bit patient with him.

No further visitors were expected at that late hour, Demetrios confided, haltingly, so, after Miss Thetis had come clattering in in her wooden sandals and whizzed straight past him in the hallway, he'd put his dusters away and gone about his usual rounds. Montacute fixed him with a keen stare and asked who else he had admitted to the house that evening. The boy replied at once and with evident puzzlement that he had let no one in besides Miss Thetis. A taxi driver had called about an hour later but had waited outside and helped Miss with her bag when she came downstairs. He'd noticed this because, drawn to his duties by the sound of someone galloping up and down the stairs, he'd waited about out of sight on the corner where the back passage joins the hall in case his help was needed.

"And what sort of help were you thinking might be called for at that hour?" the inspector asked casually.

The reply came at once with a suppressed grin: "Carrying a suitcase? All that yelling and screaming in the upper quarters, I thought someone might be going to do a runner, sir." Getting back to his routine, Demetrios told how he had fed the cats in the rear scullery, waited for them to finish, and then cleared their dishes away. By then it was time to put the cats out into the night—the Lady wouldn't have them inside the house after dark—and he'd started his tasks out at the back. Demetrios broke off to whisper hurriedly to Dorothea. She impatiently told him to just get on with his story.

Montacute was not a man to let anything slide by him and he gently enquired the reason for the boy's hesitation. Dorothea shrugged and explained that the lad had got fond of the animals and was asking what would happen to them now the professor was no longer about to care for them. He wanted

Miss Laetitia to know that he'd be very willing to take them home with him rather than kick them out into the city, where they'd starve.

Letty smiled and assured him that his offer was very generous and she'd certainly make sure the cats were not forgotten.

Her intervention was rewarded with a flashing grin and a whispered "Thank you, Mistress."

Demetrios gathered himself and told how he'd watered all the tubs of flowers, then he'd come inside again and checked that all the windows at the rear were locked, the doors bolted. The Old Mistress was very insistent on all that...she checked up on him sometimes.

Letty interrupted to remark that he was quite new in his post. She remembered that the boy back in the spring when she'd last been here was called Thomas?

Dorothea hurried to answer for him. Thomas had given notice—and returned to his own village just a little way off, on the Eleusis road. His father had had an accident at work and the lad was needed back at home. Luckily, he'd been able to recommend the services of his younger cousin. And Demetrios had given excellent service. The professor had the shiniest shoes in Athens!

Encouraged by the praise, Demetrios told how he'd gone out through the front door to check all was well and was about to come back in and lock up when he saw a dark shape on the ground under the drawing room window. He'd thought it might be a tramp bedding down for the night and the Old Mistress would never have tolerated such a thing, so he'd gone over to advise him to move away. He'd discovered Lady Merriman. And she was still alive, he'd added with round eyes. She'd recognised him and been able to speak to him. She'd told him she'd been pushed through the window and he was to fetch Dorothea and call the police.

"She said this in English?" the inspector asked quietly.

"Yes," replied the boy, and fell silent.

Dorothea clearly felt she ought to explain. "Demetrios is a bright lad! He wants to be a butler one day in a large household. That's his ambition. And we all know you need to speak English for a post like that. He's learning fast! I can't teach him much but Miss Thetis finds the time. She's been very good to him. Go on, Demetrios! Give the gentleman a sample!"

Shy but eager to please, the boy looked at them from under his eyebrows and said clearly: "May I take your hat, sir? And now the other foot, if you please. Will you come this way, madam? Her ladyship is expecting you . . ."

"There! And he understands a lot, too. He's a good listener. If that's what he says the mistress told him, I wouldn't doubt it. She said as much again when I got there but she was fading fast and I could hardly make out what she was saying. She was muttering in English."

The cook interrupted to ask a question that was on all their minds. There were other more important matters than raking over the events of last night. What about tomorrow? He wanted to know if he should at once start to look for a new post? Were they all to be turned away now the master and mistress were gone for good?

They should all stay in post for the time being, Montacute told them. Their wages would be paid until such time as the inheritors of the Merriman estate decided what was to be done with the house. It would most probably be sold by the English gentlemen who had inherited, but in the meantime Miss Laetitia or perhaps Miss Thetis would preside over the household, and Mr. Gunning would be on hand also.

A burst of muttering from Demetrios directed at Dorothea greeted this. The housekeeper, in some embarrassment, waved it away, telling them it was an indiscreet question and no business of his to ask it.

Inevitably, Montacute insisted on an explanation. Dorothea told him that the boy had been asking why the professor's daughter couldn't just take over the house and go on living in it.

"The professor's daughter?" asked Montacute and Letty together in surprise.

A further passage in Greek amongst the staff reduced Dorothea to giggles. "I'm sorry, sir, but the boy's only been here since June. You'll have to forgive him! How was he to know? He'd just about managed to work out the relationship between Miss Thetis and the professor..." Dorothea blushed and the two other servants hissed under their breath and looked aside. "I mean Miss Thetis and her ladyship...when another young girl arrived. People had told him and he assumed from the way she behaved—obviously at home here where a room was always kept for her—the one at the back—we call it Miss Laetitia's room—that Miss Letty was the professor's daughter!"

Demetrios was looking acutely uncomfortable, sliding further under the table as the explanation progressed and regretting the gauche question that so amused the adults.

Montacute kicked Letty's ankle and said calmly: "A very natural mistake. Miss Laetitia's own father and Sir Andrew were very good friends and there was, of course, a closeness between Sir Richard's daughter and his old friend, which Demetrios, among many, has observed." He directed a kindly nod at the boy. "But perhaps this might be the moment to announce some of the provisions Sir Andrew made in his will for his family and staff? Allay a little panic?"

Letty's first concern was to halt the slide of the mortified child out of sight. He was far too young to be taking on his shoulders the concerns and now the melodramas of such a puzzling foreign household, and, she guessed, probably came in for quite a ribbing from the other servants.

"Well, I wish Sir Andrew *had* willed the house to me, Demetrios!" she said cheerfully. "I'd have kept the household together, cats and all! He *has* left me one of his properties but it's too far away to be of use to any of us—somewhere up north near Salonika, though I've never been there. But the good news is—he didn't just remember his family in his will, he remembered all of you as well. Mrs. Stephanopoulos is to receive a generous sum of money in gratitude for the many years she has worked for him, and the rest of you—Petros, Maria, and Demetrios—are to have twenty pounds each."

A hubbub broke out, laced with smiles and exclamations. Dorothea produced a bottle of raki and a set of small glasses and poured out celebratory drinks for all. The first toast was to the professor with the wish that his soul might prosper, the second for the good news, and the third to Letty for bringing them the good news. They were embarking on a fourth round when Montacute and Letty took their leave.

As they climbed back upstairs, Montacute turned to Letty. "Miss Laetitia! Would you have any qualms about getting some information for me without any of the servants knowing?"

"Probably not," she said. "Ask! What do you want to know?"

"I should like to find out the home address of the boot boy. Not Demetrios. His predecessor—Thomas, I think you said his name was?"

CHAPTER 26

othing simpler!" Letty answered. "Why don't you go on upstairs to the library, Inspector? I'll bring you what you want
in a moment."

She turned back to the staff room.

"Dorothea!" she said, poking her head around the door.
"No, I don't want to disturb you again—you're all to take a half
hour off. It occurs to me that while I'm down here and standing in for Lady Merriman, I may as well initial the daybook."

Dorothea, hiccupping gently, dabbed her lips with a lace
handkerchief and raised a little finger in acknowledgement.
"Of course, Mistress! She would have counted on doing it last
night."

She took down a ledger from a corner shelf by the fireplace
and handed it to Letty.

Letty looked about her, taking in the scene, and tucked the
book under her arm. "Carry on, all of you. I'll take this upstairs with me. And take a moment to make a note of the ...
changed circumstances ..." she added confidentially.

"There you are! The daybook." Letty placed it on the desk in front of Montacute. "If you want to know what everyone ate for breakfast six weeks ago last Tuesday you'll find it in here. Weekly grocery bills...the fishmonger...the milkman... guests...who came and went...the usual things. You'll find what you're looking for at the back. Staff records. Weekly payments. Deductions for breakages—Maud was tough on breakages—and the staff's home addresses and personal details."

The inspector pounced on the book and turned at once to the back pages.

"Montacute, what do you find so interesting about that young chap?" Gunning asked.

Letty replied for him. "Changes in routine. Appearances and disappearances. That's what gets the inspector going."

He smiled and nodded in agreement as he found the information he was searching for. "Immaculately kept records. And here we have the sudden appearance of young Demetrios. Third week in June. With an address for him on the fringes of the Plaka. Stadiou Adrianou. Family name: Volos. Father Vassilios and mother Kalliopi. Father is a taxi driver by trade. Dorothea has noted that he was introduced and vouched for by the previous employee, Thomas. They interviewed no others for the position."

He riffled back through a few more pages and came upon: "Thomas. Clean record. She's noted down Andrew's testimonial for the boy. Sudden departure back home to Eleusis. Father suffered work injury and the son was needed to help out. Runs a garage. Unusual. Halfway to Corinth, they probably sell a good deal of petrol to passing tourists. Taxis? Cars? There may be a link..."

Montacute reached for the telephone and asked for a connection. "Probably all nonsense," he said casually while he waited. "But if I'm going down a hole after something nasty, I like to know that all possible exits have been blocked. Saves a lot of effort. Ah! Philippos? Montacute here. Give me Harry, will you?... Sarge! Tell me what you're busy with... Fine... Fine... Look, I want you to leave that for the moment. There's something else I want you to do. Oh... inside two hours. And what's more you'll enjoy it! I want you to drive out on the Corinth road with a young lady and fill the car up with petrol. No, that's all. Take one of the unmarked sedans. Your passenger will brief you. Pick her up... not here... um... in Academy Street. In front of the Schliemann mansion. She'll be the young lady carrying a picnic hamper. In, let's say, half an hour. You're to come back with some information for me. You'll be back in time for the meeting with the superintendent and the medics, don't worry."

"Well, I'd better start cutting the sandwiches, then," said Letty dryly. "Does the sergeant like cheese or ham?"

"No need for that. Just grab an empty basket from the kitchen. It's only window dressing. Now, here's what you're to do..."

A moment later he left the room to check on the taxi stand at the corner of the square, and Gunning and Letty sighed in irritation and relief.

"I'll stroll round the corner with you and deliver you into the hands of the sergeant," Gunning volunteered when they were alone. "I wonder if you've realised, Letty, that he's playing a game of pass the parcel?" He spoke swiftly, an eye on the door.

"What do you mean? And—am I the parcel in question?"

"I think so. You said it yourself—what interests him is change... new actors making their entrance. And it's not just Demetrios who's wandered onto this scene. *You* have arrived. *Thetis* has arrived. Both of you with a motive for spiking poor old Andrew."

"He's asked me twice now if we knew each other in London," said Letty doubtfully.

Gunning snorted. "Then he may suspect you're working together—in some sort of awful Maenad rampage. You top Andrew—not quite sure why...jealousy? revenge for a betrayal of some sort? Woman scorned? He doesn't know you as I do and what do we know of *him*, after all? The man may have some pretty primitive ideas about 'wimmin' and their emotions. He might well be not in the least surprised that a spurned woman should take it into her head to stab her lover in his faithless heart. I expect it happens every Saturday night in Beak Street, Soho. And, honestly, Letty, if what you report about Andrew is true, then it's a wonder to *me*, let alone Montacute, that the man went unfilleted for so long! And then Thetis gives Maud a push. The plotters meet back at Mrs. Rose's haven for young ladies to congratulate each other. But he's broken up the conspiracy. Thetis he's made safe under lock and key, but it's my theory he's giving *you* the illusion that you're running loose. He's even convinced you that you're being of assistance to the forces of law and order."

"But I *am* being of use. The inspector sees every advantage of sailing along in the lee of my charm and secure social position." Letty grinned. "Don't be concerned, William, I was not deceived! The man's using me as a decoy duck, an innocent-looking lure, while he stands in the underbrush, shotgun at the ready."

"And you'll have realised that he's holding you on the end of a longish leash, if I may pile up our sporting metaphors. If you're not actually in his company, he'll send you off with one of his sergeants riding guard."

"Apart from the hours I spent at Mrs. Rose's, I've been under undeclared police surveillance the whole time since Andrew died."

"And perhaps even then..."

Letty shuddered. "You're right." She seized his hands and held them to her face. "I hate this! I wish they'd leave us alone! I just want to hug you and talk. I want to do the ordinary things we were planning—watching the sun set over the temple at Sounion, dabbling in the spring at Delphi, canoodling behind the gravestones in the Kerameikos. And Thetis has given me the address of a sweet little hotel in Vouliagmeni where they smile and ask no questions. William! We could just climb into a taxi while he's got his back turned! Two minutes to fling a few things into a bag... What about it?"

"I think our romantic twosome would turn into a rather uncomfortable threesome before we'd signed the register. Don't underrate the man. I'd guess he has tentacles spreading all over Greece."

"Do you seriously think Montacute suspects me of stabbing Andrew to death?"

"Not sure. I think he's behaving strangely. For a policeman, I mean. Oh, he does everything by the book, but... well, with the attitude of one who's actually written the book. I expect him to tear it up and rewrite it to please himself at any moment. If we were on a ship I'd call him a loose cannon. Just try not to annoy him too much, Letty. I'll be here. I won't let him get away with any nonsense."

He moved to the window. "Come and look! He's back again. And what's he up to now? The inspector seems to spend an awful lot of his time on his knees, don't you think?"

Letty joined him and watched as Montacute, below the window, shuffled about on the pavings picking up something of interest and putting it in his pocket. He stood and dusted off his trousers and looked up. He smiled back at them as though he'd been aware of their presence, made a gesture, and went back a few paces towards the pepper tree. Then he was on his knees again, searching the grille and pocketing more objects. Finally he came towards the door, miming handwashing, and disappeared inside.

He bounced into the room a minute or two later, smiling with satisfaction.

"Anything interesting down there?" Gunning couldn't help asking.

"Oh, yes! The local taxi drivers would appear to be making a very good living out of their trade. They certainly do themselves proud in the tobacco department, if that's any indication. Nothing but the best for them, it seems!"

He took a couple of cigarette stubs from his pocket and laid them in an ashtray. "What do you make of these?" he asked, and without waiting for an answer: "Turkish manufacture," he said. "Look at the gold strip around the top, the quality of the tobacco. The very finest. And very expensive. Not what the taxi-driving fraternity usually smoke. And none of these has been smoked right down to the butt—we're not contemplating a smoker who has to get every last drag from his cigarette. I noticed some of these around their stand down there on the corner. And then the same thing up here. Under the tree and right outside the front door. In piles. Someone's been watching the house since the last street-sweeping was done. And, judging by the quantities buried under the grille, for many days before that. Lady Merriman, it seems, was right to be pulling the emergency cord! The house—or someone in it—*was* under surveillance. Any idea where the nearest tobacco outlet is, Miss Laetitia?"

"That would be in the café down there or—for more exotic brands—you'd have to go as far as the shop on the corner of Academy Street. I used to go there for Andrew's tins of Lambert and Butler's Navy Cut."

Montacute looked at his watch. "We just have time," he

said, assuming they were following his thoughts. "Gunning—I expect you'll want to escort Miss Laetitia as far as the Schliemann palace? I'll come with you both as far as the tobacconist's.

"Picnic basket...?" He bellowed as he strode from the room.

"Nothing to do with *him*, he claims," Montacute told them on leaving the shop. "Imported brand, possibly privately imported. Not generally on sale in Greece. He took a good look at the half-smoked one I offered and pronounced it top quality, luxury end of the market, and most likely sent straight for sale in a western capital—London...Paris...New York. Brought back into the country by a tourist perhaps?"

"That sort of thing is all the rage in London," Letty commented. "Milder tobacco—women like it...and fashionable, effete young men." She gave the inspector a steady gaze. "You'll remember our friend Mr. Melton selected a Passing Cloud from his boss's box this morning?"

CHAPTER 27

I thought I'd bring the open-top Morris," said Harry Perkins amiably, letting in the clutch. "Seeing as how we're meant to be a couple of tourists out on a picnic. If you look in the glove locker, you'll find a pair of sun goggles. With those on and your hat pulled down, not even your own mother's going to recognise you. Your reputation won't suffer being seen out with me."

"I'm sure you can only enhance it, Harry!" She glanced admiringly at the young man. "Remind me where we're headed... the Stewards' Enclosure at Royal Henley-on-Thames? Can this be Regatta Week?"

He was wearing smart civilian clothes: fashionable light flannel trousers and a navy blazer bearing the crest of a Cambridge rowing club on the breast. A boater completed the nautical theme.

He chortled. "A bit over the top? You're right! I hadn't much time and I may have oversteered. I borrowed the blazer and hat the Governor keeps at the station for sporting and festive occasions. I thought I looked creepily like Maurice Chevalier. You know..." He began to growl in a convincing accent: *"Elle avait de tout petits petons... Valentine, Valentine..."*

"Stop right there, Sergeant!" Letty interrupted. "It gets very rude after the first line. I don't wish to hear it."

"Really? Oh. I heard him at the Hammersmith Palais after the war. Bought the record and learned the words. No idea what they mean."

She didn't believe him and decided the sergeant would bear watching.

"I'll tell you when you're a bit older," she said with mock reproval, and opened up the glove locker. "Good! I like the effect," she commented, putting on the dark glasses, "and more important—the folk at the garage won't know me, either." She took them off again to direct a straight look at him. "This is a distracting piece of nonsense, you know—a wild-goose chase. Had you worked that out?"

"Certainly had! Can't tell you how much I resent being dragged away from the inspection and analysis of forty-two bags of assorted scrapings from the thickets behind the theatre!" He rolled his eyes. "And sent off into the wilderness with a pretty young lady in possession of a hamper! Who wouldn't be distracted?"

"Well, don't get too excited—the inspector told me it was all a bit of make-believe. The hamper could remain empty. But that's the spirit, Sarge! May I call you Sarge? We'll set out to enjoy it! First, though, I'd better brief you about what we're to expect and what we're to achieve at the garage..."

"Is that it? You're sure that's all? You've told me everything?" Perkins sounded doubtful and suspicious on hearing her account.

"Everything *I* know. It occurs to me that one carefully phrased phone call placed to an official in Eleusis might well have given the information we're doing a round trip of thirty miles to seek. In a fraction of the time and effort. They must have the telephone there? And some sort of police station? Or Town Hall? I'd have just got Philippos to put on an official voice and say he was the...oh...census department asking for details of local inhabitants. What's your boss playing at?"

He sighed and then smiled dismissively, reluctant to encourage her speculation. "Oh, well, let's make the most of the trip anyway," he said cheerfully. "Always good to get your hands on a steering wheel..." And, cheekily: "I'll let you drive back, if you behave yourself."

He wove his way skilfully through the thick Athenian traffic and began seriously to motor along when they cleared the northwestern suburbs and picked up the Corinth road. The sergeant looked back over his shoulder far more frequently than Letty would have considered necessary on a practically empty road. Police training, she told herself.

"That green valley we're coming up to, miss...Do you see it over there ahead and to the left? Never seen that before. I don't actually get much time to explore the country—between the job and the family I'm staying with...We seem to spend our Sundays in the Zappeion park. Taking tea."

"That's the Vale of Daphne, where there's a spectacular monastery church with the most wonderful gold-leaf Byzantine mosaics. Try to get out and see it, Harry. And please—call me Laetitia for the duration—I'm not out and about with my chauffeur."

"No, Miss Laetitia. Would you mind if I pulled off the road just round this bend? Took a few seconds to admire those trees over there?"

"Would you care to consult the Baedeker guide? I've got a copy in my satchel...They're maritime pines. They *are* rather spectacular and incredibly ancient. The very essence of Greece, I've always thought. When I'm somewhere else and remembering Greece, it's not the spiky green fingers of cypress trees against white crags, it's not even the clotted-cream columns of the Parthenon I see in my mind's eye, it's *those* magnificent shapes, in full sail against a gemlike blue sky."

They talked companionably of Surrey chestnuts and the plane trees of London, the policeman's eyes scanning the road they had turned off to nestle in the shadow of a thicket of pomegranate bushes. He watched on as three motor vehicles passed by. Two sedans, one brown open-top containing four young men singing a sea chanty, one cream Delage struggling frantically to pass them, and a taxi loaded high with suitcases and bound for the port, Letty noted.

When they moved off again she picked up her topographical commentary, though she couldn't be quite certain that her companion was listening. He seemed preoccupied.

"We're halfway there. This is rich farmland hereabouts and a wonderful sight, they say, when the wheat's waving all golden at harvest time. And this road we're bumping along on was once, in ancient times, the Sacred Way, leading to Eleusis."

"Sacred? And who would it have been sacred to?"

"The Mother Goddess: Demeter, the Goddess of the Harvest—of plenty—of animals and all living things."

The sergeant grinned in delight. "Oh, I know all about *her*. My favourite book when I was ten ... *A Young Person's Illustrated Who Was Who on Mount Olympus*. Not much about in the way of 'plenty' in the East End when I was a nipper. She was my top goddess—smiling, thick red hair, and offering an apple to the lucky young person who turned the page."

"Then you'll like the description of her in one of the Homeric hymns: 'Rich-haired, deep-bosomed Demeter.'"

"Just what a starving ten-year-old fancied for a mother!"

"And then there's her daughter—trim-ankled Persephone ..."

"Sad story! A case of abduction. Poor little girl, snatched whilst out picking flowers by a male relative, a gent called Hades. Uncle of some sort, I believe. It almost always is ... Held against her will in false imprisonment in the underworld. But her mother was a stouthearted lady who was having none of that! Tracked her daughter down and after a bit of argy-bargy with the higher authorities, got her back aboveground."

"Concessions were made, though. Persephone was let out on parole—she had to spend four months of the year back down in the underworld. And these are reckoned the bleak and fallow months of the agricultural year, the pause when nothing is growing. It's a very ancient way of explaining nature and the cycle of the seasons...probably going right back to Stone Age times. But the religious rites—the Mysteries, they call them—held every year at Demeter's temple at Eleusis were a highly sophisticated affair." Letty paused, wondering how interesting this might be for a Metropolitan police sergeant.

"Mysteries?" he encouraged. "Go on! I like a good mystery!"

"Every year in the autumn, for two thousand years, the initiates followed this road on foot from Athens to take part in a secret ceremony in the temple. They were sworn to silence on the ritual and—do you know?—in all that time no one has ever revealed what went on. It's still a mystery! The greatest philosophers and scientists of their day—Aristotle, Sophocles, Plato...a selection of Roman Emperors...everyone who was anyone throughout Europe, in fact—underwent the five-day experience."

"Entrance for nobs only, was it?"

"Not a bit of it! There was only one qualification you needed: You had to be innocent of having committed murder. That's all. Women could present themselves, workingmen, slaves—even, in later years, foreigners. And of all that assorted clientele, not one man or woman ever revealed the details of the epiphany they experienced. The most anyone has confided is a few words about changed beliefs and widened understanding. We can get no nearer than the odd general comment from men like...oh...Cicero, the Roman lawyer, for instance. I learned by heart a sentence or two of his in which he talks about the gifts the Mysteries brought. Largely because it contains my name! *Laetitia.* Do you know what that means?"

"Some sort of herb?" the sergeant ventured. "Like angelica? Cassia?"

"No! It means happiness or joy. And here's what he said: *'...neque solum cum Laetitia vivendi rationem accepimus sed etiam cum spe meliore moriendi.'* It means roughly: 'We gain from them not only a way of living in happiness but also a way of dying with greater hope.' So—joy and hope of life after death. A gift worth having! And the ceremony certainly seems to have changed people's lives. Something happened there, at night, in the darkness of the temple building at Eleusis, to sharpen the worshippers' perceptions, convince them that an afterlife exists, open them up to an otherworldly experience, and send them on their way rejoicing."

"We get that all the time when the Spiritualist Temple of the Trinity turns out after the Friday night séance! Corner of Boot Street in Balham. Next to the Flag and Lamb it is. Incidences of what you might call euphoria recorded every week. Er...there wouldn't be any involvement with intoxicating substances, I suppose—it being an ancient ceremony? Alcohol or the like?"

"The like! You may have hit the nail on the head, Harry." Letty knew when she was being teased, though the sergeant's deadpan expression was hard to read. "*Kykeon,* they called it. A drink the celebrants were given before the rites. We think it was a brew of barley and mint...perhaps a pinch or two of something special only the priests knew of. Something available to them in large quantities at any rate, since we know the numbers attending to have been in the thousands."

Perkins winced. "Thousands out and about on the roads,

under the influence of intoxicating substances? Crowd control must have been something taxing!"

They drove slowly past, the sergeant's eyes raking the ruins. "Duty first," he told himself. "We won't stop."

"Two other cars there anyway," Letty commented. "I hate crowds."

They pressed on towards the unimpressive small modern town beyond. The smartest building was the brand-new garage and petrol station bearing the name of Thomas's family. When they stopped by the pump, Harry got out and walked around the car kicking the tires. A middle-aged Greek man in overalls hurried from the gloom of the machine shop and stood by, wiping his hands on a cloth. He smiled hopefully at the sergeant and enquired if he might be of service. Harry complained of losing pressure in the rear near-side tire and the man bent to inspect it. He got up again, commenting that all appeared well. The rough road had probably forced a bit of air out but he had a pump that would rectify that. And petrol? Would they be requiring petrol? No more stations were to be found, he reported with pride, between here and Corinth. He called out, "Thomas!" and added: "My son will see to your needs, sir."

A young boy dashed up and began to fill the tank. While they waited by the churning pump, Harry engaged in manly tourist conversation with him. The growing number of motorcars on the road, the comparative speeds of the train and the car, came up for comment. Harry got around to the demands of the job and the efforts called for from one so young. Such a blessing to have a big, strapping son in a physically demanding business—his father must have been so reassured to have his help following the accident...?

Thomas looked first pleased, then puzzled. But his father had never had an accident. His father was a very careful man. Where could the gentleman have heard such a thing?

Harry managed, by playing the confused tourist with very little Greek vocabulary, to recover himself. Petrol and air were duly pumped and paid for and, leaving a good tip, the sergeant climbed back behind the wheel and set off back towards the ruins.

"Well! That didn't take long! I was almost embarrassed to ask the lad—his father looked as fit as a mountain goat—but I thought I'd better not cut corners."

"You did that well. And better safe than sorry. Thomas was genuinely puzzled. No, I fear the inspector has it right—Demetrios is a plant. He's a good listener, Dorothea said! At the door, I bet! Poor lamb! I liked him. The boy's been used. Set up by his elders to spy out the household. Probably reported every move to his father lounging about at the front of the house smoking cigarettes. But why? Do you suppose the inspector has any idea?"

"Never short of an idea!" Harry's voice had a note of pride. "I've seen the Guv juggle six! He'll sort it out."

"Well, I hope he manages to do it before some other member of the English community dies."

"Don't you fret! There's none better at the Yard."

"I'm sure. Fascinating man, the Guv," said Letty agreeably, preparing to probe. "What a pity he's still unmarried at his age."

"Not sure about that." Harry grinned and began to edge his way towards the temple ruins. "No woman would put up with him and the life he leads."

"It's probably too late, anyway," said Letty. "Army men—they get set in their ways and the police service just reinforces an established pattern. I have one or two uncles who are much the same...Not the slightest interest in women." She added confidentially: "Men's men, if you know what I mean."

"Oh, I wouldn't go so far as to say that," the sergeant said, unwilling to hear, as Letty had calculated, even the slightest smear on his boss's reputation. "He's not, um, impervious to female charms." Hearing his stilted Victorian expression, the sergeant gave a snort of self-mocking laughter and added, "Lord! You should see him sometimes on a Monday morning following a heavy weekend of worshipping at some goddess's altar! Much the worse for wear but living in a state of joy and hope, you'd say."

He fell silent, aware that he'd gone too far. Letty affected not to have noticed. "Good! So glad to hear he's halfway human," she said lightly. "I don't think you'd much enjoy working with a virtuous Knight Templar, Harry."

They sat for a moment following the line of the white marble pavement, pitted with ancient wheel tracks, along to the ruined temple. It led their gaze to a jumble of collapsed columns: the shrine to Demeter which stood upon a raised platform looking out over the slim calm crescent of sea separating it from the rocky island of Salamis.

Harry looked at his wristwatch. "Can't get the car any closer than this. Hang on—I'll just turn her round so's we've got a clear run in case we need to take off in a hurry. We're ahead of ourselves—I reckon we've got thirty minutes before we need to turn for home."

Letty noted that he placed the car in shade with the stunning view behind them and a clear but dull view of the Athens road ahead. The midday sun beat down, striking a painful glare from their rocky surroundings. Perkins took off his boater and began to fan his face, eyes narrowed and watchful.

"We can see the extent of the site in that time but you'll have to give the Zappeion Gardens a miss one Sunday and come back again to appreciate it properly. But first, Harry—the hamper! I spent a few minutes disobeying the Guv and shoved a few essentials in there. I thought we deserved it! Lemonade suit you?"

"Who needs barley broth when they can have lemonade?"

"And then I found some goat's cheese, salad bits, and a good fresh loaf. I could hack together a sandwich or two. There's even a few digestive biscuits."

His smile of pure joy would have rivalled an initiate's, Letty decided, as he swung the hamper over from the backseat.

They'd gulped their way gratefully through the flask of lemonade and were sharing out the bread and cheese when the cream Delage drew level with the entrance to the site, hesitated, and then turned up the processional way towards them.

"Drat!" said Letty. "One car. A crowd at least you can ignore—a single tourist you're obliged to exchange the time of day with. How sociable are you feeling, Sarge?"

She eyed the sergeant, who had hastily put away his drinking cup. His hand was reaching out to the self-starter and then he seemed to change his mind.

Letty decided to drop the pretence. The sergeant was a good man who deserved to know that he was not encumbered by a hen-headed female who was likely to swoon at the suggestion of danger and cling to his gun arm. She confirmed his suspicions: "That car's got two more cylinders than we have. It's faster and heavier than ours—he can outrun us or push us off the road." She spoke tersely, unafraid, unflustered. "With the top down, we're especially vulnerable. And there are plenty of nasty bends and remote places on the road back. It's one of the cars that was parked up here when we went by earlier. It followed us out from Athens, and it's a strange sort of tourist who doubles back and revisits a site within twenty minutes, don't you think?"

"You're right, miss. They've been tracking us all the way." The sergeant's face was grim. "And now they've decided to introduce themselves."

They watched as the Delage manoeuvred to place itself sideways across the narrow bit of made-up road, blocking entrance or exit.

"There are two of them in there. Men. What do you want me to do, Harry?"

She reached down by her feet and pulled her satchel onto her knees.

"For a start, I don't fancy being caught sitting here in the car, clutching our cheese sammies. Restricts your movements a bit. Do you fancy a walk, Miss Laetitia? This is probably all a load of cobblers and in five minutes when they've revealed themselves to be German archaeologists we'll be left feeling silly. But better safe than sorry, eh?"

His tone was intended to calm her but Letty saw that the young man was in a state of tense anticipation. She jumped out of the car, slipped her satchel onto her shoulder, and joined him, putting her right arm lightly through his left. They began to walk towards the truncated columns, two tourists, exclaiming and admiring. Letty managed not to look back as she heard two car doors slam shut behind them. Harry flicked a look backwards without breaking stride.

"Two, middle-aged. Walking together for the moment. No sign of papers or a guidebook. And they're not chatting and exclaiming. Armed, I think. They've got that look about them. Right hands too carefully placed, not swinging naturally. Fifty yards off and closing," he muttered.

"We're being herded away from the road and towards the sea."

"Yes. This isn't good. Listen. I want you to go, without appearing to panic, to hide yourself behind that column over there...Do you see? The tallest one, off to the left? It's solid enough to repel an assault by Big Bertha. I'll keep them busy. Stay out of their way by any means possible. Run if you have to. Drive away if you have to. No matter what I'm doing. The village is your best bet. They've got a gendarmerie there, did you see it? Make for that."

"But suppose they *are* just casual visitors with an ungainly walk...in the middle of a quarrel?" Letty whispered. "You could start an international incident if you challenged them. How can we tell?"

His eyes gleamed with purpose. "I'll test them out to see if they're innocent tourists first. Don't be alarmed. We'll know by their reaction what their intentions are. As soon as you're hidden, I'll surprise them. Go!"

He was easing his Browning from his belt and placing himself between her and the advancing pair as she walked swiftly off. He called no warning. He fired before the men had a chance to split up. The power of the Browning shocked Letty, cowering in safety some thirty yards behind the barrel; it shattered the complacency of the two men as the bullet zipped between their heads and only an inch or so above them. She watched for their reaction.

The shrieks and screams of offended tourists? A spluttering: "What the hell do you think you're playing at, sir!" A sarcastic: "I say! Geese flying low today, are they?" No. Not even the instinctive crash to the ground of army men. Without a word exchanged, the two separated and eased away in opposite directions, crouching, guns now openly drawn, to take shelter amongst the rocks. Forming a triangle with the sergeant, concealed behind a stone fragment, uncomfortably at its apex. Two shots announced to him that he was pinned down from two points. Letty reckoned that it would be just a matter of time before he ran out of ammunition or they ran out of patience.

And then? Letty's initial fear was being numbed by outrage and puzzlement. Who on earth were they? Were they road bandits out to rob innocent tourists? Steal their car? The men's own car was a good one, and they appeared well dressed. And any motorcar reported missing would be stopped at the port or the borders. They must know that. She thought: *not bandits.* Perkins had been uneasy ever since they'd left Athens. Expecting something like this? She reckoned so, and her anger started to simmer. Were they out to kill the policeman? Yes. That much was not in doubt.

The thought struck her belatedly, in all the excitement. They would eliminate him to get at the real target—herself.

Why? She had no idea. But she could work out the method. Nothing simpler. They'd chosen their killing spot well. Last summer the body of a French tourist had been found at the bottom of the steep precipice below the temple site, swishing in and out with the foam. His camera was still around his neck. Tourists equipped with the latest Kodak or Leica were seen to take enormous risks to get a sensational shot. The two men would grab her by the shoulders and ankles and swing her out and over and the last thing she would see would be the craggy cliffs of Salamis spinning between the deep blue of sky and sea.

Salamis. Letty could think of many less heroic places to die. The Athenian forces, cornered here, had turned on the invading Persians and, with immense courage and a dash of low cunning, had routed them. And she had no intention of dying at Salamis, either.

The sun beat down on her back and she shifted her constricted position slightly behind her column. What would be their tactics? She thought as her father had trained her: "Don't be caught off guard, Letty—anticipate!" They'd pick off the sergeant first, of course. And, however determined Harry was, geometry was all against him. Two would always be able to find a way around his defences, held, as he was, by the rock that at the same time protected and constricted him. One distraction or one concerted dash and the sergeant was dead.

He might take one with him but, inevitably, she'd be left facing the armed man remaining. She calculated that they would be unwilling to sacrifice one of themselves. Realistically, they'd probably shout out, offering terms, tricking him into giving up his gun—and surrendering *her* into the bargain. They didn't know the sergeant. She barely knew him herself and yet would have staked—*was* staking—her life on his loyalty.

A shot blasted against the column sheltering Perkins. And another from the second angle. None against hers. They had discounted her. They were stunning him with their firepower, she reckoned, softening him up to accept the deal she calculated they were about to offer.

Letty decided it was time to adjust the geometry and even up the odds. She slid a hand into her satchel and took out the Webley. Calculating that she was just within a reasonable range if she was very careful, she picked out and read the positions of the concealed men ahead of her by their shadows. Short in the overhead sun but enough to distinguish an elbow here, an extended foot there. One, the closer of the two, was taking such care to avoid the Browning—or, more likely, he was so dismissive of the girl's potential to harm him—he was allowing a segment of his lower body to poke out. Letty seized the chance. She took aim, breathed out slowly, and fired at the projecting rear end.

A screaming ricochet harmonised with a high shriek of pain. She fired again to confirm her views. Harry's Browning made a basso profundo contribution from the other side of the pavement. And then his voice rang out, firm and clear, shouting in English, then in Greek: "You have two minutes to get out of here. Take your wounded away. Move! Now!"

She watched the pair as they moved, one supporting the second, who was bleeding copiously from a head wound, back towards their car. A gesture from Harry kept her in her place and she peered around, watching his progress as he darted between sheltering columns, easing forward, gun trained, unwavering, on his quarry. When they drew level with the police sedan Letty stiffened with alarm and raised the Webley to fire a warning shot. Had Harry seen the danger? He had. The Browning blasted out, the bullet kicking up splinters of marble in the space between the men's feet and the vulnerable tyres, within inches of the now brimming and eminently explodable fuel tank. The shot announced that here was a confident marksman who wouldn't hesitate to put a bullet into any selected part of a man attempting to sabotage his motorcar.

Letty smiled to see the pair turn hurriedly aside and increase their pace towards their own vehicle.

Only when they moved off and turned left back towards Eleusis did the sergeant beckon her forward.

They sprinted for their open-top, praying that it would start, and moments later were pushing at top speed back in the opposite direction on the Athens road.

"Well! Thank you for showing me the Mysteries, Miss Laetitia. As you said in your commentary: a life-and-death experience. I wonder what that was all about! Anyone you know?" the sergeant enquired mildly.

She shook her head. "Bit of a puzzle! I was aiming for the man's bottom! Now—how is it he walked off clutching his top?"

"I'd say you missed. But the bullet struck rock, and a splinter got him in the forehead. The chap was losing a lot of blood. Splashed all over the pavement. Whatever happened, I think we've defiled the site."

"We've spilled blood along the Sacred Way." Letty couldn't repress a shiver. Reaction was setting in. "We won't be invited back until we've done penance."

"They say confession's good for the soul these days, too. Anything else you'd like to declare, hidden away in that innocent-looking old schoolbag, miss? Duty obliges me to ask: any other essentials for seeing the sights of the Aegean... besides a Baedeker and a popgun?"

"It's a Webley. And don't scoff! It did its job. Better than its job, in fact! If I'd hit what I was really aiming at, he wouldn't have been able to walk away." Letty pursued her dispiriting scenario: "His friend would have made a run for it and he'd have been stuck there on-site with us. How awkward! We'd have had to load him into the car, cursing and bleeding, and take him to hospital."

"Pity, that!" said Perkins grimly. "It would have given me a chance to beat some information out of him first. Lost opportunity, Montacute will say... Should never have let them get away..." Then, struck by an unwelcome thought: "The Governor! What on earth are we going to tell him?"

Letty looked at the suddenly concerned young face and reflected that the presence of two armed men bent on murder had roused no more than a stiffened jaw and a gleam in the sergeant's eye, but the thought of his boss's displeasure distressed him. Resentment of Montacute boiled within her once more. "Tell him? Hah! More truth than he cares to hear!" Letty gave Perkins an evil smile. "I'm working on a few phrases. Phrases involving 'decoy duck' (that's me)...'dereliction of duty of care towards a subordinate officer' (that's you)...'wilful endangerment of a member of the public' (that's me again). Oh, I've got plenty to tell the Guv! Can I feed you a digestive biscuit, Harry, while you drive? Action always gives one an appetite, don't you find?"

"I'd love a digestive! Thank you... Cat's paw! That's a good one, Miss Laetitia," Perkins said, rallying. "'You made a cat's paw of me!' You could always try him with that."

CHAPTER 28

"All the same, William," Letty said thoughtfully, "to attack a police inspector *once* before lunch might be written off as a misjudgement, but—twice? It begins to look like a campaign. And couldn't you at least have hit him somewhere it wouldn't show? That eye is just red and swollen at the moment, but in an hour or two it's going to be all the colours of the rainbow. And people are going to ask questions."

"I shall listen with interest to his answers," said Gunning crisply. "And if I don't like them I shall blacken the other one."

"I do wish I could be allowed to settle my own scores. Given time to consider it, I'd have come up with *something*."

"No you wouldn't. You'd have thought about it, dallied with a few entertaining fantasies involving the excruciating pain and shame of the guilty party, and then collapsed into giggles at the very notion. With you, Letty, the clouds are never in front of the sun for long. This way it's all over, sorted out in a second by one clunking fist."

"But the man knows you're a priest, William! It was hardly a fair fight."

"What *is* a fair fight? There's no such thing, Letty. Ever. The only fights are those you engage in, intending to win. And you win them by whatever means you may. But I don't need to explain that to a girl who has the forethought to slip a Webley into her satchel before leaving for a picnic. And uses it to shoot a man in the bum. Are you ever going to tell me where you got the gun?"

"It seems I'm not the only girl in Athens prepared for eventualities…"

Letty gave William information she'd held back from Montacute on their return from Eleusis. The inspector had launched into an improvised enquiry into the expedition, conducting it in Andrew's library. She and Perkins had stood one on either side of the inspector, and they'd delivered a concise, concordant, and mutually admiring account of the events in the temple ruins. William, loitering effetely by the bookshelves with a copy of Pindar's *Odes* in hand, had listened without comment, but she'd been aware of the agonised looks he'd thrown her way. So as to avoid adding to his tension, she'd deliberately played down her own involvement in the attack but the sergeant, interpreting her reticence as nothing more than good old British understatement, would have none of it. He'd launched into a highly coloured appreciation of her contribution.

When he was happy that Perkins had revealed all that could be useful to him, Montacute dismissed him with a word of commendation and the instruction to go and repeat his story to Chief Superintendent Theotakis at once, and the three of them were left considering their next move. Montacute was unusually downcast and reflective, Letty thought, and she waited quietly to hear his acknowledgement of a lapse, a dereliction of duty, a mistake. She wondered what words he would find to apologise for involving her and his officer in a life-threatening situation. It would not be easy for him and she prepared herself graciously to cut short his stumbling words.

Finally he broke his silence: "Ha! I was right!" he said with satisfaction. "Demetrios's family are in this up to their necks!"

With a snort of disgust, William had stalked to the desk, reached out, and hauled Montacute to his feet by his tie with one fist and smashed the other into his face. The two men stared at each other for a moment in silence and then, abruptly released, Montacute had mumbled his excuses and left the room, groping for a handkerchief to cover his eye. They listened as he lumbered down the corridor in the direction of the cloakroom.

"Your new friend Thetis is full of surprises." Gunning began to speak urgently, taking advantage of the inspector's absence. "This gun—which I note, in his confusion, he didn't have the gall to require you to hand over—was given to you by Andrew? Or so Montacute's supposed to think?"

"He didn't seem disposed to question that."

"Perhaps it's not the first such he's encountered? I can't think it's the only one such out there in the world, lost in the satin depths of ladies' handbags, buried in drawers under layers of scented linen," Gunning speculated.

"I find I could become quite censorious of Andrew, you know."

Gunning smiled.

"He'll be back in a minute, William. What will you do if he's decided to carry on fighting? Or arrest you? He could, you know."

"He has more sense! He's an annoying nuisance and damned careless of your safety, but I can't help liking the man. He'll see that tap as due punishment for something he feels but is incapable of expressing."

"Can it be so difficult to say: 'I'm sorry I nearly got you both killed'? He must have realised."

"Oh, yes. He was clearly shaken by what you and the sergeant had to say—he just couldn't bring himself to admit his responsibility. He's no *chevalier-servant* like me, you know, ready to apologise at every turn, flirt with ladies, leap to his feet to retrieve a ball of knitting wool. I was taught from a very young age to watch for signs that a lady was about to leave a room, and whatever I was occupied with, I would drop it and hurry to the door to hold it open for her. It's automatic with me. That's the sort of thing I'm talking about. I rather think Montacute's lip would curl at the idea of such a chivalrous response."

"Lacking basic training, are you saying?"

"Not fair to speculate from such a short acquaintance. I comment. I can't explain."

"I don't know what his background may be, but I'd say courtly behaviour has not featured in it," said Laetitia.

"But you know, Letty, you shouldn't despise that—after all, he's showing you exactly what you've always claimed you wanted to see in a man. Respect for you as the equal you are. He expects no favours, he gives none, simply because you're a female. It's an unusual trait. Perhaps we should value it."

The inspector strode back into the room holding a wet handkerchief to his face as a compress. With a flourish he removed it to reveal an eye fully closed and beginning to colour.

"Always fancied myself in a black eye-patch," he said, grinning at them. "And here's my chance. Captain Blood, I believe you invoked, Gunning, following on your first assault? With some prescience, it seems. Now, I believe I have been none too gently reminded that an apology is called for. Am I right?"

Gunning nodded. Letty stared.

"So. You have it. Please accept my regrets for involving you in a dangerous situation, Miss Laetitia, in equal measure with my thanks and admiration for a job well done."

"I'm touched and pleased to hear your courteous, if succinct, response, Inspector. The sergeant and I did what we had to do. And now I'd be interested to hear your explanation of the extraordinary behaviour of these gentlemen of the road..."

"I've been making enquiries. Telephone overheating!" he said with satisfaction. "The boot boy has a wide family. All Athenians by birth. Christians by religion—as far as they claim one. Uncles and cousins aplenty. All with solid occupations, doing well for themselves in difficult times, none with criminal records. One or two of the men have army experience, and I believe it's a couple of these you traded bullets with today, Miss Laetitia."

"But why should the new boot boy's uncles be out to kill Laetitia?" Gunning wanted to know. "It's ludicrous! She can be deeply annoying and we've all wanted to chuck her from a height, I know, but these are men who are unacquainted with her. And have nothing to gain from her death. Anything you feel you ought to declare, Letty? You didn't get involved in reprehensible activities when you were here in the spring?"

She shook her head in bewilderment.

The inspector cut in, impatient at the interruption: "I think we've got something! We had an address for Demetrios, you remember, from the daybook? I sent Philippos out to the local café in the Plaka to ask a few discreet questions. He was lucky enough to run into a neighbour with a resentful attitude. Over a second cup of coffee, the man lowered his voice and began to grumble. 'Uncanny, the way those Volos boys always seemed to land on their feet... Business about to go bust and what happens? Some guardian angel gives them an injection of cash and they're off again... Well-furnished homes, lamb joints on the table every Sunday... The missus always has the latest hats...'

"Philippos chose at this point to exceed his instructions, smart lad! He decided to follow up the financial slurs by tracking down a *rival* taxi firm. He took a ride in the cab of one of their operatives. You know how drivers like to gossip... Once around the Acropolis with a captive audience and they'll reveal the secrets of the universe to a complete stranger. So long as he shares the driver's political opinions and has an understanding ear. And Philippos knows how to offer that! Out it all came in torrents! 'That Volos clan! Those buggers get all the best concessions! And that costs money! Where does the funding come from?' The driver quoted Rumour as his source for the assertion that the money was *foreign* money. 'About time someone checked. Turkish money. Could that be legal?'

"It was said that the Volos family came originally from Macedonia. They'd had wealthy landowning relations up there before they were all cleared out. Ottoman Turks by descent. 'Well, half-and-half, probably' was the driver's opinion. 'Registered as Muslim, anyway, and we all know what happened to *them*! Put on a boat and sent back to where they came from, the Turks. To a country glad enough to have them ... so what did they think they were up to—coming back again on the sly and buying up the city?'"

The inspector sighed with satisfaction. "That was the gist of it—the rest was pure scandalous speculation—but my colleague Theotakis is on to it. Shaking out the records department."

He watched Letty's face becoming increasingly stricken as she listened to his account, making connexions. He added quietly: "And I took the step of ringing Andrew's bank and summoning up the chest he bequeathed to Miss Laetitia. They're going to get it out of their strong room. I've ordered it for four o'clock. We'll have a look inside and then send it straight back again. Their delivery service is discreet and armed, I understand. And, depending on what we find, we'll supplement with backup of our own. I'm thinking—as I see you are, miss—that it may well provide us with answers. With motive for two murders ..."

"And one attempted murder," Gunning reminded him.

"A murder as yet unachieved," said the inspector. "A murder well past what an architect might call 'the planning stage.' Works in progress and awaiting further action, I fear, Gunning."

"And, in the circumstances, you won't be requiring...?" Gunning, grim-faced and hesitant, was interrupted by a decisive reply.

"No, indeed. I'm sure we'll all feel easier if Miss Laetitia retains possession of her pistol."

CHAPTER 29

Maria was clearing away the remains of their sandwich lunch, eaten from trays on their knees in the drawing room—a scene that would have horrified the late mistress—when Chief Superintendent Theotakis was announced. The robust clouds of blue tobacco smoke wreathing his head would have had Maud running from the room with her nose in a lace handkerchief. In deference to her shade, which seemed to be never far away, Letty hurried to find an ashtray into which he might tip the spoil heaps of his capacious pipe.

"So this is where it happened?" The superintendent got straight down to business, allowing Montacute to walk him over the scene of Maud's plunge from the balcony. His commanding presence and swift assimilation of the facts of the crime scene reassured Montacute to the point where he felt able to slip into the recital a reference to his experimental ejection of Letty from the balcony.

The superintendent's eyes widened in astonishment, then narrowed again in humorous speculation. "Good Lord! And you condoned this activity, miss? Simulated defenestration by Montacute? A considerable test of nerve, I'd have thought!"

"No danger. My bodyguard was on hand to see fair play," said Letty, indicating Gunning.

Theotakis looked sharply at Montacute's black eye, sighed, and spread his hands in a brief gesture of incomprehension. He hurried on to his next point and, finally satisfied: "No, no. I'm happy to settle down in here," he said when invited to retire to the library. "That chair looks comfortable."

He installed himself in Maud's chair, unwittingly assuming her ancient authority by doing so, and indicated that they should sit opposite on the sofa. He began his summary.

"Autopsy progress, first of all. We have a completed report on the professor (here's a copy), though the examination of his wife is still continuing. Nearly there, I understand, and no surprises—broken spine, cracked skull, other internal injuries. We're just awaiting elucidation and expansion by her own medical man. More than a polite gesture, you understand—it's always a wise precaution where there's a possibility of suicide. It would be reassuring to have an informed opinion on her state of mind. And Peebles is obviously the man to supply this." He hesitated for a moment and affected to refer to a document in his file. "Reason to believe that there is a question of mental instability in the family...a grandmother receiving special care back in an institution in England, I understand from your witness, Percy?"

" 'Loopy as a crocheted doily' was the layman's term supplied by the unfortunate lady's other granddaughter."

"Ah yes...the granddaughter, presently enjoying our hospitality at police headquarters." The superintendent frowned and glanced at Letty. Obviously toning down the strength of his criticism of a colleague, he asked: "Arrest perhaps a little premature, Percy?"

"Think of it as protective custody, Markos," said Montacute. "Family under unexplained attack and Miss Templeton the next one in line, so to speak."

"Well, she gives us no trouble—for the moment. And is the source of much information regarding the two victims," Theotakis conceded. "Very forthcoming on the Merriman marriage. It seems to me we do well to hold fire on the circumstances of Lady Merriman's demise, pending Peebles's statement on the old lady's mental robustness. We must allow that Miss Templeton's opinion may well be informed by personal prejudice. Wretched man! Taking off into the country without a by-your-leave!" he said testily.

"It *is* the weekend, Markos!" Montacute protested. "And I don't think the doctor felt obliged to stand about waiting on *us*. In the circumstances. We...I...did rather muscle in and take over last night. In fact, I remember dismissing him," the inspector confessed awkwardly. "'Nothing more you can do, Doctor...Don't worry, we'll take it from here...' I remember saying. Fences to mend there, I fear."

"You agree, then—we withhold a decision from friends and family until we can speak with full authority? Family members especially are always reassured to hear that there is a comprehensible reason for taking one's own life. 'Suicide whilst the balance of mind was disturbed'...everyone understands and accepts that. Some even have the sense to take it as a warning and look into the state of their own souls."

Everyone nodded sagely.

"As to the professor...the pathologist confirms all he said at the scene of the crime. And crime it certainly was. No chance of this being a self-inflicted injury, of course. You will see from the diagram that the wound to the heart was either carefully and professionally delivered or the result of a 'lucky' stab by an amateur. Impossible to say either way. 'A single thrust penetrating the right ventricle,' according to the doc. Blade? Two-edged, bayonet-style. We have the profile and should be able to have a shot at matching it were the actual weapon ever to come to light. Death instantaneous. Some bleeding, though not copious."

"Height of attacker? Are they able to— Ah, here we are!

"As you see: Assuming the victim to have been standing at the time and the blow to have been dealt underhand"—he demonstrated a typical dagger lunge—"we must contemplate an attacker of the same height as the victim, or slightly less. Between five feet nine inches and six feet are the boundaries they suggest."

They turned over a page of the copy on Montacute's knee and read on.

"The blood samples I took from the foot of the *ekkyklema* when it was parked in its original position...?" said the inspector. "Here we are...Two blood types identified. Animal blood and human, type two, which was Merriman's."

"And if you look on, to the foot of page six, paragraph number twenty-seven, you'll see that the contents of the bottle—the swabs you took out there on the orchestra floor— conform. Animal and type two. Someone trod in the messy cocktail and then walked..."

"Or danced," said Letty. "The chorus was all over that spot, stamping and wheeling. There we were, checking people's underpinnings for secreted swords when we ought to have been looking at their shoes. Were you able to make out a pattern—a shoe shape? High heel? Sandal? Buskins? I noticed that the meticulous Melton had gone to the trouble of having a pair of leather buskins made for himself. A stickler for authenticity. Said he required the extra height the Greek boots give you to tower over the chorus. And he must be about six foot two in his socks anyway."

Montacute shook his head. "I looked at it by torchlight..."

"And I again by daylight," supplied the superintendent, "but I think we have to say—nothing conclusive. Smudges."

"But it does tell us that it was one of the company," said Gunning, confirming all their thoughts. "We're not looking for a person who sneaked onto the site from the street, did the deed, and ran off the way he'd come. It was someone who killed him and then tracked the blood of his victim and the ox blood he himself poured over the body onto the orchestra floor and then calmly got on with his rehearsal. Anybody could have wandered anywhere without attracting attention. Even a scream would have been taken for Melton's tuning up for his dreadful solo."

"Someone, at all events, that you interviewed last night, Letty?"

His question was a gentle urging to search her memory.

"Thetis," she said, "was the only one with visible stains on her clothing. But she handled the corpse—we all saw her lean over it. The robe was voluminous—it could easily have trailed in the blood."

"It did," said Montacute. "I removed it last night from her room and sent it for testing."

"No attempt to hide or wash it, I suppose?" asked Theotakis.

"None. It was lying in a heap on the floor. She just stepped out of it and ran."

"And, as Miss Laetitia was guessing, animal blood with a trace of human and makeup were all in evidence. And all could have been picked up by the contact described. As could the stains, the residue, on her leather sandals, abandoned along with the robe," he added uncomfortably.

"They are being processed as we speak," supplied Theotakis.

"But there's the knife—what did the killer do with the knife?" she asked.

Theotakis sucked on his pipe and squinted against the plume of smoke he released, then admitted: "Nothing found.

We've been combing the whole scene since first light, working outwards from the centre to the furthest point anyone could hurl a dagger." He gave a brief grin. "Troops enjoyed the dagger-hurling bit! And no damage done to the site, Miss Talbot! We even explored the channel under the pavings from the god's pillar to the edge of the *skena*. Any idea what that was all about?"

Montacute answered. "One of Andrew's conceits! It's for the libation ceremony. He dug it to carry the poured wine away from the statue. He intended to make all good after the performance, but..." He shot an apologetic glance at Letty. "I for one thought that was going a bit far. We'll just have to hope no investigator in the future mistakes it for an authentic piece of archaeological evidence."

"Ah. Well, my squad took extreme care," Theotakis said again. "We did find a few inexplicable objects I wouldn't care to mention in mixed company, along with a gold ring, an ancient and empty man's wallet, and a displaced portion of one of the priests' carved stone chairs. My man was quick to spot what that was. I've sent it along to the museum; the restoration department will know what to do with it. But, oddly, in the bushes, we came across some more shattered remains!"

He enjoyed their puzzlement for a moment and went on to disappoint them: "The remains of no fewer than three—I don't exaggerate—*three* of those heads of the god Dionysus. Swept up into a pile, as in a builder's yard. On a site cluttered with classical remains, you could perhaps pardon my chaps for passing on to the next thing, but they saw something that caught their attention."

"Which was...?" Montacute asked dutifully.

"They all had a smashed nose."

"The modern Vandal, like the original, always goes for the projecting pieces of anatomy first," Gunning commented.

Montacute was more suspicious. "Target practice, are you thinking? Any bullet holes?"

"No, nothing of the kind in the area. The noses had been knocked off by a heavy blow."

"Smashed, you say? And three of them? Andrew's bit of classical fantasy?" Letty asked.

"No. He'd hardly have left outside something so valuable as those sculptures would have been if authentic, exposing them to the elements and the plunderers. You can buy those busts in the Street of the Potters at the Kerameikos end for a few drachmas. They're very convincing! People buy them to hide amongst the shrubbery in their gardens. I have one myself," he confessed. "Not Dionysus, though! Too knowing by half! He leers at you. Always seems to know exactly what you were up to the night before! No, I choose to take my morning-after coffee on the terrace under the uncritical and radiant gaze of his half brother, the Sun God, Apollo."

Letty's head drooped. Another piece of fakery—another of Andrew's disappointments. She was beginning to wonder what exactly she would find in the chest when it arrived. More copies? More traps and deceits?

"And the drinking glasses?" Montacute remembered, searching through the report. "The two on the professor's desk? Any prints?"

"Page twenty-five, at the bottom," said the superintendent. "We tested the drink. In both glasses. Nothing but the innocent traces of uncontaminated water inside. Merriman's glass had his prints all over the outside. The other . . . nothing."

"Nothing? What do you mean? Someone must have held it? Drunk from it?" Letty objected.

"It was largely clean, miss. A lip smear on the rim, no trace of lipstick. So, no use to us. No fingerprints."

"So the guest wore gloves, or paused long enough to wipe his prints from the glass before leaving?"

"Are we surprised that the word 'professional' pops into our minds at every turn?" murmured Gunning.

"Frustrating!" the inspector summarised as they reached the end of the report. "Leave a copy with me, will you, Markos, and I'll look through again. There may be two ends in there we've failed to join up."

"Before I leave," said Theotakis genially, "just fill me in on the events of the morning, will you, Percy? I have an article to compose for the *Athens News* and would welcome a few pointers..." He turned to Letty and his smile intensified. "I hear we almost lost one of our witnesses in distressing circumstances? And on this occasion the danger was not simulated?" His tone was warm, teasing, and invited a confidence. Letty decided it would be wise never to underestimate the superintendent. "Road bandits again is what we're saying to the press, by the way. After the Delphi debacle in which the inspector played a starring role the other week, the public will shake their heads in dismay and eagerly lap up a second instalment of a story of ambush."

"You risk spreading panic with an invention like that, Superintendent," Gunning objected.

"No. No. Quite the reverse! Unfortunately, the shots were heard. And investigated! A cliff-top hiker took it upon himself to hurry to the spot and witness from a safe distance the last few minutes of the confrontation. He presented himself at the gendarmerie and gave a very graphic account of events, full descriptions of the participants, the lot! He then communicated his excitement and his anxiety on behalf of the public to the *Athens News*. No, Gunning—our hand is forced! Tourists will be reassured when they pick up the hint, ever so gently dropped, that the attack was premeditated and targeted at one person only. To be precise: at *Montacute,* who is becoming quite a celebrated man and gallant figure about Athens. Everyone is aware that two of the Delphi mob are on the loose and still being sought. Large reward on their heads! All the embassies chipped in—our foreign guests go in great fear of hostage-taking and the like. The public won't question that the thugs are now seeking vengeance in their uncouth and clannish northern way for their countrymen shot dead by the inspector. Unfortunately...can that be the right word?... they mistook Sergeant Perkins for his boss! Wearing his superior officer's Sunday-best outfit—kindly lent to him in order to impress a young lady—at the time of the attack, the sergeant drew the bullets intended for Montacute...Despite being outgunned, the intrepid young officer managed to repel the gang. Oh, there are many intriguing angles to this story! I hurry back to finish it. A word in the right ear and it could make the front cover of *Le Petit Journal*!"

Letty wasn't surprised to hear that her own practical contribution to the proceedings seemed to have been edited out. Ladylike screams and perhaps a swoon would be acceptable.

"Oh, by the way—young Demetrios..." Theotakis paused in his narrative for a moment. "That *was* the lad who attacked me with a feather duster in the hall when I arrived? Still here? I'm surprised he hasn't run off. Don't dismiss him. Leave him in place. He's a channel to the Volos men. May come in useful. I set Records to stir about in their family history as you suggested, Percy. I'll let you know what they come up with."

He turned to a fresh page in his notebook. "Now! Come along, Miss Laetitia! A few words for the editor, please, on your feelings at coming under gunfire..."

"Not sure I like the idea of being confined to barracks," said Letty when the superintendent finally took his leave. "I haven't been gated since I was at school. Still, there's my old room all ready for me here, and if one has to be kept under surveillance it's as comfortable a place as any. Will someone tell Mrs. Rose what I'm up to?"

"Don't worry about the details." Montacute was his old peremptory self. "I'll have a quiet word with Maggie. And look on the positive side—it's likely that you would have been spending most of your time by the telephone anyway over the next days."

She looked at him, questioning his certainty.

"Being Maud! The last thing we heard the old girl say was that *you* were her stand-in, Miss Laetitia. I don't suppose she ever thought it would go so far, but..." He shrugged his shoulders. "Here you are. At the centre of it all. You'll have to field enquiries about ceremonies, memorials, where to send the flowers, and so on, but, more important, it falls to you to reorganise the performance of *Agamemnon*."

"Reorganise the play? Me? Don't be silly! I hardly know it. You'll have to do it yourself!"

He ignored her and pressed on. "I think it was sensible of the superintendent to agree to the rescheduling of the first night of the play. Mrs. Venizelos was much looking forward to it...guest of honour, friend of the leading lady, and all that." He added confidingly: "It would never be made public and you're both to keep very quiet about it—but there is more than a chance that her husband will be accompanying her. The two central priests' marble seats will be held ready, anyway. If Prime Minister Venizelos doesn't turn up, then the spare seat will be seamlessly occupied by the British Consul or his representative. Some smooth-talking gent from the Embassy, Frederick Wentworth if she's lucky, will slip on his white tie, polish up his small talk, and offer his arm to the lady."

"I'd better take notes," said Letty, bewildered and uncertain. "Can it be acceptable to put on a theatrical performance a week after the deaths of the two moving forces behind it? It doesn't seem quite right to me..."

"Our views are hardly important. It's been authorised—indeed, insisted on—by the Ambassador himself, with the encouragement of the Greek authorities. The new First Lady, never forget, is half Greek, half English. There's a lot of symbolism involved, reputations at stake." He gave Letty a bland smile. "I didn't reveal the whole of the First Secretary's briefing to me this morning. But, believe me, a lot of behind-the-scenes fixing has gone on…before Andrew's murder and after it. What we're now saying is: Memorial Ceremony. Let's not forget that, for the Ancients, plays were beyond entertainment—they were a form of religious ritual. An offering from Man to the Gods and all that. They would have approved. It's this aspect that we'd like you to stress when you discuss it with friends, well-wishers, and guests alike…possibly the press. What better tribute to the professor and what better affirmation of the close cultural ties between our two countries? It will go ahead exactly as planned and rehearsed, down to the candlelit party on the orchestra floor afterwards, the champagne and the canapés, the carefully staged libation-pouring ceremony to Dionysus, and all the rest of the pretentious palaver…"

"I see. And if I miss out the last few words, I have my telephone speeches ready. I think I'll take a leaf out of the super's book and rent some space in the local newspaper. Suitably edited as to guest list, of course, I'll ask them to publish the information on the rescheduling. Date and time. Admission with invitation card only, we'll remind them. Though I suspect that security measures will be something fierce on the night?"

Montacute glanced heavenwards. "Heaven forbid that Venizelos should take it into his head to turn up! There have been several attempts on his life over the years—the ones that we know of. It makes any public appearance a problem. Steps are being taken—I can say no more than that—pressures and persuasions being applied...to ensure that the great man does *not* turn up and occupy the centre front row of the stalls on opening night. General Konstantinou, in whose lap has fallen this little surprise package, has come out strongly against an appearance by the P.M. As head of the protection squad, he's declared roundly that the site is a bear trap." The inspector breathed in deeply to emphasise his frustration. "Though you know what the man's like! All pride and dash and courage, even at his age...Listens to advice, smiles, nods, and ignores it. It can make guarding him a nightmare. State ceremonies are not difficult. People expect to see Konstantinou and his lads there in force, reassuring in their uniforms. It's the unscheduled sorties into the outside world for purposes of private enjoyment that land the protecting services with the biggest headaches."

Gunning nodded his agreement. "It was nothing more than a quiet afternoon walk in the park that gave an assassin his moment to shoot dead the Greek king, the first George, just before the war. Up there in Salonika. They caught the man. A vagrant they said. A madman with a grudge."

"Exactly what they would say," huffed Montacute. "To cover up a political assassination. The man was a Socialist and anti-Royalist. Tortured for six weeks before they threw him from a police station window to his death. We're always on the lookout for reprisals. Time for the Royal faction to make its riposte? Their hatred of Venizelos has grown no less venomous during the present King George's exile."

Letty narrowed her mouth in distaste. "I'm finding all these tales of death and vengeance depressing. And the next man who says 'Salonika' in that doom-laden tone gets a kick in the shins from me. Can we get on?"

"Well, you'll understand that if the Prime Minister does decide to throw caution to the winds and enjoy a night out with the wife, we've got trouble. Still, we're not short of seating. That place will hold thousands but the invited audience is small and select. The bulk of the seats will be occupied on the night by hundreds of police and army squaddies, all bored out of their brains, I dare say! Better order in more cushions, Laetitia! We can't risk them getting restive and fiddling with their pistols."

"Well, here's a bit of lighter entertainment!" said Gunning from the window. "If I'm not mistaken, this is Letty's box arriving. Escorted by at least half a dozen of the heavy brigade! And bang on time. Shall I ring for a cup of tea before we embark on Act Three of the professor's dramatic offering?"

CHAPTER 30

The small chest, still wrapped in its ancient rug, slipped neatly back into its place on the library floor. When the squad of bank officials had been dismissed and asked to stand ready for recall in about an hour, the two men lifted the rug by the corners and folded it away.

They stared in disappointment for a few moments at the very ordinary black-lacquered box that was revealed.

"Ah. A useful footstool," said Letty. "Though I think it may have started out as a *larnax*, don't you, William?" She flashed a glance at Montacute and added: "Burial chests. We encountered these in Crete. They usually contain cremated re-mains—charred bones and suchlike."

"Look at the length and the width," said Montacute. "Wouldn't you allow it might be a scroll chest? But the pattern on the lid—what are we to make of that?"

"I've never seen the like . . ." Letty ran her fingers gently over the raised decoration. "The sun in splendour? Or a sixteen-pointed star? Centred on a rosette. More rosettes, swags of greenery, and floral sprays twining their way around the four sides . . . stubby legs ending in lions' paws at the four corners . . ."

"It's postclassical, I think, and rather dull," Gunning decided. "Look, why don't you open it up and hope that the contents at least will be more rewarding?"

"No sign of a lock. I shall just lift it. Are you ready?"

"Here, let me take it. It may be heavier than we think," said Montacute. "Gracious! Give us a hand, will you, Gunning?" The men proceeded to heave up the lid on Letty's inheritance.

They peered down into the box in silence.

"Looks like the contents of a modest hope chest," said Letty. "All the contents of a girl's bottom drawer, carefully wrapped in white tissue paper and piled up in size order. You know—sheets on the bottom, then pillowcases, two dozen hankies so generously embroidered by Auntie Alice on top. There's probably mothballs in there, too, between the layers. But at least there's no doubt that it's intended for me. Look."

She picked up a large envelope lying across the top of the bundles and bearing her name.

Two pairs of eyes were trained steadily on her, willing her to open it.

"I'll read it aloud, whatever it is. Reserving the right to stop if it becomes what I consider personal or none of your business," she said. "It's dated a month ago. Ready?"

"My dearest Laetitia,

"I can't tell you how ridiculous I feel writing this letter of farewell and yet—I tell myself—if you do find yourself reading it one day soon, you will, indeed the world will, be thankful for my forethought and for my intelligent anticipation of dire events. 'He always had an uncanny sense of impending doom!'—yes, that's how you must tell it! But— 'craven fear and a suspicious mind' might be a more accurate diagnosis of my condition. You know me, Letty, to be a belt-and-braces man. I calculate risks, plan ahead, devise a Plan B, flirt with Plan C, and then take the plunge. Here goes!

"I promised you once a Thracian diadem. Here it is, on top, wrapped in tissue paper and cotton wool. Approach with care! It's very delicate and supremely lovely. I like to think the holy bard Orpheus himself (who was from those northern parts) might have worn it or something like it, setting the golden oak leaves atremble as he plucked his lyre. Or perhaps the witch Olympias, Alexander's fierce mother, might have slipped it over her golden hair (I'm quite sure she had fair Celtic colouring—how else to explain her son's flaxen beauty?) in order to emphasise her queenly status over the tribes of rough warriors into which she had married.

"I bought it from a trader in Thessalonike in 1917. He and his shop were destroyed in the fire of that year, though I have thought it worth keeping his bill of sale and you will find this along with other necessary documents in a file at the bottom of the box. The diadem is worth a very great deal of money but I know this will have little significance for you. It is yours now to keep or dispose of however you wish. Knowing you as I do and aware of your views on 'archaeological piracy' (I heard you call it once) I can imagine that, after a few sighs and regrets, it will make its way straight to the museum in Athens with a neat label: Gift of a Philhellene. Am I right? I cannot think that your friendship with that excellent Gunning will have done anything to reduce your high ideals and sense of fair play! (He's very ascetic, you know. He will never know how to indulge you, Letty. Are you sure you can live with that? Better send him out to play while you unpack this lot!)

"The rest of the box (which I will return to last of all) contains a mystery. Run your fingers through the contents and wonder!

"I came by them in the most extraordinary way. During the war I was given light duties by my regiment while I was recovering from war wounds. They gave me a good horse and a wide-ranging brief and a title. I was made Surveyor of Ancient Monuments, Northern Division. I had my French counterparts, and my Italian and Greek confrères, of course. Fellow academics, boon companions, but rivals, not working in cooperation. We were all of us ranging about in buccaneering style, getting shot at quite frequently (from all sides!) for our pains, sticking our *fingers into the recently revealed layers of a fascinating but scarcely known culture. When you have a standing army as diligent as the British, with its tip-top engineers and squads of stout lads needing to be kept busy, set to dig miles and miles of trenches across a countryside rich in history, then what you have is more than a defensive system—you've got the most extensive archaeological dig in progress!*

"They were not officially digging with discovery in mind, of course, but their spades turned up some wonderful objects. Many went straight into the pockets of the sappers. Some (most) turned up in the hands of the Thessalonike dealers, sold for a fraction of their value and the cash squandered on girls, Balkan tobacco, and beer. We archaeologists learned to follow the engineers. We got to know them; they got to know us and our very particular interests. The clever or disreputable among them began to anticipate our needs. (One, I'm proud to say, was seduced by the science of archaeology and went on to become a student of mine after he was demobbed.) We told them what to keep an eye out for, hinted at the most productive places to dig. You can imagine! A latrine to be sited? Well, why not put it over there behind that rather interestingly shaped mound? And as long as you're over there why not divert a couple of your best diggers to take a slice out of the cake as it were... You never know... Crude, but it was war.

"This part of Macedon is thick in burial mounds. Most, it pains me to say, were pillaged many centuries ago by the Goths and their like, passing through on their way south. Local farmers have also carried out exploratory and inexpert digs with interest solely in any contents that glittered. But—we made some valuable acquisitions. Goths and farmers didn't have my trained eye. And I was looking for other things than gold. (Though I didn't sneeze at it on the few occasions it dropped into my lap!) All my finds are accompanied by the requisite drawings, photographs, and locating diagrams. You'll find these in the large brown foolscap envelope. The best of the things I came by, working on the firm's time, went straight to the British Museum.

"You're scowling, Letty! Let me explain! We were in the middle of a war! Five armies tramping all over the ancient land of Macedon, the

Mussulman banging on the front door, the Bulgar on the back, borders shifting under our feet, capital cities going up in flames around us—I did what I could! The province of Macedonia was a very unsafe place for man and beast in those days—to say nothing of its ancient relics. My one thought was to get what I could into a packing case and on board a ship bound for London and a safe haven. If I hadn't sent them, they'd be lost to the world by now or in the Louvre or the Rome museum. And we wouldn't want that.

"*The contents of this chest were acquired by the most amazing piece of luck and by using my own money to perform the transaction. Valuable as they are in themselves, it is their historical significance which is paramount. They will lead you—or any archaeologist you may designate—to the solution of one of the classical world's greatest mysteries.*

"*I'll tell you how I came by them. I say again—I came by them honourably. (Am I protesting too much?) To tell the truth, Letty, I've always had a bad conscience about it. Did I behave badly? You must decide. It didn't feel or look like bad behaviour at the time, though war and the aftermath of war distort perception like ancient glass. They set different standards and expectations, I know that. I am conscious that I speak to a girl whose family traditions are formed by military duty and who, had she been born a boy and a few years earlier, would most probably be now lying in some soldier's grave. But I'm conscious also that, through the clear eyes of youth, she looks forward with courage and optimism. Here the generations divide. And here is one survivor who is alarmed, but in the end content, to be judged by the next generation.*

"*Now, my girl, I dash away a tear and ask you to set aside this letter for a moment and do what I know you're dying to do—unwrap some of the contents . . .*"

Laetitia had been reading the letter out loud to Montacute and Gunning, who had uttered not a single word as she proceeded. She paused and looked questioningly at the pair.

"Our old friend's here in the room with us," murmured

the inspector. "Don't you feel it? Better do as Andrew says. He doesn't take kindly to disobedience."

"He's still playing Director." Gunning smiled. "I think we should obey the stage directions. If you can bear it, Letty? Pretty emotional stuff! Is this something you'd rather do by yourself?" He reached into his pocket for a handkerchief, which she did not refuse.

"No. No. Please, both of you—stay. This letter is personal, yet not so personal that it may not be read out loud. I know he's written it in the expectation that at least William would be present. He sort of says hello, doesn't he? Did I imagine that?"

"More than hello…There was a distinct dig in the ribs aimed at me in there, I think," murmured Gunning.

"No," said Montacute. "I'm sure you're right. He loved an audience. The professor is playing to the crowd. An invited crowd. And I, for one, intend to have a front seat in the stalls. Not often the investigating officer manages to get a *victim's*-eye view of events leading to a murder. And it's happened to me twice in twenty-four hours. He's going to spin out the suspense but in the end he'll give it to me—the name of his murderer! But first, this is—and I do need to remind all of us of this at this point—a crime scene. I'm going to ask you both to put any wrappings or envelopes into this wastepaper basket and any precious items onto…um…this velvet cloth." He took a length of dark blue cloth from the top of a piano and spread it on the floor by Letty's side. "Now. Where do you want to start?"

"Here. With this." Letty picked up the topmost wrapped object. It was flat and thin, the size of a pudding plate, and surprisingly heavy in her hand. "Wait a moment, there's a label stuck over the seam, a sort of seal."

"And there's something written on it." Gunning was already reaching for it. He looked at Letty in surprise. "It says: 'No jammy fingers!'"

Letty made a soft sound and looked aside. The men caught each other's eye and decided it would be kinder not to notice her emotion. It was left to Gunning to strip away the tissue paper. They each nervously warned the others to take care and not to expect too much and then all held their breath as the object came sparkling out into the light.

No one spoke as Letty took the diadem from Gunning's fingers and very gently shook it. Tiny oak leaves trembled, individually fixed and gathered into natural clumps around a central twisted band. Here and there amongst the thickets of leaves glinted perfectly formed acorns nestling in their striated cups. The whole had the wild exuberance and freshness of a wreath hastily put together by a child playing under forest trees in the autumn. And yet the natural form was inspired and controlled by the delicacy and precision of a master goldsmith.

"Golly! Eat your heart out, Fabergé!" Gunning murmured. "It's gold. Thracian gold. So dark it almost has a bronze tinge to it. Are you going to try it on, Letty? I'll fetch a mirror."

"No!" She stopped him with a gesture. "I wouldn't have the impudence. What queenly head last wore it? I look for but I don't see a hair trapped amongst the foliage... Besides, on *my* hair, you wouldn't even notice it. Same colour. You'd just think I'd been rolling in the hay and offer me a brush. No one should wear this but Demeter herself or... a dark-haired girl. I can imagine it gleaming amongst black tresses..."

She caught the inspector's eye and knew without words that he was seeing it around the shining head of Thetis. He took it from her gently and laid it on the velvet cloth.

The second offering was encased in a red leather jewel box. Letty held up two objects to glimmer in the afternoon sunshine. Pendant earrings, again of dark gold, they trailed from central discs in swags of blossoms, fruit, and berries. Letty held them up on either side of her face, where they dangled from ear down to shoulder, and she smiled. "Lovely! But something else I can't wear...unless I have my ears pierced."

She passed one to each man and they gasped and exclaimed over the stunning workmanship and then put them down alongside the diadem.

"Percy, your turn, I think," she invited, and the inspector eagerly chose a package.

From a plain brown cardboard box he shook two matching medallions into his hand and held them up between finger and thumb. "Exquisite! Do we have any idea of the subjects?" he asked. A kindly schoolmaster who already knows the answer to his question.

"So that's where he got them!" Gunning exclaimed. "Andrew was showing me the illustrations for his work on Alexander last winter and these two featured—as line drawings. Perhaps he took a rubbing! I know who they are. The gentleman with the handsome profile and jutting beard is Philip, King of Macedon and Alexander's redoubtable father. And who knows? The lady with the deceptive simper and aristocratic Greek hairdo may well be his mother, snake-worshipping, murdering Queen Olympias."

Gunning placed the two images side by side on the cloth. Ignoring each other, the faces stared out in opposite directions.

"In life as in art!" he commented. "If this is indeed Olympias, poor old Philip finds himself head to head once again with his killer! With the wife he feared and hated. And who shall blame him! Can't exactly have been conducive to marital bliss—having to kick the snakes out of the marriage bed every time you wanted to exercise your conjugal rights. I think we can be certain it was she who arranged her husband's assassination. And who arranged for the tidying up of loose ends afterwards. The killer, having put a dagger into Philip's ribs, was caught fleeing the scene, according to the ancient sources. He was hacked to death by elements of the pursuing royal bodyguard—conveniently before a confession could be wrung out of him—and his body was ceremonially exhibited in public. The reaction of the bereaved queen to all this was interesting! It was blatantly to place a golden crown on the head of the assassin as he hung dead on his stake of shame. Pausanias, his name was. And he was a royal bodyguard, ironically. The queen gave Pausanias a magnificent send-off: She had him cremated and buried with all honours. Hard to make a clearer statement than that!"

" 'Thanks, mate. Job well done. So sorry you had to die in the process,' " said Montacute.

"Oh, good Lord!" Gunning exclaimed, brow furrowed in concentration. "It happened in the arena at Aigai, the ancient capital! Aigai. The king was stabbed to death just before his ceremonial entrance to the theatre. He was standing in the wings, waiting for the trumpet fanfare to sound."

"An unsafe place for powerful men, it seems—the theatre," Letty said quietly.

"Are you suggesting that the god of the place gets bored and likes to stage his own real-life impromptu dramas? Ghastly thought! Better say a few prayers, pour out a jug of bloodred Mavrodaphne to appease him before we go public with the play next week, are we thinking?"

Montacute grinned. "*I* leave all that nonsense to the superstitious—as I suspect you do, Gunning. I put my trust in Theotakis and his gun-toting squad."

"But who guards the bodyguards?" said Letty. "The men paid to stay close by and carry arms? The trusted ones? I wonder what persuasion she used on poor, silly Pausanias. If it *was* Olympias at the bottom of it all. Can we believe that? Look at her head! So matronly, so proper. You'd say butter wouldn't melt in her mouth!"

Gunning shuddered. "The woman was a raging Maenad! Follower of Dionysus. Adept in the arts of poisoning and other less subtle methods of killing. She'd have made Lucrezia Borgia look like a Girl Guide. She had hundreds of her own people horribly tortured and killed. The death she prescribed for the rival for her husband's affections, the young girl Eurydice—and her child—is too sickening for words. If this is indeed Olympias, we're looking at the face of the most wicked woman in history."

He picked up the medallion and held it in the palm of his hand, examining it closely, suddenly less certain. "But, I agree, this lady before us does have a certain saintlike innocence about her. I wonder if it *can* be her? Anyone like to argue that this is the rival who ousted her from the number one position at court? Young Eurydice? So briefly Queen of Macedon? Did Andrew leave us an inventory?"

"Probably in the promised envelope in the bottom. Do you have a feeling Andrew's leading us on some sort of a wet-afternoon's treasure hunt?" Letty poked about in the chest and extracted three small objects of equal size, shape, and hardness. "These would appear to come to hand next."

She unwrapped them and set them up in a row.

Gunning began to laugh. "I think he's just answered your previous question on identity, Letty! Here we have the family portrait gallery, no less! Exquisite ivory carving!" He took in his hands in turn each of the three ivories, the heads no larger than the average doorknob, yellowed with age and somewhat pitted but clear representations of the subjects in life. "Look at the detail and the liveliness of expression! Some Michelangelo of the ancient world produced these. But they're not idealised! We're seeing these characters warts and all, you'd say! And the artist solves the problem of identity. Here is Philip, and no mistake! Impressive, shrewd, a bearded warrior. And do you see the nick in the brow over his right eye? It's not an accidental chip—it's his famous old war wound! And the younger man...I was wondering when *he'd* make an appearance. Handsome, clean-shaven—and that's very unusual for a man in his early twenties, which this one appears to be. Who in the world wouldn't know *his* face? The unruly hair, the arrogant tilt of the head, the eyes gazing always over the horizon, the sensuous lips slightly parted in some emotion—"

"What a modern face! He could be my brother!" Letty interrupted. "I've seen his double many times. Chaps like him tend to row at stroke in the Cambridge boats—humming a little Bach as they swish along."

"It's Alexander," Montacute said, mesmerised by the little carving. "And look here, if I place the third one right next to him—"

"Oh, goodness! Yes! That's where he got his looks! The artist's seen it...the resemblance. She has the same arrogance, the same wide eyes—though hers are focussed, clever eyes—the same full lips...It could only be his mother, Olympias. And yes—view her in profile and it's the lady on the medallion," Letty confirmed.

Montacute chortled. "I could draw up a suspect identification sheet from these! Monsieur Bertillon could get out his measuring tapes and, citing nose length, distance between eyes, width of brow, pronounce with certainty on identity! A shared identity. Philip, from this evidence, could well not have been the father—but this was certainly his mother!"

"After all these centuries we're looking at them again: the world's wickedest woman and her egomaniac of a son," murmured Letty. "And they have the faces of angels."

More coins—silver tetradrachms and gold staters—and more medallions joined the earlier ones on the velvet and were followed by intact and ravishingly beautiful pieces, all small: a painted funeral vase; a slender *lekythos* in which Letty could almost persuade herself she could still smell the heady eastern perfume, long diffused; and, the last object to surface, a golden wine cup. It was decorated with the graceful form of the young Dionysus, who, with enigmatic half-closed eyes, was about to take in marriage the hand of Ariadne, princess of Crete, abandoned by her Athenian hero, Theseus, and here modestly hiding her lower face with her veil. Their wedding guests, satyrs and nymphs, posed lasciviously in the background, anticipating the drunken revelry, their limbs entwining with the wandering tentacles of ivy and grapevine as well as with each other's.

Stunned by the glitter and glory of the workmanship crowding the velvet cloth, Letty leaned over the chest and took hold of the last of the packages. Small and light. As she removed the last layer of tissue paper, she almost dropped it in her shock and instinctive shudder of revulsion.

CHAPTER 31

Recovering herself, Letty held it out, cupped in her hand, and managed to speak in a reasonably calm voice. "Ah. If these are what I think they are, then they may be part of the original contents of the chest. *'Larnax'* was my first thought and I say again: funeral receptacle. Similar in purpose to the ones we encountered in Crete, William. Andrew was telling us: The Macedonians cremated their royal dead and buried them in the mounds that still dot the landscape—perhaps these burnt fragments were what he found in this particular chest?"

"Looks awfully like the stuff I periodically dig out from the bottom of my toaster." Montacute looked at it, unimpressed. "But what's that larger piece?"

Letty stroked the slender brown object gently with a trembling forefinger and smiled in wonder. "That's as near as I shall ever get to shaking hands with Macedonian royalty. It's a finger bone."

"Proximal phalanx," Gunning specified, peering at it. "There are some more quite large fragments but that's the clearest. I wonder who it belonged to?"

"I think we can guess who *Andrew* thought it belonged

to!" Letty said. "He's been leading us through this! Softening us up for a revelation we might just be unprepared to swallow. That would always be his style . . . catch his audience in a story-telling web. And I think we've earned the right to read his ex-planation, don't you? The brown foolscap envelope placed so teasingly right at the bottom? Shall we have a look?"

"By all means. But, Letty, go back to his letter first, will you? I think we ought to obey the stage directions!"

"So dramatically and meticulously given," agreed Monta-cute. "Let's travel a little further with the professor, shall we? Play his game a little longer?"

"The smallest and the choicest of the artefacts I came by, I leave for you, Letty. Should you choose to spirit them away to England, you will find them eminently smuggleable. I'm sure you'll find a way if you wish to. Assigning ownership in these politically troubled times will not be easy. I've done my best to supply the paperwork you may need: bills of sale and deeds to the property west of Thessalonike where they origi-nated. All these glorious things and, indeed, the estate where they came to light are yours because you will know how to deal with them. It's im-portant that you have the house and the acres of farmland surrounding it. It is the most exciting prospect I came across in my months of fossick-ing about in Macedonia. And, if all continues to go well, you may as-sume ownership and arrange to dig where you please. I have moved heaven and earth over the years to bring this to a satisfactory conclu-sion. I've wheedled, promised, threatened, bribed, and suborned, and finally, I have the deeds in my hand and am about to slide them into the foolscap envelope.

"It's a distressing story and any surge of triumph and pride in my achievement is instantly swamped in a wave of sadness. I met Soulios Gunay (the name will mean nothing to you) in an antiques dealer's shop in the old city in the centre of Thessalonike in 1917, during the war. He was selling and I was buying. Modestly gratified and standing between us was the dealer. Difficult times. Gunay, a local farmer, was

experiencing some financial problems and was offering for sale the lekythos you will have admired. I bought it, for a generous amount, and both he and the salesman were pleased with their day. I chased after Gunay when he left and we had a cup of coffee together. You can imagine with no difficulty what we spoke of!

"The upshot was—he invited me to visit him at his farmhouse west of the city and look over some more of the goods he might have for sale. His family had farmed the land—which was extensive and productive of olives and fruit—for many generations, and had made a habit of collecting together any objects found on the property. He hinted at precious metals and exquisite workmanship. These objects he was holding in reserve, fearing some dreadful turn of events which might make it necessary for him to realise their value in the saleroom in order to finance the farm. In this he was right, except that his fears did not go far enough... Poor chap! He was to lose both his assets and his land by a cruel blow of Fate.

"No! Why blame Fate? It was by the hand of Man that he lost his belongings, his livelihood, and eventually his life. He lost everything at the stroke of a pen, the signature of a fellow countryman he trusted, on a document drawn up far away on the shores of Lake Geneva in Lausanne. The Exchange of Populations Treaty of 1923.

"Swept on by my army life—I was needed back in Athens—it was more than five years before I saw Gunay again. I rode up to his farm and found him in despair. His papers had come through. He and his family—he had a beautiful wife and two charming children—had received their marching orders. Since they were registered as Muslim, it had been decreed that they were to set off at short notice, load whatever possessions they could onto a cart, and get themselves to the port, where they would board a Turkish boat bound for a homeland which was not their homeland. They were assured that a similar property and life would be provided on the other side of the Aegean Sea. Their own farm would be taken up by refugees of Greek origin who were performing the same manoeuvre in the opposite direction.

"There was no arguing with the authorities. Two armed Cretan *gendarmes were standing about looking threatening, to make sure the family obeyed the decree. I had to act quickly. I don't think I gave it a minute's thought. I made him an offer for whatever artefacts remained to him and for the estate itself. I agreed to pay him at the port in gold coinage before he sailed. He trusted me. He handed over—for what they were worth—the title deeds to his land. I was as good as my word. Don't ask how I came by the sum of money. I'll just say the British presence still in the area had large reserves at its disposal and my credit with the Government has always been good. Shh! If the words 'cloak and dagger' come to mind, then your mind is a very suspicious one! But if events have put this letter in your hands, it doesn't matter much anymore, so I'll say: Suspect all you wish, double your suspicions, and you'll be in the target area . . ."*

"What *is* Andrew suggesting?" Letty broke off to ask. "That he was some sort of a . . . spy?"

"Undoubtedly," said Montacute. "An agent of the British Government. Political? Military? High up, I'd guess, judging by his free-ranging ability to go about the place under cover of archaeology, buying up property, defying the Lausanne convention, and borrowing army resources. I don't like to think of the favours Merriman must have called in . . . the arms he must have twisted to get what he wanted . . ."

"Not high enough, it seems from what he says next!" Letty read on, skimming down the page. "Problems . . . sticks poked into wheels . . . applications delayed in Embassy in-trays . . . I can imagine the sort of stuff. It must have driven him mad! No wonder he was spending so much time in Greece. But perseverance, or whatever else it was he was using, seems to have paid off. Listen!"

"And the upshot is: The house and land are now officially recognised as mine. I don't feel too badly about this because I bought with honest intent. Many properties were the subjects of deals of a clandes-

tine nature at this time, and many unfortunates did not do so well as Gunay—though his luck was to run out. Sadly, the family died on the journey to Turkey. There was a report that the boat on which they travelled was ravaged by disease and all the passengers died of it—those who had survived the appalling crossing. Gunay's land has not suffered. Assuming ownership as I did, I arranged with the local placement bureau for Turkish refugees—a farming family—to be installed for a reasonable rent, and there they still are.

"And the point of all this . . . and the part which gives me a twinge of guilt . . . is the answer to the questions I'm sure you've been asking yourself as you unpacked these pretty things. There are at least four tumuli on Gunay's land, possibly more. Indeed, I have, through the years, imposed on the tenant farmer the task of preserving the mounds untouched (on pain of eviction). And I have checked periodically that he has performed in accordance with my instruction. One tumulus I believe to be in its original state, undisturbed by man. I want you, Letty, to disturb it!

"You will have guessed that I have identified this site as the burial place of the Kings and Queens of Macedon. Its excavation could be as thrilling to the world as the revelations from Mycaenae. And as rich in gold! It was the custom of the royal family to be buried near their capital of Aigai (some few miles distant from the site) and in a particular way. The bodies would be cremated, the burnt remains gathered up and placed in a ceremonial box—a larnax—and placed along with sumptuous grave goods in a space built and decorated as a room. I have caught glimpses of the most wonderful wall paintings in other tombs of Macedonian nobles, but sadly raided and defaced. In the middle of a battlefield, all I could do was pop the lid back on and mark them down for further and better investigation at a later date! Heartrending!

"If I am to believe Gunay—and I do—the portrait busts and the collection of gold and silver coins you have just examined came to light in one of the mounds on his property. Having no interest in archaeology and not much knowledge of the ancient history of the region, he kept most of the objects and sold off some others but left the remaining tomb

untouched—'Just in case...' Safer than a bank, he must have assumed.
Not an unusual sentiment from a countryman. I've known peasants
the world over who keep their precious goods under the mattress or
buried in a jar in the back garden!

"You will have assigned a date to the coinage..."

Letty gave a guilty gasp. "Have we?"

Gunning ran his fingers through the coins again, paying
attention to the markings. They waited for his decision.

"Up to and including and quite possibly beyond Alexander," he pronounced. "But how would *we* know? The professor's playing with us again! The coins minted after the death
of Alexander the Great, who was number three in the lineup of
Alexanders, went on showing his face on the front, usually in a
lion's-head helmet, through the reigns of the next two or three
kings, including his own brother and his son, the number four
Alexander, who reigned very briefly. It would take an expert to
judge. Here, Montacute...what do you make of this one?"

Montacute peered and shrugged. "You're asking the
wrong bloke. Takes me all my time to tell a half crown from a
two-bob bit. It's silver with the goddess Athena on the back
like a lot of the others, but it seems a bit different from the
rest...The face on the front is Alexander, I'd say, but he looks
rather sterner, older than usual—and what's all that outcrop
behind his head?"

"I think it's meant to be a ram's horn, signifying the god
Ammon. He's done up as Alexander the Deified. He's turned
into a god—one presumes *after* his death."

"Let's assume we've failed that little test and go on to the
next thing, shall we? Letty?"

"...which leads me to infer that the burial represented here, by
these goods, postdates the death of Alexander, and yet is a royal funeral.
His mother died some years after her son. Subject to further investiga-

tion on the spot, I'm suggesting that we have here some of the contents of the tomb of Olympias. One of the raided mounds?

"But the intact tomb? I say again: It was the strong custom of the Kings of Macedon to be buried near their home, alongside their fathers and grandfathers. No one has ever located the last resting place of Alexander. He died in the East, in Babylon, and there are convincing accounts of the mummification of his body by experts in the practice. It is suspected—and for excellent reasons—that he was laid to rest, possibly along with his great golden catafalque, somewhere in Egypt. In Alexandria? At the oasis of Siwah? The world's most energetic and knowledgeable archaeological sleuths have dug about in every likely Egyptian location. Even Schliemann with his acute nose for buried gold snooped about and came up with nothing! Merriman toiled for years! Exploring, following up clues and whispers of clues, and I found: nothing. Significant? Letty, it's my opinion that if there had been something to find in the burning sands, it would have been found.

"I'm proposing that the remains of Alexander lie in the deep soil of his homeland, alongside his grandfather, his father, and his mother. The richest man the world has ever known was returned there by a supreme piece of sleight of hand on the part of his general Perdikkas and buried with all honours by his own mother. And Olympias would not have stinted on the splendour of the funeral rites for her beloved and only son! Perhaps she had the taste to refrain from the ceremonial cremation and bury her son intact as she last saw him: his youthful body preserved forever, covered in gold and draped in purple cloths.

"I'm proposing that the golden youth you so despise is, at the end, in your hands, Letty!

"Deal with him appropriately, won't you? Many, many men have admired him down the centuries, you know! And still do! Ask Gunning!

"I resist my impulse to plead for him one last time—to stress the enormous influence he was on the ancient and, indeed, our modern world, the way in which he spread Hellenic culture throughout the East, replaced Persian and Egyptian magic with Greek science and *mathematics, introduced Greek ideas of medicine, law, meritocracy, and justice. I, instead, appeal to your female and romantic instincts. He loved literature, he loved his horse and his dog. He was courteous to women and generous to his friends, and he was fond of his mother."*

"Pompous, patronising old juggins!" Letty exclaimed, thrusting the pages at Gunning in disgust. "Oh, Andrew! If you're still lurking about somewhere in the shadows—pin your ears back and hear this! That metallic tinkling you hear is the remaining scales falling from my eyes! Romantic female indeed! I expect clever, ambitious Olympias had the same problems with the men who surrounded her, running her life. How dare you make such assumptions about me and my prejudices? I begin to think you scarcely know me... *knew* me. Do you seriously think my opinion will be softened because a man loved his horse and was fond of his mother? Do you think I'm capable of such triviality of thought? And incapable of understanding that a man can be a baffling mixture of goodness and evil? Good Lord! I don't have to assign the man a pass mark in humanity as judged by the morality of a later era before I'll be prepared to dig up his bones!"

Montacute frowned, irritated, she thought, by her tirade. "Shall we let Gunning read on for a while?" he asked politely.

Gunning was ready to pick up the hint.

"He was a good son. He constantly sent home the pick of the plunder from the cities of the East he conquered to his mother in Macedonia. Olympias wrote to him regularly and he always paid attention to her advice and suggestions. And he had a sense of humour you would have appreciated. One day, needled beyond reason by his mother's demands, he waved her latest letter at his friend Hephaestion and grinned. 'She asks a lot in return for the nine months' board and lodging she gave me,' he joked.

"This, Letty, is the elusive man I have tracked for years, eager to

find some last trace of him. With luck, I shall be here beaming and smiling when you return from Crete and, when the moment seems right, I shall propose that we go north and make the discovery together. If things do not go so well for me, it will be up to you to implement Plan B.

"You must go under the aegis of the British School and liaise with the Embassy. You will find many people eager to help. Use all authority you can come by and insist on an armed guard. Take all possible care.

"I think I saw him again the other day. And again yesterday. Soulios Gunay. I had thought him dead. If this is indeed Gunay, and not my shocked imaginings, why is he in Athens? He should not be here. Why does he not greet me but stare through me, turn, and hurry away? I'm sick with apprehension—"

"Heavens! Go on, William," said Letty.

"I can't. There is no more. It ends abruptly. Not even a signature. The folds are not even—it looks as though he pushed it hurriedly into the envelope."

"The banker's men were probably rattling at the doorknob," suggested Montacute. "You've seen them—they run on clockwork and wait for no man!" He glanced anxiously at his watch. "Had enough excitement for one day? Prepare yourselves for one more! Miss Letty, pass me that paper knife from the professor's desk, would you?"

Knife in hand, he turned his attention to the black chest. "Before this gets carted off . . . you're forgetting what our lawyer friend told us. The professor was insistent that the new owner should pay some attention to it as well as the contents. And I think I know why."

"Hey! Stop that!" Letty called. "You're not going to attack it with a paper knife! I won't let you!"

"Only way. I'll be discreet. The lid, I couldn't help noticing as I cracked my muscles to lift it, is extraordinarily heavy. The surface is painted to look like ebony, but really it wouldn't deceive an infant. That's a coat of relatively modern paint, I'd say, hardly more than camouflage. And if what I'm thinking is right, then it should scrape off very easily. Because I'm also thinking that paint never adheres very successfully to..."

He stretched himself out on the floor and scraped away at a section of the underside of the back of the chest, a spot between the two rear legs, his head at a neck-breaking angle. "...to metal," he grunted, after a moment's suspense.

He lifted his head. "To be precise: to gold. It's gold, man! Solid bloody *gold*!"

CHAPTER 32

The Cretan gendarme who manned the front desk in the police lockup checked for a second time the visitor's credentials. In no hurry, he studied the immaculate figure standing aloof, uncommunicative, glancing in a marked manner at his expensive Swiss wristwatch and tapping his shiny black shoe.

"And does the prisoner wish to see *you*?" the Cretan asked with deliberate lack of deference. He had decided the visitor represented everything he despised. "She has not requested it."

"Immaterial," said the visitor. "Get on with it, man!" He passed an envelope over the desk.

The explanatory note, written in Greek, on headed paper, and signed with a flourish, was studied with exaggerated interest. Careful and professional to the bone, the policeman required the visitor to take a seat while he made further enquiries. He ignored the sigh of irritation and avoided the haughty stare that greeted his decision. "Constable!" he called over his shoulder. "Take this note to the commander."

He turned to the visitor, who had chosen to remain standing. "And now we wait."

They waited.

Ten minutes later a note came back from Superintendent Theotakis, and the bearer was Philippos.

We have to allow this. I'm sending you an English-speaking officer. It is a condition of the meeting that the sergeant sits in on it.

With all precautions taken and the female wardress standing by, the visitor and Philippos were escorted to the cells.

Thetis looked up eagerly from her book when they appeared. "Oh, I say! This is as bad as the London omnibuses! No visitors for hours and then four turn up at once! Are you an execution squad? A bridge party? I don't wish to be unwelcoming, but—this is a very small cell, you know. There's only space for two at a time with me in here...Let's see... I'd say the sergeant is an essential element— Come in, won't you, Philippos? Good to see you again! Tell me—how's little Ioannis?"

Philippos grinned, happy to play her game. "He's much better, miss. The honey and lemon worked a treat."

"Relieved to hear that! It can't have been much fun... Now, Kyria Papadopoulos can occupy her usual chair in the corridor, which leaves standing room only, I'm afraid, for the envoy from the British Embassy."

The constable with the keys fell in with her suggestions, locking her in with the two men and ambling off again down the corridor.

Thetis turned with outstretched hand and a mischievous smile to the visitor. "My husband! Agamemnon! *'I hail my lord, safe watchdog of the fold,'*" she added, slipping at once into their edgy onstage relationship. "Sorry I can't offer you a red carpet on which to place your polished Oxfords and—nowhere really to sit. You'll just have to plonk yourself down on that stool over there. Now...Philippos, do you know Mr. Melton? No? Then allow me to present Geoffrey Melton from the Embassy.

Diplomat of some sort, he tells me, and—actor. Yes—actor of some distinction. Mr. Melton finds himself in the enviable position of playing both my husband and my lover. Geoffrey, this is Sergeant Georgios. He speaks excellent English, so watch out! If you try to bully me, I shall have a witness. Now, gentlemen, what may I offer you?" She glanced around the austere cell. "Boiled sweet?"

Melton sighed and muttered Agamemnon's line: " *'There speaks my wife and the speech—like my absence—far too long!'* "

Suppressing a bark of laughter, Philippos selected a cherry flavour from the bag she held out and, murmuring his thanks, went to perch on the end of the narrow bed. Melton rejected the sweet but made the misjudgement of automatically taking up her offer of a seat on the small three-legged stool she politely pulled forward for him. He folded himself onto it like a piece of collapsible campaign furniture and found he was unable to work out what to do with his long legs. His knees were level with his ears. He separated his legs and, obviously judging that by this masculine pose he risked presenting an offensive spectacle, he at once brought his thighs together and slid them to one side. Not happy with this effeminate side-saddle presentation either, he began to wriggle. His eye level was a good three feet lower than that of the prisoner who chose to stand, with regal composure, looking down at him.

"And now, why don't you tell us why you've come?" Thetis said with the annoying briskness of a nanny. "And *do* stop squirming, Geoffrey, dear!"

Her tone triggered a violent reaction. With a shout of rage, he uncoiled himself and rose to his feet. He kicked the stool away from under him, narrowly missing Thetis, who neatly sidestepped. His angry presence filled the small room with such menace, Philippos leapt up, alarmed, gun in hand and trained on Melton. Melton held out a palm to him in a restraining gesture and began to speak in a voice only just in control. His words were icy, his sentences so short as to verge on rudeness. "Sympathies for your predicament...efforts being made at the highest level...negotiations with the Greek government..."

Thetis calmly tilted her head up and looked him in the eye. "Geoffrey, if your next sentence doesn't include the words 'at liberty,' I don't want to hear it and shall ask the sergeant to escort you off the premises."

He gave her a tight smile. "Then I'll quickly say: 'at large.'" He clicked his heels and sketched a sarcastic bow. "And very soon. The papers are being prepared as we speak. You will be released, probably on bail, pending further enquiries, and will be expected to keep to a designated address and timetable. Part of your timetable—and this is important—will involve the further preparation for and appearance in the first night of the play *Agamemnon* in the role you contracted to assume and in the associated ceremonies that have been planned for the hour or so afterwards. Everything is to go ahead exactly as discussed." He stared at her for a moment. "Don't get into any more trouble or attract the attention of the forces of law and order in any way. The queen's presence is a vital element, I'm sure I don't need to remind you."

"No indeed, Geoffrey. But the king it is who dies, remember. The queen lives on for a while, to die upon another stage."

"There's no consolation for you in delay."

"No, I agree." And she added in her theatre voice: " *'There's no escape, my friend, not by delaying.'* Cassandra, poor dear, knew that."

" *'But the last moment should be savoured,'* " he responded with the next line of the play.

" *'My time has come. There's nothing to gain by flight.'* "

" *'You have a brave soul and a gallant heart,'* " he concluded, and nodded to Philippos, indicating that the interview was over. He turned to the door and then paused dramatically. "But the discipline of a headless chicken!" he spat.

Puzzled and beginning to lose the thread of the dialogue, the sergeant, in relief, shouted through the bars for the key.

CHAPTER 33

They watched from the library window as the banker's men struggled out carrying the chest, wrapped up securely once again in its concealing old rug, the ends stuck down with parcel tape, and manoeuvred it into the back of the van they had parked in front of the house.

Letty expressed all their thoughts: "Do you think it's perfectly safe? It must be worth a king's ransom."

"Andrew considered it safe. Yes, I think it's better off in a strong room in a basement somewhere under Syntagma Square. Not so much fun as on display here, but—safe. Not so the owner, though, I'm afraid. Perhaps we should stuff *you* away in a basement under Syntagma for the foreseeable, Miss Laetitia?"

"You think this Gunay fellow has returned after all these years...can it be six?...in search of what he considers still to be his? That he's cutting a deadly swath through the Merriman family and its heirs?"

"It's hard to see how he might think he could retrieve anything," said Gunning. "Andrew has everything signed, sealed, recorded, and tied up in red ribbons. Impossible for Gunay to get his hands on it again in the political and legal circumstances. He must know that."

"They're off." Montacute turned from the window with a sigh of relief. "Oh, yes. I'm sure he would know that. Which would make his behaviour doubly puzzling. But there, in the back of that lorry, goes a very compelling motive for murder. And I'm thinking there are those closer to us than Gunay, whoever and wherever he is, who might have got wind of Andrew's intriguing possession and aim to draw some benefit from it."

"Don't be silly!" Letty protested. "If that's so and you're looking for a suspect, you need look no further than me! *I'm* the one who's inherited all that. No one else benefits."

"But no one, including yourself, was aware of that—beyond the lawyer, of course, and if my judgement of that tight-mouthed young man is right, he wouldn't vouchsafe the time of day to a watchmaker. On the other hand..." Montacute speculated, "if the said young man were to suddenly discover he's in love with Letty, cosy up, and seek her hand in marriage, I might admit to a suspicion. In fact *any* man fancying his chances with Miss Talbot and having prior knowledge of Merriman's affairs must find himself topping my list of suspects," he said, with a mild smile for Gunning.

"You forget, Montacute, that as far as the world was concerned, Andrew's estate went to his widow and, inevitably, after her death, to the nominees of *her* will. Go and arrest Maud's six cousins!"

"I've got *one* of them under lock and key...just give me time!"

Letty was saved from hearing more skirmishing by the shrilling of the telephone.

Montacute answered. "Markos! Oh, really?...I hope you sent...Philippos...good. Put him on, will you?

"No, no! Stay!" he told them, grinning, as they prepared to withdraw. "You'll want to hear this! Miss Templeton has had a visitor. She spent a compassionate five minutes with Geoffrey Melton.

"Ah, Sergeant! Tell me all that passed..." He began to frown. "You're sure that's all? Just quoting lines from the play at each other? Well, I suppose it saves you having to think up conversation... And he told her to stay out of trouble with the law... she was needed onstage next week. And her release was imminent. Just being the Embassy's mouthpiece, then. No more? How did they interact? He kicked a stool at her? Well, one can't be surprised. Is she all right?... He called her what? A fowl without a head, did you say? Are you sure of that? Give it to me in the English he used... Ah, 'as undisciplined as a headless chicken.'... Oh, it's just a saying..."

He signed off and put the receiver down.

"Well, the news of her release has been broken. I'm wondering why Melton should have been chosen as the Bringer of Jollity. They're not particularly friendly."

"That's wonderful!" Letty said. "When may we expect to see her come home... back...?"

"I've decided to leave her there for another night and get her out in the morning. Perhaps you'd come with me to spring her from jail, Miss Laetitia? She can help you with the arrangements for the funerals and the rescheduling of the performance from here. Can you get along with her in the circumstances?" he asked awkwardly. "She can be a bit difficult."

"Of course I can. There's a mountain of work to be done and not much time. It'll take two. And Thetis has established some good connections in the city. That will help. There's no rivalry between us, you know, Inspector. No bad blood. No one's going to have hysterics or the vapours or show their claws."

"I'm sincerely glad of that," said Montacute. "Wouldn't know where to place my money."

"But why leave her there overnight? If the papers are in order, you could let her out straightaway, couldn't you? If I'm required to stay in this sorrowful house I'd be glad of company. I'd rather not be here by myself after dark."

"Oh, of course." The inspector rubbed his forehead and for a moment his exhaustion showed through. His face was looking increasingly unshaven as the five o'clock shadow crept over it, darkening the hollows, and his eye had taken on a sinister depth of colour. "Sorry, I wasn't thinking. Could be alarming, I suppose, rattling around in this great barn. I'm leaving you a constable, but I understand that while he can fight off flesh-and-blood villains, he mightn't be much use against an attack of the heebie-jeebies and the collywobbles."

"And the blue funk—don't forget that!" Letty advised kindly. "All conditions to which we females are woefully prone," she explained to Gunning.

The inspector looked at Gunning. "Well, that settles it. Gunning must move in. Hardly right for him to do that if you're here by yourself, Miss Laetitia—all alone with your nyctophobia—but if Miss Templeton were here as well, you could all chaperone one another. It would be just about acceptable in the circumstances. Very well. We'll go and get her out. While Gunning goes up the hill to fetch his kit."

He blinked and groaned wearily. He ran a hand through his springing black hair and touched the skin below his eye with exploratory fingers. "Lord knows what she'll say when I arrive at the jail looking like this! Sporting all the colours of Van Gogh's unwashed palette."

"Oh, if you turn up rattling a bunch of keys in your hand, I don't think she'll even notice," said Letty comfortably. "And if she does—well, she's a lady! Far too polite to draw attention to a temporary facial blemish honourably acquired in the pursuit of your professional duties."

"Gracious, Percy!" Thetis exclaimed cheerfully. "I could stick a frame round your head and call it 'Sunset Over Sounion.' What a shiner! Come inside and tell me about the exciting day you must have had. Letty! Good to see you! I say— it wasn't *yours*, was it? The fist that put the inspector's lights out?"

Montacute sighed and ignored her. He indicated that Letty should occupy the chaperone's chair outside the cell door and went inside, leaving the door ostentatiously open. Thetis settled down on the bed, feet together and hands folded on lap, and left him standing in the middle of the floor. She looked up eagerly. "Do you want me to sign something before you let me go? Are we off, then? May I go back to Kolonaki? Have you worked out what really happened to Maud?"

Puzzled by the inspector's silence, she turned to Letty. "You didn't crush his windpipe as well, did you?"

"We've all had a taxing day, one way or another, Thetis. Bear with the inspector, will you? He's tired and trying to find words to discuss a bad situation without giving too much offence. I think."

"Exactly so." Montacute nodded at Laetitia, and turned from her, effectively cutting off further contributions to the interview. Letty took a book from her bag and pretended to study it with absorption.

She stifled a yawn as Montacute fumbled his way through the formalities of release and bail conditions. She listened with greater attention when he embarked on a summary of the lawyer's information regarding the contents of the two wills, her eyes on Thetis's face. Astonishment and—yes—she was quite certain—guilt in swift succession were what she detected. Thetis had been unaware. No one was *that* good an actress.

"Stop!" said Thetis. "Will you repeat what you've just said, Percy? Forgive me—it's a lot to take in when you announce it baldly, just like that. But perhaps it was your intention to startle?

"So," she said slowly, when he'd gone over the ground once more, "I'm to have a ridiculously large amount of Andrew's money? To invest? Sorry. I'm rather shocked to hear this."

"So will be many people," said the inspector. "They will ask why. What could possibly be the reason for such generosity? Why so much to a girl he'd known for so short a time? A girl not related to him by ties of blood? They may begin to speculate as to the very particular ties that linked Sir Andrew with the recipient. A passing and illicit amour? That will be the first thought. Those who have been close to the professor will reject it. There have been many such in his life, and they are not remembered in his will. What can be so special...? Their thoughts may circle back to their original consideration: a blood tie—"

"Oh, Letty! You told him! How could you?"

"No. Miss Laetitia did not reveal your guilty secret, Miss Templeton. I'm a detective. You seem to forget that. I detect. I'm not guessing, I'm deducing that you had told Sir Andrew that you were expecting to present him at some time in the next few months with an offspring. And by your words just now, you confirm it. Gentleman that he is, he took the appropriate steps to provide for you. Am I right in my conclusions?"

Thetis nodded miserably. "I shouldn't have told him. He shouldn't have done that. I can manage. I couldn't have known that he'd die..."

Strange mutterings, Letty thought, were coming from Thetis. She seemed to be taking no pleasure, not even experiencing any relief, at the thought of her financial security. In her situation, with no reliable income and a child in the offing, Letty would have grabbed the money with both hands and made a run for it to somewhere congenial. The south of France was a good place for a war widow with child to live a full and pleasant life undisturbed by public opprobrium. Everyone you met down there had something to hide. Letty decided to draw a few survivors of disaster into the conversation to encourage Thetis, when she had her by herself again. And she wondered, not for the first time, why the inspector had dragged her along to witness this disturbing scene.

"I shall give it back . . . No, no, it would revert to Maud and my appalling cousins, wouldn't it? I shall give it to charity. Such a sum would fund the new gynaecology unit at the hospital for ten years. Seems appropriate in the circumstances." Thetis was muttering to herself and Letty had to concentrate to work out what she was saying.

She was relieved to hear Montacute voice her own opinion: "You're not to say that! Remember the source of the money—Merriman's—not yours. It should be spent exactly as he wished, which is clearly in the support of his unborn child. The *child*, Miss Templeton! This should be your only consideration. Even knowing the man as slightly as I did, I'm ready to say he would have delighted in its existence, would have become the father that every new soul deserves."

Letty wriggled in her seat. The passion was rising in Montacute's voice in what she considered an unseemly and puzzling way. He was a police officer after all, not the girl's confessor.

"Nonsense, Inspector! Where have you been living? Cloud-cuckoo-land? Andrew would have considered his financial contribution sufficient to expunge his guilt and responsi-

bility and would have erased the whole affair from his mind...
The man was still in love with Letty, you know— You hadn't
guessed? After all these years! Maud was certainly aware...I
think even Letty suspects. No, he wasn't thrilled when I gave
him the news. He would never have mentioned the other possibility, of course...far too principled—though that is the
path I decided on when I encountered his lack of enthusiasm."

"'Possibility'?" Montacute seized on the word. "What do
you mean? Speak plainly, woman!" His voice crackled with
anger.

Letty suddenly realised why she had been dragged along.
She was the safety chain in the express train. He had known
how the interview would go; in fact, he had been resolved on
pushing it in a direction he had decided on and away from official witnesses and police note-takers. He had been aware that
this unprofessional head-to-head confrontation, stoked as it
was by unguessed-at passions, might speed madly out of
hand. A timely tug on the alarm handle available to passengers
in every carriage was the only gesture that could stop the express if it seemed to be running away.

"It is by no means uncommon in these enlightened days,
Inspector, for women to take matters into their own hands
in such circumstances and bring them to a satisfactory conclusion."

With these words Thetis had lit his blue touch paper, evidently. "Satisfactory?" he bellowed. "For whom? For the poor
little mite, losing its life on a backstreet abortionist's table?
The mothers lose their own lives, too, as often as not! I've
closed down dozens of these butchers' shops! I've seen the results of their activities. I forbid you to contemplate such a
double murder. For such it would be."

"I had in mind something a little more civilised," retorted
Thetis, refusing to respond to his rage. "A Swiss clinic...
something of that nature."

"The same butcher's shop but with white uniforms and ether instead of sacking and brandy," he growled. "Have you no regard for new life? The child is there. It exists. It will grow into a person worth having. It is a gift and you might one day, if you can curb your scything tongue and learn a few pleasant ways, find a father to share it with you. A good man who would love it as his own—"

"Fat chance!" Thetis rolled her eyes and sighed. "There are no such saints in this world."

"Bloody well are!" Montacute snarled shockingly. "I've known one! The best!"

As he seemed about to take hold of Thetis and shake her— or worse—Letty pulled the handle.

The two women listened as Percy stomped away down the corridor. He had calmed himself at once at the pressure of Letty's hand on his arm and, mumbling an apology for his ill-considered language, granted them a few minutes' private conversation. Letty settled down next to Thetis on the bed.

"Thetis, are you going to tell me why you were lying to the inspector? And to me? *I* rather expect to be lied to, but I'm amazed that you should try it on with old Eagle-Eye."

"Lying, Letty? I'm not sure—"

"Come off it! It doesn't exist, does it? You're not pregnant—not the slightest bit! Were you deceiving poor Andrew in order to—what's the word?—shake him down? Bet that's it! He was halfway to divorcing Maud anyway...he just needed a bit of a push. Maud was the stick. And you provided the carrot."

Thetis looked at her in surprise. She gulped. Tears began to trickle down her pale cheeks. Letty did not look away. Actresses, she understood, were adept at this sort of thing.

"How did you guess?" Thetis whispered faintly.

"Not difficult. Had I been desperate and in your position, it's just the sort of underhand trick I can see myself playing. I'd have told myself, if conscience had troubled me, that I would be giving Andrew exactly what he had always wanted and a much happier situation. I might even have believed it. It might even have been true."

"No. You mistake me. I meant—how did you guess I wasn't pregnant?"

"What? Don't be so thick, Thetis! Crikey, I'd thought you an effective conspirator and woman of the world, but I begin to change my mind. You're really nothing but an amateur. You invite me to hunt through your undies in the bag in which you've packed your contraceptive device. Latest model! Well, that gave me pause for thought, after your revelations the night before. And then you come down to breakfast and tuck into scrambled eggs, goat's milk, bread and honey…coffee… and Lord knows what else you mightn't have put away if the inspector hadn't interrupted. You don't behave like any other woman I've ever seen a few weeks into a pregnancy!"

"Ah! I couldn't resist the scrambled eggs!" Thetis smiled and dabbed at her tears. "I should have accepted a small crust of dry bread and a cup of herb tea. The *device,* as you call it—I'd forgotten it was in there. Hadn't used it in ages. They're jolly messy and notoriously fallible anyway. I decided to become pregnant. And, Letty—all the signs were there! For a time. But, perhaps I willed it so. If there was deceit, I was myself deceived before anyone."

"It's the power of the mind," Letty said with a rush of pity. "I'm constantly told. It can harm or heal without our consciously willing it. Even women—perhaps especially women, it's asserted—fall unwitting victim to unseen mental forces. But you have a much deeper medical knowledge than I…you must know this?"

Thetis admitted as much with a wry smile. "It's called

'amenorrhoea.' You'll find it in any medical textbook. You'll find it amongst battlefield nurses. The stress, of course. It can come as an astonishing but blessed relief. But it never occurred to me that this phantasma was presenting itself to *me*. Why would it? No bombs. No shells. No screams. No blood."

"No physical stress, I agree, but I say again: The mind exerts its own powerful control over our bodies. As does guilt," she thought it right to add.

"I *wanted* it to be so," Thetis whispered. She shuddered. "All that rubbish I had to listen to from Montacute! The even worse rubbish I had to repeat to him! Trapped by my own lies. Regret that! Now he thinks I'm a monster. When ... the reverse is true ... I'd give my own life to save a baby's ... any baby's ... Truth is, Letty, I'm rather desperate to have a child." She turned eyes dark with pain on Letty's shocked face. "You've no idea how heart-wrenching it is to work every day with the newborn scraps! I can save them, cuddle them, love them, but they aren't mine. I desperately want to hold one of my own. Can't explain it. It's a feeling that takes you over, consumes you. Nothing you can do to fight back."

"Have you spoken of this to anyone?"

"I'm alarming you, aren't I? I'm sorry! A blurted confession to a passing acquaintance in a prison cell—it's not exactly the right way of going about things these days, is it? I should be reclining on a tapestried chaise longue whispering my thoughts to a cigar-smoking, bewhiskered old gent who'll say, 'There, there ... You're suffering from a touch of hysteria, my dear.'" Thetis gave a snort of derision. "Who would understand? No one would be prepared even to listen, Letty. *You* clearly don't want to hear this but at least you're not hurrying away in disgust."

"I hope you'll think of me as a friend, Thetis, and allow me to say: Wouldn't it be a good idea to distance yourself from daily reminders of what you long for?"

"No!" The exclamation was shocking in its intensity. "I won't give up my hospital work … It's what I'm good at. I do believe I'm achieving something. I'm not just meddling—do-gooding—standing by with the jug of hot water, you know, Letty! I observe, I reason, I record. I'm going to write a book to challenge the whole ethos of the so-called experts. You can't understand! The ignorance! The unconcern! The waste of life!"

Uneasy and not perfectly comprehending such violent emotions, Letty asked calmly: "So, you chose Andrew to complete your schemes?"

"It didn't feel like scheming, if that's what you're suggesting. But, yes—Andrew, I'm sure I don't need to spell it out for you, would have been the most enchanting of fathers. And, I had thought, a wonderful husband." Thetis looked away, hiding any glimpse of a sudden self-awareness from Letty, but Letty's sharp ears picked up the slight overemphasis in her tone as she struggled on: "I was very fond of him. Truly. But how can I begin to tell that Puritan out there that my sinning was not the result of overwhelming temptation—it was committed with malice aforethought? And then the fruits of it lied about? He'll assume I fabricated the whole thing to avoid a murder charge. He'd be counting the Commandments I've broken on the fingers of two hands! I'd be consumed in an outpouring of fire and brimstone."

"His reaction was certainly beyond reasonable," agreed Letty thoughtfully. "Didn't you think? The man's a volcano. And they go off, not because of any outside trigger, but because of an internal pressure. I think that little outburst tells us more about *him* than you, Thetis."

"Well, I was jolly glad you were there to put a bag over him." Thetis sniffed. "Do you think I have grounds for an official complaint?"

Letty studied her, wondering whether the girl could possibly be as unaware as she appeared. "You owe that man an apology and an explanation," she said coldly. "He's a good man. I don't like to watch you making a monkey of him. At the very least, you've been wasting his time. I'll tell him myself if you don't."

Thetis sighed. "Oh, very well. I'll do it. Tomorrow."

"And this time I refuse to stand by in your corner holding the towel. When he turns up in the morning I shall make an excuse to leave the two of you alone to slug it out together toe-to-toe. I'll give you ten minutes. That should be long enough."

CHAPTER 34

Thetis had a charming way with her, Letty decided, hearing her embarking on the twentieth telephone call after breakfast. Low and full of controlled emotion, she responded warmly, she was grateful and understanding, she cut seamlessly from the pleasantries to the important part of her delivery: the rescheduling of the play and a repetition of the invitation to attend, warmly given.

Taking a breather, she replaced the receiver and consulted her list. "We're doing well, Letty. Halfway through those with telephones and no one's backed out. It's a case of: 'Oh, by the way, could I possibly bring along my colleague...my sister... my dentist...a party of ten...?' Ghouls! It's going to be the social event of the year and for all the wrong reasons! They've all heard the stories! Just wait to hear the hissing intake of breath that greets the appearance of the body in the bathtub when it trundles onstage! How are you doing?"

Letty put her pen down. She'd brought a folding desk into the library to join Thetis, who'd assumed command of the telephone. "Oh, getting through it! I'm fighting on two fronts. There's the funeral front and the first night. Funeral's no problem. Small and discreet ceremony on Wednesday and the undertaker does just what his name suggests. Good man. Flowers...church...all arranged. I'm engaging that Greek priest with the wonderful voice—Andrew would have loved that—I've sent William off to the Cathedral with a note." She looked at her watch. "I'm guessing he's stayed on for the service. All that incense and the thunderous baritone—it ensnares him every time!"

"What about the play?"

"Hardly much of a problem. I have Maud's notes and address book." Letty laughed. "The woman could have been a field marshal, you know. Her army would have been always in step and well victualled."

"But marching in the wrong direction."

"Well, I'm appreciating her attention to detail. We're promised cushions by the hundred...Geoffrey may be reassured that his pig-sticking can go ahead; if he's got the heart for it, he'll have his carcase."

"Knife?" Thetis asked. "Are they going to let him have that knife back?"

"Not much use without it, I'd have thought. I'd better check with Montacute...No refreshments, I decided, for the crowds. Just champagne and canapés for the Prime Ministerial party staying on afterwards for the libation ceremony. Maud knew how to delegate, which makes things a bit easier...She notes that Hugh Lattimore has this in hand. The ancient and holy ceremony comes under 'Stage Effects,' apparently! I suppose that's right. He's down here as 'plaiting the ivy wreath for the god's head' and unblocking the drainage channel. Lucky old Hugh! I'll go over it with him, just in case...his last effort with the body in the bath rather misfired. It would have made better sense historically, I suppose, to have arranged for the ceremony to happen *before* the play...you know, an offering up...Hope you like what you're about to receive, Lord Dionysus...More authentic? What do you think?"

"Oh, don't let's even consider it!" Thetis spoke sharply. "Keep it simple! We can't contemplate a single change at this stage. It would be disastrous!"

"Just a thought. A rambling, silly thought. I agree—we probably want to avoid having the possibility of P.M. of Greece parading about before a full audience, playing High Priest, lit by arc lamps, the target of all eyes, and Lord knows what else. He must stay discreetly within the protection of his thick marble seat, flanked by bodyguards, until the arena's been cleared, and then stroll across the orchestra to pour the wine and trickle the honey. I think we'll leave out the honey, don't you?"

"Good idea. As I say—keep it simple. But the wine, Letty... have you...?"

"It's done. Almost. I've asked the merchant to offer us some dramatically bloodred stuff. His darkest. He thinks I'm a bit mad and insists on bringing round a few samples to make sure he's got exactly what I want. I thought I'd order a whole case so the party can join in. Always such a disappointment, I'd have thought, to watch good wine being poured away into the earth, even if it is going to the god. Might at least enjoy a drop ourselves!"

Thetis paused and then, in an offhand voice: "Oh... Letty... thinking of personal security... the gun you so kindly took from my bag—do you think...?"

"Of course. Hang on, I've got it right here."

Letty fetched her satchel and took out the gun and the toffee tin full of ammunition. She found she was surprisingly reluctant to hand it back to Thetis and watched her slip it into her pocket with regret.

"Do be careful, Thetis! It's loaded. I fired off two bullets, but then I cleaned it and reloaded. Safety's on but be aware that you've got a full complement in there. Didn't you notice the added weight?"

"Glory be! You actually *fired* this thing? At *someone*?" Thetis said. "I'd better put it away in the drawer."

"It was a kindly act you had no idea you were committing, Thetis, putting that gun in my hands! I owe my life and that of Sergeant Perkins to it. . . . Have you ever been to Eleusis?"

Before she could finish her story the telephone rang.

"But of course," purred Thetis into the receiver. "Please put her on . . ." She turned and pulled an excited face at Letty. "Helena! How good it is to hear you . . ."

Letty grinned and went to answer a light tap on the door. Demetrios stood there looking anxious. "There's a wine merchant down below wanting to see the mistress about a case of Mavro . . . Mavro . . . ? He's got the samples you asked for."

"Ah! The Mavrodaphne," said Letty. "That's what I ordered. Go and tell him I'll come straight down."

"He's at the tradesman's entrance, miss," said Demetrios, and hurried off ahead of her.

Thetis put down the telephone, smiling and pleased with herself. She was still smiling when Montacute thumped up the stairs and came into the library.

"Excellent news, Inspector!" she said. "I'm about to make your day! Where's Letty got to? You must both hear this."

She went to the door and shouted down the corridor for Letty. "Letty! Come on back! Great news!" Seeing Maria whisking by, she called to her. "Maria! Find Miss Letty, will you? She's probably gone to her room."

"No, miss, she's downstairs with the wine man."

"Oh, Lord, yes. Tell her to come straight back up to the library when she's finished."

"Whatever's going on?" The inspector was mystified.

"Percy! I can't keep it to myself a moment longer! Oh, where *is* Letty? I need to share a triumphal hug!" Thetis eagerly took the inspector's hands in hers. "I shall have to make do with you!"

Montacute leapt backwards in alarm and remarked that he was quite prepared to wait to share the news, whatever it was, with Letty. Disappointed, Thetis restricted her chatter to an outline of their morning's work. Finally, sensing they were running out of acceptable conversation, Montacute remarked that it was odd that Letty had not arrived. Where had Thetis said she'd gone? She'd not left the house, surely, against all instructions?

Thetis shuffled her feet anxiously. "Well, no, Percy. She wouldn't do that. I know what she's up to. She's hiding somewhere about the place."

"Hiding? What do you mean? Who's she hiding from?"

"From you and from me. She read the riot act to me at the jail yesterday and told me I'd better get on with a confession I have to make to you . . . or else. We agreed that as soon as you appeared this morning she'd discreetly make herself scarce and leave us together for ten minutes."

"Confession?" Montacute leapt on the word. "You're confessing to something more? Something that's going to take ten minutes to express?"

"Oh, Percy! Ten hours wouldn't be long enough!"

Montacute looked at his watch. "I have observed Miss Letty to be a punctual young lady with a keen sense of timing. We may count on a further eight minutes. You'd best get started."

CHAPTER 35

So . . . Tell me: how long have you lived in Athens, Mr., er . . . ?"

"Gunay," the man sitting beside her in the taxicab replied. "Soulios Gunay."

The youth driving the cab flicked a glance behind him and grinned unpleasantly. Lacking a roll on the drums, he underlined the announcement with a sharp tug on the steering wheel. Letty bit back a yelp of pain as she was jerked sideways against the gun barrel sticking into her ribs. Large old service pistol. Six-inch barrel. Probably a Smith & Wesson. She'd heard him click the safety off. How firm was the trigger? One more maniacal swerve like that, a moment's inattention, and she'd be a late entrant on her own funeral list. In a momentary hysteria, she clearly heard the priestly baritone sounding out the Hymn for the Dead. Surely they wouldn't bury her alongside Andrew and Maud? Letty shuddered. Her mind was racing but her body was restricted in its movements, unable to take action—an uncomfortable struggle which resolved itself in a futile attempt to chatter. She had decided that she might be being kidnapped but that was no excuse for bad manners.

"How do you do, Mr. Gunay? Laetitia Talbot. How nice to meet you at last. Why don't you tell me how I may help you? If you wanted to speak to me confidentially, you only had to ask. We could have gone to a café. There's a—"

"I had envisaged a quieter place," he interrupted. "For our private conversation. Take the next right, Stefanos."

Letty was speaking in her Cretan-accented Greek, Gunay with what she guessed to be a heavy northern intonation. If they both kept it simple, they would probably understand each other. In any case the gun was speaking volumes.

"We are going out into the country. A pleasant way to spend a Sunday morning. I thought we'd give Eleusis a miss today . . . You, I understand, have already left your mark on the architecture of that charming spot. No, we're going in the opposite direction. To Sounion. The 'Sacred Headland.' The temple to Poseidon on top of the cliffs is a sight to behold. I have it in mind to make an offering to the Sea God. He is a greedy god who likes to take more than is his due. His foaming maw is always open. The place gets very busy in the afternoon but at this hour, when the population is mostly on its knees or cooking lunch, we should have it to ourselves."

Well, she could be forgiven, Letty thought. The man had looked every inch a merchant when he presented himself at the back door. The doffing of the hat, the slight bow, the obliging smile. The unemphatic invitation to approach his stock in the boot of his car, just around the corner. And then, suddenly, the gun in her side, an arm twisted behind her back, and a one-way fare to a deserted beauty spot.

Letty reasoned that this man sitting next to her—unemotional, unremarkable—was the one behind their troubles. The deaths of Andrew and Maud—and soon her own—were to be laid at his door. If he'd attacked her in the street, if he'd ranted and raged and struck her, she would have been better able to fight back, she reckoned. Anger calls up anger. His obdurate calm, his cold assurance, were those of a priest leading a potentially skittish heifer towards the sacrificial altar. But

Letty had caught the blood scent of previous victims and would stretch out her neck for no man.

"Not *another* cliff top? You're running out of inspiration, Mr. Gunay. After such a dramatic start, you let yourself down. The body in the bathtub was certainly an eye-catcher, the defenestration of Lady Merriman a piece of considerable daring. But so far you seem to be botching my disappearance. I'm wondering why you're pursuing me with such vigour? Why me?"

As she asked the question, a very convincing answer came to mind.

"Why me?" she repeated more firmly. "What have *I* ever done to deserve such treatment?"

He smiled. A handsome man at one time, she judged. Dark hair, greying, lean face lined with care, the leathery skin of a man of the outdoors. The eyes were concealed, evasive, hard to read. She glanced down briefly at the hand holding the gun. Immaculate. Possibly even manicured. Not a man of the soil, then. His light summer suit was of the best-quality linen, his shirt fresh and starched. In the close proximity in which he was holding her, she detected a whiff of French cologne and a trace of expensive tobacco.

"You have *done* nothing. But you *have* something of mine, I understand."

"Ah! That wretched little Demetrios! He hurried to you with the news of my surprising inheritance? I'll have something to say to *him* when I get back!"

"No. He has gone away. He has performed his last service. For you and for me. Unless . . . But do not think too badly of the boy—it is thanks to him that you are not already dead."

"You're going to have to explain that."

"My plans were, as you have guessed, to kill Merriman and his charming wife. Two lives. And then his daughter. Three lives."

"But I'm *not* his daughter! Never have been!" Letty burst out in relief. "This is an awful mistake you're making!"

"Yes. I know that. Thanks to Demetrios, I know that. He hurried to tell us our error. Unfortunately, our attempt to kill you off at Eleusis was already in train before he could transmit his message to me. His father and his uncle were already on the road and had their instructions. He was concerned for you. Split loyalties...always a danger...it was time to withdraw him. I wait, but do not hear you enquire about the health of the man you shot?"

"I don't give a spit for his health! Why on earth should I? He didn't have one of my bullets in him anyway...Your useless gunman was hit by a shard of marble from a temple column. The goddess intervened. Blame it on the goddess!"

The car veered wildly again, throwing her violently to one side and back again as the villainous-looking youth at the wheel made his views clear.

Gunay reached forward, slapped him on the head, and hissed a vicious warning. Then: "You must forgive him. You were speaking of his cousin."

"So. If it's my lack of sympathy you've got a grouse about— put me out here and I'll walk back. As penance. On my knees, if you like. I'll guarantee to visit the patient in hospital and apologise, as you're so concerned...Big bottom, hole in the head, he can't be too difficult to find...Cousins! Troublesome nuisances! Look—if it's a vendetta against the Merriman family you're waging, I don't qualify. I say again: *I'm not a blood relation.* Not a drop in common. I can offer you five male cousins from the female line all arriving by boat next week," she added hopefully. "And well deserving of extermination—golfers all, I understand."

"No deal," he said.

The car hit the open road and accelerated aggressively eastwards in the direction of Cape Sounion. The donkey and foot traffic they encountered veered off the road out of their way, alerted by the blast of the horn. Gunay clicked the safety catch back on his gun and slid it away in his pocket, confident, Letty realised with a chill, that there was no possibility of her escape.

"No deal," he repeated. "Lady Merriman's cousins are of no interest to me. But there *is* an arrangement I want to offer you, Miss Talbot. In return for your life."

CHAPTER 36

Montacute raced back upstairs for the third time and asked for Theotakis's number.

"They've got Laetitia Talbot," he said.

He spoke clearly into the telephone so that Thetis could follow the conversation. "That little shit Demetrios lured her to the back door. She went off with the wine merchant, according to the maid who was out at the back emptying a brush pan into the bin. She didn't see the car—it was parked around the corner—but she heard it. Engine left running. No, of course not! I've checked with the firm. The owner is at home having his breakfast and was planning to come over to see Miss Talbot in an hour or so. Not much of a description from Maria. Can't blame her. He looked just like what he said he was...presentable...well-off...Greek. Medium height, dark skin, Sunday-best clothes...Yes, I know...just like a thousand other blokes out and about this morning...A quarter of an hour ago? Let's say a bit more." He glanced guiltily at Thetis. "Say twenty-five minutes. I was distracted. Roadblocks? Can we get the roads watched? No idea in which direction... could be anywhere."

He listened for a moment, his eyes on Thetis's stricken

face. "Look—is this the right moment, Markos? Can't this wait? I must get out and— They've found something? The name I gave you matched one on the records. Which records are we talking about? Turkish? Ministry for Exchange and Resettlement? Soulios Gunay. Tobacco farmer. Ah. And the Ministry of Internal Affairs…related to the Athenian Volos family. Demetrios! I'll have his hide! Do what you can in the Plaka, Markos. You've got their address. I'll screw a few thumbs around here."

As he put down the receiver, Montacute's eye was caught by Letty's satchel hanging on the back of her chair. He opened it up, running a hand through the contents. "Well, that's one thing at least! It's gone. Her gun. She must have got it in her pocket."

Thetis opened her eyes wide, then shook her head in evident puzzlement.

The sound of a cheerful rendering of "Onward, Christian Soldiers" on the stairs made them freeze with dismay and indecision. Gunning came in and shot a look at the silent pair, noting that they took an unnecessary two steps away from each other on his entrance. "Ah!" he said, raising his eyebrows, "this is where I leave in haste, having scribbled a note: *Vicar called. Sorry to have found you out.*"

"No, Gunning. It's a case of offering the other cheek. Here it is. Take a swing."

"Good Lord, man! What are you on about? And please put your ugly mug away. I've seen enough of it for a lifetime." He looked at them steadily, the good humour fading from his face. "Now—which one of you is going to tell me where Letty is?"

"Not your fault, Montacute. Nor Letty's, most probably." Gunning glanced at his watch and spoke swiftly, his voice tense but positive. "I'm not going to blame her. She does take risks, but always well-calculated ones. If she's been snatched, it must have been done with some skill. And you say she's got her Webley with her? Could do more harm than good. And it's very likely this Gunay, we're saying? Seems quite a leap...but where else do we have to jump? Tell me what steps you've taken..."

He listened without interrupting to the inspector's recital, then: "Now, a minute's quiet planning is worth more than a week's thoughtless dashing about, Letty always says. Roadblocks are going up, but we're half an hour behind them at least. And it's a Sunday...officers not at their desks, cars being serviced...you'll have a job to get anything like a useful level of response. They're well out of Athens by now. The other centres will be alerted? Corinth? Piraeus? North of here, what have we? Delphi? Marathon? Oh, Lord—Thessalonike, if you keep going long enough. Your chaps have details of the car they're using? Cream Delage, isn't it? No one will be particularly concerned that a foreign girl's gone off for a jaunt in a jazzy motorcar with a gentleman. Happens every Sunday."

"That's how they'll see it," the inspector admitted. "Probably stop them and sell them an ice-cream cornet."

"Montacute, I'm assuming the worst possible intentions behind this disappearance. And this is a pretty weird sort of bloke we're contemplating...I'm trying to put myself into his skin...We have to think he's going to kill her and dump the body. His first thought was a cliff top at Eleusis. That sets his style. Simple. Dramatic. Undetectable. But he's a devious villain—clever enough to get hold of Letty, and she's not easily deceived...*I'm* thinking that *he's* thinking we'll cross that scenario off our list. And he seems to be a bloke who has to get his own way. He won't have enjoyed being thwarted—and by a woman—made to look foolish in front of his men. One of them injured...He'll want to win the last trick. With a flourish. 'This is how you do it, boys!' he might even be saying at this moment." Gunning frowned, wriggling his way down into the criminal depths of an unknown man's mind.

They waited to hear his conclusion.

"Look, Montacute, you may think this sounds a bit mad, but—what would you say to zipping off to Eleusis when Philippos gets here with the car? That's where we should direct our firepower. He's going to get it right this time. Cock a snook. He's taken her to Eleusis."

Montacute nodded grimly. He seemed to be aware of what the suggestion had cost Gunning, whose every instinct must have been to put himself in the front line, dash off instantly, and carry out his own plans.

They all started on hearing a car hoot by the front door. Montacute paused long enough to say decisively: "That's Philippos! Agreed, then. I'll go westwards, on the Eleusis road. The port and the southerly exits will be covered. Possibly not the east—leads nowhere. But then, that may be what he's looking for...a road going nowhere..." He hesitated for a moment. "Why don't you get the Dodge out and see what you can see along the Sounion road, Gunning?"

"Good idea."

The words were crisply delivered but they rang hollow. They avoided each other's eyes, each aware that there were no good ideas left to them, merely futile time-occupying schemes. But if the troops are agitated, give them a channel for their agitation.

As the inspector clattered down the stairs, Thetis and Gunning exchanged anguished looks.

"Letty has some regard for him, you know. And so have I. If anyone can find her, he will," Thetis murmured. "But—Sounion! End of the world! Frightening place! I'm coming with you, William."

"No. No. You stay here by the telephone, Thetis."

"Then at least give her my good news when you find her, William. And you *will* find her—hang on to that! Wait a minute . . . I'll run down to the garage with you and tell you the news as we go."

It had all taken so long. Gunning had fumed as he hurried around the corner to the garage, butting against the tide of noisy worshippers turning out of church. He'd cursed as the car failed to start, had forced himself to breathe deeply when he was held up at a crossroads. He only began to cease gnashing his teeth when he was at last out on the open road.

No easy progress here either, though. He'd taken the road to Sounion, following the rocky spine down the centre of the promontory. Skirting round the bleak bulk of Mount Hymettus, he had expected the road to be empty but after a few minutes, when he spurred the car up to twenty miles an hour, he had to rein it in to negotiate a file of mules laden with firewood, a herd of sheep, and several black-clad old ladies with supercilious stares, riding sidesaddle on donkeys and determined to keep him from overtaking. He was on a wild-goose chase but activity, almost any activity, was the only response to his tension and he couldn't stop. He pressed on, heartsickeningly certain that Laetitia was lost to him. He was tempted to pull off the road and offer up a quiet prayer but dismissed the corrosive old superstition as a weakness.

He pulled off the road anyway to calm himself and check the distance on the map. He sat watching as a herd of silky black goats poured past him. Big and muscular, they raised their heads to stare at him with mad amber eyes. They buffeted the car, they scratched it with their horns, all deliberately done, he was sure. They went on their way, resenting his foreign presence in his stinking modern machine. He breathed in with relief when the last one had gone by. A trace of their feral odour lingered, laced with the scent of herbs they had crushed under their hooves. He moved away from the car and sat with his back to it, hearing nothing now but the distant call of a shepherd boy, echoed close at hand by the desolate cry of a meadow pipit. The countryside had turned into a garigue of low scrub starred with golden crocuses and autumn cyclamens. To left and right, where the land dipped down into a valley bottom, he caught glimpses of a dark blue sea.

A sea which pounded itself into foam at the foot of sheer cliffs. Cliffs which stretched for mile after desolate mile. Would he catch sight of her body? What had she been wearing? He had no idea. It was well over an hour since she'd disappeared. Time enough to reach the headland. There was nothing he could achieve now. He was alone and adrift with his loss and grief. He plucked a small pink flower he didn't recognise. Persephone had been plucking flowers when she was snatched away by Hades. And her mother, Demeter, had been struck down by sorrow, but she had roused herself and travelled the world, shouting, fussing, demanding that her daughter be restored to her.

Gunning got up and went to the car. There was a frivolous little silver flower holder in the back, he remembered, for the delectation of the passengers. He filled it with water from the flask he'd thought to throw onto the backseat before he left and popped the flower into it. Well, it was no gardenia, but he resolved to give it to Letty when he found her.

He looked up on hearing a donkey's hooves clipping along the stony road surface. A solitary man smoking a cigarette and coming towards him from the direction of Sounion stopped to peer inquisitively at him. They exchanged greetings and the man threw his cigarette butt away. Gunning politely stamped it into the dust and then, on impulse, took his packet of cigarettes out of his pocket and offered them. The stranger got off his donkey and took one with a smile of thanks, and they puffed amiably together for a moment.

"Car broken down?" the man asked.

"No. I'm out hunting," Gunning improvised. "Couldn't help me locate my quarry, could you, I wonder?"

"What are you after? There's not much up here in this scrub...a few rabbits...partridge or two..."

"No, I'm hunting a person...I'm guessing you're a family man?" he said tentatively.

"Wife and six kids!" came the proud reply.

"Daughters?"

"Two. Fourteen and twelve."

"Then you'll understand. I'm chasing after my daughter. My eldest. And silliest. She's a total innocent and she's run off with a bloke I don't approve of. Old enough to be her father... twice married...total wastrel...perverted idiot. But one of those city smooth talkers—you know? They took off on this road, according to my neighbours. But so far no sign of them. They may be in a cream-coloured Delage."

The man thought for a moment and shook his head. "Fancy car. They know how to turn a girl's head! Nothing like that on the road this morning. Are you sure they've not headed for Vouliagmeni? A man and a girl? That's where all the nonsense goes on...Take the road to the right when you get to Markopoulo. It's not far. No, the only motor that's come past me on the road is a taxi. Out from Athens with a party of tourists."

"Taxi? Tourists? How many tourists?"

"Well, two and the driver."

"Two passengers?"

"Two. Man and a woman in the back. Sitting close together. The man had a hat on, the woman didn't. Fair hair." He looked suspiciously at Gunning's dark head. "Nothing like *you*."

"She takes after her mother. That's my Anna! How long ago was this?"

The man looked at Gunning blankly and then at the sky.

"You're a smoker," said Gunning. "How many cigarettes since you passed the taxi?"

The man grinned and showed his pack. "Five," he announced.

"An hour and a quarter?"

The man nodded in agreement.

Gunning ground out his cigarette and clapped the stranger on the shoulder. "Thank you! I may be in time!"

"Give her hide a good tanning!" called the man as Gunning fired up the engine again. "And as for the bloke—you'd do well to ..."

Gunning was glad his Greek didn't stretch as far as understanding the anatomically precise details of the advice so cheerily given, but he acknowledged the helpful spirit in which it was delivered with a wave as he let in the clutch and moved off.

"I may be in time!" he'd said. It had been a polite and convincing leave-taking. He didn't believe it. An hour and fifteen minutes ago they'd had ten miles further to travel. Even if he pushed the car along recklessly down this rough road, risking overheating and burst tyres, when he reached the headland they would still have had plenty of time to ... He refused to contemplate the scene, setting his brain instead to work out speeds and distances. He came up with the same conclusion each time he ran the calculation. If his worst nightmare came true, they would be returning from the headland, just the two men in a taxi, and he would meet it head-on just this side of Markopoulo.

He smiled grimly and accelerated. Head-on is exactly how he planned to meet them.

CHAPTER 37

ood. We have the place to ourselves. I thought before we inspect the temple we'd first go to the edge and look over the two-hundred-foot drop into the Aegean."

"Stun the sacrificial victim with a further show of the horrors on offer? No, thank you. I'm going nowhere near the edge. I'm not dressed for a cliff-top ramble." Letty glanced down at her Sunday-morning-at-leisure outfit: espadrilles on her feet—canvas confections that wouldn't last two minutes scrambling over a stony headland studded with thornbushes—baggy Chanel lounging pants in a fashionable shade of ultramarine, white blouse. Her body would be a long time crashing about in the foam before anyone noticed.

They strolled arm in arm away from the parked taxi, two tourists looking about them, enjoying the solitude and the staggering beauty of the scene. Letty gestured at the car. "Not bringing the lad along on this educational jaunt?" She was trying to hold down her panic and, by adopting a cheerfully unconcerned approach, thought she might even lead him into a more rational frame of mind. If she started to scream and run about he'd put a bullet in her in seconds. And every second counted. They'd surely known for over an hour now that she

was missing. Maria had seen her go off with this man. Montacute was on his way. So was Gunning. They could only be minutes behind. She kept herself from looking back down the
Athens road. She must do nothing to increase the pressure
on him.

"He takes no interest in the past. He is young."

"Mmm...not quite house-trained yet. I had thought so.
Look—you clearly have things to confide. Why don't we go and
sit in the middle of the temple floor? The views through the
columns are so beautiful. And, do you know? I've never been
here before in the morning. Always at sunset."

Surrounded by an expanse of white marble, she and
Gunay would offer a clearer target to a police marksman firing
from a distance, she reckoned. With a bit of luck they'd have
sent Harry. She would take care to sit as far as possible from
her companion if he acceded to her suggestion.

He did.

She settled with her legs by her side, ready to spring up
and dash to cover when the chance arose. "Now, Mr. Gunay, I
hate to start at the end of any story. Why don't you begin at
the beginning? It all goes back to Andrew meeting you in Salonika, doesn't it? Don't pull that face! You know you're going
to tell me. Because none of this makes any sense at all unless
you tell someone what's on your mind. Does that young oaf in
the car have any appreciation of what you're trying to achieve?
No. Well, I may not approve, but at least I'll understand. What
on earth did Andrew do to cost him his life, that of his wife,
who never knew you, and, potentially, me? Three lives? Is that
the value you choose to put on the contents of the funeral
chest?"

"Ah...it's surfaced again, has it?"

Surprised that he was so little moved by her mention of
the box, she enlarged: "For a moment. It's gone straight back
underground again, I'm afraid. But at least it's very safe. It's in

a bank vault. We realised it was not what it at first appeared…"

He nodded. "Gold. Wouldn't fool anyone for longer than a second. My father-in-law painted it."

"Is that what you're after? Look, Gunay: It was left to me. I'm willing to trade—my instant and safe return to Athens against the box and contents. You have my word that I'll make the arrangements for transfer as soon as the bank opens tomorrow morning. How about it?"

"I have learned the value of an Englishman's word!" he sneered. "This is not the arrangement I am seeking. Money does not interest me. I am not a rich man but I have sufficient for my needs and the needs of my family."

"What *are* you seeking?"

"Justice. A life for a life. Three lives for three innocent lives, and one above all for a nation's pains," he whispered.

"Not sure I quite understand you. Are you going to tell me the names of the three innocents, Mr. Gunay?" She asked it quietly.

"My wife, my daughter, and my son."

"Where did they die?"

"On the Bosphorus. A refugee transport ship. Bad crossing." The words were coming slowly from him. "Many died from malnutrition on the way. The water was bad. And then disease broke out. Almost everyone died. We were not allowed to land until it had run its course, for fear of its spreading to the rest of the population. We were anchored, helpless, in torment, on a ship of death. The few remaining of the thousand who had started the journey ministered to the dying and threw their bodies overboard. I could not save my family. My Katerina, my Adriana, my Andreas. I watched them sinking in each other's arms. I should have sunk with them to the bottom. I should not have abandoned them."

Letty left a long silence, head bowed.

He looked at her with narrowed eyes. "You are weeping? For people you never met?"

"For all the poor souls who died and the ones who lived on. Whether I knew them or not," she replied softly. " 'They wept and shared in human miseries,' Homer says of the Horses of Achilles. If a horse may feel pity, I'm sure you may allow an English girl to do so. We have our insights and sympathies. Please don't scoff when I say I can imagine a little of your grief. I lost my mother when I was a girl, and my only brother died, shot down in the war. I think if I were to multiply the pain I knew, I might be approaching an understanding of yours."

"You would need to multiply by two million, Miss Talbot. No one can do that. And the injustice goes uncorrected, even unacknowledged. The men who signed away Greek and Turkish lives sleep easy in their beds and climb the ladder of political success. A ladder whose rungs are slippery with the blood of children. And who is there to scream this injustice from the rooftops? The victims who managed to live this far are too busy struggling to make a new life for themselves. They bow their heads and scratch a living. I am the exception."

"You seem to have prospered in your new land?"

He grunted. "With half a million leaving Greece and one and a half million going the other way, there was no shortage of land for us Greeks. I was a farmer. Tobacco, corn, olives. I was given a piece of land twice the size of that I'd had in Macedonia. I put it all down to tobacco. A gamble, but I had calculated before I left Greece the increase in demand. I was not wrong. At a time when it hardly mattered to me anymore, Nature smiled on me. Good season followed good season. I found an abundance of capable workers, an efficient manager. I opened my own tobacco processing factory. That too thrived. I began to trade more widely. It seems that when I no longer care about success, she favours me. And now I have the time, the resources, and still the energy to right a wrong."

"Righting a wrong? Of this magnitude? Not possible. What you're talking about is vengeance. Revenge, not pure and simple but impure, complex, and ultimately corrosive. I'm not going to preach to you or even explain. I'd be wasting my time. But I do need to understand: *why Andrew?* He tried to help you, didn't he?"

"He became the focus of my hatred. With the gendarmes at the gate, he made an offer for my farm, my house, and everything in it."

"A good offer?"

"A derisory offer! It was worth twenty times the price. He said it was the largest amount he could lay his hands on and I was lucky to get cash from any source at all in Salonika at that time. I had to accept his word. No one had money in those terrible days. The Jews and the bankers who might have dealt had been burned out of their livelihoods in the fire in '17 and chaos still reigned. Paper money was worthless—when you could lay hands on it. I was to travel to a foreign country, not knowing what currency would be accepted on the journey or at the other end, open to attack by robbers and tricksters the moment we arrived at the docks. When Merriman promised me gold coins, a transportable means of exchange, what could I do but accept? I was cheated, of course. I presented Merriman's chit at the British offices he'd told me to go to. I was expected. The cash was ready—but only half the amount I'd been promised. 'Very sorry and all that, old chap, but resources somewhat stretched, don't you know. Lucky to have scraped this much together. Only possible as a personal favour to old Andrew.'"

"How perfectly ghastly. But I don't think Andrew was aware of that chicanery. He was an honest man, you know. I'm sure he did his best." She spoke quietly, aware that her defence could have sounded warmer.

"And then the thieves, the confidence tricksters, the

beggars, moved in. And worst of all: the so-called officials who are sorry but they have to charge you for a billet on the sheltered side of the boat, supplies, a drink of fresh water, and, in the end, a burial sack...I arrived with empty pockets and an empty life. All I was capable of feeling was a festering hatred of the man who had taken my farm and its rich past. That especially. It was my wife's father's land. Their family had tended it for centuries. They looked on themselves as guardians of the tombs and guarantors of their peace. And now here was a cheating Englishman, on his way already to the ironmongers to stock up on his spades and shovels. Booking a swift passage back to London in packing crates for the treasures that he'd dug out of the soil of my homeland. Pillager! I blame him for my loss."

"You are still angry. Has killing him and Maud in any way been a solace to you?"

He turned to look at her in wonder. "I am delighted that they are dead. My spirits lift. They will lift further when I have dealt with the one who now holds my property; they will soar when—" He broke off and shook his head. "Your Western mind would not grasp this feeling of elation."

"No. You're right. Why don't you explain to me what you meant when you said earlier that you might trade my life for something or other? Tell me what you have in mind."

"Trading is my profession these days, Miss Talbot. If you attempt to bargain with me you will surely lose."

"We've come all this way. I'm ready to listen to you at least."

Without turning her head, Letty listened for the sound of a vehicle on the road. She heard nothing. Any minute now, surely?

"No one is coming, Miss Talbot. Concentrate on the business in hand, will you?"

"So—reveal your terms. If you won't accept a gold chest

full of valuable and beautiful artefacts, I can't imagine what else I may offer in return for my life."

"Let us look on this as a piece of bargaining between business associates. Imagine a pair of scales. Two pans which must balance to the satisfaction of both parties. Into one pan I put—your life. A weighty enough contribution and, really, I need say no more. It's up to you to provide the counterweight. But I'm a generous and right-thinking man. I would not seek to punish an innocent party unless it were absolutely necessary in the pursuit of a higher good. I will help you. And a good trader—which I am—knows exactly how to sweeten the deal. I offer you an incentive. And here it is: I will reveal to you the identity of the person who killed Andrew and Maud Merriman. Yes, both. They died by the same hand. And that hand was not mine! You will need proof of my assertion. I can supply it. Or rather Demetrios can supply it. If you can fill your pan to my satisfaction, I shall be gone from the country before you get back to Athens. I have a passage on a boat from Piraeus. I shall be sorry to miss your play on Saturday. I'm sure it will be a memorable performance. But you will not see me again. More to the point—nor will the Athens police."

"Are you telling me Demetrios had some involvement with this disgusting affair? He's just a child!"

"Not in the slightest. The deaths would have occurred whoever was boot boy at the Kolonaki house." He gave one of his rare smiles in self-mockery. "Two premature deaths, unplanned by *me,* and which could well have amounted to a considerable inconvenience. What I'm telling you is that it is to Demetrios you must apply for the evidence of guilt. He came upon it in the course of his household duties—which he performed diligently, I understand. When we have shaken hands on this, I will give you an address where he may be contacted. He has instructions to respond only to you. Go yourself. Send no one else. They will not find him. You will go unharmed."

"You have my interest," she said with a formal bow of the head. "Now, tell me what you want in exchange?"

Letty listened in growing astonishment as he set out his requirements.

Revving his engine aggressively, Gunning stormed dangerously into the village of Markopoulo. Ready to charge headfirst into an oncoming ton of metal, he had been thwarted. No taxi had appeared. Disgruntled, he stopped at the crossroads in the centre, an object of curiosity to the old men sipping coffee in the *cafenion* and of opportunity to the gang of small boys who gathered around the motorcar making rude comments they had no reason to suppose he understood.

He raised a shout of laughter when he quipped back at them in their own language. He added to their hilarity when he told them he was looking for a girl.

"My *daughter*, sons of hyenas!" he yelled good-humouredly. It had worked once, why not again? He fished a photograph of Letty sitting uncomfortably on a Cretan donkey and showed it to them. "She's been kidnapped by some city slicker who's run off with her in a taxi. There's a reward for any lad who can tell me if he's seen them."

The leader stepped forward importantly. "Sir, we have not seen your daughter. But we have seen a taxi. Oh, just now. Five minutes ago?" He turned to his friends for confirmation.

"That's not right. It was nearer fifteen! Christos's ma had just called him in, remember? She always calls him at one on the dot." The objection came from a smaller boy wearing a pair of spectacles repaired with a strip of elastoplast.

"That's right." The leader considered for a moment before agreeing. "Fifteen minutes, then."

"You're pulling my leg! I passed no taxi on the road out from Athens."

"That's because it didn't go down the Athens road." The leader took up the tale again, speaking with exaggerated clarity for the bumbling foreigner. He pointed round the corner. "It went down there. That's the road to Vouliagmeni, on the coast. And from there it goes to Piraeus."

"Thanks, lads!" Gunning put his hand in his pocket and took out a fistful of drachmas. He handed them out, to the glee of the company. As he started for his car the small boy who'd corrected the time seized him by the sleeve. "Sir!" he said, blinking earnestly, "the taxi did go that way but there was no girl in it. Just two men, the driver and one in the back."

Somehow, in the depths of his despair, Gunning managed to dredge up more coins from his other pocket and hand them over with his thanks. His thanks for delivering the most chilling news of his life.

CHAPTER 38

Gunning sat hunched over his steering wheel, head drooping, eyes shut, oblivious to his surroundings. Fifteen minutes. The rat would be in Piraeus in no time at all. Piraeus, gateway to the Mediterranean. Boats leaving every few minutes for a hundred islands, for Turkey, Europe, Egypt, America.

And good riddance to him. Gunning's concern was all for his victim. Letty must have died in the last hour. In the time that had been lost in Athens. Calming himself, Gunning made himself ready to do the only thing left to him: reach the coast and lean out over the cliffs, calling hopelessly into the void. Mewing into the wind like a seagull. Perhaps, when no one answered his call, he would complete the action she herself had interrupted all those months before in Cambridge. He'd been resigned to his death and planning for it, when she'd stepped in, a stranger, full of joy and optimism, and she'd offered him half a crown and a reason to go on living.

He'd accepted both. But he had always known that it was her presence that linked him to life. Without her, he had no reason to go on. He'd kept the half crown. It was always in his breast pocket with her photograph. He would put the coin into his mouth before he leapt from the cliff top. Keep the

Ferryman happy. He smiled bitterly as he remembered that it was from this headland that Theseus's father, King of Athens, had hurled himself to his death in despair, thinking, mistakenly, that his son had died in Crete. Well, he'd be in good company.

"Sir! Sir! You all right?" The voice was anxious. Squeaky. Gunning turned to smile at the little boy with the broken glasses.

"Not very. No, son. Rather upset, in fact." There was no point in pretending otherwise. Those earnest eyes saw a great deal through the ill-fitting spectacles.

He suddenly realised that the boy was grinning.

"You haven't noticed, have you? Look! Up the road! Sight for sore eyes, eh? That what you're looking for?"

Gunning followed the grubby, pointing finger.

He stared, gulped, stared again, and turned back to the lad. Solemnly, with tears beginning to trickle, he extended a hand and made the sign of the cross on the boy's forehead, murmuring words of blessing.

He let in the clutch clumsily and juddered off, wiping his eyes on his sleeve. Two hundred yards away. A hundred. Absurdly, he drove at a slow speed so as not to frighten her. She recognised the car but he waved anyway. Drawing level with Letty, he jumped out and pulled her into a tight embrace, distressed by what he saw. She was exhausted, panting, hot, and limping. Her feet were bleeding, her shoes in tatters. But she was laughing.

"Couldn't run...Came as fast as I could...He chucked me out two miles up the road so that he could get away to Piraeus. Gunay! Utter bounder! Water...did you...?"

He helped her into the back of the car and produced the water flask.

Letty sat close to him for a few moments, relishing the familiar safety of the man and the car. "Water never tasted so good!" she said, handing back the cup. "No man ever smelled so good! And no flower ever looked so jaunty." She took the pink bloom from the holder and sniffed at it. "I don't know this one."

"It's a welcome-back-to-the-world gesture from Demeter," he said.

"You were expecting me to resurface, then?"

"Of course!" He told a comforting lie. "The goddess and I—we never lost faith."

After a few moments he decided she looked resilient enough to be asked: "What would you like me to do? Where would you like me to take you?"

"I'll tell you what I *don't* want you to do, and that's set off in pursuit of Gunay. He's heading for Piraeus—at least he said he was . . . But you're not to go after him. He's armed, for a start, and to go on—I promised we wouldn't. Part of the bargain."

"Bargain? I shall want to know all about that. I think I'd better take you to some quiet place where we can talk," he said.

"Please—not Sounion!"

"No. I've had a much better idea. When I've turned this crate round we're going to go left at the crossroads in the village and make for Vouliagmeni. They'll have the telephone there. We can report back to Theotakis." He grinned happily. "And then, duty done, dogs called off, we can have the rest of the day to ourselves. We can start with an ice cream and later have a meal of some sort and then hire a room for the rest of the day to recover. What about it?"

She smiled. "Very nearly perfect! Could we do all of those—but in reverse order, William?"

"Exactly what I had in mind, but I hesitate to put the suggestion to a girl who's been run away with once already today."

"Then I'll snatch *you* away. Think of it like that."

"Oh, Letty, as we pass through this village—Markopoulo, it's called—I want you to wave happily at the inhabitants, especially the small ones. They think you're my runaway daughter. Can you manage that?"

"I have your number for you ... sir." The desk clerk at the Hotel Apollo was frostily polite.

Gunning locked glares with him as he took the instrument from his hand. "Police headquarters? The Reverend Gunning here. Pass me Detective Chief Superintendent Theotakis, will you? ..." He spoke with emphasis and in Greek, an eye still on the clerk. "Ah, Markos?" he said confidently, remembering with an effort the superintendent's Christian name. "William here. I have Laetitia ... safe and sound but a bit the worse for wear. I'm ringing from the Hotel Apollo in Vouliagmeni. Her guide and driver have gone on via the coast road to Piraeus. Forty minutes ago. She'll give you the number."

Letty took the phone and gave the taxi number. "Got that, Markos? I'll pass you back to my husband," she finished firmly.

"... Yes, there is something you can do," said Gunning. "Letty's exhausted by her cliff-top ramble ... twisted ankle, lacerated feet ... looks like something the cat brought in ... you can imagine? She needs to rest for a while before coming back to Athens. Problem is—neither of us thought to bring a passport and we're being looked at somewhat askance at the reception desk. They're minded—and who shall blame them?— to tell us that they don't have a room spare. I wonder if you could say a few words regarding the integrity, bank balance, and general social standing of the Reverend and Mrs. Gunning? Thank you ... much obliged."

He passed the instrument back to the clerk. "The Athens Criminal Investigation Department would like a word," he said with a smile.

Letty woke to a glow of well-being and late afternoon sun. Concerned blue eyes above and a downy pillow below.

"Even heaven has its price. However much is this costing, William?"

"Not the faintest! And we haven't finished yet. I've ordered up some food and more champagne. Will red mullet—I chose it myself in the kitchen—some roast chicken and a salad do you?...A month's pay? Something like that. Discretion, Dom Pérignon, and French bed linen—they don't come cheap!"

"Had you thought—we haven't got any money with us? I've nothing but what I was standing up in—that ghastly tattered heap on the floor there—and you never have anything but coins about you."

"Don't worry! When I crept down to view the fish I telephoned Kolonaki. Got hold of Thetis. She was there with Montacute. They're sending Harry out with some banknotes and a bag of things Thetis is sorting out for you. She was worried about you checking into a hotel without luggage."

Letty gurgled with laughter. "She's packing for *me* now! That girl and I will soon have no secrets from each other."

"Not so sure of that..." he began. "I can tell you something that might rather surprise you—"

But, for once, Letty wasn't about to listen to his gossip. Her laughter had stopped abruptly. "Luggage! Good Lord! He was *lying*! I thought so but I couldn't put my finger on it... William, pass me that bathrobe, would you? I can't think, naked."

"Who was lying?"

"Soulios Gunay. He said farewell, in rather a marked manner, I'm now thinking. And said he was catching a boat at once from Piraeus. But, William—there was no luggage in the luggage compartment in the taxi."

William was not impressed. "He'd sent it ahead."

"Yes, of course—the larger pieces that are to go in the hold—anyone would. But anyone would at least have a smaller case or bag to hand, and he hadn't even an overnight bag for his shaving kit and cologne. And Gunay is a well-groomed man. He travels with more than a toothbrush in his pocket." Eyes glinting, Letty came to a conclusion. "He's still in Athens. He hasn't got to the end of the line yet."

"Dangerous for him. The police know so much about his background. Why would he risk staying on?"

"Because he's got one more killing on his list! I'm trying to remember ... He made one or two odd remarks ... Strange how danger sharpens your perceptions ... I really don't think he could be bothered to chuck me over the cliff, you know. When he knew I wasn't Andrew's flesh and blood I ceased to count as a victim in his scheme of things. But being the man's heir—well, that put me in a different category completely. I was someone he could bargain with once he'd frightened the life out of me with a sight of the drop into the Aegean—"

"Ah, yes, this bargain, this pact with the Devil, are you ever—?"

"Soon ... soon ... That'll keep. Listen—Gunay didn't kill Andrew and Maud and he's given me the means of proving it. I intend to do that tomorrow morning. Though he had been planning their deaths. He lost his wife and two children in the expulsion from Greece. He was seeking three victims in retribution."

"Two down and one to go, are you saying?"

"Not that simple. I offered Maud's cousins and he wasn't the least bit interested. I think he wrote off the third. He's a merchant, William; he would know when the moment had come to cut his losses. You see, he's not a wild-eyed madman. He's rational. Ready to adjust. And very closely focussed on what he wants to achieve."

"You make him sound damn dangerous."

"I believe he is. And I believe he has something more in mind. I'm a minnow in his scheme of things, a sprat to catch a mackerel. His sights are on something—someone—infinitely grander. He's blaming someone for the whole fiasco. And not just a small cog in the wheel like Andrew..."

"Whom he denies killing?"

"Yes. He spoke of Andrew and Maud. 'I'm delighted they're dead,' he said. 'My spirits lift. They will lift further when I have dealt with the one who now holds my property; they will soar when...' And then he stopped. Something like that. Wait, wait—" She held up a hand to silence William. "And he was talking about the injustice of the deportations: '...And the injustice goes uncorrected, even unacknowledged. The men who signed away Greek and Turkish lives sleep easy in their beds and climb the ladder of political success. A ladder whose rungs are slippery with the blood of children.' That's the way he spoke. Elemental. Ponderous. Though perhaps he was keeping it simple for me."

"And you're gathering from all this turgid verbiage that some politically successful chappie is about to come a cropper while Gunay stands by hooting with laughter?"

"No. William, he's not standing by. He's actively going for the moving force! 'Three lives for three innocent lives, and one above all for a nation's pains,' he said. Which *one*, William? Oh, my God! Who signed that wretched treaty?"

"Treaty?"

"You know what I'm talking about!"

"The Lausanne agreement. Well, Greece and Turkey, of course, and various representatives of the Great Powers."

"Names, William! Whose signatures? Who picked up a pen, signed the document, and set two million people on the move? And sent Gunay's family along with many thousands on both sides to their deaths?"

"Crikey, girl! I'm not the *Encyclopaedia Britannica*!"

"You're the nearest thing I've come to it in my life. Well, no... actually my father is nearer."

"Well, if you're lining up ducks in a shooting gallery, I can tell you that many people were involved in the planning. Lloyd George way back, Lord Curzon concerned about British access to the Black Sea, Venizelos worried witless about the massacres of Greeks in Smyrna, the evictions the Turks were already perpetrating... his hand was forced... Fridtjof Nansen, the Norwegian hero, was doing what he could on behalf of the League of Nations..."

"You know what I want! The signatories."

"The three I can remember are: Eleftherios Venizelos, naturally; his opposite number Ismet Pasha, representing Turkey; in the British corner, the Right Honourable Sir Horace Rumbold."

Letty smiled. "Somehow I think Sir Horace is not on Gunay's list. Nor is this Ismet Pasha... Gunay would arrange to kill a Turk in Turkey, surely?"

Gunning nodded. "Sounds reasonable to me."

"He wants to kill Eleftherios Venizelos." Her voice was hushed. "I'd never understood that strange phrase the Watchman uses in the play: *'I have the weight of an ox on my tongue.'* But I had to shift a great weight to say those words, William."

"And, sadly, I can't argue with them. I think you've probably guessed what he's up to. We'll warn Theotakis."

"William? You don't seem very concerned! Can't you see that his only chance of getting the Prime Minister in his crosshairs is when he shows himself in public? You said it yourself—assassinations take place in public spaces: a stroll in the park, a railway station, the theatre. He's arranged to kill him at the performance next Saturday. Perhaps Demetrios had time to report back his keyhole evidence, but I think Gunay knew the play was going ahead anyway. Yes! He mentioned the Saturday performance! He knew!"

"He couldn't possibly—"

"He did! And *I* didn't tell him. He must have got it from someone on Thetis's telephone list. She was at it for two hours, telling people about the change of plan. One of her contacts who expressed surprise, then delight, and then reached for his diary and wrote in an entry must have passed on the news. Perhaps Gunay's organisation is just that, and has deeper roots and wider branches than we guess at?"

"The Embassy, the Army, and the whole of the Police Force are aware."

"Ah. Yes. But I say again, William: You don't seem very concerned."

"I'm *not*. Sorry, Letty!" He was grinning at her. "If you'll let me get a word in edgewise…There's something you should know. I have something to report, too! You were snatched away just moments before the good news came through to Thetis on the telephone. Come and have a hug and stop frowning! All's well! What you and Gunay both were not to know when you had your cliff-top summit meeting is that Helena Venizelos has finally talked her husband out of attending. An excuse will be made—probably on the grounds of a recurrence of the dengue fever he's just recovered from. Everyone will be frightfully disappointed—not least Gunay!—but they'll settle back with a sigh of relief to simply enjoy themselves. The only explosions they'll need to be nervous of will be coming from those infernal flashbulbs the *Athens News* cameraman uses!"

"And the social and cultural event of the year will appear

on the front pages the world over...or round about page seven in the case of the London *Times*." Letty spoke with forced cheerfulness.

Gunning picked up her lingering uncertainty and said again, warmly: "It's going to be all right, you know. Your hero and mine—he simply won't *be* there in the arena, offering himself as a target, for any of Gunay's apes to take a potshot at!"

CHAPTER 39

ox up the cats, will you, Maria?"

Letty noted the dismay on the maid's face and the delay before she whispered: "Yes, Mistress."

"Oh, don't bother. I'll do it myself. They know me better. Just put some food out for them, something delicious, shut the kitchen door, and I'll come down in five minutes and catch them. William?" she called from the drawing room. "William, where are you?"

"Yes, Mistress? Do you want me boxed up as well?"

"No, twerp! But I do want you to escort me through the Plaka. It's very early... six o'clock. Thetis isn't even up yet... We should catch young Demetrios before he goes out on his errands."

"You know where you're going?"

Housewives brushing steps and watering gasoline cans still bright with summer flowers stopped to watch them as they walked through the sun-dappled narrow streets, Letty with map in hand and Gunning with squawking wicker basket. It seemed that an island village had been pricked out and transplanted onto the thin and rock-strewn soil at the foot of the Acropolis, thriving in places where roots had struck, decrepit and dying off in others.

After a good deal of argument—"I told you to keep the Parthenon at your back...No, turn the map sideways now... Haven't we just passed that old man...?"—Letty declared they had reached the street Gunay had mentioned.

"There! It must be the house in the corner...Do you see? I'm supposed to turn up unaccompanied, so I think you should skulk here by the fountain and keep an eye out while I introduce myself. Not sure who I'll find inside. This isn't the address Theotakis had for the Gunay clan."

"How would we know where they all are? I expect there's quite a web of them. Let's hope this isn't the home of the one you shot."

Every inch the cheerful English matron, Letty knocked on the door and spoke to the woman who opened it a crack. She made some play with the cats, who, strangely, thought William, seemed to offer some sort of a passport. The door opened wider and the Greek housewife came outside and looked around. Gunning gave her a cheerful wave and turned back to his newspaper. Seemingly satisfied with what she saw, the woman went to knock on a door two houses away, opened it, called out a name, and went inside. The familiar form of Demetrios appeared, tousle-headed and pulling on his shirt. He greeted the cats with delight, took one out and draped it around his neck, and stroked the other. After a moment for the reunion, Letty firmly put them back in the box again and placed it on the doorstep.

She strolled a few paces off with the boy and went to sit with him on the empty steps of a café not yet open for business. The talk was earnest and, in the case of Demetrios, accompanied by a good deal of gesticulation. A lot of finding and fiddling and polishing seemed to be going on. Finally,

Letty spoke quietly to him and shook his hand. She got up and asked a question about the cats. Demetrios nodded, picked up the box with alacrity, and went back inside.

It wasn't until she turned to him that Gunning realised the extent of Letty's distress.

With frozen features and barely able to find her words she said simply: "We must get back and see if he's telling the truth. I know in my bones he is, but my head and my heart will not accept it. Poor Andrew! He must have suffered!"

They sat uncomfortably in the drawing room making conversation. Thetis had joined them after breakfast and they waited for Montacute to arrive. Letty had refused to discuss her conversation with Demetrios and insisted on the inspector's presence before she started on an explanation. She had also insisted that an urgent summons be made through Montacute for Dr. Peebles. The doctor, still a little peevish, Montacute reported, conceded that he might be able to fit in a visit after he had attended to two emergency house calls in the area. They might expect him towards ten o'clock.

Montacute arrived just before nine. He made enquiries about the state of Letty's health and listened to her account of her abduction. She moved swiftly through the events, clearly preoccupied with other matters.

"But never mind all that—it's Gunay's little surprise we're gathered to unwrap this morning. I've seen Demetrios, who, he claims, holds evidence of the deaths of both Andrew and Maud. At least, he doesn't hold it—he discovered it. It's right here in the house. We've been walking past it every day. I haven't investigated yet. I thought we'd do it together. Will you all come down to the hall with me?"

They followed her down the staircase to the black-and-white-tiled hallway and looked about them at the unremarkable space. A gilt French side table held a bowl for visiting cards and a vase with a spray of flowers. A long-case clock ticked solemnly in a corner. As they stood in silent puzzlement, the clock whirred and clicked, cleared its ancient throat, and began to chime nine.

Letty waited for it to finish before pointing to the one other piece of furniture the hall contained. Every hallway had one, seen on every entry but unremarked by anyone: an umbrella stand. This was a capacious cylinder of beaten bronze and contained two carefully rolled umbrellas—one man's large black one and a lady's shorter green one. The heads of three walking canes projected: one ivory, one silver, and one carved ebony.

"I won't touch it. I leave it to you, Percy," Letty said.

"The umbrella stand?" he said. "But we've turned it out. It's been checked."

He advanced on it, lifted it, and turned it on its side, tipping the contents onto the floor.

"Not as thoroughly as young Demetrios, apparently. He was always looking for jobs to do. Keeping the hallway neat was one of his tasks. The day after Andrew and Maud died, he decided the umbrellas looked untidy. They'd been carelessly rolled. He unfastened them and rerolled them to his satisfaction. As you see them now. Having time on his hands, and no Maud any longer to catch him idling and shout at him, he paused to play with the walking canes. Pretty handles, you notice. The ivory-topped cane—exotic carving of an Indian goddess, I think—was Andrew's father's old cane. He never used it."

"Rather fascinating object for a young man of twelve," Montacute remarked.

"Or any age!" said Gunning, picking it up and examining it.

"The silver one was left behind by a guest at their last

soirée. The ebony-headed cane belonged to Maud," Thetis explained. "Very *Art Déco*. Was she ever pleased with it! Used it every time she left the house. She was using it on the night Andrew died."

"And *that's* the one that caught Demetrios's attention," Letty said. "Will you take a closer look at it, Percy?"

With a face where dread struggled with eagerness, Montacute picked it up. "Heavy," he commented. He ran a forefinger over the elegantly carved hand grip. He turned it in his hands and inspected the silver ferrule at the end. "Ah!" His fingers slipped, questing, along the length of the cane and caressed the carving again. He twisted the handle and grunted in frustration. "How in heaven's name did the lad ever find the place? Good God! There it is! Stand back! Don't crowd me!"

With a slicing swish, he drew a slim length of metal from the cane. Metal whose gleam was dulled by a dark brown stain.

"Very short blade for a sword cane," he commented. "But deadly. The best-quality Toledo steel, five inches long, bayonet shape with a blood channel along its length. And it hasn't been cleaned."

Thetis stared at it, turning pale. "You'll have to excuse me," she whispered. "I think I'm going to be sick."

They retreated back up to the drawing room, Montacute taking the cane with him.

"Andrew liked to think the women in his life were protected," Letty said. "Maud hadn't the wits to use a gun, so he must have found this disgusting implement for her. I've heard of sword sticks . . . my French grandfather was reputed never to leave the house without one. But that was Paris in the days of the apaches. Whatever was Maud doing using one?"

It was Thetis who answered her question: "Those tourists who were kidnapped and murdered. Maud was quite spooked by that. It's when she started to carry that thing about with her. She told everyone she had arthritis. Perhaps she did. How would I know? I never really listened! Percy, that's Andrew's blood on that blade, isn't it?"

He nodded. "Tests will reveal, and all that...but yes, I think we can assume the worst. I say, Miss Laetitia, do you think you could cast your mind back over the evening in question...I know you've already given a clear statement but in the light of this evidence...?"

"Yes, of course. We weren't concentrating on Maud particularly, were we?" Letty frowned, remembering. "She got to the theatre early and went, shall we say, to confront Andrew in his lair backstage. To beat him about the head with her discovery that he was not only having an affair with her cousin but was contemplating divorce in order to marry her? She was always creeping about. She could have overheard something? Perhaps Andrew himself, pushed beyond endurance, told her he wanted a divorce? She would never have tolerated that. He poured out a glass of water for her. She was wearing gloves, so...no prints. They quarrelled. He was subservient to her usually, I think because he pitied her, but he had a razor tongue and occasionally could strike with it. I've heard him do that. Perhaps he said something that tipped her over the edge. Years and years of suffering his infidelities and now to crown it all—the shame of divorce. I'm sure that would have been the trigger."

Montacute groaned. "Something snapped! How often I've heard that! The sword stick clicked and she stabbed him. Slim blade, you see. One lucky thrust would do it. Straight in and out. A single stroke powered by insane rage. She was a tall woman, the wound's in the right place. And then, the next stage is normally—panic sets in. And in the rush of energy that comes to people in extremis, she hauled him about and put him in the bathtub. Giving her time to think and plan."

"And then she tapped her way across the orchestra and sat down by my side, ready for the rehearsal," said Letty.

"Leaving traces of blood as she went," said Montacute.

"And then she gloated!" Thetis snapped. "All that bereaved-widow stuff she put on for us! The tapping of the tub and the 'Joke's over, Andrew!' nonsense. The clutching of the bosom and the 'Take me home now, William'! Devil! I wish I *had* pushed her out of the window! She sat there, smirking in her black gown and her pearls, provoking me. Taunting. She was spilling over with hatred. Quite mad. I'm only surprised she didn't attempt to kill me as well."

"Thetis," said Letty thoughtfully. "Can we be quite sure she didn't try?"

A tap on the door announced that Dr. Peebles was waiting below.

When he was shown up, the doctor introduced himself to everyone and, with a meaningful glance at his wristwatch, agreed that he had arrived earlier than anticipated. One patient had made a recovery in the night and he was ahead of time. A brisk Scotsman, he was not prepared to be at the beck and call of the English policeman, apparently. Now, could he possibly be of any assistance at all to the Athens police? he asked waspishly . . . They only had to ask . . .

Montacute rode the implied criticism good-naturedly and asked him to reveal what had passed between him and his patient on the night of her husband's murder. He stressed that absolute openness was vital, as the life and liberty of another depended on his statement.

Mollified, the doctor launched into his recital. "A word first about Lady Merriman's general condition. In a word: poor. She was a concern to me. She had a few peripheral and

nonthreatening ailments ... age, don't you know ... we all have
our twinges and this climate is sometimes a bit harsh on an
English constitution, but she had a quite serious heart condition. There were signs some months ago of the way things
were going. I had warned her to take things easy, but—you
know what she was like—never still. Indefatigable. I think also
she secretly considered herself invulnerable. I was summoned
to attend her at about eight on the night she died. She had just
returned from the theatre, where the discovery of her husband's murder had been made. She was agitated. Very. Her
heart was—a layman might well have said—at bursting point.
She had clearly suffered the most enormous stress. I offered
her a sedative, which she refused to take. I was angry at the rejection of assistance. I told her the truth, which perhaps a doctor ought rarely to do ..." He hesitated.

"We know how provoking she could be, Doctor," Thetis
murmured, encouraging him.

"And the truth was ...?" Montacute prompted.

"That she had only days to live. Perhaps hours, if she refused to cooperate with her medical advisor." Peebles drew
himself up to his full height and spoke in a tone of defiance. "I
advised instant admittance to hospital. I offered to drive her
there. When this was rejected, I offered to stay on. My patient
rejected my help and dismissed me. This is all duly noted in
my record of events. What you must know is that her heart
was strained beyond repair and about to give out at any moment."

The affair still rankled with the doctor, Letty judged, and
she was relieved to hear Montacute speak with understanding:
"Doctor, that is all very clear. And your valuable information is
vital to our enquiry. Would you be so good as to send in a written version of what you have just told us? And, in the matter of
conscience: We accept that you did all you could. When the

full truth comes out, I think you will see that, in the circumstances, Lady Merriman was the author of her own misfortune...and that of others."

Letty felt guiltily that they had not done enough to mend fences and, as he prepared to leave, said the first thing that came into her mind: "Doctor, I don't know if Maud invited you to the first night of the play she was working on? I know she meant to. We'd be very pleased to see you there if you could come. And stay on for the ceremony afterwards, in her memory and Andrew's?"

Surprisingly, he smiled and agreed that as he was free that evening...yes...he'd be delighted.

When the doctor left they sat in silence, stunned by the unpalatable truth they were facing.

Montacute spoke first. "We should have listened to Aeschylus. He was giving us the clear answer all along. It was the spurned, resentful wife who wielded the blade. Maud was the real-life Clytemnestra. We ought never to have suspected the concubine. She was merely playing the part."

"I beg your pardon!" Thetis said sharply. "Do you mean *me*? Percy! If I thought for one moment that you seriously considered I was capable of murder...Well, I'm not quite sure what I'd do, because I'm not the vindictive type, as I hope you have now grasped."

Letty hurried to say: "You were very nearly her victim too, Thetis. She *did* try to kill you. In an indirect and devious way. She finished off Andrew and by her exertions practically finished herself off as well. The doctor told her she was dying and so she decided in her evil, bent way to use her own death against you. She refused treatment. She intended to control her own end. I think she tried to needle you into killing her, but as you merely screamed at her in rage and left, she did the next best thing. She took hold of your sword and held it in her hand when she leapt from the balcony. Unaided by anyone. If she died at once, the police would find the sword and ask questions. As you did, Montacute. But, even better for her, she survived long enough to spit her poisonous denunciation into your ear. She was dying *and* taking Thetis down with her."

"Anything to cause a little pain," whispered Thetis, head drooping. "I'm ashamed to have any blood in common with her."

To Letty's surprise, Montacute turned to Thetis and put an arm around her shoulders. He bent his head and whispered into her ear. She snuggled her head closer.

Gunning caught Letty's eye and sprang to his feet. "Good Lord, Letty! No one thought to order tea."

"And it's Monday morning. Maria's out shopping. Shall we go down and invade the kitchen, William? I say—will you two excuse us if we dash off and make a cup of tea?"

CHAPTER 40

T he funeral service took place on Wednesday. No requests had been made by either occupant of the two gilded coffins that stood surrounded by lilies in front of the altar, so Thetis had agreed with Letty that the smaller of the two cathedrals on Mitrolpoleos Square was the more suitable for the informal gathering of friends, scholars, and British grandees.

Andrew Merriman would have approved. The tiny Byzantine church had very ancient origins. It stood on the site of a temple to the goddess of childbirth, whose authority and patronage had passed seamlessly with the centuries to Saint Mary, just as the stones and marble had been reused to form the fabric of the later church buildings. Sir Andrew would have loved the incense and the resonant priestly voice. He would have been charmed and flattered by the eulogy that Gunning had given with apparent spontaneity.

Letty had no concern for Lady Merriman's conjectured approval. She had, however, agreed to speak briefly about Maud, since Thetis had refused the duty. She managed to deliver her short address with dignity, and her appreciation of all that Maud had done to foster the arts at home and abroad was sincere.

Two coffins lay side by side but only one would rest in Greek soil.

Thetis had been adamant. "I'm not burying them cheek by jowl. I couldn't save him in life; the least I can do now he's dead is rescue him from an eternity of Maud. I'm shipping her back to the family vault in Sussex. It'll cost the earth but who gives a damn? And it's what she would have wanted," she'd added with mock piety.

And Letty had sat in the scented darkness, eyes on Andrew's coffin and weeping tears of sorrow and rage.

"Fiend! Traitor! Lovely man! You brought much happiness into my life but, at the last, you've brought me a heap of troubles. With your scheming and your acquisitiveness. You've caused me to bind myself for two years to a man you swindled and destroyed. You've left me to work off your debt of honour. All I want is to go back to Cambridge and drag poor William to the altar. I don't want to go to Salonika!"

CHAPTER 41

ell, that's the British for you!" Letty remarked to Gunning with satisfaction as they took their seats for the first performance of the play on Saturday afternoon. "Awkward customers, barrack-room lawyers when things are going well, but when there's a crisis, there's none like them for putting their backs into something. It's going to go well, you know, William! I'm probably breaking all the theatrical rules by saying so, but really—what a splendid effort!"

Two days of rehearsal had gone like silk. All had turned up on time; all knew their lines and positions. Their performance was intended as an offering, not to Lord Dionysus, but to Sir Andrew. It was an honouring; it was a farewell. Letty had feared that, without the professor's unifying presence, the play might fall apart, torn this way and that by several egotistical forces. But she was delighted to be proven wrong.

Hugh Lattimore, the stage manager, had shown a firm decisiveness that she had never guessed lay below the hesitant exterior he'd previously shown. In fact, she rather thought he'd oversteered when he appointed her his assistant and took to calling her "Letty, dear" in the overfamiliar way of the theatre-struck.

"Where's my ASM?" he'd yell. "Ah, there you are, Letty, dear! I need a hand over here with the drains. I prefer to think of them as the god's entrails. Come and help me lift these pavings and shove a broom handle through...You may think me fussy but I've found all sorts down here...dead cats, empty bottles, discarded sandwiches...Can't risk any embarrassing eructations sounding from the bowels of the earth on the night, can we?"

"A gurgling god? That would certainly shatter the solemnity," Letty agreed.

"Well, that's clear." Hugh got up from his knees, dusting off his hands. "What's next on poor Maud's list? Bless the dear lady. How we miss her..."

"It's: 'Ivy wreath, Dionysus, for the head of,'" Letty supplied sarcastically, glancing up at the god.

"Ah. Enter a *P* for postponed. I shan't do that until the morning itself. Freshness, you know. He wouldn't like to be seen in a wilting wreath." He peered upwards. "I make a habit of checking his nose regularly, too."

"His nose?"

"Shameless vandals!" he hissed. "Nothing safe around here! Noses—and any other projecting bits—come in for the attention of silly little boys. I've had to replace him. Luckily, there's never a shortage of statuary in this town! But all seems well now."

"Right. Then we've got: 'Lighting, safety of...'"

"Off we go, then. Know anything about arc lamps? And the flares that the chorus use? Better check them. And the safety containers for the matches? We wouldn't want anyone shouting out 'Fire!' in the middle of a packed house, would we?...I suspect more people have died of boredom than fire in the theatre, but one takes no chances! Look, I hardly dare mention this, but—the dummy? Do you feel up to it? All that blood again? Bit much to ask a girl, eh? Feel free, Letty dear, to say 'No, I couldn't possibly...'—I'd understand."

Letty toyed with the idea of the next body in the bathtub answering to the name of Lattimore.

Louis Adams had fallen silent as Hugh Lattimore had waxed voluble. He'd put aside his quibbling and his cynicism and seemed to be calmly prepared to do what was expected of him and go over the top with the rest of the company when the whistle blew.

Geoffrey Melton minced professionally through the proceedings, managing to upset no one. He even toned down his death screams in rehearsal in deference to sensibilities, though Letty suspected he'd give it full throttle on the night.

Thetis, on the other hand, was practically unhinged, Letty had decided, and tried to avoid meeting her on the set. A bundle of nerves one minute—"But I'm always like this at rehearsal, darling! Part of the job. You don't know actors! You should have seen me before *Clowns in Clover*! They tell me I was impossible!"—and joyous the next. Usually when in proximity to the inspector. Letty had to admit that their appearances together onstage were electric.

And here they were. Minutes to go.

Guests had been required to run the gauntlet of pairs of keen-eyed troopers and, in a spirit of jolly cooperation, had raised no objection to opening up evening purses and turning out pockets. "It's just a pipe, Sergeant. Like to see it? It's not loaded! Ho! Ho!"…"Opera glasses. I say, is that allowed?" Even the newsman's camera had come in for a detailed inspection before he was ushered to a seat in the front row. Letty had given an encouraging wave to Dr. Peebles, who, with an ironic smile, had stopped to open up the bag of professional equipment that always accompanied him.

Helena Venizelos, the guest of honour, had entered on the arm of Freddy Wentworth and they had settled in the priests' marble chairs, thoughtfully lined with silk cushions by Letty. Well, no assassin worth his salt was going to mistake that very

English figure for the Greek Prime Minister with his bald head and emphatic white beard. Freddy was looking magnificent, Letty thought, with a lump in her throat that might have been pride. Tall, straight as a ramrod, elegant in his evening suit and medals, his fair head shining copper-gold in the slanting sun. Letty wondered fancifully what his answer would be if she dashed up and asked him to marry her, and grinned.

She guessed she'd be gruffly denied access to the First Secretary by his Embassy bodyguard. That was what she assumed him to be, the grey-haired man in discreet attendance on Wentworth. Never more than two feet away from his charge, the aide reviewed the company with flinty eyes, assessing and moving on. She froze as they trained on her for a moment, identified her, made a judgement, and dismissed her with unflattering speed. Wentworth himself, Letty noticed, was clearly mindful of the presence at his back, even waiting for his nod before stepping through the stately ritual. Letty knew the feeling:

Always keep a hold of Nurse
For fear of finding Something Worse.

Gunning leaned to her and whispered: "Special Branch is with us, I see. Only one of him but I'd say that old thug was worth a company, wouldn't you?"

"I don't know what effect he has on the villains but he seems to terrify Freddy!"

The First Lady was looking ethereal in a carefully chosen dress which must have cost the earth and was probably from the House of Worth in Paris. It was slim, white, and anklelength but without a hint of classical parody—Helena's delicate tribute to the occasion. Silvery slippers on her feet and around her throat, a single row of pearls.

They had walked in between two ranks of Greek Army

men, all chosen for their astonishing good looks, Letty could have sworn—though William had said chosen for their marksmanship. Twenty men with sidearms, all General Konstantinou's protection squad. The numbers of soldiers had been reduced to this token presence in line with the cancellation of the Prime Minister's appearance. A small squad but impressive, the men went to station themselves at the ends of the rows with two directly behind the guests of honour.

For a dizzying moment, Letty, in her place three rows behind, was rigid with apprehension. She remembered the young Alexander watching the slaughter of his father, Philip, in the theatre at Aigai, up in Macedon. The assassin had run, pursued by his fellows in the Royal Guard. But to what end? The murderer had been silenced, cut to pieces before he could speak. And who was guarding this impressive contingent tonight? She relaxed a little on recalling that it was Konstantinou himself who had advised against the appearance of the Prime Minister. With a self-congratulatory flourish when his advice was acted on, according to Montacute. The general deserved praise, she thought, for his arrangements. Evident but not intrusive. The men seemed, in fact, to have been granted permission to enjoy their evening. They had been given programmes and were studying them eagerly. There was a hush of expectancy over the arena and Letty could feel a surge of goodwill and silent encouragement rising up from the whole audience.

The sun began to dip towards the horizon and the Watchman came grumbling onstage, stretching his arthritic old joints.

" '*Aiaiee!*' " The sudden screech jangled Letty's nerves, although she was expecting it. " '*Look! Over there! The beacon! There's the queen's signal! The king has taken Troy!*' "

And the play took fire.

The audience sighed and groaned and gasped. Much noisier than a London audience, but Letty thought she had never heard a silence so deep as the one that greeted the entrance of the bathtub with its ghastly cargo. Her hands were shaking and she could not bring herself to watch as the bleeding limbs were once again revealed. Thetis must have an iron self-control, she thought, to be able to do this again without a quiver in her voice. She looked at the queen, for queen she was at that moment, and acknowledged that by the alchemy of acting, the young woman had been transformed.

No one wriggled, no one toyed with a pistol. No one died of boredom, fire, or gunshot. The listeners responded with emotion to the cruelty, the danger, the betrayal, and the death onstage and, when they came to the very last lines, were ready to hiss the villain, Aegisthus, with pantomime enthusiasm when he insulted Montacute's Leader of the Chorus: " *'You insubordinate dog! How dare you hurl abuse at me—your master! I'll make you pay, you old fool!'* "

Murmurs of admiration supported Montacute as he spoke back with reckless defiance: " *'No Greek worthy of the name would grovel at your feet!'* "

And a sharp intake of breath greeted Clytemnestra's closing line to her lover as they walked off together in savage triumph, followed by the hatred of the crowd: " *'Oh, let them bleat! They can do nothing. It's you and I who have the power now!'* "

A standing ovation; a chorus of bravos; relief to have got through it; a cast, unmasking, in a line, hand in hand, red in the face, sweating and deliriously happy, were Letty's impressions of the final moments.

The theatre audience flowed away with surprising speed along the cleverly architectured stone pathways. The crowd left chattering, smiling, and, Letty guessed, eager to share their experiences with friends. They'd had a memorable evening. The next performance would be to a full house. They'd be sitting in the aisles!

And now they could throw off their heavy outer garments, unbutton, and enjoy the cool evening air on hot limbs. The guardsmen left their positions and went to occupy the front row, clearly still on duty, still quietly obeying orders, but the cast and backstage crew, buoyed up by their success, gathered noisily on the orchestra. They mingled with the guests of honour, chattering and modestly receiving compliments. And, after a suitable interval and a few glasses of champagne, Letty would judge the moment right to summon Henry Beecham. Doubling as a waiter, he would bustle forward carrying the ceremonial offering of wine for Dionysus.

She looked up at the voluptuous features of the god. His wreath was fresh; long trails of ivy and laurel had been set to wind their way down the column, to gather in a riot of greenery at the base.

Lattimore spoke suddenly in her ear. "Splendid job, Letty dear! An artistic touch..."

"What do you mean, Hugh?"

"The swathes of autumnal foliage you've draped around him. Very evocative of his early origins. The Green God indeed! He appreciates it—you'd swear he'd enjoyed his evening, wouldn't you? And more to come, of course! The *bonne bouche*!"

"But, Hugh, it wasn't *I* who..."

But he was already hurrying off to his next duty, leaving her with a growing feeling of unease. Anyone could have hidden a gun or a knife under that exuberance of vine leaves. Letty decided to keep a sharp eye on any man or woman who approached within arm's reach of the statue.

She looked again at the god. Hugh was right. The deity did look pleased. At home in his greenery. But how could he fail to be entertained? Drama, good company, and wine. Was there anything they had failed to offer the dark god?

She watched from the fringes of the group, smiling at the sight of Helena Venizelos chattering with Thetis. Thetis had retained her queenly robes and was every inch an equal for the First Lady. Slender white next to voluminous purple, dark heads together, nodding and laughing. It seemed a strong relationship.

Montacute had taken off his grey cloak and was standing with Freddy Wentworth and Geoffrey Melton, eyes darting everywhere, empty hands loosely by his sides. Letty looked at the group of three impressive men in puzzlement for a moment and then realised that what had snagged at her attention was the reduced height of Geoffrey. He too had disrobed, kicked off his high buskins, and was standing, relaxed, thumbs hooked casually into his belt. Taking artistic liberties a little too far? Letty thought so. She looked afresh at the pared-down figure, athletic in plain khaki shirt and trousers. Standing firmly on big bare feet, eyes raking the auditorium, he appeared to form a guard with Montacute, one formidable man on each side of the First Secretary.

Freddy's guard dog, uncomfortable with the grouping, Letty judged, was prowling the stage behind them.

Louis Adams was suddenly at her elbow. "More champagne for the ASM?" he asked. Members of the cast had volunteered for the task of carrying around the refreshment trays on the insistence of Montacute. No strangers in the role of waiters had been allowed on the set. Everyone at present in the theatre was known by name and reputation to the Greek and British authorities.

"No, thanks, Louis. I'm saving myself for the red wine. It's rather special. We'll have that in—about five minutes. Can you warn the other waiters to stand by?"

The signal came from Hugh Lattimore. Positioned behind Dionysus, he waved to Letty to indicate that all was in order.

Jugs, bowls, bottles, and drains were ready for the libation ceremony. Letty caught Freddy's eye and nodded. He stepped forward, the immaculate host, and announced that it was high time the God of the Theatre received his due.

His due. His due! Too late, Letty remembered the one traditional offering they had never thought to serve up for the god that evening.

CHAPTER 42

etty accepted a glass of bloodred wine from the tray when it appeared at her side, as did everyone else. Everyone apart from Melton and Thetis, she noticed uneasily. Both refused with a discreet shake of the head. Then she remembered Thetis was to hold the silver bowl while Helena Venizelos poured the libation into it before tipping it away into the channel in the earth. She would need to keep her hands free and her head clear. A sensible precaution.

Freddy was at his charming best. His clear tenor penetrated even Letty's distracted brain. "An ode to the god of the evening—a modest offering, courtesy of those wonderful bards: Homer, with a bit of help from Orpheus and patched together by dubious rhymester Wentworth. Not often I have the chance of speaking in such a sonorous amphitheatre . . . it makes even *my* voice sound godlike." He waved an arm around the theatre in an encompassing gesture and stopped suddenly, his attention caught.

"But—ah!—I see we have an audience of one? A solitary spectator!" He shielded his eyes from the glare of the lights and looked upwards into the auditorium. "Sir! Welcome!" he called out with the jovial aplomb of a Master of Ceremonies.

"Yes, you, sir, in the back row. What shall we guess you are? Aficionado of Aeschylus, Devotee of Dionysus? Or did you merely fall asleep in the last act? Whoever you are—do stay for a while. I press you into service as adjudicator. Which of the players wins the laurel wreath for elocution this year? That is the question. And the required answer is: Wentworth!"

As Freddy prepared to launch into his ode, Letty turned and sneaked a glance upwards at the stray spectator on whom Freddy had so firmly (deliberately?) turned the spotlight. A lonely figure on the topmost rank of seats got to his feet and bowed in a stagey way, responding to the challenge. Did Letty imagine that he was looking directly at her? The man raised both his empty hands in a meaningful gesture of innocence or surrender. It occurred to her that this harmless figure who appeared, thanks to Freddy's joking inclusion in the ceremony, to everyone else to be a plant, a part of the proceedings, was known to only one person in the gathering. To her.

Soulios Gunay.

Lying, murderous Gunay. Anonymous Gunay. No one else had ever set eyes on him.

Letty froze. She licked her dry lips and looked frantically about. What to do? Scream? Cut Freddy off just as he was getting started? She turned her head once again to Gunay. Quietly seated now, he was calmly watching. He'd indicated by his gesture to her that he was no threat. He was simply watching a space from which his target had been withdrawn. No danger. Why then was she feeling such a paralysing terror? Why hadn't she launched into a hysterical denunciation? Shouted accusations of kidnapping and murder?

An unarmed man was watching a space empty of interest for him, she told herself again.

A hand reached for hers and dragged her towards the edge of the orchestra.

"William! Up there ... That man! It's—"

"Shh! Quiet! Keep your head down! Don't interfere, Letty. Stand behind me and don't move. We're just the chorus in all this. Leave it to those who wrote the script. Freddy has him in his sights. Listen! He's just getting into his stride," Gunning said.

Clearly revelling in his priestly role, Freddy began to belt out his tribute to Dionysus:

> "I call upon the roaring god,
> Ivy-crowned, splendid son of Zeus!
> Savage, secretive, shape-shifter,
> Dual-natured Dionysus!
> Lord of Laughter and of the Dance!
> You delight in the fruit of the vine,
> You feast on raw flesh!
> Come blessed and leaping god
> And bring much joy to all!"

Everyone turned, raised a glass, and drank a toast to the god. Thetis and Helena moved towards him, gliding along with the dignity of priestesses. They looked up dutifully at the sneering stone features, they poured and lifted with large gestures in a ceremonial way and murmured a chant, as had been rehearsed. The classical beauty of the women, the colour of the costumes, the musical sound of the ancient Greek they were uttering, were casting a considerable spell, attracting all eyes.

The newsman, for one, was beside himself with rapture. He brandished his camera and elbowed a guest out of his way to get the angle he wanted just as Helena held out the bowl and tilted it away from her. The red wine glinted and gleamed as it streamed down into the earth.

A shot, a scream, a blinding flash. The column rocked forward. The stone god crashed to the earth a split second before the single shot sounded. The weight of stone smashing onto pavings and the blast of a high-calibre revolver combined to deafen and knock the breath out of everyone who heard. Their eyes were dazzled by the magnesium flare of the flashbulb. Letty darted forward, blinking and moaning, moving against the crowd of onlookers pushing their way in panic away from the scene. Men and women, in their terror, were rushing to hide wherever they could and, finding little in the way of cover, were throwing themselves to the ground.

She was horrified by the sight of Helena, a spreading red stain on the front of her white gown, flying sideways and down away from the statue. She had fallen and now lay motionless on the floor. The silken wings of Thetis's robe fluttered down protectively over her, inches from the column and the splintered head.

In hurling her friend to safety, Thetis had put herself straight into danger. Letty saw her try to wriggle free of the weight of marble that pinned her to the ground by one leg. But Thetis seemed to be wriggling with another purpose. She pulled the Webley from her robe, swivelled as best she could, and raised her weight onto one elbow. In an agonising effort of concentration, with a steady hand, she fired off all six rounds into the bushes behind them. An unfathomable roar rang out and a body crashed through the undergrowth beyond the arc of lights.

"*Stay!*" One word from William kept Letty back as he dashed with Montacute across the arena. Wentworth was already there, struggling with the column.

"Lever!" yelled Gunning. "Louis! Get that plank over here!"

"Raw flesh!" Letty cursed the god in her heart. "You had to have your raw flesh! Your human sacrifice. A body torn to shreds and bleeding before you!"

She looked around desperately. Were she and Thetis the only ones who'd heard the first shot, eclipsed as it was by the more dramatically visual collapse of the statue? Was that stain on the front of Helena's dress spilled wine as she'd assumed, or was it more sinister than that? But someone else had noticed. The guards were on their feet, crouching, guns in hand. At a signal from their officer they hurried to form a protective circle around the floor while he charged across the arena in the direction of Thetis's shots, to plunge, in lone pursuit, into the undergrowth behind the statue. A shot and a scream rang out. The finality of a calculated second shot from the same deep-throated gun followed and then silence.

Was it all over? Letty wanted it to be all over. But Dionysus was a god who demanded a triple sacrifice. And he was not yet satisfied.

Geoffrey Melton, revolver in hand, had run on silent feet to the edge of the orchestra. Placing himself behind the stem of one of the lamps, he twisted it around until he had what he wanted in his sights.

Soulios Gunay, still smiling, squinted affably into the searchlight. He got to his feet, presenting himself, a standing target, and he began, sardonically, to clap: a Roman Emperor applauding a performance put on in his honour. He seemed content with the scene of carnage and chaos on the stage. At the moment the Browning boomed he held out both arms, directing the bullet to his chest, welcoming his death. One shot. Gunay's shoulder jerked. A second. Gunay collapsed soundlessly, sideways onto the marble seat.

When Letty turned back to the arena, it was to see two guards returning from the wilderness, carrying along between them a lifeless body. Directed by their fighting cock of an officer, who still had his gun in his hand, they dropped it in the middle of the stage.

The terrified cast and their guests picked themselves up from the floor, sensing that the last shot had been fired, and began to creep slowly forward, eyes watchful and staring, drawn to see who had uncorked the bloodbath.

CHAPTER 43

"Peebles! Are you there?" Montacute put back his head and shouted. "Dr. Peebles!"

"I'm right here at your side, man," said a calm voice. "I've checked the First Lady and she's fine. Just winded from being hurled on her back by this valiant Valkyrie here. Not hurt in the least. The dramatic red stain is no more than a bowlful of red wine. Careful! Careful!"

He hovered over Thetis, hands reaching for her limbs while the stone rocked dangerously above.

"One more heave!" yelled Gunning. Many hands strained down on the end of the plank and others pushed at the tipping column. "Clear the area!" They skipped out of the way as it crashed down inches from Thetis's feet.

Peebles leaned protectively over her, feeling the limbs with delicate hands, calling out instructions and telephone numbers for the ambulance. "No significant bleeding," he reported. "These stiff robes were some slight protection. Silk? It can keep out an arrowhead! But it can't do much against a heavy weight. I'm afraid there are broken leg bones. Crushed kneecap. The foot seems all right—the wooden-soled sandals she's got on saved her from the worst. Pass me my bag. I left it over there in the front row. She's going to need a shot of morphine."

Someone was trying to lead Helena from the scene but she broke away and came back to kneel by Thetis's side and clutch her hand.

"Don't worry. I'm fine! Go now! Get away from here," Thetis managed through gritted teeth. "God, it hurts! Who did I shoot? Was it that little shit, Lattimore? Creeping about in the shrubbery! This is the moment where I spit on the corpse if someone'll help me over…Percy! I can't…" She groaned and lapsed into unconsciousness.

"Me? I heard that! She's blaming me?" Hugh Lattimore struggled forward, pushing his way through the crowd, spluttering with indignation. "How dare she! Will someone kindly tell this lady when she wakes up that I had nothing to do with any of this. *I* didn't push the statue over. In fact no one did! I was watching. There was no one but the two ladies within twelve feet of it! Wentworth was nearest and he didn't touch it! It just crashed down! Act of God, you might say!"

At his words, Gunning exclaimed and moved over to the base of the column, eyes covering the ground. He tore up festoons of green foliage and stirred about until he found what he was looking for. He picked up an object, winding out a length of rope that held it. "A wedge," he said. "Tug this out and the whole thing collapses. You!" He rounded on Lattimore. "Shut up! Stay exactly where you are and hold yourself ready for questioning by the inspector. At the very least, you're a close witness of all that transpired this evening."

He returned to Montacute, who was holding out Thetis's arm for the doctor's needle. "Stay with her. I'll go and see what the guards have brought in. Don't worry, Percy—that young major seems to have everything under control...though you may need to put the cuffs on Melton, who's gone quite mad and has been taking potshots at the one-man audience. Now, where the hell is *he*?"

CHAPTER 44

here was no sign of Melton, but the man he'd shot was coming into the spotlight, descending the marble steps, carried along like a wild boar by arms and legs. The body bumped and swayed with the stately tread of the four troopers who held it.

They put him down by the side of the first victim.

The crowd approached tentatively. No one called out in horror or even surprise. Heads were shaken, a puzzled murmuring began. Montacute tore himself from Thetis's side and made his way over to take charge. He moved people back a short way from the two bodies, knelt, and checked to confirm that they were, indeed, both lifeless.

He got to his feet, cleared his throat, and voiced the question on the tip of everyone's tongue: "Who in blazes have we got here? Will someone kindly put a name to these two?"

Shrugging shoulders, raised eyebrows, bleating denials, and finally silence were his response.

Letty pushed through to the inspector. "I can identify this man. The solitary spectator. His name's Soulios Gunay and he's a tobacco merchant. From Turkey." She felt bound to add, out of a scarcely understood respect: "But he's really a native of Macedonia."

"Good God! This is him?" Montacute snorted and harrumphed. "I had imagined someone more formidable. Um... thank you, Miss Talbot. Perhaps you would hold yourself ready to make a statement later?"

Freddy Wentworth was suddenly with them, leaning over the other body. He stood up again, a spectral figure, white in the face, his evening suit thick in stone dust, his shirt stained with spilled wine and blood from his cut hands. "And I can identify *this* man. The one in the shrubbery." He spoke quietly to Montacute. "But would prefer to do so in private, Inspector, if you wouldn't mind. I will just say that he is known to the authorities. And those same authorities will expect you to deal... diplomatically... with the remains in the prescribed manner."

Unsatisfied and in a mood to challenge any authority that got in his way, Montacute shouldered Wentworth aside. Deliberately trying to puncture the diplomat's discretion, he began a provoking recital of the victim's wounds. "Shot through the shoulder... small-calibre weapon... probably a consequence of Miss Templeton's sharpshooting."

A murmur of approval went up from the crowd.

"Another..." He turned the corpse over onto its front. "The second, I'm assuming... from a more powerful pistol, caught him in the back as he fled." He looked at the major's gun, which was still, discreetly, being held in his hand. The major nodded crisply in acknowledgement of his contribution.

"Well done, sir!" someone said from the crowd, and this was echoed by other admirers.

"The third—and the coup de grâce, I'm thinking—was administered by a steady hand and the bullet passed through the victim's temple." Again the major nodded.

"He got what he deserved!" a voice commented stoutly.

"*Assassin!* That's what he was. Here to shoot the Prime Minister, no doubt. And as he wasn't present, the fiend went for his wife, poor lady. You're jolly lucky he didn't have a go at you, too, Wentworth!"

"Scum! Thank God the military were here!"

"Albanian, probably. Troublemakers! Look at that evil face! Makes you shudder! Odd, though, don't you think? Anyone noticed? He's an elderly bloke...What would you say? Fifty? I thought assassins were all young hotheads? University students and the like."

"If we were told his name we probably wouldn't be able to pronounce it," someone drawled. "I expect we'll have to wait and read it in the *Times*."

Hating them, hating the place, Letty reached for Gunning's hand and whispered in his ear.

"I simply can't think why London bothered to issue you with handcuffs, Montacute! You don't appear to have made much use of them! One young heroine incarcerated for the best part of a day by mistake and that's about the sum total of your law-enforcing, what?"

Wentworth was blustering, Letty considered. Probably nerving himself to tell them a walloping great lie to cover up some machinations his diplomatic staff had been involved with. She decided not to ask him to marry her. The thought of being hitched to a man who lied for a living was unappealing.

They were sitting around a polished table in one of the state rooms of the Embassy in bright morning light. Civilised, reassuringly official surroundings. Murmuring staff had supplied them with pens and notebooks and blotters. Coffee and shortbread had been served. An aide had apologetically slid under their hands a government form, which Wentworth had waited for them to sign before he began the meeting. "Would you mind? Official Secrets Act and all that nonsense. Can't even begin until you've scribbled on it and returned it to Swinton…Thank you all so much. Now I can stick you in the Tower and cut your throats or something if you divulge a word."

The First Secretary, clearly fully recovered from his ordeal of the previous evening, was freshly bathed and smelling faintly of Trumper's best hair oil. Freshly briefed also, she didn't doubt. The telegraph between Athens and London must have been running hot overnight. She, Gunning, and Montacute had been summoned to appear before him to be fed the official line.

"But first—may we hear the latest news of Miss Templeton? You were at her bedside for most of the night, I understand, Montacute? Very devoted."

"She's doing well. She'll be in plaster and on crutches for the next six months but she's a strong girl. She was lucky. There's a surgeon in the city, a friend of Doc Peebles, retired but with extensive experience of war wounds, who was able to dash along and operate. He saved her leg. But she won't be striding the boards for a while yet. Thank you for enquiring, sir."

"I hope I would always show concern for my staff, Inspector." Wentworth smiled.

"What? Freddy! What are you talking about?" Letty asked.

"It's a deep state secret, but I'm perfectly certain the lady herself feels little allegiance to the state—any state—and will soon, herself, blurt out the truth of the matter! Under pretext of being under the influence of some opiate or other, perhaps?" He seemed pleased to intercept Montacute's guilty start.

"I anticipate her account: Recruited in London, she volunteered to be seconded to my staff here in Athens for the duration of a period of acute danger to the life of the Prime Minister."

"Recruited? Volunteered?" Montacute's tone was blistering, lacking any deference. "Miss Templeton was *coerced* by the bullying servants of a corrupt Home Office! Five years in Holloway prison or do as we suggest ... A fine notion of secondment!"

"Come now! She was offered a most respectable and worthwhile assignment, Montacute. Any patriot would have considered it an honour to accept. She was fully briefed and trained in the use of countersurveillance and firearms. And, in the event, you cannot deny that she performed her duty most nobly!"

Montacute was not placated. "She was fond of the woman she was protecting and would have given her life in her defence anyway. You were lucky there. Suppose your 'target' had been some loathsome ingrate—you'd still have twisted her arm."

Wentworth did not deny the accusation; he tiptoed around it. "We were indeed fortunate that a genuine friendship blossomed between the two. Infernally difficult to supervise and shadow a female, especially here in Greece. And this was no product of the seraglio we were protecting! Here, there, and everywhere on show in public places. Street soup kitchens in the Plaka one minute, dinner parties in Kiffissia the next! Protection could only be undertaken by one of her own sex and one who blended in with Madame Venizelos's chosen background and extracurricular activities. We do not normally recruit females for such work. We were lucky that Miss Templeton's particular abilities came to our notice at the right moment."

He leaned confidingly to Montacute: "Probably premature to make any mention of an honour in the offing, but ..."

"The right moment, you said, Freddy?" Letty challenged, sensing they had him on the retreat. "How did you know that Venizelos was in danger?"

"Ah. We had a murmur ... no, for once it was more than

that... clear indications from the very highest authority, back in England, that a plot to assassinate him was—once again—under way. But this time, we were up against something more threatening than the usual student-inspired revolutionaries. There have always been signs, Laetitia, that the Royalist party... you understand to whom I am referring when I say..."

"I have sufficient knowledge of Balkan politics," Letty lied. "Do get on with it, Freddy."

"...would go to any lengths to remove the P.M. from power with a finality, but their attempts have always been easy to counter. This time... For a start there was money behind it. And the originator tapped into an increasingly strong Europe-wide linkage. We suspect, if we were able to track it back far enough, we'd find the Kaiser himself in the middle of the web. He is known to be actively pursuing the signatories of the Versailles Treaty... an implacable fellow who has not yet accepted that for him the war is over... And Venizelos has always been his enemy, the royal family of Greece his silent supporters. But the *originator*, the moving force behind all this—and I know you will surmise, Letty, that I am speaking of your friend Gunay—insisted on orchestrating the attempt himself. For personal reasons, which I do believe you could make clear to us?"

"That's true," said Letty. "But I'm sure we're all aware..." She ignored the attempt to divert her into an account and waited for him to carry on.

"And, being a complete unknown, and a clever unknown, he might well have succeeded." He left a pause and then allowed himself a little modest self-congratulation. "A cold, scheming brain fuelled by a deep personal motive, in the driving seat of a well-funded political organisation, run by the German and Greek military. Formidable opposition, you will say! And I will agree. Hard to crack!"

"And was poor Thetis shoved all by herself into the front line to counter all this firepower?" Gunning asked. "Was she also responsible for the Prime Minister?"

"Ah, no. He had his own shadow. You may have noticed him playing rather an assertive role towards the end. Melton. Our Invisible Fixer. They come in useful at times like this." He smiled dismissively. "We knew an attack was to take place. We knew the organisation would go on and on with these attempts until it was pulled up at the root. And that is what everyone longed for! The final and total annihilation of this noxious nexus." Receiving no answering smile, he pressed on: "It was decided this time, with the full knowledge and cooperation of the Venizelos couple—who don't lack courage—to let things proceed unchecked. The network would, it was calculated, reveal itself as it played its hand.

"Inevitably, an assassin would creep out of the woodwork. With a bit of luck, he would be taken alive and be required to account for himself. Melton was brought in to exercise his very special skills in matters of this nature. It's what he does. There are some men who don't object at all to dirtying their hands in the name of their country." He hesitated for a moment to flick an imaginary speck from his cuff with a manicured fingernail, expecting—inviting, perhaps?—a scything riposte from Montacute.

Into the sullen silence, he went on: "The Prime Minister's appearance at the play was the perfect opportunity for the organisation. And our man, believe me, was ready to put his body and his gun between the P.M. and any assassin who dared to put his head above the parapet." His voice curdled with patriotic pride.

"Geoffrey Melton? Can we be talking about Geoffrey Melton? I can see him torturing a luckless creature or two in a twisted way, but gallant self-sacrifice?" Letty huffed. "Can you be quite certain of this, Freddy?"

Wentworth gave her a smile tight with secret knowledge. "The gentleman has an impressive record of service to the state...for one so young..." was all he cared to add. "But this whole affair was what you might call a setup. A rat trap. The Venizelos pair were the willing bait and Melton the killing blade in a trap set by us."

"Whoever *you* are! But the Prime Minister backed out at the last minute and the network knew that!" Letty objected.

"Good Lord!" said Gunning, suddenly inspired. "Because *he* was never the target! It was *Helena* they had in their sights all along!"

Wentworth nodded and waited for Gunning to pursue his theory.

"It was Gunay's twisted thought, wasn't it? His own wife had been lost and he'd suffered her loss for years. He knew Venizelos had mourned his first wife for a quarter of a century. Uxorious chap! He could imagine the shattering effect of losing a second wife, and he relished the thought of the old man's suffering his way to the grave."

"And *politically,* it was an astute move. And this is what appealed to the Royalist faction who couldn't care less about the P.M.'s sensibilities. He's an old man now. Supported, strengthened, motivated by his active younger wife. I think it's clear to all that he would have given up and retired back to his flat in Paris had she been taken from him in this way."

"And who would benefit? George the Second! He'd be invited back from wherever he's got to in Europe to take up the throne again! Disgraceful, shameful affair!" Gunning fumed.

"You express His Majesty's own thoughts exactly!" Wentworth sat back smiling, waiting for their reaction.

"What are you saying? That King George was aware...?"

"Yes, he was. An officer from the German armed forces visited him in London with a proposal. Told him what was about to be done in his name. We run a line of remarkably effective temporary valets...they say a man has no secrets from his valet. True. No surprise there. But we were astonished when the king himself strolled down Saint James's and paid a call on one of our top men. The strength of his honour was being sorely tested, he proclaimed. He had personal dragons to fight. Time to do the right thing...(I think we have Wagner to thank for this rush of noble sentiment to the head.) He would derive no satisfaction from the assassination of an old man's wife, however much his enemy. He scorned it for a dishonourable act! He—correctly—predicted the country would ascribe the deed to him and turn from him in revulsion. So George came clean. Confided all. Demanded absolute discretion, naturally. And here we are!" he concluded, beaming around the table and gathering his papers together. "Being absolutely discreet! Thank you all so much for dropping by—"

"No! Here we aren't! Not yet!" Letty burst out. "Freddy! You're keeping something from us! You knew him! Are you ever going to tell us who he was—the grizzled old goat who aimed a bullet, to say nothing of a ton of rock, at Helena? And Thetis?"

"Ah yes." Wentworth's expression became less unctuous. "Albanian bandit whose name escapes me? Would you believe?"

They glared at him in hostile silence.

"Won't quite do, Wentworth," said Gunning.

"No, I thought not. Well, that's what you'll read in the papers. May even prove to be one of your old sparring partners, Montacute! Busy boys! If these blokes exist—and we only have your word for it—they must be laughing their socks off when they read about their continuing exploits in the press. Oh, very well. Here, take a look at this. Top Secret, of course. Swinton has your signatures, I remind you."

He passed a sheet of paper to Montacute. A sheet of typed

paper with a photograph paper-clipped to the front. They leaned over Montacute's shoulder to inspect it.

"That's the man!" said Letty. "The man who was dancing attendance on you last night. What a villain! He actually *looks* like someone who'd put a bullet in you as soon as look at you! Gunay, I begin to think, could never have killed anyone face-to-face. Not even a weed like me. So he hired this ruffian to do the dirty work. Who is he?"

Montacute pushed the photograph aside to reveal a sheet from a Home Office official file.

"Good Lord!" he said, stunned, and passed it to Gunning. "This is a bit hard to take! Did you have *any* idea, Wentworth? This is going to do you no credit when it gets out."

"'Rose to the rank of major in a very illustrious British regiment?'" Gunning read out. "'Special Branch experience...' Five years with those bully boys...Scottish father, German mother...Name of Grant. 'Attached latterly to the British Embassy, special duties.' Nothing out of the way there? Means nothing to me, I'm afraid. But why? Why on earth would such a man attempt political murder?"

"Money and danger? Those eternal incentives? Old soldier with a chip on his shoulder, you know how it is...Expected to go higher. Passed over...Strong fighting instinct. Aggressive, ruthless. No outlet for it these days...May have had some family connection through his mother with the Kaiser's mob." Wentworth paused to assess the level of disbelief in his audience. Then he sighed. "No? Well, we haven't got to the bottom of that quite yet." He grimaced and added, disarmingly: "We're still working on a convincing story." He stirred uncomfortably in his seat and leaned towards them. "Look, there's an outside possibility that he may have been obeying orders from on high. I mean, higher than we have cognisance of..."

"'On high'?" Montacute was scoffing when he cut him off.

"How high? You mean the top floor of the War Office? So damn secret they don't even know who they're meant to be themselves? There are always fanatics up there—Royalists by instinct, most of them, feudal-minded fossils who still tug forelocks and bend the knee. Men who despise the idea of democracy, let alone a Republic. And they're always ready to meddle. Always ready to send a man over the top with a hand-shake and a patriotic tear in the eye. And the right phrase ringing in his ear...Scottish, wasn't he, this Grant? One of the Bonnie Charlie brigade, no doubt! You'll probably discover a white cockade next to his heart. Lord! I could have been one such myself if I hadn't seen them coming! And this poor bugger, Grant, was their triggerman, the one who set up the killing scene at the theatre."

"The maintenance man, according to the night guards, who have been interviewed afresh. They shared many a bottle with him after hours. They hadn't thought to mention it be-cause he was, after all, just a Briton like the rest of those lu-natics...This one came in occasionally to check up on security. Had a full set of keys and all...They actually heaved on a rope to help him reinstate the statue when it toppled over." Wentworth shook his head more in sorrow than in anger. "We asked questions your squad appear not to have thought of, Montacute."

"Already on the inside, he could operate in total anonymity and security from a base right here in the Embassy under your nose, Wentworth," Montacute countered.

Wentworth flinched.

Letty was unsatisfied. Freddy had coughed up this infor-mation too easily, she calculated. And he was diverting Percy, running him down safe channels of his own choosing. En-meshing him in a private duel. A slippery customer, Went-worth, she guessed, who had one last wriggle left in him.

"All the people you've mentioned so far, Freddy, have been

pawns," she commented, stepping between the drawn swords. "Essential perhaps at times, but expendable. There's someone else...behind all this, just out of sight..." she speculated. "No! Listen! None of us in the company even recognised this Grant. He was never there when we were about. But someone knew *every* move we made in the theatre, rehearsal times, plans for the libation ceremony...Things he couldn't have learned in a boozy after-hours exchange with the Greek watchman."

Wentworth began to rise to his feet. "All surmise," he said dismissively. "I think we can safely leave it there. You have the names you wanted. Now—if you wouldn't mind..."

They sat firmly in their places.

"No, Wentworth. Letty has it right. Give her another minute and she'll be along the trail like a hound," advised Gunning pleasantly. "Listen to her—she's usually worth hearing."

"*Lattimore!*" she exclaimed. "He really didn't take part in the killing, but he did make a contribution! His big mouth! He was teaching English to the family of General Konstantinou— a wonderful way to get information from him! 'Do tell the children all that you did today...so good for their English.'"

"And the General listened!" Montacute fixed Wentworth in his seat with his sharp words. "And used the information and passed it to Grant. Who planned accordingly; who experimented after hours on-site with wedges and angles and ropes until he had it right. And then he put his simple gear back in the storage shed where he'd found it. He brought down Dionysus as nothing more than a distraction. It was the *shot* that was meant to kill her. If a woman's lying dead under a heap of stone, everyone in range is going to assume in the confusion that she's been crushed to death. They're going to crack their muscles and dig with their hands to release her body while the perpetrator slides away under cover of the chaos into the bushes unnoticed. And who comes out of all this smelling of roses? The *General*, who, in his infinite wisdom, ensured that the Prime Minister was dissuaded from appearing. A distancing move. How we applauded his caution! He didn't care—he was the only man who knew, apart from Gunay, that the Prime Minister was not a marked man anyway. Konstantinou, eh? Poor old Wentworth! You've got your work cut out smoothing this one over. Your Invisible Fixer still on the books, is he? Hang on to him, you might be needing him!"

"Oh, it's the assassination in Macedon all over again," Letty said quietly. "And Grant himself was doomed. The gunman was never going to be captured and questioned. The bold young major made absolutely certain of that. Carrying out his General's orders. What's the betting that *he* modestly accepts a rise in rank after a decent interval? Does this violence never end? Oh, I could weep! What has been achieved? What are we left with?"

"You need me to spell it out?" Wentworth was losing patience. "We're left with a World Statesman and his wife unscathed. We're left with the unmasking of a particularly nasty and dangerous element right here in Athens and a whole network which is, even as I speak, being rolled up throughout Europe!"

Letty was silenced by the truth of this but Montacute was flashing with anger. "No, Wentworth! What we have on our conscience—those of us who have one—is a young woman who may never walk again. Smashed to the ground and crippled by a distraction! A woman who was press-ganged into a damned dangerous job by a callous Home Office that can't even live by its own rules. We're left with a very angry policeman who was sent out here to do nothing more than stand by with the handcuffs. A cardboard cutout, an acceptable face of officialdom, providing a reassuring presence. After all, the *Embassy* can't go about arresting anyone in a foreign country should they be left, by some lapse of judgement, with an undead villain on their hands. Better have on tap a compliant bobby. Just in case.

"And what's your bobby left with? The assurance that the royal families of two countries will be graciously thankful for his efforts! No crowned head need be embarrassed by a messy and uncalled-for killing. Well, I said it at the time and I say again: Sod the royal families!"

A self-destructive speech which would be followed within twenty-four hours by instant recall to London to hear of his dismissal from whatever government post he at present occupied, Letty reckoned, aghast at the inspector's flourish.

Montacute got to his feet and stormed from the room.

Letty and Gunning stormed with him.

"The Grande Bretagne bar is that way, old man," said Gunning, grasping him by the elbow. "It's a bit early for a pink gin but I think we've all earned one!"

CHAPTER 45

Are you ever going to tell me what your unholy bargain with Gunay consisted of?"

"William! I'd have thought an afternoon of dalliance at the Apollo, wallowing in scented French linen, befuddled by a bottle of the management's best fizz, would have put such matters out of your head. I'm not going to talk about it. I'd rather think about what we're going to have for supper."

He sighed in irritation. "Thought as much. You've been very quiet lately. You're planning something. And I don't think I shall like it. Listen! Whatever 'bargain' you made was struck with a gun at your head, made with a villain who is, in fact, dead. So, on two counts, your 'bargain' is null and void. You owe the man nothing. Not even a backward glance."

Letty considered for a moment, unwilling to spoil a magical afternoon with a mention of plans she knew would make him furious. "You're right. Of course, you're right. But Gunay was a bit of an enchanter, you know. He's influencing me from beyond the grave."

Gunning snorted in disapproval of her fanciful notion. "He—"

Letty put a hand over his mouth. "He asked me to do something he knew I would want to do anyway. Not *want*, particularly, but feel I had to do. He was enticing me to take a path I had already travelled halfway along."

Gunning thought for a bit and then said: "And I think I can guess what you'll find at the end of the road…"

"What I'll find, William?" she asked tentatively.

"What *we'll* find. You're not going up there without me trotting at your stirrup, miss!" And he intoned: "To Salonika!"

Letty shuddered. "You don't think we could entice Montacute and his Browning to come along for the ride?"

Gunning laughed. "No chance of that! He hasn't travelled further than a few yards from Thetis's side since she was laid low! And I think never will. I say, Letty, you haven't…I mean…you two are pretty thick…has she dropped any hint that…?"

"The word you find impossible to mouth is 'matrimony,' William. Marriage. Has he? Did she? When will they? What will the World say? And I have to say, honestly, I'm not sure! I think so. It's hard to tell. Thetis raves so! Last time I was by her bedside, she'd just spent two hours in his sole company. Well, she wasn't paying much attention to *me*!"

"And, of course, one doesn't like to ask outright."

"No. But she did say some revealing things! 'Just imagine, Letty,' she said with a sigh, 'I shall have him all for my own!' And then: 'I shall be able to nibble bits of him whenever I like!'"

"Good Lord!"

"Can *you* imagine, William? *Nibbling* bits of Percy?"

"Well, no. I've never found coppers particularly palatable. Tell you what, though…If your imagination should prove not to be up to it, I'm perfectly prepared to offer up selected parts of me for experimentation."

AN ESSAY BY THE AUTHOR

The world of the historical detective writer is an *Alice-in-Wonderland* one. Where does reality end and imagination take over? If you've done your job, the reader should hardly be able to spot the interface. It's all a sleight of hand, but there are rules—largely self-imposed in these forgiving literary times—and fair play is my censor.

The background, the setting, and the political storms growling in the background are always as accurate as I can make them. They generate the story. The peripheral historical figures encountered did or said or behaved as described, in accordance with their generally accepted character. Where they interact with the heroine or hero, as one or two do in this book, we are inviting them into make-believe and must treat them with absolute respect.

Three characters from the past inspired this tale, and their historical paths may be traced by anyone who, as I do, enjoys bolting down the rabbit-holes of history to see where they will lead me.

The earliest is the constantly magnetic figure of Alexander of Macedon. His homeland, the traditional state of Macedonia to the north of Greece, became a battlefield during the early years of the twentieth century. I had always envisaged this as a mysterious land of myth, the preserve of Dionysus the Dark God, the haunt of eagles and the home of Greek-speaking warrior tribes, and here I was, at one moment in my research, having this same land laid out for me with a soldier's eye for terrain. Brigadier Sandilands of the Northumberland

Fusiliers describes with a jaundiced eye the deprivations of the British Salonika Army, who found themselves sequestered here in 1915 and set to fight the Bulgarians (whom they admired) and the mosquitoes (which they feared greatly). Disease-ridden, badly supplied, and with not much grasp on the overall strategy, hundreds of British engineers were busying themselves digging trenches across an archaeologically rich land. And the Tomb of Alexander, much sought after, has to this day not been located...Another rabbit-hole opens.

The two other historical characters who influenced the book are a twentieth-century couple: a prime minister of Greece and his first lady.

He is Eleutherios Venizelos, world-renowned revolutionary, politician, and hero, and there is a wealth of information on him. For the *Times of London,* he was "The Great Cretan"; for *Time* magazine (in 1928) he was "greatest of living Greeks, a nimble old man of ready wit."

But it is his wife, the glamorous and mysterious Helena, who fascinated me. In 1921, in London, the rich and stylish Mayfair lady Helena Schilizzi, half Greek, half English, married the much older man she had been in love with for ten years. Londoners, who have always loved a good romance, gave the couple an enthusiastic send-off as they left to spend their honeymoon in California.

Back home in war-ravaged Europe with her husband taking a leading role on a dangerous political stage, Helena proved herself to be an inspiring consort. Intelligent, energetic, and fearless, she shared her husband's public life, knowing that he was perpetually the target for an assassin's bullet. She was the moving force behind many good works, sponsoring valuable scholarships (still in use today), endowing hospitals, and providing health care for the thousands of needy who flooded into the capital, Athens. A role model for any first lady!

She would have been much admired by Laetitia Talbot, I thought. And there it is—the descent into Wonderland. Helena, the historical character, steps—literally—onstage in my story. She appears gracious, beautiful, brave, and charismatic, as she was in life, and in borrowing her corporeal essence for a few pages, I trust I have not offended her Shade.

The attempted murder described in the book is an invention but not an outrageous imagining, as the reader may guess, judging by the following account of an actual attack which was to occur some six years after the event in the book. We have Venizelos's own crisp words to a *Times* reporter:

Athens, June 7, 1933

My wife and I were returning to Athens when I saw a green seven-seater car. The assassins allowed my car to pass and then, placing themselves between my car and that of my escort, began firing. Remembering the attempt made on my life at a French railway station, I took my wife in my arms and we both crouched on the floor of the car.

The assassins had by this time reloaded and they kept on firing for three kilometres. All the time I kept asking my wife whether she had been hit, but she replied in the negative.

When the firing recommenced I saw blood and understood that my wife had been wounded.... I urged my chauffeur on with cries of "Quicker, Jianni!" and notwithstanding his plight, he accelerated and drove us to the Evanghelismos Hospital.

The chauffeur had been shot through the arm. Helena had, in silence, been struck by four bullets. She recovered. Both Helena and her husband would die of natural causes three years later.

Three historical characters and one chilling historical theme provided the impetus for the book. The theme is a heart-breaking one. The events briefly described, which constitute a motive for a crime, actually happened. Considering their devastating impact on millions of lives and not so long ago, these events are little known outside the Balkans.

The affair is named, inoffensively enough, "The Population Exchange Between Greece and Turkey" of 1923. A treaty was ratified in Lausanne by top European politicians. What this devastating document authorised was nothing less than ethnic cleansing and the displacement of over two million people. Selection for enforced emigration was by religion. Half a million Muslims living in Greece (largely in the north and Macedonia) had to move to Turkey. One and a half million Greek Christians (in addition to the million who had already been thrown out or massacred) were expelled from Turkey.

Thousands set out in boats to cross the Aegean, leaving everything behind. Of those lucky enough to survive the diseases and privations of the sea voyage, many arrived homeless and destitute, abandoned by their political masters. For years, Greece, the much smaller state receiving vastly disproportionate numbers, was unable to cope with the huge influx, and the streets of Athens were crowded with Turkish-speaking immigrants who had to resort to begging to survive. In the rescue efforts, an international force—largely from the United States—worked valiantly to provide medical help. The accounts of an American doctor, Esther Lovejoy, are at once horrifying and inspiring. This tough lady was a survivor of the massacre of Smyrna, where she, the only foreign doctor left in the city, was caught up, taken for a Greek, and clubbed by a Turkish rifle. She records watching helplessly one day in 1923, as a refugee ship listed badly off the coast, its captain signaling: *Four thousand refugees. No water. No food. Smallpox and typhus fever aboard.* Esther and her colleagues were there on the quay-side to rescue those who were eventually able to stagger off the ship when it docked.

I'm listing below three works that readers intrigued by this little-known period of history, which has such chilling lessons for our own age, might like to dip into.

Salonika, City of Ghosts by Mark Mazower. Harper Perennial, 2004.

Certain Samaritans by Doctor Esther Lovejoy. MacMillan, 1933.

And a wonderful book on the population transfers, objective, sensitive, and meticulously researched, is:

Twice a Stranger by Bruce Kent. Granta Books, 2006.

ABOUT THE AUTHOR

BARBARA CLEVERLY is an award-winning writer of eleven novels, including the acclaimed Joe Sandilands series, which includes the *New York Times* notable book *The Last Kashmiri Rose*. She lives in Cambridge, England.